Indigo

AN URBAN FANTASY NOVEL

CASSIDY STEPHENS

Copyright © 2023 by Cassidy Stephens

All rights reserved.

No part of this book may be reproduced in any form or by any electronic or mechanical means, including information storage and retrieval systems, without written permission from the author, except for the use of brief quotations in a book review.

❦ Created with Vellum

INDIGO is dedicated to my sister even though we don't always get along. I love you so much. You are my purple.

I hope I can be your blue.

You were red, and you liked me because I was blue
But you touched me, and suddenly I was a lilac sky
Then you decided purple just wasn't for you.

— "COLORS" BY HALSEY

Preface

For as long as I can remember, my favorite color has always been blue. That has been my only answer ever since I was a little kid barely able to talk. I became connected to this color in a spiritual way. My wardrobe was blue. My walls were blue. At the time, even my eyes were blue.

Everything was blue, as Halsey expresses in her song "Colors" from her debut studio album.

As I grew older, that began to change. My irises became hazel. I began to wear darker, more mature, clothing. While the confines my room remained blue, my eyes grew fixated on other, more important, things in my life. I prioritized school over my family, and the people around me above myself. I had no time to explore what I truly wanted to do with my life.

They say blue is the color of creativity. What happens when that creativity is inevitably snuffed out by the cruelty of the world around us? Within the four walls of my blue room, I often wondered this myself, so I did what I do best and wrote about it. INDIGO is the story of a girl who feels like she is trapped on the opposite side of the glass, peering through the transparency to view the world around her as she should be living it.

Rather than remaining in the dark, she forces herself into the light where she belonged all this time. Being plunged into a world she knew nothing about was not as simplistic as she imagined. Add on the fact that she has been blessed - and cursed - with experimental supernatural abilities the make the rift between her and the real world even more vast.

Paige O'Connell is a complicated girl for many reasons beyond our mortal minds, but I can only imagine that we see a lot of ourselves underneath the shield she places around herself. She is the embodiment of her magic - her *purple* magic - and nothing can change that no matter how much she wants to lead a life of normalcy.

That is...until she is intertwined with blue and indigo splashes onto the canvas of reality

Prologue

The mist in the cold midsummer air was silent as it whisked throughout the damp city. Leaves in the midst of their transformation from the default emerald pigment to numerous shades of red, orange, and yellow. Every couple of steps, pedestrians hardly seemed to notice their desolate, yet meaningful hues; how it bled into the canvas viewing the masterpiece the setting sun painted overhead.

Despite the beauty in the sky, the city below was all but calm. Every building, vehicle, and sidewalk down to the very individuals occupying it had a story to tell, and the pen exploded mid-sentence. Ink splattered all over the map of Arkford. To put it simply, the metropolis was a scribbled mess. Pedestrians crossing the streets led to cars blaring their horns in order to arrive at their destinations quicker. Exhaust from the tailpipes of said vehicles clouded the air around them. It only took one person to destroy what nature had graciously provided to them.

This was exactly the case in the city of Arkford. Nature had been abruptly shoved to the side to make way for society's take on the ideal landscape. Instead of bushes, trees, and plants, hardly any grass coated the tiny medians that dotted the landscape. It was a depressing way to live and nobody realized it. All the people of Arkford wanted to do was to rush–rush to work, rush to their places of residence, and rush to bed only to do it again the very next day.

Hardly anything got in the way of the people's routine, but on this particular day, it would for one person who had no idea she was making a difference.

Black curls framed the dark face whose chocolate eyes were fixated on the sidewalk in front of her. Her heels clicked and clacked against the concrete with each step. Like the flock of other pedestrians around her, this woman was a sheep in the midst of its herd. Unlike the others, though, the woman had a thought of leaving the ninety-nine and embarking on her own once she saw another refugee in the crowd.

Her eyes softened when the outline of what she thought to be a harsh vision became a reality. There, sitting against a brick wall of a large building blending in with all of the others was a girl who could not have been older than eight. Her brown hair was tangled and matted in a poor excuse for a bun on the top of her head with loose strands framing her face, which was covered in dirt and grime from the world around her. She wore a large black sweater that could have swallowed her up if it were not for the jagged rips and tears in the stained fabric. The shivering girl buckled over a gust of wind rattling through her bony frame.

The woman stopped right there on the sidewalk. The child was all by herself in a big city with nothing but her cardigan to keep her company. Ebony curls bounced freely as the woman approached the little girl since she could not think of anything else to do. She watched as the child pitifully picked at her calloused fingertips. Everything about her silently screamed for help.

"Hello, Sweetie," the woman gently said. When the girl's eyes fearfully snapped up to meet hers, she was quick to console her. "You look cold. Are you alright?"

The child nodded, but when a strong gust of wind throttled by, her small frame began to shake.

"Oh, Honey...," the woman cooed with pity. "Have you been out here very long?"

Once again, the little girl nodded.

"How about we get you someplace warm," she suggested. The child failed to respond, which prompted her to ask, "Are you able to speak?"

"My mommy told me not to speak to strangers," a small voice retaliated.

The woman was taken aback. So, this child *did* have a guardian...or so she thought. "Where's your mommy, Sweetheart?"

"I-...I don't know," mumbled the girl in defeat.

Oh, dear. The woman in her thirties was in disbelief. She looked at the child with a different emotion that she was not expecting. The poor girl shivered relentlessly. Even the coat she was swaddled in did not provide shelter from the uncannily frigid air. The woman knelt down to her level with nothing but kindness and compassion in her warm brown gaze that could have lit a fire in the child's heart with her offer.

"Are you hungry? Maybe we could get you something to eat and then go find your mommy."

The child was quick to shake her head. Tears began to build in her eyes as she replied, "I don't know...Mommy said I shouldn't follow strangers. She told me she'd be back soon."

"Honey, we'll get you something to eat and then we can

find your mommy," the woman proposed. "If you want, I can leave you alone, but at least let me get you some dinner."

"Well...," the child paused, her heart beating in her throat. "I *am* really hungry..."

The woman outstretched her hand to the shaking girl. "Come on. Let's get you something to eat. What are you in the mood for?"

"Anything..."

"Okay, let's find you something. C'mon, Sweetie."

Even though the child was hesitant, she clasped onto the woman's hand. Oxygen rushed through her like a drink of ice cold water cascading down her parched throat. The little girl followed the nervous woman down the sidewalk as they rejoined the flock of pedestrians who were in too much of a rush to notice the world around her. The child had no idea how to react to this woman holding her hand and guiding her through the crowd.

The child was anxious–there was no doubt, but when the sight of a familiar red and yellow fast food restaurant came into view, her stomach rumbled hopefully. The woman seemed to notice, but even if she didn't, the child seemed to gravitate towards it. Her long, unkempt brown hair blew in her face with each step, but she did not seem to care. The woman caught on and brought her inside.

"What do you want, Sweetie?" the woman asked once they entered the short line.

"Um..." The little girl thought for a moment. "A chicken sandwich and fries sounds really good right now...if that's okay."

The woman nodded, and once the two of them reached the front of the line, she requested, "Hi, I'd like a chicken sandwich with large fries and...what do you want to drink?" she directed her question to the child at her side.

"A caramel hot chocolate, please," the child politely replied. "...It's my favorite."

"And a caramel hot chocolate," the woman finished.

"That'll be seven eighty-three," the male cashier dully replied.

The woman did not hesitate to take her wallet out of her purse and remove her credit card. The child watched with wide eyes as the woman instantaneously inserted her card into the chip reader and paid for the small girl's meal without thinking twice. She looked uncertain when watching the adult and the cashier conversing about the number of her order and when to receive it. Guilt flooded through the child's veins.

When the two walked away from the register, the girl uttered, "Are you sure?"

"Oh, Honey, of course I'm sure," the woman confirmed brightly. The smile on her face did not say otherwise. "It's the least I could do."

The little girl slowly returned the gesture. In her brown eyes was a beam of hope that was not there before. Instead of having nothing but the torn, weathered jacket draped on her shoulders, there was a woman there who cared about her well-being. She did not think of anything else but that ray of aspiration for the future until their order was called and a bag of food along with the child's favorite drink was retrieved.

"Thank you," the little girl gushed once her meal was handed to her.

"You're very welcome." The woman reached for her phone in the pocket of her coat and looked at the time. "It's getting late. After you finish your food, let's find your-..."

The woman stopped when she looked over her device and noticed the child that was in front of her two seconds ago was gone. Not a trace of her was left behind. The woman looked around frantically for the young girl, but she had completely vanished from sight. Oh, how the woman worried as she searched for the giant coat that had engulfed her helpless, bony frame. After a while, she had given up, figuring the girl had simply found her mother and gone home.

At least, that was what she hoped had happened…

Little did the woman know that in a dark corner of the restaurant, a young woman with long, blonde hair, hazel eyes, and a mended black sweater was seated enjoying the very same meal she had ordered along with one defining feature–a caramel hot chocolate steaming on the table.

Chapter One

ULTRAVIOLET

Paige O'Connell wished the world around her would change.

Seated in one of the only trees in the metropolis of Arkford, she watched as there was nothing but busy folks rushing to get from one place to another. Bitterness fluttered in her chest when she noticed how everyone was ignoring their surroundings and only focusing on themselves. That was a bit hypocritical, though, because she was doing the same.

It was not her fault, however; she needed to in order to survive—much less thrive.

Paige scowled as a couple walked under the branch she was straddling comfortably. Her eyes followed the man's hand that was not holding his partner's as he took one last bite out of a half-eaten apple and tossed it on the ground. Before it contacted the concrete below the couple's shoes, though, an opening was created in the sidewalk. The apple fell through and vanished. Neither of the two pedestrians noticed it. They could not have cared less.

Just like the opening in the concrete that had just closed,

another emerged directly over the male pedestrian. The half-eaten apple core fell through and landed directly on his head before vanishing like it was never there. Once the two round objects smashed into each other, the man cursed and caught the apple in his hands.

"What the hell?" he spluttered and threw the apple into the grass.

For a second time, the ground opened and swallowed the apple up. The air above the man's head transformed into the second opening of the portal that was impossibly created. The half-eaten apple core knocked the man on the head for a second time.

"Oh, for the love of-" the man began to start a fight with the browning fruit.

"Honey," his female partner replied calmly, "forget about it and let's go home. I'll be making a nice dinner."

The man ignored his girlfriend and continued trying to throw the apple on the ground. The same result occurred every time. The man was sure he was beginning to get a bump on his head underneath his fedora from how many times the apple hit it. About the eighth time that this happened, the man looked like he was about to scream from frustration. His muscles tensed so much that he began to shake. His mind started to descend into insanity.

"Y'know, you could throw it in the trash can over there, dimwit," a female voice snarkily commented from above.

The man looked up at where the voice came from, but Paige had disappeared from the tree. She was still there, but just...not visible. She had seen the entire thing and had caused it to begin with. A satisfied smile grew on her face as the man frantically looked around to see no one. Instead, he stomped over towards the nearby trash can before grabbing his wife roughly by the arm and dragging her away.

CHAPTER ONE

"Hey!" Paige snapped. "You let go of her."

"Where the hell is that coming from?" the man screeched.

"Who's saying that?!"

Paige hopped down from the tree - still not visible to the public eye - and walked over to the frustrated man. She took one look at him, his girlfriend, and then her eyes landed on his reddened complexion that was darting everywhere. Paige's hazel gaze narrowed into slits. She could easily make one of his cheeks a beet maroon. Before she could control what happened next, her invisible right hand lifted and smacked the middle-aged man directly in the face. It was enough to knock him backward at least two steps.

"What the-"

"Don't finish that, you selfish pig." Paige was firm with him directly before she grabbed his collar and shook him. "Got it?"

The man looked like he was about to retaliate, but in a blink of an eye, Paige was gone–for real this time. A similar opening like the one that engulfed the apple swallowed Paige and she fell through the sidewalk only to land in another portion of the city. Paige almost smiled to herself. The thrill of teleporting from one place to another gave her an adrenaline rush. She felt like she could do absolutely anything in that empowering moment.

Paige continued to walk through the city without looking back. She had no need to because the chance of anyone following her because she was a lone female in public was impossible. Why? Because she could not be seen by the naked eye. Paige loved her cloaking device–herself. She could go wherever she wanted whenever she wanted. It was something she took a bit too lightly sometimes.

What she did next was one of those times.

About ten minutes later, Paige found herself standing - invisibly - in front of the same red and yellow restaurant as the day before. She heard her stomach rumbling and decided to do something about it. Her hand slipped into one of her pockets... then the other...and then the rest of them. There was nothing there. She scowled at the fact she was broke.

"*Great. Now, I have to go through all that trouble again,*" Paige thought scornfully.

Once Paige was sure she was out of sight by walking into a dark alleyway, she morphed her appearance into the same little girl with a torn black sweater, matted brown hair, and a broken expression. Just like yesterday, she made herself visible and began walking towards the fast food restaurant. Instead of sitting outside in the cold, though, which she regretted doing the last time, she walked inside. Paige faked shivering and made sure her lips had a tainted blue color to resemble the "chill" she felt from the sporatic gusts.

The small child stood in the long line and waited patiently for at least fifteen minutes until she reached the register. Paige clasped her hands together and looked at the menu with wide eyes. The same cashier that was there yesterday looked her up and down with a puzzled look in his stoic eyes.

"What can I get for you?" he asked blandly.

"I-...u-um..." Paige feigned an anxious stutter. "I-I'd like a chicken sandwich with fries and a caramel hot chocolate, please."

After inputting her order into the register, the young man's eyes narrowed in suspicion. "Weren't you here yesterday? Where's your parents?"

"I-I don't know..." Then, Paige grumbled internally, *"And it's none of your damn business."*

"That'll be seven eighty," the cashier informed her.

The small girl checked her pockets even though she was sure there was nothing there anyway. After looking through both of her jacket pockets and the pockets of her worn pants, she looked up at the impatient man with eyes as wide as saucers–the old "puppy-dog eye" trick.

"I-...I'm so sorry, Sir, but I don't have any money." Paige's bottom lip trembled.

"Then, I'm sorry."

Wait...this was not how it was supposed to go. Usually at the sight of a poor, hungry child, people would be running to help. Instead, this cashier had no sympathy in his eyes. At that moment, Paige really did wish she could buy the meal herself. Even at the age she truly was, she could not afford food from even a fast food restaurant. No money of hers could have been spared due to the situation she had been thrown in.

Paige tried one more time to receive pity with her ginormous, pleading eyes. "Okay, then," she mumbled tearily. "Thanks anyway."

The little girl was about to walk away and out of the store when the man behind her in line spoke up before she could take a step. "Don't go! I got it."

Paige turned around to view a man who looked to be in his late thirties smiling down at her with his wallet in hand. He had small seedlings of black hair growing on his mostly bald, dark-skinned scalp. Kind brown eyes were all that the child could focus on right then and there. Paying for a stranger's meal did not look like an inconvenience to him at all. That was exactly what Paige's rumbling stomach needed.

"Are you sure?" the small child could not help but ask.

"Of course," the man replied cheerily. He inserted his card into the chip reader and paid for her meal without a second thought.

As soon as the transaction was completed, Paige whispered, "Thank you."

"Not a problem! Now, enjoy." He smiled at her.

The little girl smiled back as the man handed her the

receipt with her order number on it. She hurriedly trotted over to a vacant table in the restaurant and sat down. Her feet swung joyfully while she waited for her food, which did not take any more than seven minutes to make. When her number was called, she dashed up to the counter, showed one of the restaurant's employees her receipt, and took her tray to her table, where she began to heartily enjoy her lunch.

Paige morphed into her original form when she was sure no one was looking her way. In those few minutes of solitude she had, she still did not feel at peace. She had everything she needed right then and there—a roof over her head, a drink to quench her thirst, and a warm meal to keep her stomach at ease. It was not enough to settle her mind, though. Something felt off, and that feeling was not going to go away until Paige discovered exactly what it was.

The world around her was spinning. Paige could hardly stomach her food as her gut screamed at her that there was something out of the ordinary. She continued to eat her food despite her belly wanting to spontaneous join a gymnastics team. Paige knew she needed it. She had not eaten since the kind woman from yesterday paid for her dinner and offered to help find her mother. Paige felt bad for lying to the woman. She needed food, though, and if lying was what helped her, then lying was what she did.

A sudden screeching of rubber against asphalt jerked Paige out of her imagination, which turned out to be more of a reality than she thought. That sinking feeling in her chest grew stronger as she looked out the window to view a city bus rounding the corner with more speed than it could handle on its own. The bus tipped over just enough to keep it on its four wheels as it sped down the street in front of Paige's window. Passengers screamed in fright and when Paige looked at the driver's seat, the man behind the wheel looked as if he was in astounded dismay while trying to bring the vehicle to a halt.

Paige knew what to do despite her mind yelling at her to sit down and enjoy her food. She did not give her imagination another chance to take over as she passed through the closed window. The teenager winced as she felt her molecules and matter passing through the glass unnaturally. It was an uncomfortable sensation, but it was one she had to get used to. Before she forgot, Paige made herself invisible to the public eye. Publicity was the last thing she wanted.

"*Okay, Paige,*" she encouraged herself anxiously. "*You've got this. It's just a runaway bus...with at least fifty people on board.*"

She found herself taking deep breaths while taking off on a sprint towards the bus. The fastest human merely reached twenty-seven miles per hour while the city bus had just passed sixty. Paige concentrated just like she did each time and created an opening in her path while calculating where the other one would be. Paige slammed her eyes shut and grunted against the change in energy around her body that occurred until she emerged from the other end of the portal that led to the interior of the bus.

Paige dashed up the aisle and towards the front of the bus where the driver was struggling with keeping it on track. She eyed the steering wheel, which the driver was trying to maneuver but it seemed to be stuck as well as the brake. Without giving him any warning, which she probably should have done, she opened a portal just like she did for herself and transported him to one of the empty passenger seats. Like she expected, the man shrieked.

She sat herself down in the driver's seat. Paige frowned and sighed with disgust when she realized her legs were too short to reach the pedals. "Oh, you've *got* to be kidding me," she mumbled to herself.

Instead of adjusting the seat - which she had no time to do now - Paige leaned back in the seat and slammed her foot onto the brake, which did not budge no matter how many times she tried or how hard she pushed it. Paige attempted to move the steering wheel, which was also stuck in its place. Along with her breathing beginning to get heavier with every attempt to stop the bus failing, Paige looked up and noticed that they were headed for an elevated, curved overpass.

Paige was out of options now...all except for one. It was the last resort for several reasons: the most important one being the attention it would bring to the incident. Paige had no idea what else to do, though. It was not just her in danger, but several innocent pedestrians. The thought of a single one of them being injured or worse torched her mind like a wildfire and turned all of her caution to ash.

The passengers' screams were ear piercing as the bus started up the incline towards the curve in the overpass. Paige had less than five seconds, which she used wisely. She did not let herself be doubted once more as she spread her hands out and generated an ultraviolet energy force field around the entire bus the very second it broke through the road barrier and began to fall over the edge. The bus was caught in midair to everyone's relief.

Paige underestimated the total weight of what her energy field was carrying. She let out a labored, volumed screech that blended into the others as the force field began to flicker from the strain. The bus fell downwards a couple of yards - probing more screams from the interior - but was caught once more in midair. Paige began to slowly lower the bus toward the ground at least fifty feet below. This pattern continued - the field flickering and waning, the bus falling a yard or two, and passengers screaming for dear life - until all four wheels touched the ground. Not a scratch was on the bus' exterior.

Paige sighed deeply in relief while the passengers - including the driver - began to cheer, whoop, and holler in celebration. She deliberately made sure she had left the bus the way she came before any more trouble was caused. When she reappeared outside, she noticed large crowds of overseers approaching the scene. Several cars pulled over and some civilians even climbed on the tops of their vehicles to see what was going on for themselves. Paige only had one thought on her mind as the crowds pushed closer.

"I have to get out of here-"

Before the city square could suffocate her, Paige fell through yet another opening in the ground and landed directly in the vacant seat where she was when she left. Her food was still in front of her, but it did not look as appetizing anymore. Paige slumped down in her seat while she attempted to catch her breath for at least five minutes. Not everyone could say that they lifted a bus full of people—even with the help of an abnormal electrical field. Well...it was normal to her. Paige was proud of her abilities, but she knew she had to be careful, which was why she was determined to remove her physical transparency before doing anything else.

When she finally determined her heart was beating at a semi-normal rate, Paige stood up and grabbed her bag of food in one hand and her warm drink in the other. Paige kept her head high and her posture straight. She took a sip of her caramel hot chocolate the moment she pushed open the glass door of the restaurant and the chill of the outdoors hit her in the face. It took hardly more than ten seconds for her cheeks to become pinkened from the chill. It was an abnormally cold autumn.

Despite everything tormenting her mind at once, Paige looked completely ordinary. She took a large bite out of her chicken sandwich and relished in the taste as she casually walked down the sidewalk. Paige almost wished she was normal as she blended into the other pedestrians and her straight honey blonde bangs blew into her face. She quickly decided that that word was very overused. What did "normal" mean anyway? What was "normality?"

Simply, though; that was a word that worked better for Paige. If only those seven letters applied to merely one aspect of her being.

Chapter Two

ORCHID

The flickering light bulb hanging from the ceiling in the center of the windowless room was antagonizing. Each time it faded, even for a second, Paige felt like following in its footsteps. She wanted to be anywhere but here. The cool air ebbing from the vent overhead was suffocating rather than soothing. Its icy fingers wrapped around her neck and strangled her to the point where she could not answer the question she was just asked.

Paige glared up at the failing light bulb. Just one small movement would make its light go out in an instant. It was a swinging temptation like a monkey in search of a banana. Paige wished ever so dearly that she could reach up and shatter the light bulb to put it out of its misery. It was lifeless, dangling like a corpse from the ceiling.

A snapping of two fingers brought Paige back into her undesired reality. Paige's gaze shot up to meet the man whose little gray hair he had left hung by a thread to his scalp. Her eyes were scornful while his were devilish and impatient at the same time. He knew she had no answer to what he had just asked, but he also wanted her to conjure up something more than a sob story to explain her actions.

"Well, Miss O'Connell," the man - Dr. Kelley - probed. "I'm waiting to hear from you."

Paige was too busy fiddling around with a self-created forcefield about the size of a baseball floating between her hands. She pretended to be oblivious. "About what?" she asked, not taking her eyes off of the energy ball.

"You know what." Dr. Kelley did not look amused.

"No, I don't."

Dr. Kelley's eyes narrowed at the girl who couldn't care less. "Tell me what exactly was going through your head when you decided to pull your little stunt earlier."

"Nothing," Paige retorted blandly.

"You mean to tell me that *nothing* was on your mind when you passed through a window, somehow got onto a runaway bus, and held it with a *giant* force field where *everyone* could see it?!" He raised his voice with each word spat.

Paige held the force field sphere in her hands and finally met his eyes when a few droplets of saliva hit her face that she had to wipe off. "I couldn't just sit there and watch as it hurtled over the barrier."

"You could've thought of a better way to go about with this," argued Dr. Kelley.

"I did the first thing I thought of."

"The first thing you thought of was publicizing your abilities in front of the whole city? The whole *state*? Maybe even the whole *world*?"

"I couldn't just let those people die!" The sphere quietly shattered as Paige rocketed to her feet, knocking the wooden chair she was formerly seated in onto the floor with a crash.

"Tsk, tsk," the doctor scolded. "Because of your "heroic" actions, we are all over the news."

CHAPTER TWO

Dr. Kelley stood from his seat and powered on a television on the adjacent wall with a remote he had in his pocket. Paige watched as the television flashed to life and a news channel appeared on the screen. The headline below the reporters read, "Supernatural Phenomenon Saves the Lives of Fifty-Two Civilians." Paige fought the urge to smile at the title, but what the reporters were saying made her heart drop to her churning stomach.

"We're coming to you live from Arkford's Town Center with a mind-boggling story that fifty-two passengers have just witnessed," the female reporter with bouncy brown hair exclaimed breathlessly.

"You're telling me, Rita!" the male reporter on the other side of the split screen gushed. *"It's not every day that you see a runaway bus—much less a mysterious energy field carrying it to safety."*

"Just ninety minutes ago, a hijacked city bus raced down Main Street and towards a curved overpass overlooking the sea," Rita recalled the incident. *"We have no idea how the bus became undriveable, but one thing's for sure: Something - or someone - put it back on track."*

A video taken on a phone camera replaced the reporters on the screen. Paige watched as the force field she created around the bus flickered and faded on occasion but remained in one piece as the public transport vehicle was gradually lowered to the ground. Paige felt her breaths quicken just watching the shaky footage like it was happening all over again.

"This force field-like object appeared out of nowhere and lowered the bus to safety," Jack - the male reporter - explained the obvious. *"None of the passengers were hurt except for a couple of bumps and bruises, which is much better than the other outcome that could've occurred. What caused this incredible phenomenon, and will it happen again?"*

Paige could not control her grin when she heard the report of no civilians being injured. Dr. Kelley lowered the volume on the television and glared at Paige, whose eyes were glued to it as she continued watching the report. He sat down and calmly clasped his hands together on the desk that separated the two.

"Well?" the doctor questioned, snapping her out of her trance. "What do you have to say for yourself?"

Paige did not even bother sitting down, instead leaning forward and resting her elbows on the table at his eye level. "I'd say I'm some sort of a hero," she replied smugly with her hands cradling her chin.

"Wrong!" Dr. Kelley yelled. "You may have jeopardized our entire mission!"

"*Your* mission," she corrected.

"I'd watch your tongue, O'Connell. It's *our* mission."

Paige's heart rate accelerated once she felt a sharp tingling in the back of her neck. She knew exactly what it was, and it was one of the only things that would instill fear into her very being. Paige glared at the balding man across from her. The doctor had a wicked smile on his face, like watching her begin to crumble before him made him stronger. The buzzing sensation grew stronger with every second that Paige's mouth was sealed. It was only a matter of time until she would cave. He knew this. Everyone knew this.

"Okay, okay! It's our mission–just...just turn it off," Paige demanded between gritted teeth.

A mere second later, the tingling stopped. "That's what I thought." sneered Dr. Kelley with no remorse. "I don't have any new assignments for you, but count on this: if you step out of line one more time, you know what's coming."

"Yes, Sir." Paige's muscles tensed.

"You've lost this month's pay, also."

The teenager's heart sank even further. "What?!" she yelped. "But I need it!"

"You should've thought through your actions better," countered Dr. Kelley. "Hopefully this will ensure you have learned your lesson. Understand?"

"But-"

"Do you *understand*?!"

Paige lowered her gaze. "Yes, Sir."

"Good," Dr. Kelley concluded sternly. "Now, get out of my sight."

Paige stood to her full height - which she thought was embarrassingly miniscule - and whirled around to leave the room. As she did so, though, a small energy field the color of orchid began bubbling in the light bulb hanging in the center of the room. The more steps she took, the larger it became until it eventually shattered from the pressure. Glass shards spilled all over the desk in front of Dr. Kelley and the whole room went dark once Paige slammed the door.

The outside world was just like it always was. Everyone was in a rush no matter what time of day it happened to be. Paige despised the way everyone needed to fend for themselves in the city of Arkford. She found it stupid and demeaning, especially when she was quite literally by herself. Nearly everyone else had families to return to every evening. Paige wondered how civilians would be able to work and leave their homes for the day. What were families for if you had to work and barely see them? Was it worth it?

Paige was clueless.

She tried not to think about the antagonizing world around her as she made her way back to a familiar building. She had lost count of how many times she walked down this route, especially after days such as this one. Paige stuffed her hands in the pocket of her black sweater as she walked down the sidewalk where she had memorized every crack and blemish. Her blonde bangs blew into her eyes. She knew she needed a haircut, but she also knew money was tight. A haircut was the least of her worries right now.

Paige trudged through the heavy glass doors of her apartment complex and ignored the receptionist at the front desk like she always did. The woman was always typing away on her computer anyway, and Paige was not one for small talk. Instead, she walked straight for the elevator and pressed the button to summon it. Thankfully, the contraption was already on the ground floor, so the doors opened within a few seconds. Paige walked inside and pressed the button to the twenty-sixth floor.

The teenager was grateful that the elevator had recently been prepared. For the past month or two, the elevator was squeaking and struggling to transport its passengers throughout the building. Being on such a high floor made Paige nervous in the first place. The elevator only made it worse. She tapped her foot while impatiently watching the floor numbers rise on an old-timey screen above the elevator doors. When they finally opened, she dashed out and hurdled towards her apartment.

Paige's living quarters were small for the average person, but just the right size for her. It was a two-room apartment with a miniature kitchen and living area combination along with a bedroom through a door on the left. The bathroom was connected to the bedroom, which was absolutely perfect for her. Paige had to admit to herself that she hardly spent time in her apartment. Giving her a roof to sleep under was all it was good for. That did not mean she was ungrateful, though. At least paying for it was not an issue.

Paige decided not to bother with dinner. She had no food in

her pantry anyway. Instead, she grabbed a remote off the coffee table, flopped down on the sofa in her living space, and turned on the television. She flipped towards the local news station, which was still broadcasting the story of the bus nearly falling from the overpass. Paige began to play with an energy orb as she watched the television with a smug look. The bus driver that she had teleported out of the way was speaking to the reporter.

"*Next thing I knew, I was out of the driver's seat and sitting in a passenger's empty seat in front of the bus!*" the driver voluminously exclaimed. "*I don't know what happened, but as long as my passengers are safe, I'm happy.*"

Paige smiled at that. She continued tossing the force field sphere around and watching it float between and above her hands. She began passing it from hand to hand like a basketball player getting ready to attempt a three-pointer. The news reporter continued speaking as she began to space out, regaining her attention.

"*That surely is something, isn't it? There seems to be some sort of unnatural phenomenon going on here. With the giant orb lowering the bus and the driver somehow teleporting his way from the steering wheel, we have no idea what's going on and what - or who - is responsible for this. Is there some sort of superhero in our midst? We have no idea!*"

A superhero.

That was a term Paige never used to describe herself. What she did that day was a heroic act, no doubt, but did one good deed make her a superhero? After all, Paige *did* trick innocent citizens into buying food for a "poor girl," but that was specifically so she would have some sort of means of survival. That was where Paige was bamboozled.

Not everyone was perfect, though. Paige knew that for a fact. In fact, she considered herself the epitome of imperfection and paradoxes. What made a hero? Was it heroic acts, a heroic personality, or something more?

"I'm no hero," Paige grumbled silently. *"If anything, I'm a thief."*

She had to decide where her priorities lay. That meant sacrificing a lot of things that Paige was not ready for yet. Then again, what was life truly about? Was it about fighting to survive? Paige thought back to the Arkford pedestrians rushing home to their families after a long, hard day at work. Maybe having a family *was* worth it. Paige would not know, though. It was a long story that she was not ready to tell.

Paige popped the energy orb and watched as it crumbled to nothingness at her fingertips when another headline caught her eye: "Supernatural Forces May Be A Danger To Society."

The teenager blinked at how quickly the news changed from positive to negative. She hated how people who knew nothing about a situation made assumptions without conducting further research or thought. Paige thought the urge to toss another field of energy at the television screen and instead picked up the remote to turn it off. Once the intimidating headline disappeared from view, Paige leaned back into a comfortable, seated position with one thought on her mind.

"I need to be more careful."

Little did she know this was merely the beginning.

Chapter Three

AZURE

A stomach rumbling in her ears was one of Paige's least favorite sounds.

There, she sat–once again in a tree overlooking what Arkford had to offer. Paige felt safe being above the crowd where she could see everything that was going on at once. The factor of control was important to her. Unfortunately, it led to her tummy growling like a starving kitten without a mother more often than not.

Just shy of thirty days ago, Paige vowed to herself to be more careful of her actions. Getting on just about every news station in the country was not what Paige - or whom she worked for - wanted to do. Publicity was dangerous–Paige knew that by now. She never realized how truly important her monthly pay was since now, she had to fight to survive another week. Without the little food she was able to purchase with her salary, Paige needed to get sustenance some other way. That way was her least favorite.

Theft.

Paige's legs dangled and swung from her perch while she

watched the scene below her unfold below her black worn-out Converse. She enjoyed viewing the small park near the center of Arkford. It was one of the only places with an abundance of trees, bushes, grass, and any sort of tranquility in the urban landscape. It was a nice change from normality.

She took a large bite out of an apple she was holding in her right hand and chewed at the piece in her mouth almost silently. The scenery below reminded her of a bustling marketplace. In fact, that was exactly what was going on underneath. Booths of every shape and size were set up in a large square around the park, which had been set up as a temporary shopping center. Everywhere Paige looked, she saw goods and services being exchanged for green paper or invisibly through credit cards that she desperately needed.

Paige looked at the apple that she had just taken from the cart by the foot of the tree she was invisibly lounging on. Guilt clouded her subconscious with every bite, but her stomach's need for fuel took over once it was sustained. Soon enough, all that was left of the apple was the core. Paige debated on eating that too, but she decided against it, instead dropping the apple into a trash can below. She watched as the poor middle-aged man who ran the apple stand nearly flinched out of his shoes when he heard the thud.

She knew what she was there to do. Even though it would have been considered wrong in the eyes of the people, it was necessary for her well-being. Paige dropped down from the tree branch and landed quietly as a cat in the grass. Still invisible to the public, she unzipped the large compartment of a backpack that was on her left shoulder and began pocketing a few of the applies from the poor man's cart.

"*I really am the bad guy.*"

Paige's inner voice kept repeating itself in her ears as she darted from cart to cart, booth to booth, taking as much food

CHAPTER THREE

as she could fit in her worn backpack. She had been doing this for years, but it never got better. Sometimes, times got tough, though, and she did not have any other choice for herself. She needed to think about what her body physically needed. The emotional and mental qualities took a bit more time that she failed to have.

Paige continued to pickpocket each and every booth, taking just enough so the products' vacancies would be unnoticed. Her backpack was hardly able to be zipped shut by the time she was done, and when it finally did, she began to leave the bustling park. Weaving around crowds of people was difficult, even when invisible to the public. Paige tightened the straps of her backpack as she made her way towards the exit. The quicker she got out of there, the better.

Her clean getaway was almost a reality until she heard a small voice from a few booths over. Paige turned to her right to view a small boy and his mother, dressed in rags that Paige had only experienced wearing whilst in one of her most frequent façades. The both of them seemed strapped for cash, the mother's face covered with dirt and grime and the boy wearing shoes with half the soles missing. She frowned and stopped in her tracks when she saw the scene unfold.

"Mama, I'm *so* hungry!" the child whined desperately. "Can we *please* get something to eat?"

The weary mother with brown hair in messy strands framing her face smiled sadly at her son. "I'm so sorry. I thought we had enough."

"But there's loaves of bread right there!" The little boy pointed at a nearby cart that Paige had already taken from and began to drag his mother towards it. "Can we *please* ask the man for one? He won't mind!"

Paige almost smiled at his innocence. The man in charge of the bread cart scowled down at the boy who was staring up at him with hopeful eyes. The weary mother smiled apologetically at the large, beefy man that Paige found disgusting to say the least. Black hair covered his tan arms and overgrew his face. His nose was comically large.

"No money–no bread," he denied their silent request with a firm, deep voice.

"Please, Sir," the little boy persisted despite his mother tugging him back, "can we please have one? You have a huge cart, and we would love something to eat for lunch."

"Jimmy, we're going home," the mother whispered to her child.

Jimmy's lip quivered and he pointed at the man. "Why won't he let us have one?"

"Because not everybody in this world will go out of their way to help those in need," the mother replied, "and that's okay. We're all trying our best and this man needs money too. He's working really hard just like we are."

"B-But Mama..."

"Come on, Hun," his mother coaxed him away from the man who was staring them down with his beady black eyes.

Paige watched scornfully as the mother and son duo walked away from the bread cart. The man, looking satisfied with himself, continued to mind his own business, waiting for more potential customers to feed his hungry ego. Even though Jimmy wanted so badly to turn around and ask the man minding the bread cart one more time for a small helping for he and his Mama. Instead, he held her hand and walked by her side towards the exit of the marketplace.

Paige could not watch and do nothing any longer. Instead, she opened her backpack, took out one of the two loaves of bread she had stolen from the very same cart, and lightly tossed it over to the mother and son. It had become visible once it left Paige's grasp. The loaf of bread hit the boy's weathered shoe and he stopped in his tracks at the contact. Once he saw the loaf of bread, his eyes lit up and he picked it up off the ground.

"Mama!" he exclaimed happily. "Look what I found on the ground!"

His mother turned to him and blinked confusedly. "You found that on the ground?" she inquired, quite unsure.

"I did! Can we take it home? *Please*?"

After one look at the bread and then at her son's pleading eyes, she smiled and nodded. "Yes, we can. Hold onto it tightly, now."

The two of them began walking again, but with more of a spring in their steps this time. Jimmy looked like he was about to jump for joy with the small bit of food in his hands. The boy began chattering about something unintelligible to Paige, who was growing further and further away from the duo. A subconscious smile grew on her face when she realized what she had done: she had helped two people in need. They were just like her, after all–looking for mere scraps of food in order to survive. Paige then realized something else with a pang.

She was a hypocrite.

Paige did the wrong thing morally to do the right thing in her heart. How was that being a "good" person? Sure, she provided comfort to those who needed it, but in doing so, she stole from someone who also needed the profit. Despite his differing outlook, it was not right to steal, yet she did it regardless.

The teenager hoisted the backpack back onto her shoulders. Paige felt like her spine was threatening to snap in half from the weight. She began to leave the marketplace anyway, since she could not risk any more time than she needed. Paige knew her theft would not be noticed - at least not right away - so she needed to be as far away from capture as possible. No matter how many times she did this very thing, it never got easier.

Paige half-walked, half-dashed in the general direction of her apartment complex. This was the only way her pantry was filled, especially when she lost a month's worth of pay. Paige remained out of sight as she walked down the busy streets. Every so often, she had a scare where she either barely, or nearly bumped into someone while invisibly striding down the street.

She was tired of living like this, having to scrounge around for food every chance she was not clouded in fatigue. Paige angrily glared at the ground as the backpack on her back grew heavier with each step. Guilt circuited through her veins instead of the crimson red courage she needed to keep herself going. Each step became more labored than the last. Nearly thirty days ago, Paige thought she was a hero. Now, she was falling apart quicker than she could put herself back together again.

She continued to walk and brush off the hunger and fatigue that rested on her shoulders. When something caught her eye, though, Paige stopped in her tracks. She was not one to sightsee, but a certain billboard caught her eye. Paige read the bold white lettering atop the navy-blue background.

"Find Your Path at Azure University! Fall Enrollment Open Now."

"*My path?*"

Paige was intrigued. She caught herself reading the headline several times. She was quite curious as to why the sign caught her eye in the first place. Then again, Paige had no idea where her path was leading her in the first place. Maybe Paige needed extra assistance–a compass that would guide her in the right direction. She was clueless as to where she was meant to be. It was possible that even a shred of "normality" would be enough to steer her back in her lane.

When someone bumped into her invisible frame, causing her to stumble forward, Paige knew she needed to make a decision, and she did so in a matter of seconds. For once in the past month, Paige knew exactly what she wanted - and maybe needed - to do next. Instead of continuing towards her apartment, she booked it in the opposite direction. Her backpack suddenly became light as a feather as the straps bounced against her shoulders with each striding step. She darted around the bustling pedestrians without a second glance... well, maybe one or two so someone else would not collide with her.

Paige felt herself begin to sigh with relief when the fabric of the people began to thin out into fringed threads. The building she despised but needed was inside. It did not look like your usual high security building. Instead, it resembled more like a weathered brick warehouse that was at least four stories. Nobody knew about the basement of said building except for explicit individuals. Paige was blessed and cursed - in a way - to be one of them.

The atmosphere grew thicker when Paige passed through it. The iron bars making up the surrounding fence of the storage warehouse were like feathers against her skin. Despite the simplicity of it all, Paige never got used to it. She morphed through the fence and then the locked, heavy door like it was a light weighted curtain. It hardly fazed her as much as it used to, but by the time that miniscule feeling collided with her senses, she was already inside.

Paige allowed herself to become visible once she was safe within the walls of the suffocating building. She had been inside hundreds - if not, thousands - of times by then. It never got brighter. The dim lights residing on the ceiling were all that lit the lobby. The floors were a drab beige carpet that Paige could not tell whether was stained. The walls were bare of any pictures, but instead were inhabited by the occasional window. The room was empty other than the receptionist's desk. Paige ignored the fact that the woman at the desk looked like she wanted to be anywhere but here. She felt the same, but only allowed a firm look to be present on her face as she approached and leaned against the desk.

"I'd like to speak with Dr. Kelley," Paige demanded before the receptionist could question her presence.

The receptionist blatantly pretended to be typing on her computer to delay her reply. "Dr. Kelley isn't in right now," she responded without making eye contact. "If you want to set up an appointment, leave your name and number on-"

Paige slammed her fist down on the desk so hard that she thought she heard the wood splinter under her touch. The receptionist gasped in fright and nearly flinched out of her seat. She was struggling to keep her glasses on her face, but Paige was completely calm. When the receptionist finally had the nerve to look into the teenager's eyes, all she saw was impatience. No remorse, no sympathy, just...impatience.

"That wasn't a request." Paige blew her blonde bangs out of her face. "I'd like to see Dr. Kelley now. It can't wait."

The receptionist stared at her blankly. When Paige failed to get an answer, she leaned closer and made sure her voice was heard. "I *need* to see Dr. Kelley."

"I-..."

"Please," Paige winced from the simple word emitting from her gritted teeth and watched as the receptionist continued cowering before her.

The woman reluctantly nodded from behind the desk. "You know where his office is."

That was enough confirmation for Paige. She dashed down

CHAPTER THREE

the nearest hallway, which happened to lead to the office she was searching for. Paige had walked that very same path countless times. In fact, it hurt for her brain to wrap around the endeavor entirely. What was she doing in the first place? Dr. Kelley would surely deny her request.

"*I have to try,*" Paige encouraged herself.

She hated having to take orders from a man who could hardly keep what hair he had left on his head. To put it frankly, he was disgusting. His skin was whiter than his teeth which were deteriorating day by day. The bags under his eyes never disappeared, just like his stingy attitude towards everyone who refused to abide by his expectations. Paige had experienced that many times. She did not want *it* to occur again.

Paige stopped by his office, nonetheless. She needed him whether she liked it or not. One of her hands, which were already tightened up into clenched fists, began rapping loudly on his iron door. Paige lost count of how many locks were on each entryway–even the restroom. Paige about that feature of the building the hard way. Instead of simply walking through it, which she was tempted to do, she waited on the other side just like she always did to show respect. Even if the man was a balding pathetic excuse for a person, Paige couldn't risk punishment.

"Enter," Dr. Kelley's monotone voice boomed from the other side.

Paige watched as the locks on the door came undone one at a time. She wondered how he did that in the first place. Maybe it was a new technological feature that she had not heard of yet. Then again, she had not been to his office in quite a long time. She avoided that room for many reasons which were valuable and crucial to her. She ignored the raging voice in her mind as she walked into the office once the thick door slid open on its own. She fought the urge to wince when her eyes caught the man sitting at a large desk in a swivel chair. Three computer monitors almost blocked her view of him, which she wished would vanish entirely. Paige swallowed down her nausea and approached his desk.

"You know I'm a *very* busy man, O'Connell." Dr. Kelley set down his stack of paperwork that he was assessing. "What is it?"

Paige straightened her posture. "I have a request," she stated bluntly.

"You came down to my office during my *working hours* just to ask me a question?" Dr. Kelley spat with his saliva landing on at least one of his monitors.

The teenager almost flinched but stood firm. "Yes, Sir."

"Very well," the doctor sighed laboredly. "What is it?"

"I'd like to enroll in Azure University," exclaimed Paige loud and clear.

Dr. Kelley looked like he wanted to spit out a drink he did not have. "Excuse me?"

"I'd like to enroll in Azure University," Paige repeated without a moment's hesitation.

"Why in the *hell* would you want to enroll in a university?" Dr. Kelley inquired. "You have everything you could ever want right here–a free apartment, food, and comfortable living."

"Comfortable living? *Comfortable living*?!" Paige's voice rose with each word. She slammed both of her hands onto his desk. "For the past month, I've been having to fight to get what I need to survive. I just had to steal food from the marketplace this morning." Paige threw her backpack down on the ground with a thud as she continued to shout, "I'm *starving*! This isn't comfortable living at all! You don't know what it's like having to beg for food like a commoner. I *am* a commoner."

Dr. Kelley rolled his eyes and stood from his chair. He towered over her diminutive stature. "If you want this, then

CHAPTER THREE

you need to watch your tongue. You already have an apartment that's fully paid for along with a few luxuries. Don't forget that I can take it all away just like *that*," he threatened her while snapping his fingers. "I can make you much worse off. Do you *want* to return to a cell?"

"I haven't forgotten," she quipped snarkily, "and I didn't ask for any of those things. I sure as hell ain't complaining, but I just want to live a normal life for once. Getting an education would help me do that."

"You haven't even graduated high school, much less intermediate or elementary," argued Dr. Kelley. "What makes you think college will help you if you know absolutely nothing?"

The teenager started to bargain. "*This* is my chance to learn. I'll go on more missions. I'll have a smaller cut of monthly pay. I won't spend money on textbooks. I can-"

"Enough."

Paige clamped her mouth shut. Dr. Kelley had been very thoughtful while Paige continued to list things she could do in order to achieve her goal. In fact, he thought about it quite a lot. The teenager in front of him had a lot of potential, even some that she neglected to see in herself. Maybe this experiment would be beneficial for the entire organization.

"This could...be something to consider," Dr. Kelley noted out loud.

"...What do you mean?" Paige inquired with wide eyes.

Dr. Kelley sat back down at his desk and clasped his hands together. "I'm ready to make a deal with you, O'Connell."

Paige stiffly sat down in a chair across from him. "What is it?" she asked.

"I will submit an application on your behalf to Azure University for an undeclared major. Even if you haven't received a high school degree, I can pull some strings. When you want to update your major, talk to me and I'll consider it,"

Dr. Kelley proposed. "Your class schedule will be chosen by me and there will be no excuses for absence. Along with this, you'll provide two thirds of your monthly allowance for us instead of fifty percent. Along with this, you will have a special allowance to *only* be used on groceries. Does that sound sufficient?"

Paige blinked at the man across from her. For her entire life, he had only offered himself as a controlling boss-like figure, as if she was an employee. In a way, she was, but for what point? She had no idea. All she knew is that it was her only choice. She stared at Dr. Kelley with her lips parted in a dumbfounded look.

"Are you being serious?" she finally uttered out.

"I am." Dr. Kelley flashed her his yellow, toothy smile. "There is...one condition, though."

"There it is." Paige's hopeful expression softened into a stoic one. "And what is that?"

"You must conceal your identity. Once you come up with a false alias, we will provide all of the required documents, such as a driver's license, passport, and birth certificate. You must always keep this identity while on school property, but you may return to your true physical form elsewhere. If I find these policies to be violated or that you have not been vigilant to others around you, there will be *severe* punishment. Do you understand?"

Paige ever-so badly wanted to question Dr. Kelley's reasoning for these rules, but after she considered what exactly she was getting herself into. Maybe it was the best idea for her to conceal her identity. After all, publicity was not what she - or the organization - wanted. Instead, she needed to focus on her studies rather than running from the news. Nobody knew what she looked like, but what if starting fresh would be the best thing for her?

CHAPTER THREE

"I understand, Sir," Paige replied without breaking eye contact.

Dr. Kelley outstretched his right hand. "Do we have a deal?"

Paige looked at the wrinkly...thing extended towards her. One of the last things she desired to do was touch such a slimy, disgusting creature. Things could not be how she wanted them to be all the time. With this thought in mind, she leaned forward and shook the doctor's hand with an iron grip.

"Deal."

Chapter Four

BLOND

Paige adjusted the thinly rimmed square glasses on her face for the umpteenth time that day. It was currently seven thirty on a Monday morning. The last thing Paige wanted to do at the beginning of the week was be conscious at the crack of dawn. Sleep, even though she got very little, was very important to her, especially since she was still a teenager. While she was not acquainted to those of the species, she acted like one.

Somehow, the glasses on her face were still sliding down her nose even after she adjusted them. Paige's face scrunched up in a scowl as she continued to get herself comfortable. When she was finally satisfied, she stepped back and looked at herself in the mirror. Paige had to do a double take - or even a triple take - when she saw the figure looking back at her. A head of poofy black hair paired with brown eyes, clear skin, and a formal outfit was not what Paige was used to herself looking like. She was adorned in a navy-blue blazer overtop a white tank with matching dress pants. Paige also wore black flats–she hated how heels felt on her feet.

CHAPTER FOUR

Paige ran her brush through her hair again. She thought her new black curls would smooth out rather than remaining in place. Her straight, blonde hair with bangs was never that unruly. Paige ultimately decided that it was enough of a change for her to be unrecognizable...even to herself. She blinked once at the mirror, then twice, and then three times before confirming what she saw in her reflection was - in fact - real.

Despite looking the part, Paige was nowhere near ready for what was awaiting her. She picked out a beige tote bag that she discovered in a lost and found bin inside the city library that had the quote *"I cannot live without books"* by Thomas Jefferson. Paige had no idea who that man was, but he seemed scholarly, so she took the bag to put her few belongings in. She threw in a notebook that she bought for three dollars at the local pharmacy along with a small pencil case filled to the brim with mechanical pencils, extra lead, erasers, and pens. Paige could not promise that she bought absolutely everything. She also put her new wallet along with a fake driver's license, a student identification card, and a debit card that hardly had any money on it.

Paige slung the tote bag over her shoulder and assessed herself in the floor-length mirror once again. She looked like a completely different human being, which was what she was not used to. She adjusted her square glasses once again before finalizing her self-inspection.

After taking a deep breath, Paige exhaled through her slightly chapped lips, "Perfect."

She pulled her tote bag up to rest more comfortably on her shoulder and turned around before she could over-assess herself in the mirror's reflective - and selective - surface. Paige grabbed her apartment keys from the counter and strutted out of her living space without a second glance to her unmade bed or the untouched rest of her apartment. Paige locked the three locks to her door and stuffed the keyring in her tote bag to mingle with her other belongings. Paige was thankful that she chose to wear heel-less shoes as she padded quietly towards the elevator and pushed the button to go downward.

One elevator ride that seemed to be an eternity later, Paige found herself briskly striding through the lobby and through the heavy double doors. The warm late-summer air hit her like a pile of bricks. It was a similar feeling to the one she had when her old-timey analog clock began blaring relentlessly with alarm until she smacked the top of it. Little did she know that just over an hour later, she would be having the same emotions as she made her way across the bustling city of Arkford.

The landscape around her was just as it always was. Pedestrians littered the sidewalks and filtered out into the crosswalks and streets, which caused the boatloads of traffic to honk their horns and yell in distress. Paige resisted the urge to clamp her hands on either side of her head to block out the sound. No matter how many times she walked a similar route, she never got used to the hustle and bustle. Paige preferred a solitary lifestyle.

Unfortunately, what you wanted often was what you could not have.

Paige ignored the rumbling in her stomach for the time being. She decided to wait until lunchtime to retrieve something from the college cafeteria. Whether it was the legal method or not, Paige refused to care. She would sustain herself in any way she could whether it was the right thing to do or the wrong thing.

She could not find it in herself to critique the life she lived. Paige had no one to look up to. She lived by herself and had her own space, which she would always be grateful for. Despite having constraints on her life to begin with, Paige felt a certain amount of freedom and that was barely enough for her. With this new identity, Paige could finally be visible to the public without fear of publicity, especially after the bus incident. Paige could not bear to risk it–not just for herself, but for those putting the very limits on her shoulders.

Azure University seemed to blend in with the rest of the city apart from the fact there was a generous, square field of perfectly trimmed grass and two sidewalks circling it. The both of them met at the front of the school, which consisted of a staircase and double doors that were tall, elegant, and brown. They were propped open to likely welcome the new freshman into the Fall semester.

The building itself was a diamond in the rough. As opposed to the countless skyscrapers and buildings that would make a dinosaur claustrophobic, the university looked to have about four floors and was composed of three large buildings surrounding the field. The three of them were connected by outdoor walkways. The biggest of the trio, which was in the middle, had a massive round courtyard framed with bushes, benches, floor-to-ceiling windows, and the hallways leading to the classrooms on the main floor. Of course, all Paige saw on the interior was one hallway into the administrative wing to get her photo for her student identification card.

Paige had no idea what to think, or expect, as she walked across the right-leaning sidewalk next to the field and towards the double doors. Once she entered the premises of the building, she was knocked back by either the cool breeze of the air conditioning or the large crowds of people flooding the lobby and hallways. The three receptionists at the curved front desk were very busy accommodating each student's needs. She decided not to waste her time there and speed-walked past the lobby to figure things out on her own.

She strode through the hallways while fumbling for her notebook in her tote bag. She had written down her class schedule, the room numbers, and the professors' names. Even though Paige was not a forgetful person, she preferred to be more prepared than not. She read the first class's name on her list as "HIST 121 - United States History 1" which was one of the general education courses she did not have the luxury of choosing.

Instead of dwelling on it like she wanted to, Paige walked straight to her classroom, counting the room numbers in her head as she went. She was thankful that her class was on the first floor, hence the "one" at the beginning of the room number. It was quite far down the hallway and Paige wished she could simply become invisible and weave through the groups of people. This was a high-risk factor, though. Paige needed to be as normal as possible or there would be severe consequences.

Normalcy was what she wanted though...right?

Paige put that thought on hold when she reached her classroom. She took a deep breath before enclosing her hand around the knob and pushing the door open. The room was not crowded, but it was not empty either. About half of the seats were taken, which was overwhelming in itself. Paige was not used to being in an environment like this at all. Instead of focusing on that, though, she found a seat near the door of the classroom and sat down. Paige leaned her tote bag against the chair she was seated in after she scooted it forward.

The teenager paid attention to no one and everyone at the same time. She kept her eyes on her notebook and mechanical pencil that she placed on her desk but noticed that most of the students had laptops in front of them. Paige never thought about how she might need one; she had never used one before. She never had any requirement for one. Instead, she opened her notebook to the second page - the first occupying her schedule - and began writing a header: "HIST 121 - 8/24." When Paige looked up after quite a bit of labored writing, erasing, and writing the same thing again, she noticed more people were in the room.

Paige frowned when she saw someone wearing pajamas.

She ignored the people around her - her *classmates* - the very second her professor walked into the room. He was a tall, lanky man who appeared to be in his late fifties or early sixties. His hair was completely gray, but he was not balding and gross like Dr. Kelley. Instead, this man was dressed neatly in a light brown blazer and matching pants. He wore a black tie over his white button-up shirt. He carried a briefcase that matched his tie. When he approached the desk at the front of the classroom, not many people looked up. Paige did, though. She adjusted her glasses right when they were about to fall off her face.

"Good morning, scholars!" the professor exclaimed in a brighter voice than Paige expected. "I'm Dr. Michael Jenkins, but you can call me Dr. Mike for simplicity's sake. Welcome to the first portion of United States History!"

Paige blinked at this older man with nothing but surprise in her eyes. All she had expected of her professors was for them to be strict and demanding when it came to an introduction. After all, that was all she was used to, especially with Dr. Kelley.

Dr. Mike continued, "It is my goal to teach you the wonders and joys of American history while giving you the option for open discussions about your interpretation of the events that have occurred during the development of this wonderful country–the land of the free and the home of the brave."

"*Land of the free?*" Paige fought against grumbling. "*Ironic.*"

"Now, let's do a quick roll call and see who's here–shall we?"

Nobody in the classroom really had a choice because the eccentric professor began calling off names from the sheet listing them that was in his hand. After each name was called, a student would reply with "present," "here," or a pathetic little finger-raise. Dr. Mike smiled as he called out each name and saw that someone was present until he got to the fourth name on the list.

"Peyton Finlay?" When no one answered in at least five seconds, he continued. "Okay...is Penny Hamilton here?"

Once again, there was silence in the classroom. Paige thought that name sounded familiar, but she was sure it did not belong to her. She looked around at the other students. Nobody spoke up. Dr. Mike scanned the classroom and was about to continue going through the roll when Paige realized something important: Penny Hamilton might not have been her actual name, but it was the name matching her picture on her student identification card.

"Present, Sir," Paige breathlessly interrupted Dr. Mike as he was calling out the next name.

The professor turned towards Paige and nodded in her direction. He gave her a friendly smile, which Paige returned only because it was a kind gesture. Otherwise, the facial expression would be out of the question. As soon as his attention was waived, Paige stared down at her notebook. She pretended to know what she was doing while the professor finished his roll call and began with his lecture.

"Now, I'm sure many of you are taking this class just because it's required for your general education courses," Dr. Mike half-joked, "but, does anyone plan on becoming some sort of History major?"

A couple of people raised their hands. Paige was not one of them.

"Ah, good! A few of you are. As most of you probably know by now, History is a very broad subject. In this class, we will be covering the time from the early Pilgrims first settling on Plymouth Plantation to the Civil War. It truly is amazing how much the United States has grown and developed over the-"

Dr. Mike was interrupted as the door to the classroom abruptly opened. When the knob hit the wall with a loud *bang*, Paige almost flinched out of her seat but managed to keep her composure when she realized who exactly was now in their presence. It was just a harmless boy in his late teens rushing to class five minutes later than the start time. His backpack and blond hair bounced as he dashed towards one of the only empty desks in the room. Paige was thankful it was not next to her, but instead, it was directly behind her. He dropped his backpack down beside his chair and scooted the object in with an ear-piercing scrape against the floor. Paige cringed at that.

"Sorry I'm late, Professor!" the boy puffed as he got himself together. "I slept through my alarm and I had a flat on my bike so I had to pump the tire back up before I left. There were so many cars on the road that I had to take the sidewalk. won't even mention how bad the traffic was–oh wait...I just did. Oops."

"Well, this kid's annoying," Paige grumbled to herself.

Dr. Mike was all smiles, though. "Oh, it's alright–especially since it's your first day. You must be Peyton Finlay. Welcome to United States History. We were just getting started with what this course covers."

"Okay, Professor. I'm sorry again," Peyton apologized with a sheepish expression.

When Peyton scooted his chair forward for a second time, Paige gritted her teeth in annoyance. She decided right then and there that Peyton was her least favorite person in that classroom, as well as the only person she could accurately pin a name tag on.

Dr. Mike continued on with his lecture that was somehow somewhat interesting. Paige took note of every single word he said. She ignored how badly her right hand cramped as she filled up page after page with notes. Paige had no strategy except making a bulleted list with her chicken scratch handwriting that she wished she could more than barely read. Paige's eyes darted from the whiteboard to her notebook to make sure she doodled every detail, dotted every "i" and made sure there was a period at every sentence. Paige wanted this, after all, and she was not going to take advantage of the system.

Eighty-five long minutes and an excruciatingly cramped hand later, Paige was relieved to hear the words: "Alright, class–that's all I have for you today! See you Wednesday." She stuffed her notebook into her tote bag and hoisted it onto her shoulder. Since she was close to the door, she snuck out of the classroom with ease, but not after she shoved the stubborn wooden doorstop underneath the door.

Paige decided right then and there that she was quite hungry. The smell of food wafted in the hallways despite it being just prior to eleven o'clock in the morning. Paige made the decision to follow the alluring scent down the hallway. She weaved around the occasional college student - Azure University was not the largest of schools - and made her way around the campus without realizing it. She remained in the same building but made her way to the cafeteria wing.

She stopped in her tracks in the large doorway that granted her access to the university café that she had no idea existed. Paige's stomach rumbled at the promise of food...which was about to be broken when she discovered the price next to each item on the wall menu to her left. Paige frowned at the fact she hardly had any money on her. She was always subconsciously taught to save whatever money she had in case of an emergency.

"*Is this an emergency?*" Paige asked herself. When her stomach rumbled a second time, she fought the urge to smack it. "*Oh, shut up.*"

This was indeed not an emergency.

Instead of implementing the procedures in case of an emergency, Paige decided to go a simpler route. She padded towards the nearby ladies' restroom and slid in. Paige's gaze darted around to ensure she was alone before putting her perfected cloaking device to good use: her ability to make her appearance transparent. Invisibly, she headed towards the door and instead of opening it, she simply walked through it. Paige winced ever so slightly as her body adjusted herself to pass through the wood. Thankfully, someone's life was not at stake this time. Instead, it was her stomach.

Paige waltzed towards the university's cafeteria/restaurant and made her way towards the ordering station. It was like a buffet catered to the civilian's needs. Paige had never seen so much food in her entire life. Small containers of sandwiches, burgers, fries, small salads, and other sides that Paige did not know the names of. Her jaw dropped as she looked at the options, but her heart was the next body part to plummet when she saw the two cash registers near the exit.

Instead of letting herself question how she was going to go about with this predicament, Paige walked straight into the room filled to the brim with options for lunch and began taking one of nearly each item. She was very thankful that once she grabbed an object, it became transparent just like her. There were others in the line to retrieve their items as well, so one of each item missing without being paid for was inconspicuous.

Paige held as much as she could in her two hands and walked over to one of the empty tables in the corner of the seating area. When she was certain no one was looking and was instead focused on the food in front of them, she reappeared as a functional member of society. Paige sat down at her table and picked out a cheeseburger and fries to devour for lunch. Since she did not want to look suspicious, she began putting the rest of her food - thankfully in sealed containers - in her tote bag.

The sight before her was mouthwatering. Before Paige could stop herself, she took a large, hearty bite out of her burger. The savory flavor melted on her tongue like an ice cube. Paige caught her emotions subconsciously lifting from the food entering her empty stomach. She never realized how much being hungry affected her attitude towards things. The cheeseburger was disappearing from her plate quicker than she expected, but she stopped mid-bite when she began to witness a scene unfold out of the corner of her eye.

"Hey, there!" the friendly brunette cashier chirped. "Is that all for you today?" When the customer nodded, she gestured towards the screen displaying the amount he owed.

The tall, lanky blond boy nodded and gave her a polite smile. "One second."

Paige found herself watching the conversation intently. She recognized the blond to be Peyton from her History class that morning. She noticed how his grin slowly dropped as he searched through the pockets of his jeans and then his coat. His face was paler than it was that morning when he walked in late.

"I'm so sorry. I can't seem to find my wallet," Peyton admitted shyly. "Give me a second to check my pockets again."

CHAPTER FOUR

"There's no rush," the cashier assured him.

Peyton briskly rummaged through his pockets. His face became paler still when he realized his wallet was nowhere to be found. He even turned each of his pockets inside out to ensure his predicament was real.

He looked up at the cashier and forced a smile. "I'm so sorry...I must've forgotten it at home," he sheepishly apologized. "Sorry for wasting your time."

"No, it's o-" the young woman looked like she was about to say something else, but Peyton was already gone.

Paige's lips curved into a frown as she watched Peyton stride out of the buffet without looking back. His hands were stuffed in his jacket pockets and a sheen of embarrassment flooded his face. Peyton's eyes watched his shoes while he walked out of there empty handed. Paige wondered why she cared—it wasn't like this was her problem.

She was even more surprised when a sharp *"Hey!"* left her lips when he walked by her table.

Peyton whirled around when her dominant tone reached his ears. He had a confused look on his face and his eyebrows were scrunched together. His expression intensified when he realized Paige was staring right at him. He pointed to himself and mouthed *"Me?"* to double check whether she was speaking to him.

"Yes, you," asserted Paige and pointed to the chair across from her. "Get over here."

The blond boy was skeptical. He looked at the girl in the navy-blue blazer and square glasses like she was an alien. Still, Peyton approached her table with his hands in his pockets and his posture just the slightest bit slouched. He opened his mouth to greet her, but she simply pointed to the chair again.

"Sit down."

Peyton did not have it in him to argue. Instead, he plopped down in the empty chair Paige had gestured to.

The puzzled boy shuffled his seat forward. "Uh...do I know y-" he started, but he was interrupted.

"Chicken wrap."

"I'm sorry, wh-"

Paige's eyes narrowed before she took another bite of her burger. "That's what you wanted, is it not?"

"Well, yeah, but—wait. How'd you know?" spluttered Peyton.

Paige decided not to answer his question. Instead, she reached into her tote bag that was hanging from the back of the chair and pulled out one of the containers she stored inside. She opened the top and studied it before pushing it across the table. Peyton eyed the container and opened it only to reveal a chicken wrap just like the one he had ordered but could not afford.

Peyton looked at the food and then back at Paige. "Where did you get that?"

"Bought it," Paige easily fibbed. When Peyton hesitated, she pushed it closer to him. "Go ahead. Take it."

"Wait... Are you sure?"

Paige rolled her eyes when his stomach rumbled. "I wouldn't have offered it to you if I wasn't."

"Well...thank you," Peyton shared his perplexed gratitude and picked up the wrap out of the container. "I can pay you back, you know."

"Don't bother."

"No, I mean, when I get my wallet back, I really ca-"

Paige stuffed at least three fries into her mouth. "Just take it. Don't worry about it."

"Okay...thank you," Peyton reiterated. There was a brief

silence that he wanted to fill when the two began to eat their lunches, so that was exactly what he did. "Oh, I'm Peyton."

"I know," Paige simply replied in between two bites of her burger.

Peyton's brows almost lifted off his head. "*Huh?* How?"

"We have History together."

"*Oh!* That makes so much more sense!" Peyton exclaimed to Paige's annoyance. He blushed when he realized *how* she would have noticed him. "Yeah...I was late on my first day."

"I noticed."

Peyton averted eye contact. "It's been quite a morning." Paige wanted to prevent him from explaining further, but he did anyway. "I slept through my alarm, had to pump up a flat, and then forgot my wallet. What's next?"

Paige shrugged as if he was searching for an answer.

"Hopefully nothing," he continued when Paige failed to speak. "Anyway, what's your name? I feel kind of rude just talking about me and not even knowing who you are."

"It's Pai-" she started, but then cut herself off when she realized she couldn't use her actual name. "Penny. Penny Hamilton."

Peyton's mouth stretched into a grin. He had finally gotten something out of her! "Well, Penny Hamilton, it's very nice to meet you. Lunch is on me next time."

"Likewise." Paige focused so much on keeping her sarcasm to a minimum that she did not even hear Peyton's proposition.

At least someone was being civil with her even though he was quite annoying.

The two of them ate their lunch with not much more than silence. Peyton's river of words had run dry since the two had already been somewhat acquainted and Paige simply wanted to eat her lunch, so that was exactly what she did. She was grateful for the lack of conversation. Talking was the last thing she wanted to do when it was completely unnecessary. Even after she finished her food, she was quiet.

The café was full of mostly incoming freshmen who were trying to find their way around and loved the smell of fresh - *actually* edible - food in the late morning. Paige knew she was one of them, but she had more security knowing she was not the only one struggling. This was what she wanted–to be normal, and if this was being normal, she was starting to become acquainted with it. Maybe she was right to long for it.

Peyton balled up the wrapper lining the styrofoam container that was holding his chicken wrap right before he pushed his chair out and stood up. "Thank you very much for the lunch, but I should get going to the computer lab and get some homework done."

"The computer lab?" Paige asked before she could stop herself. "How come?"

"The assignments are online," Peyton explained like it was no big deal.

She was perplexed. "Why can't you do your assignments on paper and turn them in when you arrive at class?"

Peyton gave her an answer that Paige was not expecting.

He *laughed*. Did Peyton find the situation funny? Was Paige's confusion amusing? Insecurity flooded throughout her along with a sprinkle of panic. She had been caught.

"No, Silly," he chuckled warmly. "I'm sorry for laughing–I just thought you knew that Azure University became completely digital this year. I'm a sophomore. Last semester, I had some paper assignments, but now, everything's done online."

Paige's mouth opened and closed like a goldfish.

Peyton's frustrating grin was back on his face. "Well, so long! It was nice meeting you."

Paige watched as Peyton walked away from the table with

his backpack on his back. She was stuck in yet another problem, but this time, an idea flashed in her mind right in the nick of time. Paige grabbed her tote bag, threw it over her shoulder, and didn't bother pushing her chair in as she dashed after the boy who left her more annoyed than enlightened. Once she was right next to him caught his questionable gaze, she proposed her next move:

"I think I'll tag along."

Chapter Five

CYAN

As soon as Paige and Peyton left the lunchroom, the former began to regret her decision of joining the latter. She was very awkward around people, especially those who were somehow in a ten-foot radius of her. The question of "willingly," though, was unanswered.

Paige relished in the fact that the hallways were peaceful. Azure University was not a very large school, which was surprising because of the city's large population. Paige expected a massive number of students–more than enough to keep the buildings cramped. She had to admit that her first class was about the size she thought–about twenty-five to thirty students were on Dr. Mike's list. Being in a less populated space than the city itself was reassuring.

Having someone talk her ear off...was a different story.

"So, what's your major?" Peyton asked Paige after rounding another corner.

Paige was disinterested. "Undeclared."

"Oh, neat!" Peyton was the exact opposite of her. "Do you have any idea what you're going to declare your major as?"

"No."

"Oh." The blond gave her a sideways look. "You know, I'm getting my degree in Human Physiology."

"Fascinating."

Peyton's grin was back on his face. "It is!" he agreed brightly. "I'm hoping to become a doctor, but I have no idea how to get there from here."

"Join the club," Paige muttered irritatedly.

At that moment, she had no idea why she decided to join Peyton except as a learning experience. Yes...that was it. Paige was there to learn, which was what she needed to do in order to have more of a normal life. That was what she wanted, so that was what she was planning to get. A silly boy her age was not going to get in the way–no matter how annoying he was.

"Check it out–we're here!" Peyton piped up after a couple more yards of silence.

Paige stopped and looked through the doorway. In front of her were several rows of tables each containing at least four desktop computers apiece. The room itself was bland, only having one window at the back. It was well lit; there was just enough to give the room a comfortable, cozy feel. The only thing that Paige could think of to make it better would be some blankets and pillows. Comfort was a priority.

The teenage girl said not a word as Peyton led her inside. She did not want to say anything to him, frankly. Paige was unsure if it was her instinct or something else keeping her from propelling forward, but she trusted her gut. Peyton picked a seat near the back of the room next to the window. Wanting to be polite, Paige followed after him and took a seat next to him. She was delighted to discover that the chairs had wheels on them. Paige began scooting around until she was completely comfortable.

She caught Peyton giving her a sideways look before he

dragged his gaze to the computer in front of him. He pressed the power button on the bottom of the monitor and Paige almost flinched when she watched the screen come to life. Paige failed to catch herself watching letters and numbers pop up on the screen as Peyton logged into the computer with ease and began clicking away at what she assumed was the internet.

Paige turned to her own screen and took a deep breath. "Okay...I can do this."

She found the power button in a matter of five seconds. She pressed it and watched as it turned blue along with the screen. Paige's eyes lit up brighter than the computer itself. Now, there was a bigger problem...

How was she supposed to log in?

Peyton turned in her direction when he realized she was staring puzzledly at her computer. "You know, you use your student number to sign in, right?"

"Uh, yeah," Paige deflected almost...*anxiously*. "I just...don't know where to find that."

To her surprise, Peyton seemed friendly about it. "Oh! I had trouble finding it the first time too. Do you have your student ID with you?"

Paige nodded and sifted through her tote bag, which was still filled with containers of food. She was trying not to feel awkward while doing so. Thankfully, she pulled her wallet out of the bag and opened it to reveal her fake driver's license and student identification card. She studied it and realized there was a number at the bottom. Paige slowly typed the number into the computer's login screen, only using her two index fingers. She was unaware of how Peyton was watching her with quizzical eyes.

"You got it?" he asked her with scrunched eyebrows.

Paige nodded without giving him a second glance. Instead,

she focused on the screen ahead of her that had become the desktop background picture along with several symbols. She clicked on a colorful one that seemed intriguing and discovered it opened right where she needed it to–the internet! Paige was lucky that the internet's home screen was set on the school's student login. She used the number on her identification card once again and created a password with more difficulty than she wanted to admit. When she got to her first assignment, she frowned.

"...Discussion...board?"

"Yeah," Peyton confirmed, revealing the fact he had been watching her the entire time. "Have you done one before?"

"No."

"Do you know how they work?"

"No."

Peyton scooted his chair towards her monitor. "It's not bad," he started to explain while pointing at the screen. "See that paragraph? That's your topic. Your job is to answer the questions there in about two hundred and fifty words."

"That's stupid," Paige deadpanned.

"I know," chuckled the boy to her left, "but they're assigned for almost every class. You'll get used to them."

Paige willed with all her heart and soul that Peyton would leave her alone, which was what he did next. She almost exhaled loudly in relief when he turned back to his own computer to continue with whatever project he was working on. Paige decided to do the same, especially since this situation could not get any more awkward.

...Or so she thought.

"Why did the Puritans sail from Europe to North America? Compare and contrast the Puritans from their nation of residence. Explain why freedom was so important to them and provide specific details," Paige mumbled to herself.

She stared angrily at the paragraph like it was a vulture looming over her head and waiting for her to lifelessly collapse. Paige knew that this material was simple, hence it being from the first unit of her very first college class that civilians in pajamas were allowed to attend. She yanked her notebook out of her bag and scanned her notes, but in her haste, all of the words blurred together. In fact, several people from her class had already contributed to the discussion. Why couldn't Paige answer the question like everyone else?

Peyton's expression morphed from wary to concern when he saw the slight panic in her eyes and her complexion as sickly as a ghost's. "Is everything okay over there?"

Paige did not reply. She either did not hear him or just wanted to ignore him. It was most likely the first because the very second he opened his mouth, Paige launched from her seat, shoved the chair in, and marched out of the computer lab.

Peyton's jaw dropped to the floor when she turned the corner. He had no idea what happened or why Paige - or Penny, to him - was so upset. Maybe she needed some extra help with her homework? There was no shame in that—absolutely none. Part of him was tempted to follow her, but the other part told him to stay put.

Penny was really something. She was dressed very nicely for her first day of university. Did she not realize that she could be whoever she wanted? There was something off about her, but Peyton had no idea what it was. He decided to trust his instincts and leave Penny be for the time-being. He did not know of anything else to do other than work on his own schoolwork and not let himself be concerned for a girl he hardly knew.

So, that was exactly what he did.

Peyton did not let himself get distracted by the situation that made him more embarrassed than haunted. He completed the discussion board assignment for his history class that he shared with Penny before shutting off his computer and calling it a day. Thankfully, he only had one class on Mondays and Wednesdays, which was already over. Peyton worked more efficiently in a quiet, cozy environment like the computer lab.

It hardly took any time at all for Peyton to pack up his things into his backpack and to do the same as Paige did at least half an hour prior. He walked down the house with his eyes glued to his smartphone. It was like his neck was created with a slight slouch to it that was prevalent whenever he was looking at the small screen. Peyton had the school practically memorized by now—he knew every twist, turn, and doorway without removing his gaze from the electronic. It was second nature to him.

Peyton strolled towards the bike rack outside the double doors of Azure University's main lobby. A sleek cyan bicycle was waiting for him in the spot furthest away from the entrance of the school. Peyton usually tried to take the spot closest to the doors, but since he was late, that was not a possibility. He brushed that thought out of his blond head while unlocking his bike from the chain he had around it. He put the combination lock in his backpack like he always did, pulled his mode of transportation out of the steel rack, hoisted one leg over, and pedaled off.

The crisp air beat his face like it was a branch whose leaves were about to fly off into the breeze, never to be seen again from between the skyscrapers making up Arkford City. His hair blew into his eyes with each turn and gust of wind. Peyton ignored the street laws of sitting in parked traffic at every red light. Instead of doing so, he pedaled down the sidewalk and skidded around every person that might have been in his way. He was never caught. Lots of other people did it as well. He would just be another one of the bunch.

Peyton simply did not care for sitting in traffic for at least half an hour a day when his house was only a fifteen-minute bike ride away.

A breath of relief left Peyton's lips as the urban scenery became merely a backdrop to make way for the nearby suburbs that he was used to. He was very thankful to live at least somewhat away than the hustle and bustle of Arkford's center. The sun was shining without the cloud of pollution and the birds were singing over the quiet sound of his bike chain rotating. He caught himself steering too quickly into his driveway at the corner of London Place and York Street and had to slam his foot onto the concrete to keep himself from flying into a bush in front of the front porch.

Peyton inputted the code for his garage door and wheeled his bike inside. Since his small mode of transport neglected to have a kickstand, he simply leaned it against one of the many bookcases lining the right-hand wall of the interior room. The garage was a mess. There was no chance that one of the family's two cars would be able to fit inside. Instead, his father's hardware supplies covered the walls among abandoned bookshelves along with the washer and dryer, a couple of white plastic laundry baskets, and some other knick knacks.

He hopped up the three wooden stairs leading into the house and opened the door, which always had an odd sound that seemed like knuckles cracking when it moved. Peyton made himself known in the kitchen by dropping his heavy backpack on the floor next to the table near the entrance. His mother, who was seated in one of the living room chairs to his left, looked up from her crocheting and smiled at her son.

"Hi, Honey!" she exclaimed cheerfully. "How was class?"

Peyton returned the gesture. His mother looked just like him—or he looked just like her male counterpart. Her blonde hair reached her shoulders, and her brown eyes were a radiant copper like the edges of a polished penny. Her smile was the first thing everyone noticed about her. Peyton wished she did not work solely behind a screen so everyone could see her ethereal face.

"It was good," Peyton honestly replied. "If I wasn't late, it would've been better."

Peyton's mother, Caroline, set down the blanket of yarn she was creating to focus on her son. "It's not your fault your bike had a flat. I'm sure your professor understood. If not, he's a...turd."

"Mom," Peyton laughed at her horrible excuse for a profanity, "he told us to call him Dr. Mike and he's really nice. He's not a turd. I promise."

"Good, or we would've had a problem."

Peyton grabbed an apple from the fruit bowl on the kitchen counter and took a large bite out of it. "You could totally beat up my professors," he chuckled with a full mouth.

"I know I could," Caroline confidently declared.

Peyton smiled down at his mother who was at least six inches shorter than he was. He remembered when he was so excited to be shoulder-height, then chin-height, then eye-level. Now, he towered over her small frame at nearly six feet in height. Just two inches to go and he would have broken the barrier. Peyton clearly got his height from his father, who was about his size but with more muscle and structure rather than Peyton's...not so sculpted physique.

Peyton flopped down on the couch adjacent to his mother's chair and looked in her direction as she spoke and crocheted at the same time, "So, did you see any of your friends?"

"Mom," he argued playfully, "I only have one friend and he lives next door. He doesn't have any classes today, and even if he did, he'd probably sleep through them."

"I don't understand children these days." Caroline shook

her head. "How in the world can a twenty-year-old sleep through an entire day?"

"Leo's nineteen, Mom," retorted Peyton. "Do you even know how old I am?"

"You're twenty, Pey."

"And you still won't let me have a beer."

"The minimum age is twenty-one."

"Oh, come on! Dad would let me have a sip."

"Dad's not here."

Caroline gave her son a stern but teasing look. "Okay, Mister Casanova," she decided to lovingly change the subject. "Did you meet any new friends today?"

"Uh, not really." Peyton's mood dropped to his shoes in a matter of seconds.

His mother instantly put down her crocheting but neglected to secure her hook. It fell from the footrest and clanged against the wooden floor which made the both of them flinch. Caroline simply picked it up and set it on top of the blanket she was making before standing up and walking over to her son on the couch. Caroline sat down next to him.

"What's wrong?"

Peyton just shook his head. "Nothing, Mom. It's been an interesting day."

"Something seems off, Pey," Caroline persisted. "What's going on? You know you can talk to me about anything."

"I know, Mom."

Caroline gently ruffled her son's hair that was almost identical in shade to hers. "If you don't want to talk about it, that's okay. I know college is hard, but you're trying your best, which is all your father and I ask from you. We trust you."

"Thanks, Mom." The corners of Peyton's lips quirked upwards.

"It's what mothers are for." Caroline grinned back. "Now,

how about we watch a show or something? Unless you have homework, of course."

Peyton pulled his legs up on the couch cushion so he was sitting cross-legged. "That sounds great," he confirmed brightly.

Caroline placed a chaste kiss on her son's forehead before rising to her feet and returning to her usual chair in the living room. She picked up her crocheting at the same time Peyton grabbed the television remote and flipped to their favorite streaming service. He chose a show both enjoyed and would have fun watching together while his father was at work.

Even though the humorous sitcom was playing on the television screen in front of him just mere minutes later, Peyton's laughs feigned to be completely genuine. He kept wondering what had happened in the computer lab to make Penny storm off like that. Maybe she felt stupid for not knowing what a discussion board was. Maybe she did not want to be associated with a clumsy guy who forgot his wallet at home. Something was off, but he tried not to worry about it as he relished the moment with his mother.

There was always tomorrow, anyway.

Chapter Six

XANTHIC

Peyton breathed in the fresh late summer air as he walked down a concrete path he knew all too well. It was a nice change from the urban landscape where he went to school. He would not change a bit of it, though, because having such a rushed, stressful place nearby gave him more appreciation for the neighborhood he was able to call home. He wished he could have been outside longer, but his destination resided right in front of him.

His blond hair bounced as he stepped up the four stairs to the front porch. The wood creaked under each footstep and every so often, a board had a crack in it, but that was what gave this house character. Peyton paid it no mind. It had slowly been weathering down but still looked like a treasure in his eyes. Why? Because this was one of Peyton's favorite places in the world.

He knocked on the door several times. When there was no answer, Peyton decided to knock again a couple of times. Once again, there was no reply. He knew this was complete tomfoolery because the person he wanted to see was *always* home unless he had a class or if there was something else going on.

Peyton was not fooled. His best friend *never* had anything going on.

"Leo! Wake up!" Peyton shouted and banged on the door, but it was to no avail.

He frowned at the door in front of him. Peyton now had only one option left, which was to dig through his pockets for his keyring and find the special one that fit into the lock. It took him no time at all. In fact, the key stood out as a bright, vibrant red among all the others. Peyton inserted the key into the lock and turned it sideways. The door swung open without a hitch.

Peyton easily walked inside and shut the door behind him. He knew every inch of the place–to the unusual sight of a record player and two full bookshelves of records in the living room to the stainless-steel appliances and countertop in the kitchen. Peyton dashed up the carpeted stairs without a look back. Instead of heading towards the room he was initially going towards, he stepped into the bathroom, grabbed the random cup that always seemed to be in there - this time, it was a Star Wars cup with Darth Vader on it - and filled it halfway with cold water. Then, he began tiptoeing towards the bedroom next door.

He pushed the door open, which was surprisingly silent, and walked inside. The sight before him was just as he expected. Someone was swaddled in blankets with their shut eyes and snoring mouth faced towards the door. A brown tabby cat slept peacefully curled up at the person's feet. Peyton smiled at how tranquil the situation was, and how he was going to break the silence with one swift movement. When he was close enough, he leaned down, held the cup over the boy's head, and dumped it all out.

"What the-?!" the boy jerked upright and scared the cat off the bed who ran out of the room with a shrill *mrow!*

Peyton just laughed as his friend screeched profanities left and right. He swatted the pillow he was laying on in every direction, which Peyton barely dodged. Water dripped from his ginger hair past his brown eyes and down the old t-shirt he was wearing. He tossed his blanket off of him with kicking feet and shielded himself with a giant teddy bear that was the closest thing to him. Somehow, the bear had a menacing look on his face.

"Who's there?!" he demanded. "What the hell's going on?"

Peyton bent down to his eye level and grinned. "Morning, Leo."

"*Peyton*! Oh, my God! What the hell was that?!" Leo threw the poor teddy bear on the floor, his eyes heavy with sleep but alert at the same time. "I thought you were a burglar!"

"With the way you slept through me banging on the front door, the burglar would've cleaned out the whole house by now," Peyton teased.

Leo just glared at him.

"Even the cat was out like a light," the blond thoughtfully noted. "How do you do it?"

"Magic."

Peyton rolled his eyes and clasped his wrist, successfully yanking him out of his bed. "C'mon, Sleepyhead. We've got class in half an hour."

"Half an hour?!" Leo shrieked in dismay. "Why didn't you get me forty-five minutes ago?!"

"Not my responsibility." Peyton shrugged. "Now, go on!"

Peyton struggled not to laugh while he watched Leo frantically rummage around in his dresser drawers to pick out an outfit. He dashed into the bathroom and Peyton was not even sure he took a shower since less than five minutes later, he walked - or hopped, more rather, since he was trying to pull a sock over his foot - out with hopefully brushed teeth and a slightly wrinkled outfit consisting of a red Under Armour sweatshirt and a pair of jeans Leo seemed to wear every single day of his life. Peyton only smirked when he realized Leo neglected to do anything with his hair.

"You know you still have bedhead, right?" he questioned.

Leo thought about it for a second and then turned around to walk downstairs. "I don't care."

The two of them briskly scurried down the stairs. Leo struggled to pull his shoes on as quickly as he would have liked to but failed miserably since he was in a hurry. Right afterwards, he grabbed his wallet off the table and put it in his pocket along with his phone and hurried over to his cat, who was sitting peacefully on the living room couch licking his foot. The cat squealed when he was picked up by the redhead, but he quickly settled down once he realized the human holding him was his best friend.

"You be a good boy, Ollie—okay?" he asked the furry animal in his arms despite not getting an answer—or at least a verbal one. When Ollie rubbed Leo's chin and purred, the latter smiled brightly. "I'll take that as a yes. See you when I get home."

Leo deposited Ollie right back on the couch where he was comfortably seated before. After a quick check that Ollie's food and water bowls were both full, he grabbed his keys, slung his backpack over his shoulder, and dashed towards the door leading to the garage with Peyton in tow. He hit the button to open the large door upwards to reveal the outside, but he hardly took that for granted because he grabbed the handlebars of his cherry red bicycle and pedaled under the door before it fully opened.

"Hey, wait up!" Peyton yelled as he ran after Leo and shut the garage door behind him.

Leo looked behind his shoulder for a split second. "That's what you get for pouring water on my head!"

Peyton sprinted after Leo before taking a detour to his own house. He opened the garage door with an app on his phone, ran inside, and came pedaling out on his own electric blue bike and a backpack on his back. The two of them began cycling together towards the urban area that the both of them dreaded. Peyton and Leo grew up together in the suburbs, but since Azure University was one of the nicest - and surprisingly smallest - universities around, the two of them decided to give it a shot despite the abrupt change in environment.

Peyton fought the urge to scoff for two reasons; the first being that the city was approaching the two of them quickly while they rode their bikes, and the second one was that Leo was creating more of a distance between them. Peyton must have truly underestimated the fact that Leo was in a rush because he was finding himself huffing and puffing to keep up.

"Good grief!" Peyton wheezed when he was directly behind him. "Wait up; will you?"

Leo snuck a glance over his shoulder again and reluctantly agreed. "Okay," he dragged out the word.

Peyton almost sighed in relief when Leo slowed down, but that exhale was caught in his throat when he sped off after a split second of calm before the storm. The distance between Leo and Peyton's bicycles grew larger with each second passing, but Peyton pushed through and began catching up. The two of them entered Arkford's urban district and instantly hopped their bikes onto the right-hand sidewalk.

With Leo in the lead, the two boys weaved around pedestrians who were taking their sweet time either walking to work, having a shopping spree, or were simply out and about.

CHAPTER SIX

Some of the people walking amongst the concrete jungle were furious and shouted as Leo and Peyton sped and skidded past them without a look back. This was something they were used to, and it was a sacrifice they were willing to make if they refused to sit through traffic on the road itself.

"Hey, watch it!" a middle-aged woman with her blonde hair cut in a bob screamed at the two of them as they rode by.

"Sorry!" Peyton shouted in reply and then mumbled, "Karens."

Leo questioned from up front, "What?"

"Nothing."

Before Peyton or Leo knew it, they had arrived at Azure University's campus. It truly was like an oasis in a desert choking from the fumes of its own self destruction. The both of them hurried to lock up their bikes, sharing Peyton's combination lock like they always did when they rode together. The two wasted no time shoving the double doors open and sprinting down the hallways around several of their peers who were annoyingly taking their own sweet time.

Two flights of stairs and two young adults trying to catch their breath later, they found themselves in front of their Advanced Chemistry classroom. Leo looked upon this room with distaste while Peyton proved to be the opposite. He practically dragged his other half through the propped open door and sat down at a desk in the front row of the filled classroom. Nobody liked the front row...except for Peyton.

"Nerd," teased Leo while sitting down next to him.

Peyton ignored his best friend. Instead, he unzipped his backpack and plopped his laptop on his desk. He typed in his password and opened up a perfectly prepared document that included the start of his Chemistry notes. He typed in the date while Leo appeared to be doing the same. The both of them were right on time because their new professor, whom nobody in the classroom had ever seen before, strutted into the classroom. He fit Leo's "nerd" criteria more than Peyton did with his thick, black-rimmed glasses, gelled brown hair, and a plaid collared shirt along with a bow tie and dress pants on his twig-like figure.

"Good morning, class," the man in his thirties greeted before checking his watch. "Or should I say afternoon?"

Leo blinked puzzledly until he checked the time on his laptop. His eyes widened and he opened a messaging app that he and Peyton used to communicate during classes. They had been doing this for at least a couple of years now. He typed out a quick message and sent it to Peyton, who clicked on the notification that popped up on his screen and read it.

"Dude! You didn't tell me I woke up after noon!"

Peyton smirked and sent a message in reply. *"Not my fault. We're lucky we're on time."*

Leo's gaze turned towards Peyton's after he read the text. Peyton just smiled while Leo was trying to contemplate how exactly he slept in so late. Leo loved to sleep. He savored every bit and piece of it that he could during the weekend. The summer was a masterpiece painted with the colors of Dreamland.

The topic was soon dropped when the man at the front of the room continued to speak. "My name is Professor Jesse Bryant, and I will be teaching your Advanced Chemistry class this semester."

"Oh, really?" A sarcastic text from Leo popped up on Peyton's screen.

Peyton sent a couple of crying laughing emojis in response.

"Now, if nobody has any questions, we'll start with looking through the syllabus." Professor Bryant powered on the classroom computer as well as the setting to project the screen onto the whiteboard at the front of the class. "Please open your syllabus that I've sent to your Azure email address."

Everyone did so. As soon as Professor Bryant started talking, it seemed like he would never stop. For eighty-five minutes straight, he spoke about the fundamentals of Chemistry, the class learning objectives, the essays and lab reports that would need to be written each week, and some other important things listed in the syllabus. He barely took any questions because no one was brave enough to raise their hand. Peyton understood what was going on, though, so he kept to himself. Leo, on the other hand, was trying not to fall asleep in front of his computer monitor.

Speaking of which, the redhead magically started paying attention the second that Professor Bryant exclaimed, "Well, that'll be all for today, folks. I'll see you all on Thursday and then on Friday for your first lab."

As soon as Professor Bryant finished his lecture, the entirety of the classroom was in a magical hurry—including the man in charge. He gathered his paperwork into his briefcase that he carried, snapped it shut, and then left the room before anyone else did. Peyton blinked as his quick action. He thought it was a little bit unprofessional, especially since at least one student might have had a question after the class period.

"Well, that was a bore," yawned Leo.

Peyton stuffed his laptop into his backpack and zipped it. "How'd you manage to sleep through most of it?"

"I fell asleep?!" Leo exclaimed in horror.

"No, you moron."

Leo smacked Peyton upside the head. The blond whirled around to retort, but Leo beat him to it. "Once again, that's what you get."

"Whatever." Peyton started leading the way. "I'm getting lunch."

"I'm going back to sleep."

"But you have another class," retorted Peyton, astonished.

"The library exists," Leo reminded him. "They have cool bean bags I can take a nap in."

"What about your class in a couple hours?"

"I'll set an alarm."

Peyton looked at Leo, who yawned again, before agreeing. "Okay, then. I'll see you later?"

"Yeah, sure."

The two of them clasped their dominant hands together and gave each other a "bro hug" as they called it. A lot of young men their age did it to greet and say farewell to each other, but neither of them knew exactly what it was. Peyton watched as Leo turned around, waved over his shoulder, and then headed off towards the library, which was on the first floor of the center building that made up Azure University's campus.

Peyton stared after the nearly empty hallway until he got bored of realizing Leo was not going to return for lunch. He himself decided to shift his field of vision and walk the other way, and when he did, he nearly jumped out of his skin with fright. There, about a yard in front of him, was the ebony-haired Penny Hamilton. She wore a comfortable black knit sweater and a pair of medium-washed jeans along with black flats. It was a drastic change to what she was wearing yesterday, which was practically a suit.

"Woah—uh, hey," Peyton stuttered out once he realized she was standing no more than three feet apart from him.

Penny's voice was almost robotic as she replied, "Hey."

The young woman studied Peyton's figure. He seemed nice enough. Despite being startled out of his shoes, he still had a friendly demeanor about him. That was exactly the reason why Paige felt guilty about escaping the computer lab the previous day. Peyton had done nothing wrong. She was just...embarrassed. Paige thought fitting in would have been easier, but now, what if Peyton found her to be odd? He was the only person she knew outside of the organization.

"Is...," Peyton's voice wavered, "...is everything okay?"

"Huh?" Paige was caught off-guard. "Oh, yeah. I was looking for you."

Peyton's eyebrows shot up. "You were?"

"Yes."

"...Why?"

"I think...," Paige trailed off. *"How does it go again? Oh, yes! That's it!"* She adjusted her posture and looked him directly in the eye. "I think we got off on the wrong foot. I wanted to apologize for my behavior yesterday."

"Your behavior?" Peyton asked incredulously.

"Yes, my behavior." She took a deep breath and then explained, "I shouldn't have been so short. I left the room quickly and without reason. For that, I apologize."

Peyton blinked at her once, and then twice before it sunk in. "Oh, uh, it's okay. Don't worry about it."

"So...um...are we good?"

"Yeah, we're good."

Peyton could see the girl's anxiety physically deflate from her system. He had no idea that Paige spent almost the entire night rehearsing what she was going to say to him in order to make things right. If Paige wanted a single chance at fitting in with Arkford's civilians, she needed to try harder than ever before. She hoped the dark bags that had been produced under her eyes from lack of sleep were not too noticeable. Thankfully, Peyton didn't seem to care.

"Would you like to get lunch? I'll pay since I actually have my wallet this time," he joked.

"Is he inviting me for lunch? That's what normal people do! Right?" Paige forced a small smile onto her face. It was an

expression she was not used to. "If you're offering...then yes. I'd like that."

Peyton grinned at her. "It'll be my treat. Now, come on."

Paige followed Peyton towards the university café more eagerly than the previous day. She stuffed her hands into the pockets of her fluffy sweater that matched the dark hue of her hair almost perfectly. Peyton's strides were much larger than hers, so she had to fight to keep up. In fact, he was over a head taller than her. The top of her head barely reached his chin. Paige failed to notice that Peyton was watching her out of the corner of his eye. There was something about her that was unique.

He was intrigued to say the least.

"So...," Peyton started. "Did you get that discussion board assignment done yet?"

Paige instantly looked up at him as the two walked. "I did, actually," she honestly responded. "I came back to the computer lab last night after my two afternoon classes and finished it."

"You know, you don't have to be embarrassed if you can't figure out something. I was like that when I started here last year," Peyton assured her with genuinity.

"I know." Her complexion pinkened at that. "Are you...are you a second-year student, or whatever they call it?"

"I'm a sophomore, yes. I thought I told you that yesterday. I should be in my third year, but I took a gap year after I–watch out!"

Peyton was about to finish his statement when he realized Paige was about to walk directly into the doorframe of the café. He firmly, but gently grasped onto her arm and yanked her out of the path of the wooden barrier. Paige's eyes were so wide that they looked like they were about to fall out of their sockets. She fought the urge to fight against the grip he had on her

CHAPTER SIX

appendage, but once he let go, she discovered what exactly happened. She hadn't realized that she was looking right at him during the majority of their short journey in the hallway. If Paige's face was heating up before, it was a tomato at that moment.

"Thanks," she gritted out between gritted teeth forced into a polite smile.

Peyton shrugged. "You're welcome, Penny."

Paige and Peyton said nothing else as they entered the café, claimed a table, and waited in line. The former noticed that the latter decided on a chicken wrap just the same as yesterday along with fries and a soda while Paige wanted to try something different. She found herself looking at the prices rather than the actual food, which was why she decided on a side order of chicken tenders and a small order of fries with water as her drink. Peyton looked like he wanted to ask about it, but he must have changed his mind since he said nothing when the two reached the cash register.

She watched as Peyton easily paid for both meals with some sort of card in his wallet. Paige figured this was a credit card that she had heard about in conversations. She had seen some other people use these cards to buy products at stores, but not often. She was used to green paper money or coins. Huh. This technology was fascinating to her, but she felt too embarrassed to ask about it.

She held that thought as the two of them sat down at the table that they claimed with Peyton's backpack in one chair on Paige's tote bag on the other. They sat down at their respective seats and put their food in front of them. Paige was about to dig into her meal that she had been looking forward to for the entire day, but then stopped before she could take a bite. She looked at Peyton, who seemed to be doing something on his small cellular device...what was it called? Oh, yes! It was a phone. Paige had never used one before.

"I wanted to thank you for lunch," Paige spoke up once Peyton put his phone down.

It's not a problem," replied Peyton with his signature grin that Paige couldn't decide whether irked or intrigued her. "Besides, you paid for my lunch yesterday."

"Yeah..." Paige's voice grew quiet with the realization she could have been caught in a lie, "...paid for it."

An awkward silence flooded the table after that. The two of them decided to start eating their lunch. After at least two bites of his chicken wrap, though, Peyton inquired, "So, Penny, where are you from?"

"Here," Paige lied with her mouth full. "You?"

"I've always lived in the suburbs outside the city," Peyton explained. "It's very nice out there. Have you been there?"

"No. I've always lived in the city."

"Man. You know, you could always stop by if you wanted to visit the suburbs. I mean...if you wanted to."

Paige shrugged off the offer. "Thanks."

Peyton took another bite out of his chicken wrap and chose to ask another question. "So, what are your interests? I know your major is undeclared, but what do you do for fun?"

"Uh..." Paige wracked her brain helplessly. What *did* she like to do? "I'm still figuring that out," she answered truthfully.

"Oh, I see."

Once again, silence littered the awkward environment that Paige accidentally brought forth. Peyton must have thought she was a "weirdo" as some people called it. No matter how many conversations she heard while on her undisclosed missions or assignments, she never figured out what *she* herself enjoyed. Was it simply lurking around in the shadows?

Luckily for her, the boy sitting across from her did not seem

CHAPTER SIX

to mind. Instead, he began talking about what he liked to do. Paige discovered that he enjoyed the idea of being a doctor, which was a complicated job from what she heard. She also found out that he had another friend, which was not surprising. Peyton looked like the type of person to make friends. Was that what he was doing with her? Were Paige and Peyton friends, or was Peyton only friends with Penny? The thought hurt her brain throughout the entire conversation.

Meanwhile...in an undisclosed place, neither Paige nor Peyton knew they were being watched. A dark room was filled with only the light of at least six computer monitors mounted to the wall. One of them was pointed directly at the table that Paige and Peyton were enjoying lunch at. A desk rested underneath these mounted monitors with a keyboard and another monitor that looked to be displaying a database of some sort. Two men sat down in front of this extravagant display and watched their every move.

One man leaned towards the other and asked, "Do you really think this is a good idea?"

"Of course," the balding man with a spine-chilling xanthic grin confirmed. "After all, we need someone like this for our next project."

"Is he really the right one?"

Dr. Kelley turned his rolling chair towards his partner. "He's *perfect*," he asserted, his eyebrows slowly lowering. "Gullible, a bit reckless, but also intelligent."

The doctor's partner was still unsure. "If he's smart, then he'd catch on."

"That's why we need to do this quickly."

"But-"

"You'll see," Dr. Kelley cracked his knuckles and typed something into the mainframe. "Take it from me. It's easier than you'd think."

Chapter Seven

AQUA

The last thing Paige was expecting when she entered her History classroom was for Peyton's seat to be empty. She was nearly late herself, just like he was the two days prior, but surely someone would learn from their mistake the first time, right? She sat down at her desk which was a row in front of Peyton's and removed her notebook and a pencil from her tote bag that was resting beside her chair.

Paige thought back to her journey just minutes before. She had somehow managed to sleep through her alarm set on the clock next to her bed. Then, she threw on whatever clothes she had that were at least somewhat matching. She wore the same sweater as the previous day. It was quite comfortable and it was her favorite. Paige did not care enough to wear a blazer if others in the same room were in pajamas. That was where she drew the line.

Dr. Mike entered the classroom and set his supplies down on his desk. "Good morning, scholars," he greeted the class cheerfully. "Today, we'll be beginning our discussion about the Puritans. Now, I assume you all have some sort of background

CHAPTER SEVEN

in American History in grade school, so this should be more of a review than anything."

"*Nope,*" Paige internally grumbled.

Paige tried her best to pay attention to Dr. Mike's lecture, but since she did not have the proper background like everyone else in the classroom, she found it difficult to keep up. Azure University usually required a high school diploma, but since Dr. Kelley pulled a few strings for her advantage, she was here. Paige felt much less than qualified as she wrote down facts and definitions that she hardly understood. She made a vow to herself to improve her knowledge of United States History.

The sudden sound of rain pattering down on the cozy classroom's roof strengthened the gratitude Paige had for her ability to move quickly through the streets. Of course, she could have generated an energy field to protect herself from the droplets, but she had enough publicity as it was. Stories of the runaway bus still made the news and the occasional dinner table conversation. Practice made perfect when it came to hiding from the world, and she surely had enough of that. The thought of Peyton being caught in the rain strengthened her theory that he had been held up. That was most likely what happened.

In the meantime, Paige continued to write down every single little detail that Dr. Mike threaded into his blanket of speech covering the class. Page after page in her notebook became filled with bulleted lists, underlined definitions, and circled factoids. Paige had had no time for error when it came to school. This was what she wanted, and she would achieve the results she desired because anything other than success was not an option. The organization already was making several exceptions for her as it was.

Paige caught herself looking over at the door to her left just in case a certain lanky boy with blond hair happened to walk through it. It was not that she was interested in his character in any way. Instead, she just wanted to make sure she was doing the right thing by acting like a normal civilian in an academic environment. Maybe Peyton was too "weirded out" - as someone her age would possibly say - by her. If that was the case, what was Paige doing wrong?

That thought haunted her all the way to the café after her History class ended. Still, there was no sign of Peyton as she invisibly walked through the doors, grabbed what food and drink she wanted, and reappeared out of sight of the student body. She sat in the corner of the café and merely watched as her peers paid for their lunches. Paige wished she could do the same, but that was simply not possible in her mind. She had no job and no time for one either. Besides, Paige did not want to waste her life doing something she hated. Then again, the morality of theft was not the ideal path to take either.

Paige did not even notice the taste of her hamburger and fries as she continued watching the entryway to the café for any sign of Peyton. He was the only person she knew, and even though she would never admit it, maybe he was a little bit of a friend. Regular people had friends, or at least that was what Paige had believed for her entire life.

When it came to those standards, she had never been a regular person.

The blonde - well, black-haired girl now - tossed the trash from her meal in the garbage bin near the exit as she walked out but left her lemonade in her grasp. Paige made her way to the nearby computer lab to complete some much-needed research for her History class along with the other three she had in the past two days. She was thankful that no one was in the cozy room since Paige was going to be in there for quite a while.

Paige sat down at one of the tables near the back and

placed her lemonade next to the computer monitor. She looked around on said monitor and found the power button. Paige's face lit up right when the screen in front of her did. Since she had done this before, she quickly logged into the computer, went onto the university's website, logged into that, and found a list of assignments in the order of their due dates. That was perfect! Paige clicked on the assignment with the soonest due date and groaned when she realized it was another discussion board.

Nevertheless, Paige read the description and was prepared to do her work. "Introduce yourself," she mumbled the instructions. "Where are you from? What are your interests? Do you have any educational goals? Career goals? Describe yourself in a hundred and fifty words or more. Shit."

She blankly stared at the instructions in front of her. How was she going to answer *any* of these questions? Her English class knew just about as much as Paige did. After at least five minutes of just watching the screen like it was magically going to be filled with words, she decided to do the only thing she could do:

Lie.

Paige typed and typed until her fingers were sore. She had no idea how long she had been working on that assignment, but, somehow, she ended up with a hundred and fifty words on the dot. She read it back to herself and tried to digest if the information she offered to the computer was understandable.

Hello to my fellow classmates. My name is Penny Hamilton and I'm a freshman here at Azure University. I've been home-schooled for my entire life by my mother and father while the two of them balanced busy jobs. I taught myself most of the time. Because of this, I'm awkward around people, which is why I am quiet during my class sessions. I like doing things the old-fashioned way with a pencil and paper because that's what I grew up doing. This discussion board assignment is something new to me, so I tried my very best to accommodate the instructions' standards. My interests include going on nice walks in the city when the weather is sunny. I like going to the marketplace and seeing all of the good food. I don't really have a hobby other than that. I hope to meet some new friends during this educational academic journey.*

"It's not much, but it'll have to do," Paige thought once her inner voice finished speaking. She pressed the submit button and decided that was the end of it.

Paige leaned back in her rolling chair and stretched her arms out. She had done this assignment all by herself! She fought the urge to stand up and dance around at the realization she had completed something that pertained towards her goal. If this was what normal people did, then Paige thought she was doing a good job of it. She sat back up straight and her eyes caught the yellow tint of her lemonade. Paige picked it up and let the soothing liquid wash the walls of her parched throat.

She nearly spat it all over the computer screen when she heard a voice from the doorway, though. "You know, drinks other than water aren't allowed in the lab."

Paige craned her head around the computer monitor to view a carrot-top of a young man leaning against the door frame. She studied his confident figure with his hands connected to his phone that he was half glancing at. Paige's black eyebrows lowered and blended in with the thin frames of her glasses. She was stock-still. Who did this boy think he was? Maybe he was trying to give her a warning, but Paige *hated* being told what to do.

"Good grief, I'm not gonna tattle on you if that's what you think." The boy's smirk was somehow not menacing. "I'm just warning you."

Paige's brows shot up when she realized she was glaring. "Oh... Well, thank you," she replied quickly.

"Not a problem." The redhead walked into the room and leaned against a table a couple of rows in front of Paige's. "My advice? Bring a cup that isn't transparent. The professors can't catch you if they can't see it."

"Are they really that strict?"

"Not really. I remember getting reprimanded several times during my freshman year. Gotta help out my peers." The boy smiled and then looked her directly in the eyes. "I'm Leo Rhys, by the way."

"Please don't be awkward; please don't be awkward." Paige offered him a kind smile while introducing herself. "Penny Hamilton."

"Hey, wait–I think my friend knows you."

"...They do?"

Leo decided to sit down two chairs away from Paige. "Yeah," he confirmed. "His name's Peyton Finlay. He's a total nut. Yesterday, he walked right into my house and dumped cold water on me to wake me up."

Paige hesitated, her curly hair that she was unused to falling into her face. "He did?"

"Yup."

"And you know this...how?"

"He said something about meeting a new friend named Penny from History class," explained Leo. "Apparently that dummy forgot his wallet and you paid for his lunch on Monday. That was you–wasn't it?"

Relief washed over her like a tidal wave. "Oh, yeah. That was me."

"Yeah." Leo comfortably leaned back in his rolling chair. "I haven't seen him in quite a while, actually. It's been since yesterday afternoon."

"You haven't seen him either?" Paige was suddenly alert.

"I guess not. Wasn't he in class this morning?"

The girl shook her head.

Leo sat up straight at that. "That's odd," he commented with a complete change in mood. "I went over to his house last night to bug him but he wasn't there."

"Wouldn't his parents be concerned?"

"They probably thought he was at my house. He stays late on Tuesdays and Thursdays because of a lab he has and sometimes, he crashes at my place. Don't ask why. We're practically brothers, so we tolerate each other's company."

"So...you're saying you haven't seen him since yesterday afternoon. Is that correct?"

"Yup, that's right."

"Interesting...," Paige stated thoughtfully

"What's interesting?" Leo's lips curved into a frown.

"Nothing." She abruptly stood from her seat and made sure that everything was in her tote bag before she went to leave. "I have to go."

Leo rose as well. "Woah–you're antsy. Do you have a class or something?"

"No," Paige bluntly replied.

"Oh." The redheaded boy stopped in his tracks. Was Penny leaving on purpose just to get away from him? He brushed that thought aside. "Well, wherever you're going, good luck."

"Thank you."

Paige stepped around him and marched towards the door until she realized she was probably being rude about the whole situation. She had a choice to make: she could either turn around and apologize to Leo for her abrupt departure or continue out the door. Rather than following her heart, she chose her mind's words of wisdom and did not take a single look back. Paige had no time for any more small talk, so she was going to do something about it.

She caught herself dashing down the hallways that were slowly becoming familiar to her. Her peers and the occasional professor blended into a blur that became Paige's vision. She ignored the squeaking that her damp shoes made on the tiled floor as well as the cold droplets hitting the top of her head once she shoved open the double doors to the outside world.

Morphing into her original body was something Paige was completely used to by then. She became multiple identities as time went on, and each of them had their own feel. Penny Hamilton had a scholarly and friendly feel. Paige O'Connell possibly had blood on her hands mixed in with the pouring rain. She ignored how her blonde bangs stuck to her forehead from the downpour and the beads of sweat budding due to the sprint she broke into.

Paige knew exactly where she was going. She was a very intelligent individual. There was no way that the organization was going over her head once again. She could not let them control her life once again. Paige was not some sort of animal being let out of its cage every once in a while for some fresh air. That was what she felt like, though. College was her only freedom, where she felt like she was able to be her own person, but now, that had been taken away from her too.

She dashed down a familiar route that she never got used to. Paige hated how water soaked into her socks and drenched them as she ran through and around flooding puddles that had magically appeared from merely an hour or two of off-and-on rain. Paige's heart dropped when she arrived at the building she was looking for. Without hesitation, she hid her appearance from the outside world. Paige merely walked through the high security gates without batting much of an eye. She powered her way through the entrance and walked directly past the front desk. She had no time for speaking with a receptionist.

Paige walked down a hallway that she had not been down in quite a while. Her heart began pounding in her chest with each step. The sweat flowering on her face overtook the droplets dripping down her skin, into her clothes, and then appearing on the floor behind her. Blinking her emotion away as she went down this excruciating route. Her hands clenched into fists and loosened again several times. This became a routine of hers, which stopped once she approached the door she was in search of.

The blonde took a deep breath in and then out. Her hands trembled from the friction they put themselves through, but she could not turn now. Paige was on a mission, and that mission included skipping her other two classes that took place that afternoon. She recalled reading the syllabi for said sessions and remembered that she had five unexcused absences for each class.

This was quite inexcusable.

One by one, Paige's clammy fingers clasped onto the doorknob. She would have walked through it with ease but found that it would only cause questions for whoever - or whatever - was inside. Her transparency regained itself at that thought. She knew she had to be smart about this. If who she thought was behind the door, her abilities could not be put in jeopardy.

"*Come on, Paige,*" she spoke to herself. "*You can do this.*"

With a small *creak*, Paige turned the knob and the door slid open.

Chapter Eight

LAVENDER

An intoxicating ringing blared through a pair of ears— one being out in the open and the other pressed against a cold, hard surface. The body that they were connected to was stiff, aching when a single muscle would twitch. A groan bubbled up the walls of their throat and barely ebbed from their chapped lips.

Blond hair pressed against the forehead of this individual, coated in sweat that stuck each separate strand in a different place. Every eyelash was clamped to the other from several hours of sleep. A hand brushed the short hair out of the face of the body slowly returning to consciousness. A pair of brown eyes pried their way open to a blurry canvas of watercolor nothingness.

Peyton's gaze snapped into focus a moment later. What was once a foggy mess became a jigsaw puzzle where the last piece had fit flawlessly into place. The gray backdrop had been revealed to be a cell that Peyton had no idea how he got into. The iron bars covered one wall while the rest along with the flooring was pure concrete. The right side of Peyton's body was chilled to the bone. He fought away a shiver as he forced himself into a seated position. His head spun like earth on its axis, yet everything fell into place instead of apart. The only question that plagued his conscience was one of simplicity.

"Where the hell am I?"

Not much was on the other side of the bars from Peyton's fatigued figure except for what seemed to fill the room: prison cells. The boy's hands became clammy despite their grasp onto nothing but oxygen. Said element transitioned from thin to thick as it entered his nose and exited his mouth in tight waves. Peyton pulled himself up from off the floor and staggered off-balance to the bars themselves. He looked left and then right. It was clear that nobody else was in the room. Not even a security guard was in the premises that Peyton could ask a question to. Instead, there was an empty desk with a vacant chair overlooking the prison environment.

Peyton's lips parted. He wanted to enunciate a word, but it was too late coming from his parched mouth. Before anything could leave his larynx, the door next to the desk gradually slid open. Not knowing what else to do, Peyton fled from the edge of the cell and went right back to laying on the floor. He wondered if pretending to be unconscious would keep himself from jeopardy. Peyton laid still and ignored how the small bumps in the semi-smooth concrete jutted into the right side of his body.

"Do you *really* think playing dead would do you any good?" a female's voice inquired from the doorway.

The boy's eyes shot open. So much for that idea. "...Who are you?"

Paige shut the door behind her and casually walked over to the desk. She leaned against the wooden surface. Peyton was quite puzzled by the whole situation. Just a moment ago, he awoke on the concrete floor of a jail cell and then a blonde girl who could not have been older than him sashayed into the room wearing a black sweater over a band tee with ripped jeans and worn out Converse. Her hair was damp and so were her clothes. She must have been out in the rain. Was it raining, even?

"Someone who's *not* a moron," Paige asserted without making eye contact.

Peyton shot up to his feet and cocked his head to the side. "What's that supposed to mean?"

"Exactly what I said."

"*Who does this girl think she is?*" Peyton asked himself. "Okay, but you look *very* out of place. Do you know anything about what's going on?"

"*I* look very out of place?" she retorted snarkily.

"Now, look here–I don't know who the hell you are or what you're doing here, but I want to know why I'm in jail or whatever this is," Peyton asserted.

Paige stood up straight, looking him in the eye. "It's complicated, so do me two favors. One: don't ask questions, and two: be inconspicuous."

"Huh?"

Paige ignored his question. Instead, she walked around the desk so her bottom half was out of sight. A scowl haunted her lips when she realized the drawers each had a lock on them, but she had a way around that. Paige allowed her hand to simply pass through the wood and feel around in each drawer. When her fingers touched a frigid metal, she knew she had found exactly what she was looking for. Paige pulled her hand along with the object through the drawer. Peyton watched as Paige dangled a pair of keys in front of her.

Peyton's brows lowered. "Where'd you get those?"

"I told you not to ask questions."

"I need to know what's going on."

"I'll explain later."

"No, I need to know *now*."

"Later."

"*Now!*"

"Do you want to get out of here or not?" Paige snipped while storming towards him. She and Peyton were less than a foot apart with iron bars separating the two of them.

Peyton hesitated. He looked at the keys rocking back and forth from the ring around her index finger. The boy had no idea that Paige was so close. There was something uncanny about the entire situation, but he knew better than to question it. Peyton took a deep breath and then looked the girl in the eyes before nodding obediently.

Just like that, Paige inserted one of the keys into the lock, turned it sideways, and pulled the cell door open. She put the keys in one of the pockets in her sweater and started off towards the door she previously entered through. After she realized that her footsteps were the only ones audible, she turned around and gave Peyton - who was at a standstill - a hard look.

"Are you coming?"

Peyton awkwardly looked at the opening in the iron bars that appeared before him and stepped through it. Paige fought the urge to roll her eyes as she began leading him out the door and down a hallway. She ignored her heart throbbing against her ribcage like it was about to burst at any given time. There was a more important task at hand that did not just involve her life being rolled as pips on a pair of dice in the gamble of fate.

The two of them briskly walked side by side with Paige slightly ahead like a goose leading its skein through wisps of clouds. Nothing but the sound of two pairs of footsteps filled the scarily vacant hallway. Peyton looked around at every door, floor tile, and rut in each stained beige brick of the walls. If this was a dream, he sure as hell wanted to wake up sometime soon.

"What is this place?" he caught himself inquiring.

Paige gave him an instinctual glare. "No questions."

"You can't expect me to just follow your lead without knowing who the hell you are and what all this is."

"What'd I say about being inconspicuous?" she snapped in a hushed tone. "It's like you *want* to die."

Peyton's brown eyes were so wide they looked like peppermint patties coated in chocolate. "*Excuse* me?"

Without any warning whatsoever, the sound of sirens began blaring from everywhere in the building. The two of them stopped in their tracks after a red flashing light flooded the halls. Paige's heart sank when she realized what was going on. They had been found out. She looked at Peyton like she was a deer trapped in a pair of headlights and did the only thing she could.

"Just come on!"

Before Peyton could protest, Paige harshly grabbed onto his wrist and started dragging him along. She broke off into a jog which Peyton was forced to match. The breath was whisked out of Peyton before he got the chance to recognize what was going on. Paige increased her speed into a sprint and continued to pull Peyton along with her. She refused to let go despite whatever arguments he was about to make. Thankfully, she knew her way around the building like it was her home. In a way, it was.

"What's that?" Peyton puffed as the two ran.

"Alarms," explained Paige shortly.

Peyton managed to conjure up a sarcastic remark. "Well done, Sherlock."

"Just *shut up!*"

That seemed to do the trick. Peyton clamped his mouth shut as the two continued to sprint through the hallways. That did not change his increasing anxiety alongside Paige's own. She led him through more passages among twists and turns where Peyton was unsure how his ankles hadn't snapped while mazing down. Paige seemed to know exactly where she was going, but Peyton was unaware of anything–including her name.

Peyton bit back yet another question. He knew he was going to get shot down. Apparently, he had no idea how dire this situation was. Then again, he had no clue where he was even located–was he still in the same state? Country even? That thought whisked out of his head once Paige shoved open a door and the two of them were greeted with a downpour. Peyton knew better than to complain about the rain soaking his hair, clothes, and shoes, or his aching lungs. The agonizing sensation rose up his throat and strangled him like an anaconda. Paige, on the other hand, looked like she was not going to slow down anytime soon.

That was what he thought, at least.

Paige skidded to a stop about halfway between the door they had passed through and the iron gate they had yet to cross over. The momentum caused him to nearly fall flat on his face if Paige had not tightened her grip on his wrist and pulled him upwards. Peyton opened his mouth to question why the two of them stopped, but his inquiry was answered when the reality was revealed to him.

Countless men in dark gray uniforms, black masks over their nose and mouth, goggles concealing their eyes, and gloves on their hands surrounded Paige and Peyton. Each of them held an automatic rifle with magazines holding at least fifty golden bullets hanging out of them. The clicking of

CHAPTER EIGHT

weapons being cocked transformed Peyton's already-heavy breaths into brisk hyperventilations.

"Oh, my God. Oh, my God. *Oh, my God,*" Peyton continued to mumble under his breath with increasing volume.

Paige was completely silent except for her labored respirations. The two were back-to-back and surrounded. Everything was completely still. Even the rain falling seemed to halt in its path. The scene unfolded before anything could stop it. Peyton clamped his hands over his ears when the sound of gunfire filled the air around them. A scream fell out of his mouth and he collapsed onto the ground in a small ball. His eyes opened only when he realized none of the bullets had made contact with his body after at least five seconds of consistency.

His eyes cautiously fluttered open to notice rain - along with countless bullets - bouncing off of a lavender energy field that was tinted lilac surrounding the both of them. The outside environment became muffled and echoey because he was suddenly in a world of his own. Peyton's brown eyes flitted upward to view Paige standing over him with her hands outstretched. It did not take a genius to determine the field was her doing.

"What the hell is that?!" Peyton yelled over the bullets ricocheting from the energy field.

"Can't you trust me for five seconds?!" screamed Paige in return.

"Oh, I don't know!" His voice was full of furious satire. "What *should* I do when I'm being shot at?"

"Grab onto me."

Peyton blinked at her. "What?"

"Just do it!"

The boy asked no more questions. Instead, he clasped onto her hand and got to his feet only for his body to disappear underneath him along with Paige's. His gaze widened when he realized that the two of them had become invisible to the naked eye. Peyton's eyes darted to where he assumed Paige would be standing.

"Are we-"

"Yes, we are," Paige snapped before lowering her voice. "Don't scream."

"Why would I-"

Peyton immediately broke his unspoken promise when the ground disappeared from below them. He let out a shriek that echoed into the abyss that he and Paige were whisked into. He felt like he was flying but was well aware of the chance of falling until the bone crush. Peyton could not see how Paige was gracefully gliding through the portal she created, even when the two reappeared on the other side. He was prepared for his knees to break upon impact, but instead, they were able to merely jog out of the sideways exit onto the flat surface making up a nearby street.

Adrenaline pumped through Peyton's veins as he dashed behind Paige who was keeping a steady pace. He turned to face the building they were escaping from. The energy field had vanished and there were several bullet holes in the ground where they had once stood. A chill rocketed through his bones. His fatigued legs failed to carry him anymore.

Once the two rounded yet another corner where the building was entirely out of sight, Peyton's clammy hand let go of Paige's. His body reappeared once contact was lost. Paige halted and whirled around to view Peyton's fragile frame giving in on itself and crumpling into the grass beside the vacant sidewalk. She herself returned into view after she noticed him begin to convulse and dry heave into the poor half-dead blades.

Paige's face scrunched up as he practically spilled his guts in the grass only to roll away from the mess of sick and begin gasping for air once he was finished. She kept her distance while Peyton attempted to recollect himself. Frankly, she had no idea how to even start comforting the boy in front of her. What was she supposed to do in a situation like this?

"What...," Peyton choked heavily, "the hell... was that-?"

"Don't freak ou-" Paige softly started, but she was interrupted.

"Don't freak out? Don't *freak out*?!" he began to yell while he sat up and narrowed his gaze in her direction. "What do you mean *don't freak out*? I was just in prison, got shot at, and now *this*?! Invisibility? Force fields? What's going on?!"

Paige sat down cross-legged across from him. She tugged blades of grass out from the dirt and tossed them aside like a small child not knowing what to do at kindergarten recess. "I was trying to save your life. It worked–didn't it?"

"They were shooting at us!" Peyton waved his arms around like a confused penguin. "Why were they shooting at us?!"

"You need to calm down."

"Calm down? How am I supposed to calm dow-"

Paige lurched forward and clamped her hand over his mouth. "You need to listen to me," she gritted out. "Panicking won't make it any better. I need you to breathe. Those men work for a group of scientists. They most likely wanted to do some sort of experiment on you like they've done on me. Trust me–you don't want that."

"Experiments?" Peyton's muffled voice squeaked from behind her hand.

Paige merely nodded. "It's me they're after. They'll go for someone else sooner or later."

"But that doesn't make any-"

"Listen. It was a test. I will take care of it." Her hazel eyes were fierce. "Now, if I let go, will you *promise* not to freak out?"

Peyton nodded meekly. Paige released her grip on him. He

began coughing and reeling over to catch his breath, but thankfully for the both of them, his stomach decided not to turn itself in circles again. Paige awkwardly watched as he composed himself. She had no idea what else to do than to let him settle down.

"Can you answer one question for me?" Peyton pleaded while looking up at her.

Paige pushed herself upright. "What's that?"

A toothy grin appeared on his face—one that the girl hardly expected. "What else can you do?"

"Create energy fields, become transparent along with select things I touch, pass through solid surfaces, and teleport short distances through wormholes," Paige bluntly explained. She purposefully left out one important detail.

"Holy cow."

"How...is a cow...holy?" she deadpanned.

Peyton stifled a chuckle at that. When he realized she was being completely serious, that positive emotion vanished. "Would you prefer profanities?"

Paige just stared at him quizzically before changing the subject. "I'm walking you home. Where do you live?"

"Woah there," Peyton dismissed and got to his feet. "You might've just saved my life, but there's no way in hell you're going to my house."

"And why not?" She crossed her arms over her chest.

"I don't even know you."

"I'm Paige. There. Now, you know my name."

"I'm Peyton."

"I know," Paige replied before she could stop herself.

Peyton's jaw nearly dropped. "How would you possibly know that?"

She paused, realizing her slip up. Paige needed to think of an excuse - and fast - so, that was exactly what she did. "The

CHAPTER EIGHT

organization had a file with your name on it while I was looking through the drawers for the keys."

"Fair enough."

It was a poor excuse, but it worked out nevertheless. Peyton's jaw snapped shut when he realized if he were to ask another question, it most likely would not be answered. Oppositely, Paige thought he was an enigma of sorts. What on earth did he not understand? The organization merely wanted to test her. This has happened before. Would it happen again if Paige made any more connections with the student body?

She surely hoped not.

"Let me take you home," Paige insisted.

Peyton nodded, agreeing. Paige was very thankful for his submission, especially since she was unfamiliar with any areas outside of downtown Arkford. Luckily, Peyton led the way down a sidewalk in the direction they were traveling before he needed to stop.

The two of them walked along the concrete path in more silence than they would have liked, or Peyton would have liked, more rather. He shuffled around awkwardly as he strode ahead of Paige, who was following him without a single sense of direction. Her trust was slowly fading like early morning fog with each step they took. Paige caught herself glancing over her shoulder as the city grew smaller and smaller behind them. Peyton, on the other hand, knew exactly where he was going.

"How far out do you live?" Paige discovered herself asking.

Peyton looked over his shoulder for a couple of seconds. "Not far. I'm in this neighborhood, actually," he replied. "You don't have to accompany me, though. I'm fine."

"We've been walking for twenty minutes."

"Am I being too quiet or something?" Peyton suddenly appeared a little bit worried. "I mean, you're obviously an introvert, so should I do more of the talking?"

Paige hesitated. *"That's new,"* she commented to herself. Paige adjusted how her loose sweater was resting on her shoulders. "It doesn't matter."

"Wait, I'm sorry," he apologized.

Paige's brows furrowed. "...Why?"

"Because you said not to ask any questions."

"I meant regarding the situation at hand."

"Oh."

Silence ensued after that. Peyton wanted to smack himself for being so clingy and questionable. Then again, he had just escaped a life or death situation, witnessed supernatural abilities, and puked near a sidewalk in front of a girl. He was unsure what was the worst out of the three. Then again, Paige seemed indifferent. He watched as she walked beside him looking at nothing but her worn shoes with a neutral expression. Peyton had no idea what to do.

She seemed...lost–literally and metaphorically.

Peyton failed to answer that question because his residence appeared before him prior to him finding a chance to speak. He stopped in the middle of the sidewalk, which probed Paige to do the same. She studied the building in front of her. It was two floors with a light brick exterior and dark gray shingles on the roof. The place looked vacant, especially since there were no cars in the driveway. A sense of longing flashed in Paige's hazel irises before she was snapped out of it.

"Well, this is my place," Peyton brought up like it wasn't obvious.

Paige continued analyzing the scene in front of her. "I see," she commented. "It's nice."

"Thank you." The boy shifted from one foot to the other. "Uh, is it a long way back to your place? I'd feel bad leaving you be."

Her eyes narrowed into a puzzled glare.

"Not that I mean you can't protect yourself." Peyton put his arms out in mock surrender. "I just mean...you literally saved my ass."

"I believe I saved your whole body," Paige obliviously retorted.

Peyton gave her an odd look. "You know what I mean," he clarified. "I guess I just want to say thank you."

There was no response from the girl in front of him except an empty, unprejudiced expression.

He continued with a smile, "Thanks for helping an annoying stranger who has no idea what the hell's going on."

"You're welcome," answered Paige, who had to tilt her head upwards to genuinely look him in the eye for the first time. "And I guess you'll know soon enough."

Paige had no idea why she said what she did, and neither did Peyton. She stuffed her hands into her fluffy pockets and averted eye contact with him. Peyton pushed his hair out of his eyes and rolled his lip through his teeth.

"What does that-" he began inquiring, but Paige had already vanished just like his understanding of what this world was capable of that day.

Chapter Nine

ELECTRIC

This must have been a dream.

There, Peyton laid, face down on his bed. Somehow, he had made it above his comforter and was sprawled out like a starfish on the ocean floor. Soft snores emitted from Peyton's open mouth against his warm pillow, which had been cold once he rested his head on it. The fan overhead spun like wildfire. Since Peyton had two exterior walls to his room, it was either the warmest part of the house during the summer, or the coldest during the winter.

Either way, he was sound asleep. His mind unconsciously flipped over itself. What was going on? Peyton had no idea. He could not comprehend the intensity of the dream that he had. It felt like he had drunk several bottles of booze and had an excruciating hangover. It was not like he knew what *that* felt like, obviously.

Peyton refused to budge even when a cool hand began nudging his shoulder. Instead, he grasped onto the pillow, rolled onto his side, and dove deeper into slumber. His name was being echoed, but it was as desolate as a breeze whisking through a mountain's crevice. His blond hair fell in his face, but it was blown away by each quiet snore passing through his lips.

"Peyton," his mother repeated for the sixth time. "It's time to get up, Sweetheart."

The boy only grumbled gibberish before rolling over to face the opposite way. He seemed to go back to sleep until Caroline tried again and nudged more. "Peyton, you need to get up."

"I'm waiting for the alarm," he whined from underneath his pillow.

"It's been going off for twenty minutes."

This caught Peyton's attention. He almost headbutted his mother as he shot up in bed as stiff as a board. "What?!" he screeched like a banshee. "Why couldn't you get me twenty minutes ago, then?!"

"I thought you'd be getting ready!" Caroline yanked her son out of bed.

"You've known me for twenty years, Mom—I wouldn't be."

His mother dashed out of the room while Peyton rushed to get ready. He stripped his clothes off on the way to the bathroom next to his bedroom. He hopped in the shower for a solid ninety seconds - unfortunately with cold water - before shaking his hair dry with a towel hanging on the rack. Peyton ignored the fact that water dripped down his legs as he made his way back to his room. He threw on the first clothes he found on the carpeted floor, which happened to be an oversized olive-green hoodie and a pair of ripped jeans he wore almost every day.

Peyton ran down the stairs - taking them two by two as he went - and the aroma of breakfast wafted into his senses like the smell of fresh spring flowers. He knew at once that his mom was making one of his favorites: French toast. His nose directed him right to the granite kitchen countertop where his mother was removing two pieces of French toast from the pan she made them in onto his plate.

"Ooh, French toast!" Peyton exclaimed, quickly grabbing his plate. "Thanks, Mom!"

Caroline rolled her eyes and looked up at her son. "You'd better eat up quickly before you're late."

"Give me a break," he retorted with a full mouth. "It was *one* time last year."

"Your professor was pretty sore about it."

"Mrs. Cullen was a jerk."

Caroline laughed and it sounded just like the feminine version of Peyton. "I know, Pey. How do you know this one isn't?"

"Because he lets us call him "Dr. Mike" instead of "Professor Jenkins.""

"Point noted."

Peyton stuffed the rest of the French toast in his mouth before collecting his things for the day ahead of him. His backpack was stuffed to the brim with textbooks and papers despite it still merely being the first week of the semester. He had no idea how he was so messy–it just happened. Because of this, Peyton never bothered to clean it. It never did him any good. Besides, the only friend he had over was Leo, and the redhead couldn't care less.

"I'll see you later, Mom." Peyton hoisted his backpack over his shoulders and gave his mother a bear hug along with a peck on the cheek.

Caroline hugged her son with enthusiasm. "Love you, Hun."

"Love you too."

Peyton dashed out the door and smacked the button that triggered the garage door to lift up. He winced as it creaked and crawled agonizingly slowly to the top of its conveyor. He hardly waited for it to open before he swung his leg over his electric blue bicycle and pedaled out from the interior room. He either figured his mother would shut the garage door later, or he merely forgot. The latter was the most likely of the two options.

He pedaled as quickly as his two legs would take him. The world around him blurred into a blue, green, and brick canvas that raced past the boy who had no time to admire the paint splatters. Peyton's eyes were trained on the sidewalk in front of him. He felt like he was in a video game simulation, dodging obstacles on a racetrack while others around him were racing to get to the finish line. Peyton rode around several people walking in the same direction as he was, but slower. He was in a rush, and when Peyton was in a rush, no one could get in his way.

Before he knew it, Peyton was locking up his bike to the rack outside the exterior of Azure University. He huffed and he puffed as he dashed inside the building, not even bothering to hold open the doors for anyone that could be behind him. Unfortunately, that happened to be the case.

Peyton whirled around when a voice squealed, "Ouch!"

"I'm sorry!" Peyton hurriedly apologized to the brunette he accidentally slammed the door on.

Either way, he ran down the hallway to his classroom without looking back again and made his way to his seat next to Leo. For once, the redhead had made it to class before Peyton had. The blond gave Leo a quizzical look. The boy in the red sweatshirt was resting his head on his arms and snoring silently. His shut eyelids were turned towards Peyton's seat. Peyton succumbed to the urge to elbow Leo in the shoulder.

Just like he expected, Leo shot up with a start. His chocolate eyes were wide when he noticed Peyton sitting beside him. "Where the hell were you?!"

"Mister Rhys, please don't yell in my classroom," Professor Bryant requested politely.

Neither of them had noticed that their Advanced Chemistry professor was in the room and in the middle of their second lecture for that week. Both Peyton and Leo's heads whipped towards the relatively young man standing at his podium at the front of the classroom. He had a small remote in his hand that controlled the projector screen hanging in front of a large whiteboard.

Leo's face became as red as his hair. "Sorry, Sir."

"Not a problem." The professor smiled and continued on with his presentation. "Now, our next slide is regarding the law of chemical combination. You all should know this because of your prior experiences with Chemistry, but it's crucial to review simple terminology."

As soon as Peyton flipped open the lid of his laptop and entered his password to begin taking notes, a message notification popped up in the top right corner. *"Where the hell were you?!"* Leo reiterated his question through text.

"I pulled a "you" and slept in."

"Until the afternoon? That's late...even for you."

Peyton's eyes became saucers when he realized the time displayed on his device was nearly one o'clock in the afternoon. *"How come you didn't pull a "me" and wake me up?"*

"You know I'm too lazy for that."

Peyton glared over at Leo. When the boy finally noticed the hostile gaze pointed in his direction, he offered his friend a sheepish smile.

"I should've known," the blonde replied. *"Now, go back to sleep."*

Leo's response was immediate. *"Be nice to me."*

"Not my fault you're an idiot."

"That's rich coming from someone who slept past noon."

"You're one to talk, hypocrite."

When Leo sent back several angry faced emojis in return, Peyton simply reacted to the message with the laughing bubble. He opened his notes and began typing the date at the top of a new page before beginning to type everything that was displayed on the projector screen at the front of the class. His professor eloquently spoke about the fundamentals of chemistry, the law of chemical combination, and more aspects to review the basic material before delving into the more intense portion of the course.

Peyton rather enjoyed the lecture. He had written at least two single-spaced pages of notes in the standard Times New Roman font, size twelve. Both of his hands and all ten of his fingers were cramped and pink by the time Professor Bryant finished his lecture and told his students to have a good weekend along with the fact he will see them on Tuesday. Leo was unsure if he enjoyed or despised that tidbit of information.

"That was a snoozer," Leo commented once the two passed through the doorway.

Peyton rolled his eyes and tightened the straps on his backpack as he walked. "You've said that every time we leave a class for the past two semesters."

"And it's still true."

"And you're still a moron," Peyton retorted playfully.

"Hey!"

Peyton and Leo walked in the familiar direction of the café within the university. It felt like they were both in high school again, walking to the cafeteria amongst a bunch of teenagers. Some were mature and well put together, and some were not. Peyton thought it was quite amusing how many people decided to wear pajamas to class. Maybe they could not afford new clothes because of crippling student debt. That was a joke, of course.

"Are you actually not going to go to the library and sleep this time?" teased Peyton after the two reached the line to grab their lunch.

Leo shrugged. When his stomach rumbled, he patted it. "Duty calls."

"Of course it does."

"You know, it's not like you to sleep so late," Leo brought up the concept of slumber. His expression was more concerned than normal. "Are you okay, Man?"

Peyton shuffled forward in line when the people in front of him moved up. "You know, I had the weirdest dream last night," he replied.

"Oh? Do share."

"It was the weirdest thing." He realized he was at the front of the line and retrieved the food he wanted–his usual chicken wrap, a side of fries, and a fountain drink. "For some reason, I was in a prison cell."

Leo decided on a rather large cheeseburger, fries, and a fountain drink. "You? In a prison cell?" he chuckled warmly. "You probably got arrested for hitting someone with your bike."

"No, it wasn't that."

"Then what was it?"

"I don't know. I was just *there*."

"That's odd."

The two boys arrived at the register before they knew it. They set down their orders on the counter and watched as the cashier rang up the total price for Peyton's meal. The blond - thankfully - fished his wallet out of his pocket and paid for his meal with his credit card. Leo did the same, but with cash. He had the ideology that if cash was used to purchase something, then no money was spent since nothing was removed from his bank account.

"But get this," Peyton continued after they stepped away from the register and towards the drink machine. "In the dream, some girl who couldn't have been older than us just waltzed in, grabbed keys, and dragged me out so we could run out of the warehouse-looking building."

Leo blinked at that, filling up his drink. "Was she dressed weirdly?"

"Nope. She wore a black sweater over a t-shirt and ripped jeans." Peyton did the same.

"That's out of place."

"That's exactly what I said! She didn't like that."

"Did you get a name?" Leo inquired as the two sat down at their usual table.

Peyton set his food down in front of him. "I think it was Paige. She didn't say all that much other than arguing with me."

"Arguing? What about?"

"I wouldn't shut up."

Unfortunately for Leo, the redhead burst out laughing in the middle of his first sip of soda. The fizzy liquid projectiled out of his nose and all over his face dripping down to his neck and his maroon hoodie. Leo quickly went from a calm, composed individual to a blubbering, hysterical mess. Over half of the café's seating area turned to face them. Peyton just sat there blankly while Leo got his chuckles out.

"I'm sorry," he wheezed after finally calming down and cleaning himself off with one of his napkins. "What happened next?"

"Do you really want to know?" Peyton stoically questioned.

"I do."

"We were shot at."

Leo's jaw dropped. "Excuse me?"

"You're excused." Peyton took a bite out of his wrap. "But

get this: she saved me with this cool purple force field thing. Then, we turned invisible and somehow teleported through the floor. Then, I threw up. It was nuts!"

"You threw up?"

"Are you serious?"

The redhead shoved a handful of fries into his mouth. "What?"

"I mention weird supernatural stuff and the only thing you got from that was the fact I threw up?" Peyton was jokingly disgusted.

"Pretty much."

"Idiot."

Leo sipped on his drink innocently. "I'll pretend I didn't hear that. You're the one who threw up in front of a girl. Was she cute?"

"Yeah?" Peyton wasn't sure how to answer that question.

"You know, that force field you mentioned reminds me of what happened like two months ago," Leo recalled, "you know, with the bus. It was all over the news."

"Oh, yeah...I remember that." Peyton visibly lit up. "Maybe that's where I got the concept from."

"Probably."

"It was scary, though."

Leo's brown eyes were genuine. "Well, it was only a dream. You don't have any bullet holes in you...that I know of."

"Yeah," the blond half-heartedly chuckled.

"Don't sweat it. I have weird dreams all the time."

"Oh, you mean the time you dreamed a zebra was giving you a tour of a water park?"

Leo's face scrunched up into a glare. "Yes. Like that."

Peyton laughed as he reminisced about the memory. Leo often had unusual dreams, because, well, he was an unusual person. For one, he was the only one who had been a constant friend in Peyton's life. That was something to behold in the blond's eyes. Hardly anyone other than his parents put up with him. Peyton was surprised Leo had stuck by his side. The two were like peas in a pod...and the pod had some brown spots on it. They were imperfect, but always stuck together. To put it simply, Peyton and Leo were brothers by choice.

The two of them finished their lunch amid casual conversation. The concept of dreams had been left in the past, just like their past quarrels, no matter how playful they were. Before long, Peyton found himself saying farewell to Leo since he decided to head to the library to take a quick power nap. He himself decided to make his way to the computer lab to complete any extra work he needed to do before Friday's events. He had to play quite a bit of catch up the night because somehow, he had fallen behind.

Peyton noticed Penny Hamilton's presence immediately as he entered the cozy computer lab. Her expression was either focused or frustrated behind her square glasses. She typed furiously at her computer. The fact she was only using her two index fingers caught Peyton off guard. Peyton stepped towards her and took the rolling chair to her left.

Penny hardly looked in his direction, even after he greeted her: "Hey, Penny."

"Hey," was her monotone response.

Peyton watched her type for a little bit before trying to strike up a conversation again. "So, how's the work going?" he inquired politely.

"Fine," Penny answered.

Huh. That was unusual. Penny was often more talkative than that. Peyton opened up his school profile and began working on a discussion board assignment due that evening. There was no one else in the room. The only thing keeping them from silence was the sound of their fingers typing on their respective keyboards. Peyton noticed that Penny was a much quicker typer than the previous time he saw her. Maybe she had gotten some practice.

"Is everything okay?" After a while, Peyton decided to ask. There was most definitely something off.

"Yes."

Peyton's eyebrows lowered suspiciously. "You look upset."

"Everything's fine."

"...Okay, then. I'll take your word for it."

Peyton attempted to focus on his work until Penny stood up, packed up her things, wheeled her chair in, and walked out of the lab without saying another word. Peyton watched her leave over the top of his computer monitor. There was something peculiar about the whole situation, but he had no idea what it was. Part of him wanted to follow her and ask what was wrong, but he figured the reason she left was because she needed space, and he needed to respect that.

Little did he know that Paige O'Connell's alter ego had heard the entire conversation he and Leo had during lunch... except for the part that the whole event was a "dream" in Peyton's point of view. She retreated once she heard the scene unfold.

It was dark out by the time Peyton left Azure University. He had a Biology lab that evening, which meant he spent the entire afternoon at the school. It was an understatement to say that he was exhausted, despite the amount of sleep he had gotten. As he pedaled home, the one headlight on his bike illuminated the path before him. He was thankful for the quieter roads and more peaceful scenery, especially when he arrived in the suburbs once more.

He racked his brain for any possible reason why he had such an odd dream the previous night. There was no way that there wasn't a meaning for it. Peyton knew there was some sort of importance when it came to such things–often, these types of dreams were warnings. Was someone trying to tell him something?

Peyton wheeled his bike into the garage, which he opened using the keypad beside the door. He dashed inside and opened the door leading into the kitchen. He was instantly greeted with the smell of his mother's cooking. The whiff of taco meat - ground beef to be exact - bubbling on the stovetop was a wonderful thing to return home to after a long day of learning. He rushed towards his mother and hugged her from behind.

"Hi, Mom," he exclaimed with a grin.

Caroline turned around in her son's grasp and embraced him with just as much energy. "Hi, Pey! How was school?"

"It was good. Leo beat me there for once."

"That's not surprising, since your mother told me you woke up past noon," Peyton's father noted from the couch.

"Hello to you too, Dad."

Peyton skittered to the living room to give his father - Lucas Finlay - the same hug that he gave his mother. The brunet man looked much younger than his age. Other than his brown hair and a mustache along with some stubble, he and Peyton looked almost identical. Lucas and his wife, Caroline, had the same kind brown eyes.

"Hey, Son." Lucas tightly hugged Peyton. "Hope you kicked butt in school today."

Peyton grinned at the man about an inch taller than him. "You bet I did."

"I knew it." The fatherly figure extended his enclosed hand, which his son fist bumped. "Did anything interesting happen?"

"Not really. I just hung out with Leo and learned about sciencey stuff." Peyton left out the part about Penny's stiffness towards him.

Lucas' face scrunched up like he smelled something disgusting. "Well, I'm glad you enjoyed it. You're going to get far with that knowledge."

"Thanks, Dad. Let me know when dinner's ready."

"You got it."

Peyton released one arm from his backpack's straps as he headed up the stairs to his room. Each step seemed higher than the last. He was looking forward to hitting the hay early that night, hopefully without another odd dream. He was not used to being so busy—he was taking the most college credits this semester than ever. Peyton yawned and enclosed his fingers around the doorknob leading to his room.

The door swung open. When his backpack hit the floor, so did every notion that what happened was actually a dream. There, sitting on his unmade bed, was the blonde girl who had freed him from the cell and saved his life the previous night.

The most confusing part about all of this was the fearful expression on her face.

Chapter Ten

EBONY

For the second time in twenty-four hours, Peyton thought he was going to throw up. His entire body went faint at the sight of the small girl with blonde hair and hazel eyes wearing the same outfit as the previous day sitting right on his bed. He thought she was simply a figment of his imagination–only residing in his "dream," but no. She was here, and all too real.

Peyton tried pinching a bit of loose skin - which there was a lack of - on his arm. He wanted to wake up, to return to reality as he knew it. Instead, when he lifted his gaze from the reddened spot on his arm, Paige's searing, stoic eyes were locked upon him. There was something about them that was different from the last time he saw her. She seemed much more...unsettled. Yes, that was the word to describe it.

There she was, twiddling her thumbs in her lap. Her ankles, adorned with her beat-up high-top Converse and a pair of white socks were crossed and, to put it simply, she looked like a lost child. Her hair was slightly matted–just enough to be noticeable. The black sweater she was wearing when Peyton last saw her was tightly wrapped around her petite frame. It appeared as if she hadn't slept in days. Paige looked like a shivering corpse of a girl, paler than a ghost.

"Oh, my God," Peyton stuttered out while just standing there. He then gave himself a reality check. *"Okay. This is real. There's some girl on my bed. Wait... She looks hurt."*

The boy cautiously took a couple steps forward like he was approaching some feral animal and inquired, "...Are you alright?"

"I'm in your house." Paige's response was not what he expected.

"Excuse me?"

"Do you *not* find it unusual that I broke into your bedroom?"

"In my defense, I thought the prison thing was a dream," Peyton explained. "You know... People don't get shot at every day."

Paige just offered him a blank look.

"Never mind." The tension was so thick in the room it could have been seared with an electric saw. "What are you doing here anyway?"

"I had nowhere else to go," was her simple response.

Peyton's expression softened. "What do you mean? Don't you have somewhere to live?"

The look in her eyes completely changed. At first, it morphed from fear to simply being neutral. Then, it became... guarded. She gripped her hands together tighter than before. Paige's eyes left him for the first time to stare at her shoes, which had gone nearly as many places as she had been for the past several years. Silence loosened its clutch on the room when she finally decided to speak up.

"Not anymore."

"...What?" blubbered Peyton when he watched the hope

CHAPTER TEN

drain from her eyes that she was trying to conceal. "When did this happen?"

"Paige's gaze grew cold. "Does it matter?"

"You look like a drenched rat," he deadpanned to Paige's annoyance, "so, yes. It matters."

"I'm not even wet."

"Then what happened?"

"I got evicted," she sarcastically replied.

"Why's that?" Peyton asked, intrigued.

"It's complicated." It surely was. Paige attempted to control the fact her mind was floating back to the previous events that afternoon.

It had been a particularly normal day up to that point. Paige staggered into her apartment after a long day of trying to blend in with Arkford's civilians like a chameleon. Once the door had shut behind her, Paige reverted back to the form she felt the most comfortable in: her original body. She flung her shoes off and did not care where they ended up. She pried her socks off and tossed them elsewhere.

Nothing could replace the feeling of her bare feet, blistered and calloused sinking into the carpet coating her bedroom floor. The black sweater she wore almost every day hung on her shoulders like a dozing sloth on a tree branch. It had no care in the world, which was something Paige wished she had the ability to relate to. Instead, she did the next best thing and collapsed face down onto her unmade bed. Her blonde hair flopped every which way. Her body was like a starfish due to the way it was positioned.

Paige instantly fell into slumber. She had no idea that receiving an education would be so difficult, and - for lack of better words - exhausting. She pulled her blanket over herself and snuggled in tight. She felt like a cocoon of sorts. Despite the sun shining outside, she found herself in the realm of dreams that she seldom visited. Peace was one word to describe it. Her soft snores and the quiet turning of the ceiling fan filled the room and made way for nothing other than rest.

At least, that was the case until a sickening thud jolted her awake.

Paige shot up with a start. Her heart nearly flew out of her mouth when the same sound reverberated through the entire apartment for a second time. She silently removed the blanket from overtop her tiny frame and padded across the floor. Paige decided to investigate the matter...right after she picked up her shoes from wherever they flew. She messily slid a pair of socks and then Converse on her feet, loosely tying the laces just enough so she would not step on them.

The teenager crept into the entertainment space of her apartment. Trusting her instincts, Paige made herself transparent and stood in the doorway of her bedroom. Her entire body tensed when the sound returned for a third time. She flinched backward ever so slightly when whoever was outside started pounding on the door harder and faster. The bangs became deafening. Paige caught herself wanting to backpedal into her room, but she stood her ground. She did not know what was going on, but she had an idea.

She jumped backwards when the door slammed open. Several of the men she saw yesterday shrouded in ebony with masks and goggles upon their faces flooded into the room. Each of them was holding an automatic rifle, just like they were the previous night. The army of black-clad men who easily towered over her stormed into her apartment. Paige's home became eerily silent as the men began searching throughout it. She remained invisibly against her bedroom wall, merely watching as three of the men stomped into her bedroom, turning over every nook and cranny. One even entered her closet and the bathroom.

Paige held her breath as one of the men approached the side of the bedroom she was hiding against. His pair of goggles was mere inches from her face. Her heart throbbed in her chest as his gaze

CHAPTER TEN

scanned her invisible frame for at least fifteen seconds, like he somehow knew she was there. Once he turned away from her, Paige took a step back...followed by another and then another. The sequence continued until she was almost out of her room. She stopped dead when the back of her left foot kicked the pot containing the only plant in her whole apartment.

Everything stopped. The men searching her apartment froze along with Paige. They turned towards the broken flowerpot shattered on the carpet. Dirt and the poor plant were littered all over the floor. Paige was frozen when all eyes were in her general direction. She knew she was in a tough situation.

"Oh, shit," she accidentally said out loud.

All at once, the men began firing their automatic weapons in Paige's direction. Thankfully, her instincts and reflexes were sharp, because she managed to fall through a self-generated hole in the floor and reappear outside the doorway of her apartment. Paige ignored how the doors of her neighbors opened as she began to sprint down the hallway. She noticed a red lever on the wall to her right labeled "Fire." She knew the best thing for her to do was to make sure all of the civilians were safe, so as she ran past, she pulled the lever. At one, sirens began blaring throughout the whole complex.

Paige somehow quickened her pace once she realized she was being chased. The screams of her neighbors once they realized gunmen were in the hallway deafened her. Guilt clouded her vision. She had put innocent people in danger, but there was nothing she could do about it now. Paige's confidence soared when she noticed a floor-length window was right in front of her. Without a shadow of a doubt, she dove through it without a single scratch—merely passing through the surface with ease. She flinched when the glass shattered behind her from countless gunshots.

Millions of shards rained upon her as she fell from tens of floors up. Paige spread her arms out and crafted an energy field around her now-visible body. Said shield slowed her fall, but the ground was approaching quicker than she wanted it to. The sound of a pedestrian screaming startled Paige enough to break the protective field around her just before she hit the ground. She bit back a screech when her body made impact with an unfortunate vehicle that was in her path. Paige's ribs seared with agony as she tried to pry herself off of the car that she made a sizable dent in. Miniature pieces of glass showered down onto the poor black vehicle once Paige managed to get to her feet.

She hobbled away from the scene as quickly as she was able with one arm wrapped around her abdomen as if it would fall apart any second. Paige kept her eyes forward instead of on her fragile, broken frame that popped and cracked every time she took a step. Her teeth gritted together so tightly that she thought they would shatter like the glass twenty-six floors up. She had no idea where she was going until the events from the previous night hit her like a bus. Paige came up with one option that would have been the safest for her.

"So, let me get this straight," Peyton began after more silence than he was comfortable with. "The same men that were after us yesterday broke into your apartment and trashed it, so you fled? And you thought the best place to go was *my* house?"

"Precisely," confirmed the girl sitting like a statue on his bed.

Peyton stood uncomfortably in the doorway of his own room. "Did you just...break in?"

"Mhm."

"Okay...well...," he stumbled over his words, "are you okay? I mean, you just got shot at."

Paige gave him an incredulous look. "What do you think?"

"I mean—are you hurt?"

"Don't worry about it."

Peyton took a couple of steps towards her, a bit of worry

etched on his face. "Can you at least tell me where you're hurt so I can help you?"

"I don't need help," she hurriedly denied his request.

"Are you su-"

"Yes."

"Okay, um..." Peyton decided not to probe her any further. He fought the urge to smack himself whilst contemplating his options. "Do you want something to eat? I'm not sure how long you've been in here, but my mom's making tacos."

There was a sudden pause. Paige looked at him like he was some sort of alien from Mars or another far-off planet. She stood as still as a pillar of salt, frozen in time. Peyton shuffled awkwardly from one foot to the other. He untied his shoes and put them by his desk that was positioned on the same wall as his bedroom door. When he returned to his full height, which Paige caught herself envying, the girl's expression had become almost...hopeful.

Then, she inquired, "Are you sure?"

Peyton put his hands in the center pocket of his hoodie. His whole face lit up. She had finally said something he could understand! "Of course I'm sure." He was careful to exclaim his response in a manner soft enough so his parents would not get suspicious.

"Then...if you *really* don't mind, maybe..."

"I don't mind at all." It was hard to hide the grin on Peyton's face. "I'll be right back."

He did not give Paige any time to interrupt because he bolted from the door. Peyton took the stairs two at a time, careful not to completely blow it and become twisted into a pretzel halfway down. Peyton skidded into the kitchen and grinned when the sight and smell of fresh tacos on the kitchen. He watched as his mother, Caroline, lined up the dinner she poured her heart into on a tray on the counter. She sprinkled shredded cheese on each individual taco to Peyton's delight.

She turned around when Peyton slid to a stop. "Oh, hey, Pey!" she grinned. "Are you hungry?"

"Yeah, actually." Peyton eyed the fresh dinner with a rumbling stomach. "Could I have a couple extra? I have a lot of homework that I need to start and I need energy."

"Or you're just a pig," his father teased as he entered the kitchen. Lucas leaned over and kissed his wife on the cheek. "Looks great, Dear."

"Ew, PDA." Peyton stuck his tongue out in disgust.

Caroline could not contain her joy. "Of course you can," she replied to Peyton. "We have more than enough, but don't upset your stomach."

"Sweet–thanks, Mom." Peyton flashed her a smile and put four tacos on his plate.

"You're welcome, Hun."

Peyton wasted no time hurrying back up to his room. He neglected to see or hear his parents look at each other and then smile at their son's antics before getting their own food. The two of them were very close, even after twenty-two years of marriage. Peyton hoped that he would have that same opportunity when the time came. He needed to focus on academics first and foremost, though.

He scurried up the stairs and into his room, where Paige had not moved a muscle. She was in the same position as before, seated stiffly on his bed with her legs crossed at the ankles and her fingers in knots on her lap. As soon as she heard his footsteps, her hazel irises shifted upwards to meet his brown ones. Peyton thought he imagined some sort of vulnerability in her expression, but it quickly faded away once he shut the door behind him.

"Is it okay if I shut this?" Peyton asked, and she nodded. He

CHAPTER TEN

walked over to her and sat down on the opposite side of his bed. "I have tacos for us."

Paige studied the plate of four tacos he set between them. "...What's in them?" she cautiously inquired.

"Just ground beef with taco seasoning and shredded cheese on top. My mom makes the best tacos. Try one," he encouraged her.

Paige just watched him with a suspicious gaze as he picked up one of the tacos from the plate between them and took a bite out of it. He seemed quite delighted with the food that had just entered his system, like it was replenishing his energy in a blink of an eye. Paige could not help but wonder if that was how civilians felt three times a day when they would receive a meal. She always had to fight for food, but now, it was being offered to her freely.

"You're sure you don't mind?" she questioned again, her field of vision only on the food.

Peyton nodded and swallowed his first bite. "I don't mind at all. Take as much as you want. My mom made loads of them and she'll probably have me take one for lunch tomorrow."

"Tomorrow?" Paige skeptically picked up a taco.

"Yeah," he replied between two bites. "I go to Azure University as a Human Physiology major. It's a lot of work, so I tend to forget to bring my lunch. Mom always fusses at me because she makes so much extra food."

"Oh, no... I completely forgot about school tomorrow," Paige silently worried.

Instead of voicing her concern, she nodded and took a small, hesitant bite out of the taco she was holding. Paige's heartbeat gradually slowed each time she chewed before swallowing. A sense of relief flooded her system–it was comforting to know that something she was consuming was not stolen for once. Paige felt her body loosening and shifting. It was as if something fresh, homecooked, and free was making her want to do a happy dance.

"So?" Peyton's voice brought her out of her imagination. "Is it okay?"

Paige took another bite, unable to resist. "It's good. Thank you."

"You're welcome."

The two of them sat on the bed in silence other than the soft crunching of the taco shells between their teeth and the fan blades twirling overhead. Paige seemed more relaxed than she was before while Peyton sneakily pushed the plate with the last portion - he had only had one - towards her. Paige decided not to ask any questions. Instead, her instinct took over and she finished what was on the plate to begin with. Peyton just grinned when she picked up the final portion that vanished soon after.

By the time Paige was finished, she noticed Peyton had removed his laptop from his backpack by the door frame and set it up on his desk. He sat down at his rolling chair and flipped open the lid. Paige watched as he began typing and opened the familiar Azure University login page, which he typed his username and password into. She did not mean to be nosy or intruding. She was simply curious.

"What are you working on?" she asked to break the awkward silence.

Peyton finished typing out a sentence before replying, "It's the beginning of one of my lab reports for Advanced Microbiology."

"Oh."

"Do you want to see?" Peyton inquired when she said nothing else. "It's about morphology, which is the study of the forms of things."

"Why must you learn about that?" deadpanned Paige.

CHAPTER TEN

"Because it's Microbiology, and it's one of the required classes for my major."

"That's stupid."

Peyton shrugged and then continued typing. "It's not necessarily my favorite class, but, like I said, it's required, so I have to take it."

Paige let her curiosity get the best of her. She tried pushing herself into a standing position to observe what exactly the blond boy across the room was working on, but once her weight was transferred to her legs, a stab of pain reverberated throughout. A hiss of agony escaped her mouth as she clutched her abdomen, which was where the pulsations were stemming from. This caused Peyton to whirl around. When he realized what was going on, he rushed over to Paige and extended his arms, stifling her fall before she could hit the ground.

"Stop it–*stop it*," Paige gritted out, but to her dismay, his grip was still on her–albeit looser. "I'm fine. Let go."

"You know, if you tell me what hurts, I can help you," he offered a bit sternly. "Can you at least tell me what happened?"

"I fell."

"Now, we're getting somewhere," Peyton sarcastically thought. He was getting a tad bit frustrated due to her skepticism, but he concealed it well. He understood it, but it irked him, nonetheless. "Did you fall from high up?"

"Twenty-six floors."

At this, Peyton's entire demeanor changed into one of shock. "Holy shi—Paige! What the hell?!"

"You don't want your parents to hear, do you?" she interrupted, changing the subject.

"At this point, I don't care." Peyton's voice was firm. "Show me where it hurts."

"I'm *fine*."

"Paige, now. I want to help you."

"I can help myself."

Peyton's expression became pleading as he echoed in a hushed tone, "*Please.*"

Paige knew she was not going to get out of this situation by taking the easy route. She had already broken into the Finlays' household, consumed some of their food, - despite it being given freely - and had forced herself into Peyton's life. She could not hide everything from him, which was why she took a deep breath–in through the nose and out through the mouth and made the decision to reveal what exactly was bothering her.

Slowly, Paige pulled up the hem of her shirt to reveal a ghastly sight. Her abdomen was covered with more bruises than visible skin. The black, blue, and purple patches reminded Peyton of a rotten fruit that he would never decide to eat. This was different, though. His nose scrunched up and his entire face soured at the sight. Paige's rib cage poked through the skin and left several ruts in what would have been a smooth framework. Had she been starving herself? Did she have any other choice?

"Jesus Christ," Peyton exhaled laboredly. He then realized what his new responsibility was, especially if he wanted to go down the road to a medical career path. "Okay, you stay there," he instructed with as much professionalism as he could. "Lay down. I'll be back with some pain killers and ice packs."

"But-" Paige started protesting incredulously.

"Just stay there, please."

Peyton made his second trip down the stairwell quicker than the first. He rushed towards the refrigerator-freezer combination and opened the door to the latter. He fished at least two ice packs out of the side of the door and grabbed small towels to wrap around them from a nearby cabinet. Next, he booked it to a drawer on the other side of the kitchen.

CHAPTER TEN

Instead of picking out a few painkillers, he took the entire bottle.

"Is everything okay in there, Hun?" Mrs. Finlay asked from the living room.

The boy's gaze snapped over to view both of his parents with their eyes on the television. Thankfully, they appeared to be watching one of their favorite sitcoms. Caroline's husband had his arm gently wrapped around her shoulders. She was snuggled into his side like the two were in their late teens, just now falling in love. It did not feel like twenty-two years went by with the way they looked at one another and acted in each other's presence.

"Yeah, Mom!" he replied over the sound of laughter on the television. Peyton decided a little white lie would excuse him. "I tripped and hurt my knee, so I need an ice pack and Ibuprofen."

"Oh, alright–be careful!"

"I will!"

Peyton ran up the stairs two at a time and opened the door to his bedroom. He stopped in his tracks when all that was before him was an empty room. Frantically, Peyton ran around the upstairs hallway, checking inside every room - even the closet - before coming across the guest room. He took a deep breath, turned the knob, and exhaled a sigh of relief. Paige was seated on the guest bed just like she was on Peyton's.

"I didn't want to occupy your bed," Paige blandly clarified.

"You didn't have to move," Peyton countered before he realized what happened. "Did you–did you teleport through that wormhole thingy?"

Paige slowly nodded, as if she was trying to confirm the answer to a math problem to a small child.

"Okay, uh, lay down, then." Peyton shut the door behind him with the two fingers he had free and approached the bed.

"I've got ice packs and will get some water so you can take Ibuprofen."

"I...bu...profen?" she enunciated puzzledly.

"Yeah." Peyton shook the bottle of pills. "They're to help those nasty bruises. I take this all the time if I have headaches or something else. Did you hurt yourself anywhere else?"

"Don't think so. I told you I'm fine."

He chose not to argue. "Okay, then, I'll just get you some water."

Paige waited patiently while Peyton dashed to the nearby bathroom. The sound of the sink turning on and off lasted a maximum of five seconds. Paige attempted to coax her paranoia away, but right then and there, she had no choice. She was in a strange house with a strange family after a strange occurrence. It was not like she could fight back, so instead, she sat down on the bed and watched as Peyton reentered the room.

"Here you are." Peyton handed her the cup of water. He then unscrewed the cap of the bottle and handed her three of the small red pills. "This should help."

She cautiously studied the pills in her hand. "Are you sure these are safe?"

"Yes, I'm sure. I promise it will help."

Paige decided to take the risk. What else did she have to lose? She popped the three pills into her mouth and took a swig of water to wash them down. She placed the cup on the nightstand next to the bed which she assumed was alright since Peyton did not stop her. To her own surprise, he knelt down and untied her Converse, sliding them off her feet and setting them on the floor. Guilt stabbed her in the throat. Who was she to deserve such attention?

"Try to relax," Peyton soothed her with a kind smile. "Can you lay down for me? It'll help you feel better."

"You don't have to do this."

"Listen. I'm planning on being a doctor in the future, so this is good practice," he told her in a teasing tone.

Paige thought she was going to smile for a split second, but it never happened. A quirk upward from the right corner of her lip was all that escaped her. She fulfilled his request and cautiously laid down on the bed. At once, she soaked in the comfort it gave her. For once in her short life, she let herself fully relax. She was still on some sort of guard, but Peyton was gradually passing her test for the moment.

That was...until a cold pressure landed right on top of her bruises. Paige wanted to shoot up and shove whatever had come on top of her, but a gentle hand blocked her path. Her hazel irises met Peyton leaning over her with a kind, soft gaze she was unused to. She felt her heart pounding against his hand on her chest when she lowered herself back down onto the bed.

"I didn't mean to startle you," he said in a quiet tone. "I'm just putting a couple ice packs where it hurts. I got the right spot, right?"

Paige nodded and leaned back down so the back of her head was engulfed in a pillow once more. Despite the unsettling feeling the close contact gave her, she remained still and let Peyton position the ice packs over her rib cage. She did not want to admit it, but the measures he was taking to ensure her well-being was taken care of made her...a bit more comfortable. The situation as a whole was awkward, but only for a little.

Peyton scooted away once he had positioned both of the ice packs comfortably. "How's that? Any better?" he asked gently.

"...Uh, yeah," Paige blinked in response. "Thank you."

"You should get some rest."

Paige shuffled closer to the pillow she claimed. "Maybe I will."

"Are you alright?" Peyton's expression was sincere. "Do you need anything?"

"Oh, um...no. I mean...I'm alright, and no thanks." She seemed to be quite content—or as content as her demeanor would let her to be.

Peyton stood from the bed and backpedaled towards the door. "Just let me know. You know where my room is...apparently," he joked regarding their earlier situation.

Paige *almost* smiled. "Okay, thank you."

"Goodnight."

Instead of replying verbally, Paige nodded. Peyton shut the door behind him and left the room to herself. She hardly had time to think of anything else before her head figuratively hit the pillow, nearly at the same time as Peyton in his own room. The both of them had the same thought in their minds as they drifted off down the hall from one another:

"What the hell?"

Chapter Eleven

MAUVE

Young adults and alarms did not get along well. That was a known fact and was proven when Peyton fought the urge to throw his phone across the room. Instead, he forced himself out of bed. He was caught off-guard by the fact he was still wearing the same clothes he was the previous day. He had no idea how his parents neglected to notice how he did not come downstairs to say goodnight like he always did. The two of them were busy with work, but always made time for their son.

A yawn rattled Peyton's jaw. For once in the past forty-eight hours, he felt like he had gotten a decent night of sleep. That was, at least, until he noticed his laptop left open on his desk. Then, he realized he was completely above the covers on his bed. The most confusing thing, however, was the fact that his door was open. Gosh, Peyton must have been exhausted the previous night if he simply staggered into his room after school and passed out.

Then...the events of last night hit him like a dump truck.

Peyton launched himself from his bed without a second

thought. He padded across the creaking floor that made up the hallway and cursed at his house for being so worn down. He had memorized every crack, every step, every noise the carpeted floor made under his bare feet. The guest room was a place seldom used, but if his hunch was correct, what happened was - in fact - not a dream. He and his imagination needed a serious talk due to the tricks it was playing on him.

He rapped gently on the door to the guest room. Peyton had no idea what else to do, especially because of his spontaneous guest on the other side. He waited for ten seconds, and then twenty, followed by thirty. After that time had passed, he decided to knock again. There was still no answer.

"I hope I don't get my ass kicked...," Peyton thought to himself as he carefully twisted the knob and opened the door.

He stood awkwardly in front of the door frame where he cracked the door behind him. Peyton assessed the unusual, but relieving sight in front of him. Paige was cuddled under the blankets and clutching a ginormous pillow that seemed too big for her. She was swaddled up like a cocoon, like she had not a care in the world. Paige curled onto the feather-filled object as if she was scared to let go. Her blonde hair poked out from under the comforter. At least one strand was caught on her cheek.

"Uh, Paige?" he whispered to try to get her attention.

There was no response from the tiny figure except for a slight deepening of her respirations as she adjusted her position. She shuffled around until she got a better grip on the pillow and drifted right back to sleep. Peyton exhaled–partly from frustration and partly from embarrassment. He hated waking people up, even if it was someone he was close to. Leo was an exception, though. He could not exactly fill a cup of water and dump it on his guest like he did to his best friend not long ago.

Instead, he crept forward and tried again a little louder. "Paige?"

Still, there was no answer. Peyton shifted his weight awkwardly from one foot to the other. He took another step forward and attempted one more time along with an outstretched finger to gently poke her. "...Pai-"

At once, Peyton was flung backwards by a wall of mauve energy. He let out a yelp when his back hit the dresser on the other side of the room. The whole guest room rattled with the commotion, which provoked Caroline to yell from downstairs.

"Are you alright, Pey?!"

Peyton regained his posture and shouted back, "Yeah, Mom! I just tripped!"

He turned back to Paige, whose atmosphere completely changed in a matter of two seconds. Instead of being comfortable and relaxing for once, she was sitting halfway up on the bed with her hazel eyes wide open, her entire body stiff, and an energy field splitting the room in half. The wall separated herself and Peyton for at least ten more seconds before she realized what exactly she was doing and allowed for it to disintegrate.

"Holy-...I'm so sorry," Peyton apologized in a rushed tone. "I didn't mean to scare you, but I thought I'd wake you up before I went to class."

"Do you want me to leave?" Paige asked calmly, but almost with a hint of hope that he would say the opposite.

Thankfully, he did. "Of course not–unless you want to. My mom should be leaving for work around eight forty-five, so unless you want her to know you're here, I'd wait up here. My dad's already at work, so you don't have to worry about him."

"Are they...not friendly?"

"What?" He was confused. "Of course they're friendly. I just didn't know if you wanted privacy because you've never met them before...and I might get in huge trouble if they find out I had a girl over overnight."

Paige gave him an odd, almost demeaning look.

"Wait, no! Not like that!" he corrected himself desperately. "I just mean...I'm a dumb college student and my parents somehow trust me because I've never been in a relationship or anything. I have rules I need to follow. It's nothing about you."

"So, you want me to stay up here until your mother leaves for work?" she questioned.

Peyton thought he was in trouble when it came to Paige. "I mean, you've got that invisibility thing, so I guess not, but be careful."

Paige said nothing and simply let him continue.

"Uh, there's food in the fridge, or I can take some extra breakfast. My mom usually makes it for the two of us. The bathroom's right down the hall on your left. Oh...and if you want a change of clothes, I think I could steal some of my mom's."

"Wouldn't she be suspicious if she found some of her clothes missing?"

"...You can borrow some of mine then if you want. Whatever's in the dresser or on the floor is free reign. Most of it should be clean."

She cocked her head to the side. "Most of it?"

"Yup," he confirmed sheepishly. "Sometimes, I forget to do the laundry."

Paige nodded, which left Peyton standing awkwardly in silence once more. This time, Paige was the one to speak up.

"By the way, if you were wondering, I put the ice packs in the freezer."

"I could've done that," protested Peyton. "How are you feeling?"

"I'm fine," Paige fibbed, and she was going to keep up with the lie until Peyton's brows furrowed suspiciously. "...Sore."

"Do you want the ice packs?"

"I'll get them later."

"Are you sure?"

"Positive."

Peyton nodded at that. "Okay, well...do you need anything?"

Paige shook her head.

"I'm gonna head off to school and I should be back later this afternoon. Do you have a phone or anything?"

"No."

"I'll write my phone number down somewhere and if you need anything, just use the home phone."

The girl nodded from her position on the bed.

"Okay, uh..." Peyton adjusted his blond fringe out of his face. "I guess I'll see you later unless you're going anywhere. I don't mean to confine you or anything."

"I'll be here," Paige assured him.

Once again, Peyton nodded, and the grin that Paige was starting to get used to appeared on his face. "I'll see you later."

Paige returned the gesture, minus the smile, and watched as Peyton shut the door behind him, leaving her alone once again. It was something she was used to, and enjoyed, but not as much anymore, if she were to be honest. After what had happened at her apartment, Paige had no idea who to trust other than herself. Then again, she was in a partial stranger's house. Peyton seemed harmless, but she did not know for sure.

There was no such thing as being too careful.

That was why she remained in the guest bedroom until thirty minutes after Peyton notified her of his mother leaving the house. Despite hearing the front door open and close when the strange woman left, Paige kept to herself. She simply sat on the bed and let herself rest. The thought of returning to Azure University for her studies that day sickened her rather than being a form of motivation.

"Looks like Penny Hamilton won't make it to class today," she mumbled to herself.

Was this how civilians enrolled in school felt? The second week of the semester was barely ending, but Paige had already skipped most of a day and was about to skip a whole one. Thankfully, she did not have many classes at all on that day–only one on Friday afternoons. Therefore, she was not as worried since she already had two fifty-five-minute sessions earlier in the week. Regular people had injuries, so she could use that excuse.

Paige forced herself to her feet when she was sure no one else was in the building. A stab of pain throbbed throughout her body, but she ignored it the best she could. Instead, she picked up the bottle of painkillers that was still on the nightstand, unscrewed the cap, and spilled three into her hand. Then, Paige grabbed the cup off of the nightstand and wandered into the bathroom next to Peyton's room. She filled up the cup, popped the pills in her mouth, and downed the cup in just under three gulps. Paige was not sure where to put the cup, so she simply placed it back where it was on the nightstand next to the pill bottle.

Now, she found herself on a new adventure–finding some clothes that would be satisfactory for the lazy - no, *restful* - day ahead. Paige padded down the hallway and towards the only other room she really knew in the house, which was Peyton's. He had left the door halfway open, so she prodded it the rest of the way. She stepped inside and decided to find something that would at least somewhat fit her–Peyton said it was okay. Otherwise, this peculiar decision of hers would have been asinine.

CHAPTER ELEVEN

At least five minutes later, Paige studied herself in the floor-length mirror in the corner of the bedroom. A pair of fluffy, red plaid pajama pants adorned her short legs, more than reaching the floor. She wore an oversized black Nirvana t-shirt that almost went down to her knees. She scowled at her appearance. This would not do, especially if she had just been on an adventure across town. She was not ready to take a shower in a stranger's home, so that was off the list.

Instead, Paige wandered towards the hall closet, found a new toothbrush, and ripped it out of the package. She entered the upstairs bathroom, squirted some of the toothpaste resting on the vanity onto her toothbrush, and brushed her teeth until her arm was sore. She spat into the sink, cleaned off everything so it was as good as new, and then discovered a brush in a cabinet underneath the sink. She ran said brush through her hair until she got most of the tangles and matting out of her hair. She *almost* looked like she didn't jump out of a window twenty-six floors above ground level.

Paige limped a tad as she made her way down the stairs. Once again, she was thankful for being in an empty house. Since she was not being watched, she decided to get something for breakfast—after all, Peyton said it was alright, therefore it was not stealing. She discovered that just as he had promised, a little sticky note with Peyton's phone number rested on the counter along with a little note:

Anything in the pantry or the fridge is free reign. Have whatever you want as long as you don't clean out the whole thing. Be safe.
-Peyton

"I'm not *that* much of a pig," she grumbled playfully to herself.

Paige set the note back down on the counter and opened the pantry to find something suitable for breakfast and came across a box of fruit loops. That was inconspicuous enough. There was only one problem, though:

It was on the top shelf.

She exhaled a deep sigh and prepared for whatever absurd adventure she was about to get herself into. Paige stood on her tiptoes and reached as high as she could, but it was to no avail. She was tempted to start climbing up the shelves, even placing a foot on the first shelf above the tiled floor, but then she remembered that she had an easier way of retrieving what was rightfully hers. With a flick of her wrist, a small force field bubble formed around the box of cereal. Paige repelled the cereal box from the top shelf and let it drop into her hands.

Paige then made her way over to the fridge and opened it. People usually had milk with cereal–right? She assumed so, because a carton of milk rested on a shelf in the door of the refrigerator. She grabbed it and then began looking for a bowl. She ended up finding one that was a little too large, but she did not feel like searching for another. Paige poured herself a generous amount of fruit loops and then put milk on top of it.

Once she decided her breakfast was satisfactory, Paige retrieved a spoon and plopped down on the living room couch. She noticed three remotes on the table and thought maybe a little bit of television would not hurt. Paige picked up the largest remote and pressed the power button. When nothing happened, she frowned and tried another remote. Aha! Success!

Paige started flipping through channels with her left hand and stuffing a couple of spoonfuls of cereal in her mouth as she did so. Once she found the news station she usually watched, she set the remote down on the couch next to her and continued eating her cereal. The story that had been airing just before the commercial break continued a few seconds after the

CHAPTER ELEVEN

last ad for some sort of laundry detergent continued, and it certainly caught Paige's eye.

"We're here live outside of the Hillwell apartment complex following up on an electrifying event that occurred last night," announced Rita, the same reporter from before. *"Once again, we have documented supernatural activity."*

The male reporter, also the same as the last time, added on, *"At about six fifty last night, August twenty-seventh, an object that almost seemed like a person flew through the hallway window from twenty-six floors up."*

"At first, we ruled it to be a suicide attempt, but what happened next changed our minds from the get-go," Rita exclaimed animatedly. *"The glass didn't shatter until at least three seconds after the impact, and as this person - a young woman, it seemed like - rocketed to the ground, the same ultraviolet energy field that surrounded an Arkford city bus from two months prior was visible. Is this young woman the source of this otherworldly phenomenon?"*

"No," Paige sarcastically retorted to the screen with a mouth full of cereal.

"Even though this photo is blurry, caught from a cell phone, we can make out that this young woman is probably in her early twenties, has blonde hair, and is wearing a black sweater. If you can identify this woman, please don't hesitate to call the number on the screen," the male reporter instructed his audience.

Paige boredly flipped to another channel. Nobody knew her anyway. Besides, Penny Hamilton went to Azure University– not Paige O'Connell. She did have a bit of a problem at hand, though. She hoped with all her might that Peyton would not turn her in to the authorities. Trust was something she was not familiar with since she never needed to execute it.

Instead of focusing on the negatives, though, Paige finished her cereal and washed off the bowl and spoon in the sink. She winced when water splashed back up to hit her in the face, ricocheting off the spoon, but did not take it out on the metal object. She placed the clean dishes in the part of the double sink that possessed a dish rack.

Paige decided to explore to keep her mind at ease. It would only be a matter of time until the Finlay family returned to their residence, so she needed to remain undetected. She plodded tiredly around the bottom floor of the well-loved house until she came across a room she had not seen before. The glass door - which she found very unusual - was left open, but either way, it revealed a cozy office space. It reminded Paige of a smaller version of the computer lab, with a muted blue coating the walls, the occasional portrait of nature, and a soft glow of a fan light overhead. Against the back wall was a mahogany desk with shelves attached nearly reaching the ceiling filled with trinkets and stationery supplies.

The teenage girl slunk across the room and studied the desktop computer in the middle of it all. She shuffled around the mouse on its pad and almost flinched when the monitor came to life with a blurred flower background. Paige blinked when she realized this was only the lock screen, and there was an important thing she was missing:

A password.

Paige thought long and hard. Only a stupid person would begin entering random combinations of letters and numbers only to be locked out of the computer a minute later. She stood there and looked at the antagonizing blinking line waiting for her to begin typing. Paige had an idea–she could get some of her homework done and be productive...not without the password, though. She then got a better idea.

Next thing she knew, Paige was in the kitchen and had the house phone in her right hand and the sticky note Peyton left for her in the other. She slowly dialed the number on the landline and held it up to her ear. She listened to the monotone ringing for at least ten seconds before the other line picked up. Paige deflated with relief when she was assured that it was indeed Peyton's voice instead of a fake number.

"Uh, hello?"

"Do you know the office computer's password?" Paige asked instead of returning the greeting. Oops...she regretted that afterwards.

Peyton seemed confused. "*Paige?*"

"Who else?"

"*Good point.*" Paige sensed an amused undertone to his voice. "*Is everything okay other than you needing the password?*"

"Yes," Paige replied quicker than she meant to. "Can you tell me what it is?"

"*Um, sure. Are you ready?*"

She dashed back to the office computer before Peyton could say anything else. Paige ignored the dull pain in her ribs as she jumped into the rolling chair and positioned herself in front of the computer. "Okay, I'm ready."

"*Okay, it's 'B,'*"

Paige briefly searched the keyboard for the correct key, and when she found it, she repeated, "B."

"*U.*"

"*U.*"

"*T.*"

"*T.*"

"*T.*"

"*T.*"

"*K.*"

"*K.*"

"*I.*"

"*I...*"

This process continued until the password had been fully

typed out. Paige registered the letters and frowned when she realized what they spelt. "Butt...Kicking...Chicken? Really?"

"My mom's a goofball," Peyton laughed quietly on the other line. "*But yes. That's right. What do you need the computer for?*"

"I simply wanted to entertain myself." That statement was partly true. She *needed* to entertain herself by getting her homework done and her mind off of the situation.

"*Well, if you want some games to play, I have some things bookmarked.*"

"I'm not one for games but thank you."

"*Oh.*" Peyton hesitated. "*No problem. I should probably get back to class.*"

Paige's eyes slightly widened at the realization. "You left class?" she inquired, and then added on silently, *"For me?"*

"*Well, yeah. I wanted to make sure you were okay. Are you okay?*"

"...Yeah," she trailed off.

"*Are you sure?*"

"I'm okay. I'm sure."

She noticed a small chuckle on Peyton's end. "*Okay, well, I'll see you when I get home.*"

"See you then."

It took a minute for Paige to find the "X" button, but Peyton had not hung up until she pressed it. She set the home phone down on the desk and scooted forward in the rolling chair. She clicked on the internet browser icon and searched for the Azure University website, logged into her account, and began on her long list of homework that needed to be done. Once she began typing, it hardly stopped.

Paige didn't even notice the lingering beginnings of a smile on her face.

Chapter Twelve

STRAWBERRY

"Are you sure you'll be okay here?" Paige gave the boy across the room a scrunched expression of confusion. "I'll be fine. I was on Friday. Remember?"

"Yeah," Peyton continued, "but my parents are home. You can come with me if you want."

"Out of the question."

"How come?"

"I already told you that I want to remain inconspicuous," Paige reminded him.

"Oh...right."

Peyton thought back to the conversation the two of them had after Peyton returned home from school last Friday afternoon. He had found her right where he left her–in the guest bedroom resting up for the next day ahead. Little did he know that she had spent the entire day downstairs catching up on her - no, *Penny's* - homework and even getting ahead by half a week. She treated herself to a small bowl of pretzels around noon and Peyton brought a portion of the spaghetti upstairs that his mother made the previous night for dinner.

"Honestly, I'm surprised my parents haven't figured out there's an extra person in the house," he commented thoughtfully.

Paige generated a miniature energy field about the size of a basketball and began fiddling around with it, tossing it from hand to hand. "Are you...underestimating me?" she inquired snarkily without making eye contact.

"What? No! My parents and I are just really close, so I'm not used to keeping a secret from them."

"Is keeping a secret difficult for you?"

Peyton thought about it and then earnestly replied, "One this big? Yes."

"I can tell," she mumbled halfheartedly.

Paige thought back to Thursday, which was already three days ago by then. Her academic persona heard Peyton speaking to Leo about what exactly had happened the previous night. Of course, Paige never expected Peyton to be completely over the whole situation, but how did he not realize from Paige's requests during said exploration that she wanted to keep it quiet? She remembered silently storming out of the café and retreating to the computer lab. Then, Paige made her escape for a second time after Peyton happened to wander in there.

Peyton's head cocked to the side. It was something Paige noticed he did when he was confused. "What do you mean by that?"

"I...," Paige trailed off to think for a moment. Then, an excuse came to her. "You were quite talkative during our little expedition on Wednesday. I just assumed."

"What'd you expect me to do?" he asked a bit crossly. "Just

to be quiet and follow your lead without even knowing who you were?"

Paige poked the energy ball with her index finger and it popped, fading into petite lilac sparks. "Point noted."

Peyton took one look at her reserved face and sighed heavily. "Look. I'm sorry. I didn't mean to be rude about the whole thing."

"I'm sorry too," Paige apologized a bit plainly. "I shouldn't have expected so much."

"Yeah, you're right." Peyton ran his fingers through his hair with a hidden grin. "You shouldn't expect so much out of little ol' me when you're some badass superhero chick."

Paige's hazel eyes slightly expanded. "That's not what I was insinuating."

"I'm only teasing."

"Can I ask you something, though?"

It was Peyton's turn to be a little puzzled. "Shoot."

"...Did you just call me a superhero? Why?"

Peyton was surprised by her question. It was one of the last things he was expecting to be asked, especially from someone who had such a guarded look on her face. He all but shook his head and denied it. The statement held no disarray or any room for a refute.

"Well," he began, his chocolate eyes on hers. "You made your way into a freaky building and pretty much saved my life." He grinned at her reaction, which was filled with nothing but the opposite of her expectation. "And you saved a bus with over fifty people on board."

Paige was in a state of shock. "How did you know that?"

"Purple force field? Unexplainable strength? A mysterious disappearance? That has you written all over it."

"It...*does*?"

Peyton chuckled at this. "Of course," he confirmed to her

masked glee. "It was all over the news. Now, we - at least, *I* - know who the mystery hero is."

"...We?"

"You and me."

Peyton's grin was almost contagious. *Almost.* Paige sat there in stunned stupor. The only person who had ever considered her as a hero was herself, especially after the bus incident. She thought back to the dreaded conference with Dr. Kelley. The sinking feeling in her chest never went away. The lies he spat in her face always remained.

Paige held the force field sphere in her hands and finally met his eyes. "I couldn't just sit there and watch as it hurtled over the barrier."

"You could've thought of a better way to go about with this," argued Dr. Kelley.

"I did the first thing I thought of."

"The first thing you thought of was publicizing your abilities in front of the whole city? The whole state? Maybe even the whole world?"

"I couldn't just let those people die!" The sphere quietly shattered as Paige rocketed to her feet, knocking the wooden chair she was formerly seated in onto the floor with a crash.

"Tsk, tsk," the doctor scolded. "Because of your "heroic" actions, we are all over the news."

The news story with Rita and another reporter played on the television in the office. Paige watched the entire program - which merely lasted about a minute - with wide eyes. A grin almost as large filled her face once the announcement of no casualties or injuries was reported. Then, the balding man across from her had the ability to take it all away in a second.

"Well?" the doctor questioned, snapping her out of her trance. "What do you have to say for yourself?"

Paige did not even bother sitting down, instead leaning forward and resting her elbows on the table at his eye level. "I'd say I'm some sort of a hero," she replied smugly with her hands cradling her chin.

"Wrong!" Dr. Kelley yelled. "You may have jeopardized our entire mission!"

"Your mission," she corrected.

"I'd watch your tongue, O'Connell. It's our mission."

Paige blinked herself out of that moment and back to reality. His words flooded her mind. They were all she had known for over a decade. This was not her life–at least not now. It was only a matter of time until "something" happened again. She would not have the power to stop it. She would be the opposite of a "hero." In fact, it would be all her fault.

"Paige?"

The blonde girl snapped her gaze upward to meet Peyton's. The boy had somehow made it across the room while she was deep in thought. The plain, brown irises that were usually filled with life were replaced with a darker worry, which unnerved her. Paige was quick to snap out of it. It was something she needed to master, after all.

"Yeah?" she managed to ask.

"Are you okay?"

Paige gave him a curt nod and pretended like nothing happened. "Yes. I'm fine."

"Are you sur-"

"Yes," she interrupted his question entirely. "I'm sorry. You deserve to know what has happened and why things need to be this way."

Peyton shifted his weight to the other leg. "...Would it be too much to tell me?"

"I'll tell you when I can trust you."

"When would that be?" he inquired, visibly lighting up at that.

Paige sat criss-cross applesauce on the bed like a small

child in kindergarten. "I just met you this week. How am I supposed to trust you?"

"Well," Peyton stated before he realized the magnitude of his remark, "I trust you."

The blonde stopped fiddling around with the bed comforter. "Why would you trust me so easily?" she questioned stiffly. "I could snap you like a twig."

Peyton grinned teasingly. "Is that a challenge?"

"No," she obliviously deadpanned. "Why would it be?"

"Never mind." He shook his head, dismissing the matter to begin with. He started backing towards the door frame. "I should meet my friend–he's probably waiting outside."

"Alright."

Peyton paused. "Are you sure you'll be-"

"I already told you I would be alright," asserted Paige.

"...Alright then. I'll see you later."

Paige nodded as a proper farewell, despite the casual environment. She averted eye contact from Peyton as he left the room. He often wondered what she did while he was gone. Little did he know, she snuck into the house's office and got ahead on as much homework as she could. Penny Hamilton was nearly three weeks ahead on her college work since that was all she did during the time she was at Peyton's house. When she was unable to access the computer, she was either finding something to eat or staring up at the ceiling.

Paige thought back to the very first discussion board assignment she did. *"I really need to get a hobby,"* she thought. Normal people didn't stare at a ceiling all day.

Meanwhile, Peyton scurried down the stairs, grabbed his wallet, keys, and phone, and exclaimed a quick "goodbye" to his parents. "Mom! Dad! I'm going with Leo now!"

"Have fun!" The two of them chorused from the living room.

CHAPTER TWELVE

Peyton dashed out the front door, but not before locking it behind him. Sure enough, Leo's tan Nissan that had seen better days was parked in the driveway. The redhead waved from the driver's seat to which Peyton returned. Directly before the blond touched the handle to open the passenger side door, a horn blaring startled him backwards. Peyton glared through the window at Leo, who was trying to conceal his smile.

Peyton opened the door and shut it behind him. "You jerk."

"Wow–that's a friendly greeting," Leo retorted. "Hello to you too."

"What the hell was that?"

"Proper revenge for you dumping water on my head."

"That was several days ago!"

Leo shrugged, wrapping his arm around the chair next to him after putting the gear into reverse to look behind him. "So?"

"You suck," mumbled Peyton while typing a quick text to his parents that assured them he was with Leo.

Peyton appreciated his protective parents. The both of them loved him dearly, and even though he was two years into adulthood, Caroline and Lucas welcomed the possibility of remaining at home. Texting them to let them know he was safe whenever he arrived places was a small price to pay for unconditional love.

Leo steered the two of them out of the neighborhood and even further away from Arkford City. This was where Peyton preferred to be–away from the noise, away from school, but most importantly, away from his responsibilities. Leo's eyes were on the road ahead as they drove into a small, but familiar town with nothing but classic rock music filling their ears.

"Our usual?" Leo inquired as he steered into the drive through of a familiar red, blue, and orange restaurant.

Peyton nodded. "Yes, please."

"Is something wrong?" The car stopped behind another in line.

"No," Peyton lied through his teeth and looked straight forward. "Nothing's wrong."

"Oh, BS," countered Leo, turning the radio down.

He pretended to distract himself with his phone, which was miserably failing to adhere to the intention. "I'm just stressed with the Fall semester starting up and everything."

"But you've gotten nearly a 4.0 every semester so far," Leo argued with a chuckle. "If anyone should be worried, it's me."

"Why did you pick Advanced Chemistry again?" A small grin appeared on Peyton's face.

"Because I needed a Science with lab requirement, and I didn't want you to suffer alone."

"But you're not going to be a doctor."

"Right." Leo shrugged as they began to roll forward.

Peyton attempted changing the subject. "So, what *do* you want to do?"

Leo could not answer because his tan Nissan had arrived at the order station's speaker. He rolled down the window and waited an uncomfortable five to ten seconds before a chipper voice feigned a cheerful tone from the speaker. "*Hello, and welcome to Dairy King! What can I get started for you today?*"

"I'd like one chocolate flurry and one strawberry flurry please," Leo leaned forward and spoke into the microphone.

"*Okay! What sizes?*"

Leo looked at Peyton, who shrugged. The former replied, "Medium's good for both."

"*Sounds good! Anything else?*"

"No, thank you."

"*Perfect! That'll be eight seventy-six. I'll see you at the window.*"

Leo coaxed the car forward and rolled his window back up.

"I actually want to be a teacher," he answered Peyton's question from before.

"What?" His passenger was bewildered. "I thought you *hated* kids!"

"They aren't too bad."

Peyton's brows furrowed. "Who are you and what'd you do with Leo Rhys?"

"I've been doing a lot of thinking over the summer," Leo explained as they pulled up to the window and rolled his vehicle's down. "And, as of recently, that involves you. What's going on with you? You've been trying to fool me by being on your phone."

Peyton fidgeted in his seat and put his phone in his sweatshirt pocket. "Oh, the ice cream's here!" he redirected loudly.

"Hey there! That'll be eight seventy-six." A positive, very tiny woman with a silver pixie cut and a nametag reading "Keagan" in cursive handwriting by her shoulder exclaimed.

"Whose turn is it to pay?" Peyton hissed to his friend.

"I got it," responded Leo, who was already handing his credit card to Keagan.

"But-"

"Too late."

Keagan practically skipped over to the register, swiped the card, and then handed it back to Leo with a huge smile on her face. "Your flurries will be out shortly!"

"Thanks." Leo returned the gesture.

The girl trotted away from the window, so Leo turned back to Peyton, who was running his fingers through his hair. "I know that look," the redhead asserted. "You're nervous. What gives?"

Peyton was at a standstill. This was *Leo* who was right next to him. The two of them had been the best of friends for ages. Heck, he could tell him anything! On the other hand, though,

Paige had specifically requested numerous times for her identity to remain anonymous and practically nonexistent. She needed his help, whether she realized it or not, and Peyton was determined to aid her with what she needed.

"Do you remember that weird dream I had the other night?" Peyton inquired hesitantly. *"Okay, Peyton. Don't screw this up."*

Leo nodded. "Yeah. What about it?"

"Well, I..." he started, but once again, he was interrupted by the ecstatic Dairy King employee.

"Here you are." Keagan held out their desserts, which Leo took.

The both of them replied at the same time, "Thank you!"

"You're welcome!" The girl's smile glittered almost as much as her nose stud. "You all have a good one!"

"You too!"

Leo drove out of the drive through line and scanned the parking lot for a place to temporarily put his vehicle to rest. When he found a space near the back, he steered the Nissan into that spot and adjusted the gear into park. Eagerly, he removed his spoon from the plastic packaging it came in and stuck it in his strawberry flurry, but before he took a bite, he remembered his friend was in the middle of explaining himself

"What were you saying?" Leo asked Peyton, who looked entranced by his dessert.

The blond's eyes snapped upwards to meet Leo's. Peyton paused for a second to recollect himself before making yet another excuse: "I was just thinking about the bus incident that caused my dream," he fibbed. "I still can't put my finger on what happened."

"You know, another incident happened Thursday," Leo casually commented.

"Huh?" Peyton was authentically puzzled. "What happened?"

"Some girl was seen jumping out of an apartment building but caught herself with the same type of force field thing. Apparently she crushed a car too by landing on it before running off. I have no idea how she's still alive."

The scoop of chocolate ice cream on Peyton's spoon dripped into the cup he was holding, but he didn't notice. "My God...," he trailed off. *"Oh no... Paige's low profile..."*

"Yup." Leo shoved a mouthful of strawberry flurry between his lips. "Whoever she is, I hope she knows she's really cool. This city needs some action other than work and school."

Peyton shook that dreadful thought away. If Paige needed assistance, she knew that she could let Peyton know. Paige knew what she was doing–in fact, Peyton was one hundred and one percent sure that she was twice as smart as he was. Even though he hardly knew her, she was a unique human being...if he could even call her that knowing her supernatural abilities. Then again, Peyton had no idea how much Paige trusted him in the first place.

But on the other hand...what was wrong with a little adventure?

The blond shoveled a scoop of his dessert into his mouth and smiled. "I agree."

Little did he know that his silent proposition would become a reality soon enough.

Chapter Thirteen

BRUNETTE

Sleep was something Paige never got used to no matter how much she did it. The concept of Dreamland was foreign to her, therefore untrustworthy. The black abyss of nothingness was what she preferred to be shrouded in while in the midst of such a vulnerable state. Thankfully, that was her reality right then and there.

Floating in the void was something Paige enjoyed. It was not fear, not joy, not sadness, not anger, just...nothing. In fact, nothing was better than everything all at once. That was what this was to Paige: a desperate escape from the chaos of the world falling apart around her. In her slumber, she did not have to worry about not having a home, or even a *normality* to expect at the end of each and every day. It was, for lack of better words, relieving.

The sound of footsteps in the hallway outside the door of the guest bedroom brought her back to reality, though. Paige fought back a groan as she peeled herself out of the cocoon she made while unconscious. She learned from experience that Peyton Finlay was outside getting ready for school that morn-

CHAPTER THIRTEEN

ing. Paige pried her eyes open and let out a fatigued, but silent, yawn. She knew she had yet another mission to accomplish that day.

Paige was very thankful she had taken a shower the previous afternoon while Peyton and his parents were out of the house. She was still getting used to the grand scheme of things, especially the kindness that was given to her without an expectation of something in return. That was how things worked in the organization, but not here. Peyton was risking his relationship with his mother and father for her. How many people were like this?

She caught a glimpse of herself in the mirror. Once again, she was wearing a pair of Peyton's pajama pants and an oversized shirt of his. Paige could not continue on with simply wearing his clothes. It was too kind of a gesture. Guilt crept into her subconscious every second she thought about the boy who took her in. Was it wrong to still not trust him?

There was no time for that thought to dwindle in the back of her mind. Instead, she adjusted her appearance to be transparent and ventured to the bathroom to get ready for school. Paige either ignored or did not hear the water running in the restroom as she grabbed the toothbrush she had hidden for herself in the mirrored cabinet attached to the side wall. She squirted just enough toothpaste on her brush and ran it under the sink. Once Paige put it in her mouth, though, a sudden noise from behind the shower curtain nearly made her spit the toothpaste everywhere.

"Paige, what the hell?!" a male voice whisper-yelled over the shower.

Paige revoked her invisibility with a start, whirled around, and slowly lowered the toothbrush from her lips. Her entire face flushed pink when she realized Peyton was indeed right in the middle of a shower. She blinked once, then twice, and then three times. She had never had such an embarrassing problem of being in the same room of an unclothed member of the opposite sex.

"Oops...," she exhaled, covering her eyes with her free hand.

"It's fine, just...could I have some privacy, please?" Peyton stammered as his complexion morphed into a tomato.

"Give me two seconds." Paige stuffed the toothbrush in her mouth and began brushing like there was no tomorrow. "I'm not looking."

"Please?"

He sounded desperate, but Paige merely failed to understand. "Almost done."

"With what?!"

"Brushing my teeth," she explained with her mouth full.

Peyton sighed. "Alright, just...hurry up."

Paige scrubbed her teeth with the brush as quickly as she could for at least ten more seconds before spitting out the toothpaste-saliva mix into the sink. She ran the water and washed off her toothbrush, cleaned out the sink, filled a cup with cold water, and rinsed out her mouth. She stuffed her toothbrush back into the cabinet, put the cup back where it was, and then passed through the door, not before she whispered an apology. Peyton just sighed and continued his shoulder. Nothing like *that* had happened before.

The teenage girl scurried down the stairs as quiet as a mouse and as transparent as a ghost. Once she noticed Peyton's mother in the kitchen, she was tempted to go right out the door, but then she remembered a conversation that she and Peyton had a couple of days ago.

"Please make sure you eat something," Peyton requested of her while folding a load of laundry in his bedroom.

Paige sat awkwardly on his bed. "How come?" she asked with innocence.

"You need to eat," was his simple response.

"Why?"

That question caught Peyton off-guard. His brows furrowed as he made a likely assumption rather than answering her inquiry, "I'm guessing you probably don't eat much."

"So?" Paige fiddled with the comforter next to her.

"Can you at least try to have something every day?"

Paige hesitated. This was not something she was used to hearing. Peyton's tone was genuine. Was it a possibility that he truly cared about her? She was hardly used to eating, much less enough every single day. She had ruts and ridges in her abdomen to prove it. Nevertheless, she gave those brown eyes asking a completely different question a glance and nodded.

"...I mean, I guess."

That caused Peyton's small smile to return. "Thanks, Paige."

With Peyton's small, but meaningful, request in mind, Paige opened the pantry door while his mother was occupied with whatever was cooking on the stove, grabbed a chocolate-covered granola bar, which was the first thing she found, and made no trace of her occupancy before darting through the front door. An unfamiliar world was laid out in front of her that Paige was not quite ready to explore, but she had no choice. She had missed one day of classes—she could not afford to miss any more.

Paige attempted to invisibly make her way towards Azure University, but she soon realized how much farther Peyton's house was from the establishment than her apartment was. Her first solution was to run, but as soon as she took three or four long strides, a sharp pain in her abdomen slowed her to a stop. Paige gritted her teeth together and bit back a yelp at the pulsating sensation that refused to go away. She knew she needed to get to school, and on time too.

Then, an idea hit her. Paige grinned to herself and started forward once again, this time with one arm clasping her rips. She broke into a slow, leisurely jog and used her free hand to open a transparent portal to a short distance away—about one hundred to one hundred and fifty feet. Once Paige passed through one vortex, another one opened, therefore repeating the cycle past the unsuspecting citizens of Arkford and towards the university.

Paige halted at once when an electric blue bicycle raced past her unseen figure. She squinted and recognized the blond head of hair occupying the personal vehicle on the concrete in the middle of the city. As far as she knew, bicycles were meant for the street, but she had no time to worry about that now. Instead, she needed to do one thing:

Speed the hell up.

She continued her routine of passing through wormholes that she lost count of as her strides grew longer, quicker, and more agonizing the closer she got to her destination. Paige paid no attention to the flourishing pain in her stomach. Instead, she focused on the familiar buildings emerging in the distance. That propelled her faster. It was truly an odd sight if anyone other than herself could witness it. Paige darted out of the way of a vehicle speeding towards her as she crossed the street. She did not blame them—despite the fact she was in the crosswalk, nobody could see her.

Paige was huffing and puffing by the time she made it to Azure University's grounds which had nearly the only greenery in the urban landscape. She passed through the double doors like they were not even there. While blending flawlessly into the crowd, Paige morphed into Penny Hamilton's physique right in the middle of the commotion of several individuals

CHAPTER THIRTEEN

trying to get to class on time. She couldn't blame them—in fact, she was one of them.

Before she knew it, she was one of the only people left in the hallway. She dashed towards her US History classroom and flung open the door. To her horror, the rest of the classroom was filled and at least half of her peers' pairs of eyes turned in her direction. Thankfully, her professor ignored her and continued on with his lecture about the first settlement of Jamestown. With a sheepish, tiny grin on her face that faded in a matter of seconds, she made her way to her seat and plopped down in the chair in front of Peyton.

Paige was well-aware that she had absolutely none of her supplies, but that was no matter—she had already done the work for the next two or three weeks of this class. Not taking notes would not be much of a problem for her. Still, she wanted to make a bulleted list of points or do *something* to keep herself occupied. She did the only thing she could think of and turned around to view Peyton typing on his computer. Paige softly cleared her throat to retrieve his attention, which was successful.

"Could I borrow a sheet of paper and a pencil, please?" she whispered.

Peyton nodded and reached into his backpack, which was leaning against his chair. He retrieved a dark blue notebook and ripped out a sheet of paper. Then, he unzipped the pencil pouch he grabbed next and found a mechanical pencil. He handed both objects to Paige, who thanked him quietly. She began scribbling down on the sheet of paper even though she had already taught herself the material.

The eighty-five minutes - or however much was left of the class when Paige walked in - passed by slower than she remembered last week. Maybe it was because she was getting used to her classes, but either way, rather than notes, she had a sheet of notebook paper covered front and back with random squiggles and doodles of nothing in particular. The sight embarrassed her; she was supposed to be learning–not trying to keep herself awake.

"*Is this how other college students feel?*" Paige had a sudden revelation.

Aha! So, this was what being normal felt like!

Once class was dismissed, Paige stuffed the sheet of paper in the pocket of her black knit sweater. She promptly stood from her desk and was about to exit the room free of any unneeded confrontation until Peyton's sickeningly familiar voice cut through her train of thought.

"Hey, Penny!"

Paige skidded to a stop right in the middle of the doorframe. She flinched when Peyton slammed into her and knocked her forward. She felt the need to catch herself until a firm hand grasped onto her forearm before she could stumble forward. Peyton pulled her back upright while Paige attempted not to fight back out of instinct.

"Woah, there!" Peyton exclaimed during the interaction. "Be careful. Are you alright?"

Paige nodded since she did not know what else to do. "Yeah, yeah," she dismissed the question. "I'm fine. Hey, Peyton."

"Hey," he repeated awkwardly. "How's it going?"

"It's alright. How are you?"

"I'm pretty good."

Silence.

"*Is this how real people have a conversation? Because if so, it blows,*" Paige thought to herself as the two of them sat there in silence.

Peyton appeared as if he was going to say something else, but a group of three girls passed by the two of them. All three pairs of their eyes were on Penny's persona. At first, it was innocent, but then, the laughter started. It began as giggling, but then transformed into roaring laughter after two of them looked at their phones. Paige blinked at them and then adjusted her glasses. Maybe that was the problem. Was she seeing things? Then, she looked at Peyton, whose eyebrows were furrowed quizzically.

No, it was not just her.

Paige approached the group of girls. Two of them had brown hair and one had dark blonde hair. She made eye contact with the brunette in the middle and stiffly inquired, "What's so funny?"

"You don't know?" the brunette on the leader's right snorted through her bright red lipstick. "Out of everyone here, you should be the least confused."

The girl in the front elbowed her friend harshly. "Shh!"

"Ow!"

"Pardon?" One of Paige's eyebrows raised. "I want to know what's going on."

"Yeah," Peyton stepped forward and demanded, "what *is* going on?"

The leader of the group snatched her friend's phone, which had the desired content on it, and revealed the screen to Paige. Directly in front of her was a video posted on social media of Penny using two index fingers to type - not well - on a keyboard in the computer lab. Then, the video shifted to the library, where Penny was trying to reach a book, but miserably failed, letting practically the whole shelf fall on her head. Then, there was one more setting: the university restaurant. A video of Penny grabbing food from her tote bag was on full display with the caption: "Do we *really* want a pig on campus?"

Paige was seething by the time the video ended, but she refused to let it show on her face. This film was surely intended to poke more than "fun" in her face. Instead, she calmly looked at the leader of the three girls and asked, "You, in the middle, what's your name?"

The tall brunette smirked with dull blue eyes that had a mischievous twinkle in them, "Hannah."

Hannah's head snapped to the left when Paige's hand made sharp contact with her cheek. Peyton needed to hold her back by putting a tight arm around her. Paige attempted to land more hits on the girl in front of her, but the boy behind her prevented her from doing so. Hannah's two "friends" ran away like cowards once the slap was executed.

"Go to hell, Hannah," Paige spat in her face.

"You *bitch*!" Hannah screamed at the curly-haired girl. "You hit me!"

"And you deserved it," Peyton cut in before Paige could retort with several profanities. "C'mon, Penny, let's go."

"Look what she did!" Penny strained viciously against him.

Peyton began dragging her away from the lone antagonist in the hallway. "I know, but you can be the bigger person and forget it."

"The bigger person?" she deadpanned. "She's got six inches on me."

"Just come with me."

Paige knew Peyton was going to overpower her, merely because the two of them were in a public setting. Instead of fighting him, she let him walk her away from the whole situation with her hand in his. While the two left the scene, Paige looked over her shoulder and watched as Hannah nursed her cheek where a red splotch was already beginning to form. When the brunette looked in her direction, she matched Paige's glare with a sinister grin.

Peyton felt Penny tug against him and he only pulled her along. "Just drop it,"

"But-"

"Drop it," he pleaded.

That made Paige quiet down. She needed to remember that this was Penny that Peyton was with–not Paige. Keeping a low profile was crucial. Otherwise, he would be in grave danger once again. She was following the organization's orders. What else did they want? Paige was only one person. How much more could they expect from her?

Despite this bigger matter at hand, the social media video of her alias played on loop like a broken record in her imagination. The dull pain in her ribs was almost nothing compared to the action purely executed to hurt her - or Penny's - feelings. Never before did she realize words had such power, but actions were extraordinarily more severe. Paige was used to getting away with hiding in the shadows. Now, she understood what civilians often dealt with.

"Are you okay?" Peyton asked once the two rounded a corner. "What she did was uncalled for. I don't even know who that jerk is."

Paige nodded stiffly. "How can people be so...senseless?"

"I don't know, but usually, people in college could care less about other people. You probably won't even see her again, especially after you gave her the what-for."

"Then, why did you pull me away?" she retorted. "I would've done more to teach her a lesson."

"You would've gotten in trouble," he reasoned.

"Does that matter?"

"When it comes to education? Yes. You could've gotten kicked out of this place for physical assault."

Paige shrugged at the thought, finding a loophole. "What about the slap, then?"

"That was in self defense," Peyton explained with the

corners of his lips quirked upwards. "And it was pretty badass."

"Oh, please," she sarcastically exhaled.

"What?! It's not every day you see a catfight in the halls."

Paige blinked up at him. "A...catfight?" she questioned. "I don't understand."

"Never mind."

Paige's alter ego and Peyton walked down the halls until the former realized that she hadn't a clue where the two of them were going. When she stopped in her tracks, Peyton did a step later. He looked confused, as if something about Penny did not align with reality. In fact, not much about her made sense. It was almost as if she was pretending to be someone she wasn't.

"Penny?" He grabbed her attention. "Is something wrong... other than that video?"

Paige answered his question with one of her own: "Where are we going?"

"I was thinking about getting lunch if you'd like to join. My treat."

Paige was at a standstill. How could some people be so cruel like Hannah, but others be so kind like Peyton? She was at a complete loss for words. Her mouth opened and closed like a fish out of water. She was drowning in her own waters. Being a civilian, no matter how briefly, has given her a clear message and taught her some hard lessons, but it was all just a blur.

"I-...I can't," Paige stammered out.

Peyton frowned at that. "How come? I don't mind."

"I just can't."

"Okay, but...wait. Where are you going?"

Paige started walking the other way. She wanted nothing to do with people at the moment. "I just need some space," she explained. "I'll see you later."

CHAPTER THIRTEEN

"Okay, uh...sounds good." Peyton was very confused. "I'll see you?"

His parting vocalization was more of a question than a statement as Paige made her leave. Instead of heading to the library or the computer lab, she walked straight out the two front doors of the university itself. There was nothing she had against Peyton–it was all those three girls in the hallway. Words and actions had not been so successful in conquering the wall of her emotions, but for some reason, Hannah and her "minions" breached her defenses.

Their words were paper cuts, but their actions were stab wounds.

Paige knew she would be back to the university in time for her other two classes that day. Now, however, that was the least of her worries. She had an errand to attend to that she had been putting off for as long as possible. She held her head high despite applicating her cloaking device - herself - as she made her way back to her apartment.

The humidity that the warm drizzling rain brought forth made Paige's usually flat, blonde hair the slightest bit poofy. She shrugged her black sweater off her shoulders, but kept the latter half of her sleeves on her forearms. Paige reappeared just as she passed a tree blocking the civilians' view of her to begin with. She strutted right into the Hillwell apartment complex without a look back.

Paige stopped in front of the elevator doors and pressed the button to activate the strange contraption. Once the doors opened, she stepped inside and shut them with the interior button before anyone else could get on with her. She pressed the button for the twenty-sixth floor and tensed as the elevator began making its way upward.

She considered the options that were open to her. This was not her home anymore, hence the uneasy feeling she had in her stomach. Then, the butterflies - which were more like wasps at that point - intensified once she realized she had somewhere else to go. Was she doing the wrong thing by moving out whatever was left from her apartment after the ambush? For the first time in quite a while, true anxiety rocketed throughout her system. To put it in simple terms, she had a double life that was becoming harder to maintain.

Paige had no idea what was going to happen next, but there was only one way to find out.

The elevator doors opened.

Chapter Fourteen

CELESTE

Being a college student *sucked*. One minute, everything was perfect. Assignments were done on time, lectures were understood, and you felt like you actually knew what you were doing. Unfortunately, that glorious feeling went right down the drain as soon as the first weekend commenced.

Then, all hell broke loose.

Chaos ensued every second of every day. Life revolved around education. Nothing mattered except getting a perfect unweighted grade point average. Learning was not even the main goal anymore. Instead, turning in assignments by the end of the semester was. Peyton did not want a repeat of the previous year. He was a good student, but he enjoyed spending time on things he enjoyed rather than general education classes. Now, since Peyton was in the midst of classes for his major, he found learning to be more exciting.

That was why Peyton was pedaling as quickly as his scrawny legs could take him down the sidewalk towards his house. Even after a full day of classes, he still had enough energy to rush home and complete his work for the day before settling down for a long, much-needed night of sleep.

Peyton swung his leg over his bicycle's blue frame while the private vehicle was still in motion and slowed casually to a stop. He typed the passcode for the garage door and watched as the poor thing squeaked its way upward. He pretty much leaned his bike over the first stable thing he could find and paraded his way into the house.

The door leading to the kitchen opened with a slam, which made the woman at the stove preparing dinner almost flinch out of her socks. "What the-" she started before turning around, "Oh! Hey, Sweetheart!"

"Hey, Mom," replied Peyton, striding over to his mother and capturing her in a hug. "I didn't mean to startle you,"

"It's okay," She returned the gesture. "How was school?"

"Busy."

Caroline quirked a smile. "Well, that's to be expected. You're doing great, though."

"Thanks, Mom." Peyton smiled. "I really am trying my best."

"And that's why your father and I are so proud of you."

He blushed shyly. "Mom..." he dragged out the word for emphasis.

"It's true!" Lucas yelled from the living room where he was watching a baseball game.

"Dad!"

Caroline giggled and ruffled her son's hair. "Now, why don't you get yourself ready for dinner?" she suggested. "I'm making pasta."

"Sounds good," Peyton agreed with her. "I should be down soon."

With that, Peyton made his way upstairs and towards his

room. He was in a bit of a cheerful, but stressful mood. College did that to a person—one moment, it was smooth sailing, but the next, you felt like the Titanic. A century-old problem never went away. Whatever thoughts running through his head promptly disappeared when he opened the door to his room and saw Paige sitting on his bed for the second time. This time, however, he was calm and was not about to panic. He was used to an extra person being in the house. What he was not used to was the red and white bag sitting next to her on the bed.

Peyton shrugged his backpack off his shoulders and set it next to his desk. "Hey, Paige," he greeted her like an old friend. He then gestured to the bag. "What's that?"

"I wanted to thank you for being so kind to me," Paige emotionlessly explained. "So, I brought you dinner."

"You didn't have to-" he started, but was stopped when she handed him something wrapped in paper. He hesitantly unwrapped it and stared at the content before eyeing her. "A chicken wrap? How'd you know those were my favorite?"

Paige opened her mouth and was about to explain that she remembered from the first day of university, but then closed it. It was Penny that Peyton had met just a week ago—not Paige. She needed to be more careful, especially when it came to publicity. Instead of being honest, which was not something she was able to do, she made up an excuse.

"Lucky guess."

Peyton was unsure about the whole situation. "You really didn't have to."

"I wanted to," countered Paige before he could stop her.

"Did you at least get something for yourself?" he inquired.

Paige just shook her head. "Didn't have the money or the time. I collected as many things from my apartment as I could before picking it up," she simply explained.

To her surprise, Peyton set down the chicken wrap back

where it was. He got to his feet and then headed to the door. "I'll be right back."

Paige gave Peyton an odd look, which he turned away from as he shut the door behind him. He dashed down the stairs and into the kitchen where his mother was finishing up dinner. At the sound of his brisk footsteps, she turned around and gave him a smile.

"Are you *finally* ready for dinner?" she asked him teasingly.

"Yeah, sorry," Peyton quickly replied. "I have a lot of schoolwork to catch up on, so I'll bring it upstairs if that's okay."

Caroline frowned a bit at that. "Are you sure? We miss you downstairs for dinner."

A blade of guilt stabbed him right in the chest. "I know, but once I get the hang of getting everything done at a reasonable hour, I'll be down more often."

"Okay, Sweetie." Her lips curved upward as she handed him his plate and a fork. "Good luck with your schoolwork and let me know if you need anything."

"I will, Mom."

Peyton turned around before he could feel any worse than he already did. He made his way back up the stairs and to his room. Paige was still sitting on his bed like she was afraid to be in the room. It was as if she was in the middle of some sort of crime scene, where if one object was touched, moved, or altered altogether, the whole investigation was ruined. Peyton shut the door behind her, which was almost enough for her to flinch out of whatever trance she was in.

Paige's eyes followed the plate of pasta as it was positioned on the bed next to her. "What's this for?" she questioned almost...timidly.

"You said you didn't get anything for yourself," Peyton

clarified, gesturing to the warm food that smelled like Heaven, "And my mom made me dinner. I can't have two dinners all by myself and let you have nothing."

"...Pardon?" Her entire demeanor changed from stoicism to astonishment.

Peyton pushed the plate towards her. "It's all yours if you want it."

"You don't need to."

"I want to." He grinned that familiar smile at her. "And besides, now, we're even."

Paige cautiously moved the hot plate onto her lap. "...If you're certain."

"I'm certain."

That was all the confirmation Paige needed to let the intoxicating aroma take over her senses. At once, Paige picked up the fork provided for her and began devouring the meal she was very grateful for. That was the only way she could think of to show her thanks. She and Peyton ate their dinner in near silence. Paige noticed how Peyton periodically looked at his phone in between bites of his chicken wrap and fries on the side. Occasionally, there was a smile on his face, and other instances, a neutral look was all that remained.

Paige felt inclined to ask what exactly was going on, but promptly after Peyton realized he was being watched, he set his phone down. The blonde girl could not describe the sensation rising in her chest other than it being some sort of warmth. She felt as if she was valued. Peyton's attention was on her, despite there not being a competition between the young woman and the cellular device.

"Sorry," Peyton apologized to her. "I was just texting with my friend, Leo, about an assignment that's due on Sunday night."

Paige stared at him. Who was she for him to owe an explanation to? "Don't worry about it." She was curious, though; she had heard of texting, but had never done it before. "How...how do you do that?"

"Do what?"

"Text," she elaborated.

"Oh—it's easy." Peyton picked up his phone and opened his messages app. "See this keyboard right here?" When Paige nodded, he continued, "You type what you want to say to the person and then press that arrow to send it."

Paige nodded again. She then pointed to three yellow faces that Leo had sent in his next text. "And what are those?"

"Emojis." Peyton pressed a button to direct the screen to a vast list of emoticons. "Here. You can look through them if you'd like."

Paige hesitantly took the phone that Peyton held out to her and studied it. She had never obtained the opportunity to hold one of these futuristic devices in her hands before, so she decided to make the best of it. She scrolled through the list of emojis and analyzed each and every one–from the animals to the emotions until...

"...Is that what I think it is?" Paige squinted.

Peyton leaned over her shoulder. "What?"

He started laughing when she pointed at a certain brown emoticon with a smiley face.

"That's a poop emoji," he explained.

Peyton half-expected Paige to chuckle along with him, but what laid before him instead was a stone-faced neutrality. "Why would anyone use that?" she questioned him.

"Usually as a joke," he supplied.

Paige blinked at him. "What other emojis are there?"

Peyton smiled at this. He let Paige hold his phone while he showed her each section of emojis. Whether she realized it or not, Paige was awestruck by how much information could be stored in such a small device. She was used to using words to communicate with the little people she knew. Now, she could use tiny faces? This was amazing!

"This is so interesting," she commented while scrolling through the list of emojis and analyzing each one.

He nodded. "Yeah, I guess it is."

"You guess?"

"Well, I've never thought about it like that before."

Paige deposited Peyton's phone in his outstretched, yet patient, hand. "I bet it's nice. Isn't it?" she asked no one except her own mind.

"What do you mean by that?" Peyton's expression morphed from amused to confused.

"You and most others in this city have grown up with everything you could ever need–even things that you never *would* need. I've been scrounging around for my whole life, begging for scraps off the table from those who are more fortunate. Why? I don't have a damn clue. Some people just get left at the bottom of the barrel."

By the time Paige had finished talking, she was tensed up in the same spot on the bed that she had been ever since Peyton returned home. She glared down at the floor like it had insulted her. In fact, it had. Everything about Peyton's house was too good to be true. He had a roof over his head, a comfortable place to sleep, a loving family, and - she looked up - even a television just in his room alone. Hell, he had a multitude of clothes that he lended her in a heartbeat.

Peyton looked at her with wide eyes. "Paige, I-...I don't know what to say," he stammered awkwardly. "I'm so sorry you've had to live like that, but when you're under this roof, you won't have to."

"I don't deserve this treatment," she retorted without making eye contact.

"Oh, sure, you do," countered Peyton as he stood up and removed her plate from the bed since she was finished. "Everyone deserves the bare minimum."

"But you're providing me with more than the bare minimum."

Peyton looked directly in her hazel irises and shot down that statement: "Treating someone like they're an actual human being *is* the bare minimum."

That shut Paige up. She eyed Peyton like he was a unique specimen of some sort, like she had never seen anything like him in her life. In a way, that was factual. Paige was used to nothing but business, and anything to gain more success for said "business." She was sick and tired of living like that. That was why she sought shelter in the only place she could find that was not controlled by the organization. Paige stared down at her bare feet in shame, like she was a lost puppy with nowhere to go. Treading on thin ice caused frostbite after a while.

Peyton could hardly bear to look at her when she was like this...which happened to be more often than not. He wanted to fix it, to make a *difference* in the long, twisting and turning road that was leading Paige to nowhere other than self-doubt. She had no idea what her plan was anymore, where she was supposed to go, or who she was supposed to be. Rather than doing anything, she did nothing, which she hated and loved at the same time.

It was only when Peyton walked over to his desk and began adjusting something that Paige could not identify. She studied him as he removed two portions of the black-box-looking thing and attached what looked to be bracelets to them. Paige cocked her head to the side when Peyton grabbed the remote

CHAPTER FOURTEEN

and moved to sit down on the bed next to her. He tossed her one of the small, colored objects - which Paige now realized had buttons on them - and turned on the television.

"Am I supposed to know what you're doing?" Paige questioned stoically. She held up the object in her hand. "What is this?"

Peyton pointed to the little red object in her hand and then the celeste one in his own. "That's a controller."

"...A controller for what?"

"This."

When Peyton pressed a button on the remote, a plethora of little icons flooded the screen, making a list of several cartoon applications. Paige gazed at the television like it was magic. Peyton used the blue object - the controller - in his hand to click on one of the icons, which absorbed the rest of the features on the screen. At once, energetic music began playing and there were several options listing "Singleplayer," "Multiplayer," and other things that Paige could not quite understand.

Thankfully, Peyton turned to her. "It's a game. Want to play?"

"A game?"

"Yup."

Paige eyed him skeptically. "What kind of game?"

"So, basically, you accelerate with this," - Peyton pressed a button on the tiny plastic controller - "Steer with this," - He jiggled the knob - "Drift with this," - He pressed a button on the top right - "And you can throw stuff at people with this." He pressed the top left button.

"...With this?" Paige dangled the controller by the wristband.

"Yeah. Are you ready?"

Paige nodded and watched as Peyton pressed the button

on the screen that said "Multiplayer." A line immediately jutted down the middle of the screen. Peyton got up to sit on the other side of Paige so their view was aligned with each side of the screen. She gazed at Peyton's side as he picked a character with blond hair that looked an awful lot like him and a blue outfit. He pressed a button and there was a cheerful beep.

"Do you need help picking your character?" Peyton's question jolted her out of whatever trance the television had put her in.

"Huh? No. I got it." Paige concentrated very hard, but scowled when the cursor went in the opposite direction than she wanted it to be. "No, go the other way. Why is it-"

Her question was answered when Peyton took her controller, flipped it around, and handed it back to her.

"Oh."

Peyton chuckled at the slight misinterpretation of how to hold the controller. His brown irises followed Paige's cursor as it passed by every single character. Paige's expression changed slightly with each one, as if she found something wrong with every option. Finally, she decided on a pink character with a mushroom hat. Then, she picked a bike as opposed to an actual car. She thought it made her petite character look cooler.

Paige was a bit thankful for Peyton choosing the randomized races option since it would have taken her forever to decide what to do. The screen was hypnotizing, especially when the colorful, forest scene depicting the background for their first race was revealed.

"Friendly tip: hold down the button to go when the countdown hits one,' Peyton advised her.

Paige nodded, her eyes glued to the screen. Sure enough, numbers on the screen counted down from three and they were off. At first, Paige struggled to keep her character smoothly on the track, but once she got the hang of it, she found herself growing closer and closer to Peyton;s first-place lead. It took every bit of brain power she had to weave around the computer-generated opponents in order to catch up, and once she was in second place, Peyton's attention whipped towards her.

"What the hell-" he started to ask before he realized his character had crashed into the side of the track. He whirled back around and adjusted his car to be back on its mission–soon enough, he was in first place once again.

Paige refused to give up. She sped around the track like an expert once she got the hang of the whole thing, but then remained behind Peyton, who was very focused on the finish line in front of him. It was the final lap, and - just like the two of them expected - Peyton was in first place and Paige was in a close second. He was so invested in his own journey that he failed to notice the scarlet, turtle-shell-shaped object in Paige's character's hand. The finish line was in sight, and Peyton was about to cross it until Paige released the weapon and let it practically blow Peyton off of the track. With a satisfied smirk on her face, Paige finished in first.

When she turned to Peyton, she almost let herself smile when she saw that his jaw was on the floor. "What?" she innocently inquired.

"How did you..." Peyton was distraught. "You've never played before–right?"

Paige nodded, trying to hide the grin on her face.

His eyes lit up when he realized she possessed an expression other than solemn. "Aha! I *knew* you were having fun. I didn't know you could do that."

"Never got the chance to." She looked away.

"*That's really sad...*," Peyton thought to himself. Maybe he should try a different approach. "Well, *did* you have fun?" he asked instead of probing her further.

Paige thought about it for a good five to ten seconds. Then, her eyes met Peyton's and she nodded. "Yes. Yes, I did."

"Then, let's keep racing," Peyton grinned at her. "Ready?"

Once again Paige nodded. Peyton's smile kept itself on his face even after the brief moment passed. He eagerly clicked the "continue" button.

"Mission success. Let's hope I can keep it going."

Chapter Fifteen

PURPLE

"I'm sorry, Miss Hamilton, but I'm afraid this won't cut it," the professor loomed over the intimidated student like a wolf after a bunny.

The girl with vibrant black curls eyed the five-page essay the professor clenched in his right hand so tightly that the paper was crinkling. She adjusted the collar of her navy-blue blazer and made sure her glasses were straight. No matter how many times she had put them on, they always seemed to slide down her face at the worst times. Her black flats were glued to the floor as this woman, who was more entitled than she needed to be, narrowed her eyes at her.

Paige shifted her gaze from the paper to the woman's piercing gaze, which was at least two inches higher up. "What's wrong with it, Professor Cullen?"

"Come over here." Professor Cullen placed - or slammed, more rather - the poor stack of papers on the desk. "We need to discuss this."

"What do we need to discuss?" Paige looked her professor in the eye rather than looking at the essay.

"This essay."

No shit, Sherlock." Paige forced a polite smile on her face that Aphrodite was jealous of. "What about it?"

Professor Cullen with her bob of brown hair that reminded Paige of a robin's nest. "You were meant to discuss a narrower topic," she claimed like a poor attorney. "You need to provide a clearer example of the topic of...what even is it–moral goodness?"

Paige stiffly nodded.

"Right." The professor pointed to one of several little notes that she wrote on the sheet of paper. "I don't even see a clear thesis anywhere in this piece...or should I even call it that?"

"Goodness is something defined by the morality of the mind. Something that is beautiful isn't necessarily good because it's pleasing to the eye, but because it's relative to the subconscious' definition of good," Paige supplied.

Professor Cullen's eyes narrowed just the slightest. Paige wanted to flip her double chin over her mouth so she would shut the hell up when she retorted, "Well, why didn't you put that in your paper?"

"I did, Ma'am." Paige's tone was sweeter than sugar. Even Willy Wonka would find it distasteful.

"Show me."

Paige flipped to the third page of her paper and pointed to a sentence that Professor Cullen had not even touched. It was written in size twelve Times New Roman font at the very end of a particularly long paragraph describing the importance of what is morally good and subjectively good. The skin around her index fingernail began to redden as the circulation was being cut off. Professor Cullen - fortunately and unfortunately - relieved that pain when she snatched the paper from under her finger.

"Miss Hamilton, this thesis statement was put in the

wrong place," she explained. "It should've been at the end of your introduction."

"I was building up to it."

"You're supposed to deliver your thesis and *then* build up to it. You need to redo this."

"Then why didn't you teach us that?" Paige thought crossly. She straightened her shoulders and politely took hold of her paper. "Can I ask what grade I'd get if I don't redo it?"

Professor Cullen's head cocked to the side. "Well, I *guess* I could calculate a proper grade for you, but it would be very harsh. I don't think you'd want that."

"No, Ma'am. I don't."

"Then, you should get to work." The professor jabbed her meaty finger into the assignment. "I'll give you until Sunday night."

Paige's eyes looked like off-colored tennis balls that had spiraled right out of bounds. "What?! But that's four days from now!"

Was it just her imagination, or did Professor Cullen's smile resemble the Joker's? "Well then, you'd better get moving."

Paige hated the fact that her fists clenched and her posture stiffened like a certain funny picture - or a meme, as Peyton said - she saw on his phone. Her hazel eyes met Professor Cullen's dull brown ones that were as wicked as the Witch of the West. She opened up her tote bag with a quote from the third President and slipped the dratted essay in a folder inside the bag's contents. Paige slung the bag's handles over her right shoulder and started off towards the exit of the classroom. Before she passed through the doorway, though, she stopped in the middle of it and offered an innocent look to her "superior."

"Thank you for this learning opportunity." Her tone reeked with faux genuinity.

Either her professor did not answer, or whatever words she mumbled under her breath were incoherent. Paige stormed out of the room and marched down the hallway. Her foreign black curls bounced as she walked, as if they were streamers attached to the ceiling of a party. Paige's presence in the halls were like ocean waves gracefully lapping a beachside shore— barely there, but just unique enough to grab one's attention. Her footsteps were the pebbles being carried away by the current, battling against the white foamy hue.

Her heart throbbed like the steady rhythm of the beachside scene surrounding her imagination.Then, the tide became higher, slowly ebbing up the shore. The ocean conquered the sand like a perilous army. Success only became prevalent when the opposing side raised their white flag. Water asserted its dominance over the sand just like Paige's heart won the war against her mind. A wave of solemn solitude washed over her quicker than she could stop it.

"Am I really not good enough for that lady?"

Paige was greeted with the fresh kiss of autumn air. Despite the metamorphosis of the leaves transitioning from green to red, orange, and yellow, the lack of such was overwhelmed by the metropolis of nothing but a concrete jungle. Paige was the explorer and she and her Indiana Jones adventuring skills would get her out. Thankfully, they were brief in doing so. After at least a twenty-minute walk through the zoo of civilians glued to their cellular devices rather than the world around them, Paige found herself entering the suburbs.

A breath of fresh air in the oasis from the urban desert was all she needed to be spiraling back on track. Paige wracked her mind to keep it in alignment of where she wanted it to be. She needed to mentally prepare herself for the rest of the day that was about to unfold before her. Paige let herself disappear, both physically and mentally, into the greenery that surrounded her along with peaceful, cottage-like structures that she could only imagine in a fairytale. Every fairytale had its villain, whether it be Jafar or Mother Gothel, but Paige was far from the princess.

She felt like either Iago or Pascal instead.

Paige passed right through the closed doorway and walked through a transparent vortex directly to Peyton's room. She turned on television as well as her visibility under her biological alias when she walked past his desk and picked up the blue plastic controller attached to what Peyton called a "switch." Whatever it was, Paige liked it, so much so that Peyton allowed her to use it whenever he was not home. This was one of those instances.

She was forever marveled by the everyday experiences that civilians had and was very thankful that Peyton offered her the opportunity to witness them with her own eyes. Being sucked into a video game was not how Paige expected the rest of the afternoon to go, but she was *not* going to work on the dreaded essay yet. She needed a distraction, and that was exactly what the "switch" was meant for.

Paige played several rounds of the racing game that Peyton introduced to her what seemed to be ages ago. Time flew by like a peregrine falcon but crawled like a snail at the same time. Paige was enthralled by said game for over an hour, but it seemed like a mere ten minutes had passed when the door to Peyton's room slowly opened. Paige had learned to glance over to see who it was, but once she realized it was simply Peyton, she let her eyes resume watching the screen.

"Hey," Peyton greeted her like it was an everyday thing...in a way, though, it was.

Paige simply nodded a greeting. Her stoicism was something Peyton was used to, but it was unlike her to not say a single word in return. He decided to probe a little bit further.

"How was your day?" He asked her. When Paige only shrugged her shoulders, he tried again: "Is everything okay?"

"Yup," she replied, her eyes fixed on the game.

The corners of Peyton's lips tilted downward. "Are you sure?"

Paige nodded.

She hardly noticed what was going on around her until Peyton grabbed the remote from his desk and turned off the television. Paige's gaze darted from the black screen to the boy holding the controller, and then back again. She deflated like a balloon when the realization that she was not getting out of this situation hit her like an unwanted red light.

"Something's wrong." Peyton sat back down on the bed. Paige finally allowed herself to look at him. There was nothing but compassion in his eyes. "Do you want to talk about it?"

Paige's ears deceived her. Did she really have that option? "Not really."

"Okay, then. You don't have to."

Wow—was this really happening? Paige had to do a mental double take. "Thank you." She cleared her throat to allow the trickling river of words to flow through. "...I mean...thank you for not prying."

Peyton shrugged and smiled. His kind, authentic aura glowed like a desolate star, a single light in a world of darkness. "It's basic human decency."

"Basic human...," she trailed off only to interrupt herself. "Oh, right."

She ignored the odd look that Peyton gave her. Instead, she fiddled around with the tiny controller in her hand like it was some sort of tinker toy. Peyton silently found the childish way that Paige sometimes acted as endearing. He figured she knew no better. Everyone deserved to be a kid sometimes. Then, an idea struck him from that very mindset.

"You know," Peyton thought out loud. "How about we fix that "bad day" situation you've got going on?"

That caught Paige's attention. "How?"

Peyton stood up and slipped his checkered Vans back on his feet. "Get on your invisibility cloak and let's roll. Do you mind walking?"

"No, I don't mind, and I don't have-..." Paige hesitantly followed in his footsteps.

"It's just a saying."

She opened her mouth to retort, but then closed it again. Instead, she allowed herself to vanish right in front of Peyton, who had to do a double take at the floor where Paige was standing initially.

"You ready?" he asked her.

"Ready." Her voice reverberated from the general direction of the doorway.

Peyton unknowingly walked past her when he went to leave. "You know, the fact you can literally disappear from plain sight is kinda creepy."

"It's helpful as well." Paige's voice lowered to a whisper.

The two of them said nothing as they padded down the stairs. Thankfully, Caroline did not seem to notice two pairs of footsteps as they walked past since she only questioned her son, "Where are you off to?"

"I'm going out with Leo." Peyton inconspicuously stopped by the front door. "Is that okay?"

Caroline's pearly white smile caught Paige off-guard. She had never seen Peyton's mother before. Their blonde hair was almost identical, but what really grabbed Paige's attention was her grin. She and Peyton had the same dimples, the same closing of the eyes, and the same rosy cheeks when they expressed their happiness. Paige almost wanted to join in, but it was no use. No one would see her anyway.

"You know that's always okay, Pey," replied his mom. "You two have a good time."

Peyton refused to let himself exhale with relief. "Thanks, Mom. Love you."

"I love you too."

Peyton opened the front door, which Paige slinked out of first. He felt the tiny breeze of her long blonde hair whisk past him before he went out right after her, locking the door behind them. Once the two of them reached the bottom of the porch stairs and started walking, Paige's outline popped up right next to Peyton, who could not hide his flinching to the side.

"Jesus-" he started, but then covered it up with his signature grin. "That's really cool. How do you even do that?"

Paige shrugged. "I used to need to think about it a lot. Now, since I've mastered it, it's second nature."

"Can you make specific parts of your body disappear?"

Paige responded by rolling up the sleeve of the dark blue hoodie she was borrowing from Peyton's wardrobe and waving a transparent hand in front of his face.

"Woah, nice."

"I guess so."

Paige relished in the tranquility the cobalt night brought forth. Tiny stars speckled on the canvas of the sky lit the sidewalk that the two trod upon. A slight shiver cascaded through her petite frame every now and then, however, the incandescent glow of the occasional streetlamp soothed whatever nerves she possessed. Paige pulled the sleeves of the large hoodie she was clothed in over her trembling hands right before she stuffed them in her pockets. Luckily for her, whatever destination Peyton had in mind was in front of them. Paige was puzzled by the red, blue, and orange building lit before her.

She glanced at Peyton. "Dairy King?"

"Yeah." Peyton tilted his head towards the restaurant. "Ice cream fixes everything. Have you ever had it before?"

Paige was embarrassed to shake her head. Thankfully, Peyton did not seem to mind.

"Well, there's a first time for everything. Come on."

A little bell tinkled its greeting when Peyton pulled on the door and held it open for Paige. She felt inclined to walk in first, which was exactly what she did. An unsettling sensation flooded her when she realized the place was all hustle and bustle. This was what she was used to in Arkford City, but not in the suburbs. Paige caught herself shrinking down in the sweatshirt she found irresistibly comfortable.

Peyton's soft voice cut through her senses as smooth as butter. "Are you okay?"

Paige nodded with thinned, pressed lips. She followed him up to the counter where a small line two people deep had begun. Paige had done this numerous times before, but under different aliases. Being herself in a situation such as this seemed *wrong*. What if someone on the erroneous side of morality noticed her piercing eyes, her long hair, or even her unsteady posture? It was too much to bear.

She pulled her hood over her head.

The boy beside her laid his eyes upon the unsettling situation Paige was in. He knew better than to bring it up, so he didn't. By the time the two of them reached the register, Peyton was lost in thought. As soon as a "How can I help you?" reached his ears, a blade of guilt stabbed him right in the chest. He had forgotten to ask Paige what she wanted. Wasn't the guy supposed to order for the girl? How did this work?

Peyton cleared his throat and chose to set an example. "Hi, uh, I'd like one medium chocolate flurry and..." He turned to Paige and lowered his voice. "What would you like?"

Paige had completely forgotten to look at the menu, so she

conjured up something on the spot. "Um...do they have caramel?"

"Yes, they do," Peyton replied instead of the cashier. "And one medium caramel flurry, please."

The blonde looked the cashier right in the eyes. An eerie shade of blue was what she received in return. It seemed as if the teenage boy who had just inputted their order of flurries in the machine was on some sort of monotonous quest...a mission, perhaps. At first, Paige thought he was just consumed with his work, but there was something uncanny about the ghostly, glazed over look in his oceany irises. Paige caught herself backing behind Peyton, but she did not prevent her body from doing so.

"Eight seventy-one," the cashier emotionlessly stated.

Peyton took his credit card out of his wallet and inserted it into the chip reader. Paige could not keep her eyes off of the cashier. He looked just like a normal teenager, with brown hair and in the standard blue, red, and orange work uniform with a name tag stating "Dylan," but there was something mysteriously *off* about the glazed hue to his blue eyes. Once the dull blue irises met Paige's, though, they appeared to light up in a negative way. Paige lowered her gaze to her shoes.

The boy in front of her looked over his shoulder when he realized she was no longer by his side. "Is everything alright?" he asked once he received the receipt from the cashier.

Instead of responding verbally, Paige grasped tightly onto his hand and dragged him away from the counter. Peyton had no choice but to follow her to a table in a far corner of the shop. She sat herself down and Peyton did the same across from her.

"Okay, what's going on?" he inquired

"Keep your voice down," demanded Paige in a snippy tone. "As soon as we get the ice cream, we need to leave."

"What? Why?"

"*Should I tell him the truth? No. I don't know him well enough yet.*" Paige settled with a solid excuse: "I don't feel safe."

Peyton's gaze softened. "Is it all the people?"

For once, Paige did not feign the vulnerable expression on her face as she nodded.

"Okay, um..." Peyton thought for a moment. "Do you want to play a game while we wait to distract yourself?"

"What kind of game?"

"Twenty Questions?"

"What's that?"

"It's simple, really," he explained. "We take turns asking each other questions so we can get to know one another." When Paige's eyes narrowed, he quickly elaborated, "It's all lighthearted. If you don't want to answer a question, just say "pass." Okay?"

Paige shrugged just a little bit. "Okay."

Peyton grinned once again. *How was he able to smile in almost every situation?* "I'll start. What's your favorite color?"

"I haven't thought about it before," she honestly answered. "But...I guess I like purple."

"Hey! Blue's my favorite color!"

"Oh?"

"Yup. You know, blue and purple together make indigo."

"What's indigo?"

"It's a color between blue and purple."

Paige looked at the ground underneath her well-worn Converse. "I was unaware of such a gradient. Blue and purple... I like that."

"Cool!" Peyton seemed to agree.

Silence. *Was Paige supposed to ask a question now?* She considered asking Peyton what his favorite color was, but she remembered that he had already answered that question.

What were some simple questions, and why couldn't Paige think of any?

Then...she thought of a solution that seemed normal enough.

"What's your favorite video game?"

Peyton considered that for a second. "I like Wario Kart, but playing Singleplayer gets boring. I'm glad I can have someone to play with other than Leo. I always beat him and he gets mad."

Yes! She had started a normal conversation!

"Next question." The way Peyton treated her like an actual human being was growing on her, and quickly too. "What's your favorite song?"

Uh oh... Paige never listened to music, so how could she answer that? Her mind began to panic about how to make up some sort of excuse until...

...she realized she did not have to.

"I don't really listen to music." She decided to be honest.

Relievingly, Peyton did not look like he minded. "Oh, that's okay. I have some music recommendations for you if you'd like."

"Maybe some other time."

"Oh, well, that's okay too."

Why was talking to Peyton so *easy*?

"...I guess it's my turn to ask a question now?" Paige twiddled her thumbs in the pouch of her - no, Peyton's - hoodie.

Peyton's answer surprised her. "If you want to."

"Okay, um..." She thought hard about what else she could possibly ask him. "How...how do you know when you can trust a person?"

Paige's inquiry surprised the both of them. She knew what she was thinking, but that did not necessarily mean she had meant to say it out loud. Her words instantaneously caught

Peyton's attention, which had been on her already for the entire time they were at the table.

"Damn, that's a tough one." Peyton paused to sincerely contemplate his answer. "I guess the only people I have around me right now are my parents, Leo, and, well, you too. I've always trusted my parents because they've been there for me for my entire life. Leo took a little bit of time, but after we spent time together and realized we could be ourselves around each other, I guess that's when you could say I trusted him."

Paige voluntarily let her next words slip out. "Do you trust *me*?"

"Absolutely."

"*What?!*" She was at a standstill. "How come?"

"Well, for one, you saved my life." Peyton began counting on his fingers. "Two, you could've literally murdered me in my sleep if you wanted to. Three, you've spent quite a bit of time with me, whether it be just…talking or playing video games, and four, well, you haven't eaten all of the food we have in the pantry. The last one's a joke, of course."

A small chuckle escaped Paige's lips. It was hardly noticeable, but it was *there*. Paige caught herself averting eye contact with Peyton, but when it was regained, she noticed that he was looking right at her. This look was different from what she had experienced with the cashier five minutes before. This…this felt safe. Paige did not feel like she was in imminent danger.

Reality, however, smacked her directly in the face when Dylan's loud, but somehow bored tone cut through the air with a "Two medium flurries: one chocolate and one caramel!". Peyton immediately stood and for some reason, Paige was gradual to follow. It was only when he turned to her when she realized.

"Ready to go?"

Paige abruptly cleared her throat and nodded. "Yup."

The two of them walked up to the counter with Peyton in front. He took the two flurries off the surface in front of him. Paige was thankful that Dylan was already taking the order of the next customer and was not acknowledging their presence. Peyton started for the exit of the Dairy King with Paige in tow. She tugged on the strings of the navy-blue hoodie she was wearing to make her visible cloaking device more effective, at least until the two of them were outside.

Paige allowed herself to relievingly exhale once the door shut behind them and the situation was left in the dust. The sickening punch of actuality, though, lingered in their footsteps dotting the rustic sidewalk's tiles for the second time that night. An uncomfortable quietness remained between Peyton and Paige. For some reason, the two of them could not continue the moment that was occurring inside the ice cream parlor, instead eating their flurries in silence.

The caramel ice cream was not as sweet without someone to thoroughly enjoy it. The fog of unknown emotions, a sticky situation, and secrecy wafted through the air instead. She thought about the first question Peyton had asked her during their game. Indigo... Did that mean something more extravagant than she first insinuated? No. That was impossible.

Paige let her ice cream melt along with the flame of hope in her heart.

She hated how her life had become an illicit affair.

Chapter Sixteen

MIDNIGHT

"Being a morally good person generally means to accomplish deeds that are seen on the correct, or "right" side of reality. For example, an act of kindness towards another person can be considered morally good. As long as an action is executed that does not cause harm to anyone, including those who might be in the crossfire, but instead produces positivity, compassion, and it is considered morally good."

Paige clicked the top of her mechanical pencil and checked off one of the comments left on the stack of papers next to her. "Is that thesis statement good enough for you, Professor Cullen?" she thought to herself scornfully.

Her eyes were glued to the computer screen in front of her. In the past month of education at Azure University, one of Paige's main goals was to learn how to type efficiently on a computer. It seemed as if that goal had been achieved, since she hardly needed to look at the keyboard while she continued writing.

"To begin this essay, we are inclined to ask the question of "What is goodness?". According to the Oxford English Dictionary, the answer is simply "the quality of being good." To narrow down this definition of sorts, another question is needed. What exactly is morality, and how does it align with goodness? Morality can be defined as "a particular system of values and principles of conduct, especially one held by a specified person or society" (Oxford English Dictionary). Morality is what society defines as "acceptable" or "right." Different people have different views and values, though."

"Does that sound okay?" Paige read what she wrote silently. "Good enough."

Another satisfying checkmark next to Professor Cullen's question of "*How does morality specifically align with goodness?*" later, Paige leaned back in her chair and assessed her work. She read back what she had so far and double checked that the first page of her assignment met her professor's guidelines, no matter how stupid she thought they were. Then again, Paige had no idea how an essay worked in the first place other than through the research she did. She was learning too.

Professor Cullen did not need to know that the essay she discarded right in front of the class was Paige's very first.

Once Paige deemed her work to be satisfactory, she flipped to the second page of her essay, where there were even more comments from her dreaded professor. Paige took a deep breath and adjusted the glasses without a prescription in them to be further on her face. Her black brows furrowed as she concentrated.

"Okay, what does this comment say? I already have a thesis, proper introduction, and now I need three basic points? I thought this was a narrative essay, you-"

"Hey, Penny."

The mechanical pencil flew out of Paige's hand and clattered onto the floor. She looked up through her falling glasses and shoved them back up her nose only to see Peyton striding into the computer lab. When his left checkered *Vans* shoe hit the pencil, his pupils darted down to the floor so he could pick it up. He gently set it down on the table right by the small stack of papers making up Penny's essay.

"Oh, sorry. I didn't mean to scare you." Peyton sat down in a rolling chair to Paige's right. "How's it going?"

Paige sat back up straight in her chair. "Fine."

He did not look so sure. "Is something wrong, Penny? You looked stressed when I came in."

Instead of answering with words, Paige shoved the marked-up essay into Peyton's hands. He almost dropped the stapled stack but held it steady when he realized what it was. His brown eyes scanned the contents on the first page, then the second, the third, and finally, the fourth. Paige had no idea why, but with each silent second, self-consciousness began filling her like a flooded room in the middle of hurricane season.

"Holy shi-...let me guess. Mrs. Cullen?" he asked even though her name was at the top of the first page along with Penny's.

Paige nodded without looking him in the eye.

"Aw, don't let it get to you." Peyton swiveled more in her direction. "She's hard on everybody. I had her during my first semester and she was very picky."

"Did she hold up your essay in front of the class before dismissal saying to you that "we need to talk about it" and that it "wouldn't cut it" and that you need to redo it in four days?"

Peyton blinked once, twice, and then three times...even a fourth until he commented, "Well, no. She's a you-know-what."

"She certainly is."

He shook his head. "I can't tell you how many times she's fussed at me about work, but she did it privately. What is her problem?"

"I don't know, but I need to get this done by Sunday night."

"Bullshit."

"You're telling me."

Peyton scooted towards her computer. "So, how far have you gotten?"

"I just finished the first page."

"Okay, not bad." He smiled with authenticity. "Only three more to go. I don't understand why Mrs. Cullen was so harsh on you. I really liked what you wrote."

Paige's cheeks heated up. "You did?"

"Well, yeah. Goodness and morality is a difficult topic and you explained it well. She's just an annoying bi-"

"Yeah, I get the picture. Thank you."

The boy next to her twiddled his thumbs in his lap. It was almost like he was...nervous. Why would he be nervous, though? It was just Penny; someone he hardly knew at school who happened to do something nice for him on the first day.

Then, it clicked.

"So, I was thinking..."

"About?"

"Would you maybe like to, I don't know...come over tonight?" Peyton timidly asked her. "I mean, you seemed pretty down. Maybe a movie or something would cheer you up?"

Paige's head snapped upwards so quickly her glasses almost flew off her face. "Huh?"

"Oh, you don't have to. I'm not trying to force you." Peyton's eyes bugged out when he realized his request was out of the blue. "But, if you want something to make you feel better about the essay, the option's there." He shuffled backwards. "I mean, if you wanted to."

Paige was caught at a standstill. She was not stupid. If she had not known Peyton before, she would have immediately said "No" when it came to his proposal. Her academic persona had only seen him enough times at school to count on one hand–*maybe* two. Why should she trust him? Then again, Peyton had no idea that Penny Hamilton's true figure had been living in the upstairs guest room for a few weeks now. She knew him more than he thought she did, which was why she answered in the way that she did.

"Actually, now that I think about it, I'd like that."

The entirety of Peyton's face lit up. "No kidding?" He then composed himself. "I mean, that's awesome. I'll see you tonight? My address is 16 London Place."

"Yeah." Penny's smile was somehow different than Paige's underneath the skin. "What time were you thinking?"

"Seven?"

"Sure."

Peyton's grin that Paige was beginning to know all too well grew, making his dimples become more visible by the second. Just before it got creepy, though, he stood from his chair and brushed his bangs out of his eyes.

"I should probably catch up with my friend, but I thought I'd stop in and say hello. I'll see you tonight," he repeated.

Paige nodded, forcing her smile to be a beaming one. "See you then."

Peyton may have left Penny in the computer lab, but his optimistic mood lingered. He had acquired a liking to Penny, especially when it came to her snarky, but smart attitude. She was able to defend herself in a manner that was unmatched to anyone else he had seen on campus. In fact, he reminded him a bit of another girl he knew...

He shook his head to remove that thought from surfacing. Tonight was going to be all about Penny, and that's what mattered. He had aided Paige in every way he knew how, but tonight, he needed to make sure Penny felt loved and safe just as much as Paige. As he strode to the campus library, there was more of a spring in his step, as if he was walking across a trampoline. Peyton scanned his student identification card and the library doors unlocked. He hardly had to walk past the entrance containing a circular table filled with computers around a large column and turn right before he saw just who he was looking for.

It was Leo, sound asleep in a maroon bean bag chair with a book over his chest.

Peyton smirked at the opportunity that was now open to him. He tiptoed over to where Leo was in the midst of a peaceful slumber and decided to play another harmless prank on his best friend. Peyton lifted the tail to his backpack strap and let it hover right by Leo's nose. His steady breathing gradually became more labored and tensed as seconds drew into half a minute, until...

Achoo!

Leo lurched up with a start. He let out a large "Ow!" when his face collided with the butt of Peyton's backpack. The librarian from across the room put her index finger with a long, midnight blue nail to her lips and loudly shushed them. Peyton found it ironic that the one doing the "shushing" was much more voluminous than the ones being "shushed."

"What the hell, man?" Leo whisper-yelled at Peyton, who only grinned.

"Just waking you up...again."

"You're never in the library," he commented, fumbling with the book that had fallen off of his chest. "What gives?"

Peyton plopped himself down on a beanbag chair and fiddled with the strings of his navy blue hoodie–the same one that Paige borrowed most frequently. "Well, I may or may not have done something really stupid or really awesome."

"And what's that?" Leo stuffed his bookmark into the book, finally finding his spot that was close to the end.

"I asked a girl over."

Leo had taken his phone out of his pocket, but once the screen turned on and Peyton's words registered, the device flew through his fingers. "You *what*?!"

"I invited a girl over to my house tonight," Peyton elaborated.

"Wha-"

"Shhh!" The librarian shushed them again. "This is a library, not the cafeteria!"

Peyton and Leo looked at each other with wide eyes. Whoops.

"You did *what*?!" Leo resorted to whispering in an energetic, surprised tone.

"I'm not going to repeat myself.'

"Well, who'd you invite?"

"Penny Hamilton."

Leo's brown eyes widened so much they were about to fall out. "Her?" he questioned in disbelief.

"What's wrong with that?" Peyton retorted.

"Nothing, nothing," Leo quickly countered, "I just meant that when I met her one time, she seemed pretty...serious."

It was Peyton's turn to be surprised. "You met her?"

"Sure, I did. I think it was the day before you had that weird dream," he shrugged. "She was very curious about where you were. Are you two friends?"

"I'd say so."

"Do you like her?" Leo continued to interrogate.

"Well, yeah, but not in that way."

"That's bull."

Frantically, Peyton lurched up. "No!"

"Shh!" Once again, the frazzled librarian interrupted their conversation. "How many times do I need to tell you to be quiet?!"

Leo ignored her but kept his voice down. "Then why are you blushing?"

"I'm not blushing." His peachy-colored cheeks begged to differ.

"Oh, yes you are," Leo's voice drawled out amusingly.

"Nope."

"Yup."

"Nope."

"Yup."

"Nope."

"Nope."

"I'm not falling for that." Peyton folded his arms over his chest.

Leo chuckled under his breath. "You did before."

"That was ninth grade."

"And I have no idea how that one remaining brain cell is still alive and kickin'."

"Oh, shut up."

Leo sat up straight, rested his elbows on his knees, and cradled his chin in his hands. "So, what do you two plan on doing tonight?"

"I suggested a movie," replied Peyton with a shrug, laying back down. "Or, we could do something else. It's up to her."

"Something else?" Leo wiggled his eyebrows suggestively.

"Shut up, idiot."

The redhead smirked knowingly. "But I bet it's crossed your mind."

"Never."

"Peyton, we're teenage boys, which means one: we're stupid; two: we have brains that have minds of their own, and three: they have nothing better to do."

The blond rolled his eyes and deadpanned, "I'm twenty."

"Same thing. Better get your act together, though. Does she even know it's a date?"

"It's not a date," sighed Peyton, exasperatedly combing through his hair with his fingers to the point where the strands became unruly tufts.

Leo started adjusting the bird's nest that Peyton created on his head. "Sure, it's not," he sarcastically crooned. "I'll take your word for it, but just be yourself."

"Right. Be myself."

"I'll be right next door if you need anything."

Peyton's lips became a tight grin. "Thanks, Leo. Just don't be hiding in the bushes by the window."

"What?" Leo feigned a surprised expression. "Never."

The blond smacked the carrot top upside the head. "Idiot."

"Ow!"

"Shhh!" exclaimed the librarian.

Peyton's mind swam laps around itself for the rest of the afternoon in an attempt to ignore Leo's teasing, but endearing, remarks about Peyton's "first date." As soon as he arrived home in the early evening after a long day of classes, homework, and overthinking, he began preparing everything - but mostly himself - for Penny's visit. From the very second that he opened the door, Caroline knew there was something different with her son, so much so that she put down the blanket she was crocheting

"Hi, Pey!" she greeted her son cheerfully. "How was your day?"

"Hey, Mom!" Peyton took his shoes off at the doorway and dashed over to hug his mom, who happily accepted it. "It was good; thanks."

Caroline put her hands on her son's shoulders when she backed away from their embrace. "You've got more sunshine in your step than usual. Did something good happen today?"

"Well, actually." Peyton smiled, but he failed to look her in the eyes. "I've invited a girl around tonight. I hope that's okay." He surely was not expecting his mother's reaction.

She *squealed.*

"Oh, my goodness!" Caroline ruffled Peyton's hair enthusiastically. "This is wonderful! What time is she coming over? What's her name? Did she want anything specific for dinner? What are you two going to do?"

Peyton cautiously removed his mom's fingers from his hair. "Mom... Her name's Penny, and she...likes things to be kept quiet–at least that's the vibe I get from her. Mrs. Cullen was really hard on her and made her redo an essay in four days, so I thought maybe watching a movie or something would cheer her up."

"Well, aren't you a sweet young man."

Peyton's complexion did not hesitate to become a tomato, or even a ripe apple. "Mom...," he protested timidly. "We're just friends. She's coming over at seven. As for dinner, I don't think it matters. What were you going to make?"

"Your father was planning on grilling hamburgers. I'll go tell him." Caroline excitedly trotted to the back door.

"Mom, wait!"

Caroline swung the back door open to reveal Lucas seated on a chair on the backyard deck while reading a book. "Lucas!" she shouted to her husband. "Make sure you make four hamburgers tonight! Peyton's got a girl coming over!"

Peyton facepalmed.

"What?!" Lucas' reading glasses fell right off his face. "Say what?"

"Make sure dinner's ready by seven," Caroline instructed him. "That's when she's coming over."

Peyton's father put his book down on the small table next to his chair and stood to his feet. He walked over to his son,

CHAPTER SIXTEEN

who was standing awkwardly in the doorway. "Who'd you pull, Son?" he teasingly inquired.

"Dad!" he protested loudly.

"*Dad!*" Lucas mocked him, waving his hands around like a flustered penguin. "What took you so long, Peyton? You're twenty years old!"

Peyton stamped his foot on the wooden floorboards of the deck, letting the back door swing shut behind him. "She's just a friend, and I invited her over to cheer her up."

Lucas smirked. "Oh, you'll do that, alright."

"Dad!"

"Lucas!" Caroline smacked her husband's shoulder just as he was putting on his reading glasses. They fell on the floor again.

"What?" he innocently asked. "I'm just playing."

"You're embarrassing him."

His expression grew incredulous. "You were doing the *same thing!*"

"So?" Caroline's grin matched her son's...when he was in the mood to execute it. Now was not one of those times.

"Mom, Dad," Peyton started nervously.

"Yes?" the both of them chorused.

"Try not to embarrass me, please. She's coming over in about an hour."

"Got it!" the couple confirmed in perfect unison.

"I'll get the burgers ready," Lucas determined. He walked over to the grill, opened it up, and prepared the propane.

"I'll get everything set." Caroline wandered back inside the house and started setting the table with the finest silverware she had in the kitchen.

Peyton sighed dramatically from right where he was near the back door. The sound of his father putting the hamburger patties - that Caroline had retrieved from the freezer moments earlier - on the grill and the flame being ignited was deafening. Had he made a mistake by inviting Penny over? He figured she did not enjoy a big fuss. Then, there was Paige.

"*Oh, no... Paige...*"

Another exhale escaped his lips. How was he going to tell Paige about the spontaneous guest in the house when he already had one on his hands? She already felt uncomfortable as it was in the guest bedroom, almost never coming out of it except to retrieve food and to use the restroom. Maybe there was something she was not telling him, but it was none of his business. Either way, Peyton now had another problem to worry about: What would Paige think?

His phone buzzed in his pocket. Peyton took it out and read the message from the most familiar contact on his phone consisting of three letters and a bunch of orange emojis: his best friend's doing.

"*Good luck tonight.*"

A small smile graced his lips. Leo was one of the only escapes from his crazy reality. Peyton texted his best friend back with the only simple words he knew would communicate his situation.

"*Thanks. I'll need it.*"

Chapter Seventeen

LILAC

Peyton cleared his throat anxiously at the thought of completing the task that was now upon his shoulders to do. Each stair seemed like it was higher than the last, putting an unnecessarily large weight on him. With every step, his frame became heavier. It was almost to the point where walking was unbearable. Right when Peyton reached the very top, he rested his hands on his femurs and took a deep breath.

He did not think he was *that* out of shape.

Peyton brushed his tousled, slightly shaggy bangs out of his eyes and cracked his knuckles. Despite it only being mere minutes since this thought came to mind, Peyton felt as if it had been hours. He cringed at the memory that was formulated just seconds that slid into moments earlier. How could he have expected not one, but *both* of his parents to be on board with inviting someone new over, especially someone of the female gender? Of course, they had the wrong idea about Penny. They were taking it *way* too far. Now that he had two people on his side, there was only one more left to sway.

He stood in front of Paige's door, shifting his weight from one leg to the other. *"Just knock,"* he told himself. "It's your house. You can invite whoever you want. Oh...but I want to make sure Paige is okay with it too."

Peyton cleared his throat and quietly knocked on the door. "Paige?" His tone was soft. "Can you let me in? I want to talk about something."

There was no hesitation when the door swung open to reveal Paige laying on her back in the guest bedroom's bed. Oh, the heck with it, Peyton thought, it was Paige's room now. His parents didn't have to know. At first, he was confused about the fact the door opened itself until a small lilac energy field released its grip on the doorknob and floated over to Paige. She morphed it into a larger sphere about the size of a basketball and began batting it about like a kitten.

"Uh, hey," Peyton puzzledly stated as he shut the door. "How's it going?"

"You wanted to discuss something with me?" Paige dodged the question as well as his eyes. She instead watched as the purple ball bounced off her hands every few seconds.

The boy nodded at that. "Yeah, but...wait. Are you mad at me?"

"No. Why would I be?"

"Should I just go for it? Yes? No? Oh, what the hell-" Peyton stiffened and then exclaimed worriedly, "I may or may not be having a girl over for dinner in thirty minutes."

"Why would I be mad at that?" she inquired without missing a beat.

"Well, I just thought maybe you wouldn't be so ecstatic about...wait. *Huh?*" Peyton stopped in his tracks once what she said registered.

Paige spun the energy sphere on her finger like a cocky

basketball player would. "Why would it matter so much to me? It's your house. None of my business."

"You're taking this way better than I thought you would."

"How'd you think I'd take it? Like some sort of jealous girlfriend? Because I'm obviously *not* that."

Peyton's mouth opened and closed like a goldfish in search of its daily meal. "I honestly wasn't sure."

"Yes, you were."

"No, I wasn't." Peyton's whole demeanor changed when he realized she still would not lay her eyes upon him. "Wait...are you mad at me?"

"For the last time, *no*," Paige affirmed her true feelings. She continued batting the ball around, unable to hide the lingering smirk on her face.

"Oh, I see." The boy folded his arms over his chest when he caught on. "You think this is funny."

Paige let herself reveal the playfully devious look on her face. "Yes. Yes, I do."

"You know, I haven't seen you smile like that before."

"I smile when I find things amusing," she deadpanned.

"So, I haven't been amusing before?"

"I didn't say that."

Peyton's grin increased in size. "Paige, did you just *lie* to me?"

"I think you need to reanalyze your priorities."

"Excuse me?"

"You're excused." Paige popped the ball of energy and sat up on the bed. The boy across from her watched as tiny lavender sparkles specked around her general area of the room before they vanished into the carpet at her feet. She then finally turned to him. "So, what's this girl like?"

Peyton was caught off-guard when her little smirk refused to leave her face. "Uh, well, she goes to school with me. We have US History together. On the very first day of the semester, I forgot my wallet, so she paid for my meal."

One of Paige's eyebrows raised. "Oh, really?"

"Yup." Peyton was either oblivious or excited...or both. "So, I'm hoping I can make a good impression on her tonight. We're having burgers and probably fries, so I hope she likes that."

"Who doesn't?"

"True."

Paige swung her legs over the floor. She ignored how the socks she was wearing were too big for her feet. In fact, everything she was wearing at the moment was too big—Peyton's blue sweatshirt that she always seemed to borrow, his black sweatpants that - thankfully - had a drawstring. It made her feel tiny, but over time, appearing small did not seem so bad anymore, especially when she had someone who made her feel like a person rather than an object, or a robot programmed to accomplish different tasks.

When Peyton said nothing else and stared down at his checkered shoes, Paige brought him back to reality with a simple question: "Are you finished getting ready for her to come over?"

"Huh?" The boy checked the time on his phone. His eyes bulged like saucers. "Oh, crap! I'm sorry, but I gotta go. She'll be here any minute. Are you sure you don't-"

"I don't mind."

"Okay." Peyton dragged out the word. He backpedaled towards the hallway. "I'll see you later after she-"

He cut himself off by hitting the doorframe. Peyton's cheeks reddened at his mistake, which only probed Paige's amusement. He continued, "-leaves. Unless you want to meet-"

"I'm fine upstairs," Paige hurriedly dismissed the offer.

"Right." Peyton shoved himself through the doorway and cracked the door. "I'll see you afterwards."

Once the doorknob stopped moving, Paige rose to her feet. Upon instinct, she looked around the entire premises of the room - one bed, one dresser, one closet, and one mirror - and as soon as she confirmed she was not, in fact, being watched, she let herself transform into Penny Hamilton's body. Paige took in her new appearance at the mirror.

Black, curly hair? Check.

Brown eyes covered with square glasses? Check.

Comfortable ebony knit sweater? Check.

Paige often wondered how long it would take for Peyton to notice the knit sweater that she and Penny sometimes wore under different aliases were the same.

Once she deemed herself ready, she allowed herself to vanish. A vortex opened at her feet and she gracefully fell through it, falling through another one onto the ground at the side of Peyton's two-storied house. Paige reappeared right where she was and quickly made her way onto the sidewalk. She stopped in her tracks before proceeding to the front porch. This was it. Despite seeing Peyton just seconds earlier, Paige was somehow nervous. After all, this was not Paige who was coming over to his house—it was Penny. Would Peyton treat Penny differently than he did Paige?

That was why she was giving Peyton a test he had no knowledge of.

Breathe in.

Breathe out.

Paige was about to take a step forward, but halted when an urgent bark nearly startled her out of her shoes. She whirled around to view a male pedestrian with a large golden dog pulling him towards her. Upon instinct, Paige backed away.

Lavender energy flickered around the fingers of her right hand, and once she noticed, she hid her appendage behind her back.

"Woah!" The man skidded to a halt while his dog lurched at its leash. "I'm so sorry, Miss," he apologized. "I didn't mean to startle you."

"It's alright," Paige replied, albeit shakily. Her eyes lowered to meet the ecstatic panting creature at her feet. "He surely is...excited."

"He is. His name's Juniper. Would you like to pet him?"

Paige blinked in his direction. "I guess so. Sure."

She bent down and cautiously held out her left hand since the right was twitching behind her back, still itching to defend herself. Juniper sniffled her non-dominant hand and then, to Paige's surprise, his tongue extended from between his strong jaws and began to lick her hand. The slobbery, wet situation was uncomfortable to Paige—she had never been around an animal such as this before. With the utmost care, Paige removed her right hand from behind her back and began to scratch the loveable creature's head.

"He's nice," Paige complimented as she petted the dog.

"He is," the young man agreed with a charming smile. "So, what's your name? I haven't seen you around in this neighborhood before."

"Penny. And you?"

"Max."

"Pleasure."

Juniper propelled himself onto his hind legs and pressed his front paws against Paige's stomach. She fell backwards with an *"oomph"* and ended up seated on the sidewalk with a large dog on top of her. Paige could not hide the small grin growing on her face from the furry friend leaving his mark on her. The tiny scratches on Juniper's head accelerated into ear-rubs and pets all over his back. Eventually, Juniper rolled over on Paige's lap so she could scratch his belly.

That was exactly what she did.

Max watched cheerfully from the sidelines. "He seems to love you."

"I hope so," Paige responded truthfully.

She was so focused on the dog in her lap that she hardly noticed a second person approaching from the house she was heading to in the first place. As soon as the new pair of footsteps caught her ears, Paige's eyes snapped up to meet Peyton's skeptical, yet somehow sparkling ones.

"Hey, Penny," he greeted her with a smile that did not seem as real as usual. "Everything okay over here?"

Paige studied the way his eyebrows furrowed with both confusion and a little bit of concern. "Hey. I'm fine. Why?"

Peyton instantaneously fumbled when he saw Max, a complete stranger. He then turned back to Penny. "I just saw you outside with someone and wanted to know if you were alright."

"I'm fine. I was petting this gentleman's dog."

"Oh."

It was an understatement to say that Peyton felt stupid. As soon as it was a minute past seven in the evening, he began looking out the window to make sure Penny was not lost. When he noticed her with a strange man, his protective instincts took over and he lurched outside. Peyton wanted to slap himself, especially when Max waved with a sheepish expression. Instead, he adjusted his posture, took a deep breath, and spoke.

"I'm so sorry. I didn't mean to interrupt."

"It's alright." Paige gently coaxed Juniper off of her with one more pat on the head. "I should get going anyway. Thanks for letting me pet him," she directed to Max and Juniper.

Max took a tighter hold to Juniper's leash. "No problem. He loved it."

Paige was clueless on goodbyes, so she settled with a polite nod. She walked directly past Peyton, who nearly tripped over his own feet in order to follow her. Max watched the two of them with a puzzled expression. He scratched Juniper's head and then continued on their walk in the opposite direction. Peyton brushed his shaggy bangs out of his eyes. He wished he could look Penny in the eye when he apologized.

"I'm sorry."

Paige fixed her glasses. "For?"

"For being nosy, I guess," Peyton admitted shyly. "I just wanted to look out for you."

"It's alright."

Peyton led Paige up the porch steps, but stopped before he opened the front door. "Just a little heads-up, my parents may or may not want to meet you. They were ecstatic to find out I was inviting someone other than Leo over," he chuckled at the thought.

"It's okay. I don't mind." Paige let herself smile, even though it was tight.

"...You might."

Peyton opened the front door before Paige could ask any more questions. He stood to the side and allowed his guest to enter the house first, which she did. Paige stepped inside the familiar building that was supposed to be new to her. She had one rule to follow:

Don't get caught.

That rule was nearly broken when the urge to disintegrate into thin air washed over her. Peyton's mother was eagerly setting the table, but all movement stopped for a split second after Paige stepped through the doorway. The blonde woman who looked much younger than her mid-forties had a smile perfectly resembling her son's. She took in Paige's false, yet striking appearance with absolutely no pinches of salt.

"Oh, goodness! You must be Penny," she gushed, approaching the two of them and nearly knocking over Peyton in the process. "It's so nice to meet you, Sweetie!"

Paige returned the facial gesture, despite it being hesitant, and let Peyton's mom rest her hands on her slimmer, shorter shoulders. "You too, Mrs. Finlay."

"You can call me Caroline. That's what Leo does when he's over. Have you met him?"

"I have, yes."

"He surely is a doozy. Almost as much as this one here." Caroline rolled her eyes at Peyton.

"Mom...," her son whined.

"Now, come on in the rest of the way!" She blatantly ignored Peyton. "I just finished setting the table and my husband should be done with dinner by now. Oh! Let me get the fries out of the oven."

Paige tentatively followed Caroline through the house and into the kitchen. "That sounds very nice. Thank you."

"You're so welcome, Dear."

Peyton led Paige over to the nearest seat at the table in the kitchen that was as neat as a pin. The culinary portion of the house was Caroline's pride and joy. Even as she fanned away the slightest bit of moist steam from her face as she removed two trays of French fries from the oven, she had a smile on her face. Paige wondered how she did it. She had seen Caroline around before, but this was her first time interacting with her. In fact, it was her first time around Peyton when he was with his family.

It was a pleasant surprise, really, especially when Peyton pulled out a chair for Paige.

"Thanks," she whispered as she delicately sat down.

Peyton pushed the chair in behind her. "You're welcome."

He then sat across from her. He looked as if he was about to say something else due to the manner his lips were opening, but just before he could, a man about Caroline's age stumbled into the kitchen with a plate of burgers. Paige instantly recognized the resemblance Peyton had to his father. They had similar builds and the same hair color, but Peyton was just a tad bit smaller in the muscular department.

"Burgers are ready!" Mr. Finlay announced loud enough for the world to hear.

"About time." Caroline snatched the plate from him and began putting together a plate for each of them.

"Hey!"

Peyton leaned over and noted, "My parents are dorks."

All Paige could do was let out a tiny giggle. This was apparently all it took for Caroline's husband to look in Penny's direction. His brown eyes were as sparkly as his son's, but with more experience and wisdom in them than the young adult's. Paige could already tell that Mr. Finlay was a kind man. It was a certain sense that all three members of the Finlay Clan gave off.

"Oh, hello!" Mr Finlay greeted Peyton's guest. "I'm Peyton's dad, of course, but you can call me Lucas. Penny, right?"

"Hello–that's right." Paige did not need to be so forceful with her smile this time. It came as naturally as a waterfall over a bed of smooth pebbles, weathered to the core. "It's nice to meet you."

"And you as well. I understand Peyton met you at school?" Lucas inquired to make small talk.

"That's correct."

"That's wonderful." Lucas helped his wife carry the four plates over to the table. He set one in front of Paige, who thanked him quietly. "It's nice to have someone other than

Leo, who I assume you've met by now, to keep my boy on track."

"Dad," Peyton hissed from the seat across from Paige.

Caroline turned to Paige, who was on her right, and sighed playfully, "Boys. Just ignore them. We're so happy to have you in our home, Penny."

"I'm happy to be here," Paige politely responded.

"Dad, why must you embarrass me in front of my friend?" Peyton groaned loudly enough to get the females' attention.

Lucas smirked, putting mustard on his burger. "Because it's fun. You're easy to embarrass."

"But you never do it in front of Leo!"

"He's used to it. He's basically your brother, so I got bored and gave up."

"Dad!"

"*Dad!*" Lucas repeated sarcastically.

"Gentlemen, or should I say *boys*," Caroline loudly intervened. "How about we actually eat what's in front of us before it gets cold?"

"Sounds good to me." Lucas picked up his hamburger and opened his mouth to take a bite right when his wife stopped him.

"Not yet! Who wants to say grace?"

"*Grace?*" Paige found herself asking. "*What's grace?*"

Silence. If there were crickets in the house, they would most certainly be chirping to break it like a champagne glass.

When neither Lucas nor Peyton said anything, Caroline turned to Paige. "How about you, Penny? Would you like to bless the food?"

"Oh, uh, sure," she confirmed despite not knowing what the hell she was doing.

The mechanic whirring of her heartbeat accelerated like a station wagon desperately trying to pass through an intersection at a yellow light. Sweat beaded on her forehead, and for once, Paige was thankful for the frizzy black curls that covered it up. Her eyes expanded when Peyton and both of his parents bowed their heads and closed their eyes. Paige heard metaphorical crickets chirping obnoxiously in her mind.

Then, it hit her.

"Oh! I'm supposed to say the prayer!"

Paige wetted her lips with her tongue and nervously began to speak to seemingly no one even though there was certainly One who was listening, "Uh, God? Thank you for the food that's in front of us. Thank you for the time we have together. I hope we can enjoy tonight almost as much as our dinner. Amen."

At the last comment, Peyton snorted. Caroline whacked him upside the head. "Peyton! Where's your manners?" she scolded teasingly. She then looked at the anxious Paige. "That was lovely, Penny. Thank you."

"You're welcome." Paige attempted to hide her sheepish blush.

At once, the four of them began eating their meals. Paige decided not to experiment with any of the condiments on the table, including ketchup, mustard, and mayonnaise. The last thing she wanted was to not eat the food that Mr. and Mrs. Finlay had so graciously put together for them. Instead, she took a small bite out of her hamburger. At once, the home-cooked meal spoiled her taste buds with more satisfaction than fast food could ever give. That was because of the extra ingredient that Paige had no idea she craved:

Love.

"So, Penny," Caroline started. It looked like she barely touched her food yet. "Tell me about Azure. How are you liking it?"

Paige fought to swallow the bite of beef she had ingested

before answering. "I really like it. It's my first year of college, so I have a lot of getting used to."

"What classes are you taking?"

"I'm taking US History, Quantitative Reasoning, Introduction to Physics, and English Composition." Paige fought back an eye roll at her last selection.

Caroline bit one of her fries in half somehow daintily. "And how do you like them?"

"I'm enjoying them, but there's one professor who's been giving me a hard time."

"Mrs. Cullen, right?" Peyton darted in from across the table.

"That's the one."

Caroline frowned at this news. "I'm so sorry to hear that, Sweetie," she apologized. "Peyton had her class during his first year and she was sore about him being late once."

"That sounds like her," Paige agreed with a shrug. "I'm almost done with the essay she had me rewrite, though."

"Rewrite?" Lucas, who had been very quiet, questioned.

"Yes. I have to rewrite four pages in four days."

"Now, that's ridiculous."

"It really is."

Caroline seemed to notice the uncomfortable look in Paige's eyes since she changed the subject. "I'm happy to hear that you're enjoying Azure otherwise."

"Me too." There was gratefulness in Paige's smile.

"So, how did you and Peyton meet?"

Paige had almost forgotten how the two of them met in the first place. Thankfully, Peyton stepped up for her. "I forgot my wallet on the first day, so Penny paid for my lunch."

"You forgot your wallet?" inquired Lucas.

"Yes, Dad," Peyton exhaled dramatically. "Look, I was in a rush and left it on the counter."

"I'm not mad. Just be more careful next time."

Caroline chuckled at the interaction and curved her attention back to Paige. "Thank you for doing that, Penny. You seem very kind."

"Thanks...Caroline." Paige stumbled over the use of an adult's first name. It was unnatural on her tongue. "I hope I'm a good friend to Peyton."

"Believe me, Sweetie, you are."

Paige wanted to ask Mrs. Finlay what she meant by that, but the sound of Peyton and Lucas bickering once again over something miniscule derailed her train of thought. The rest of the dinner was spent in casual conversation, with Peyton and his father biting remarks back and forth about miscellaneous topics while Caroline and Paige watched amusedly. Upon occasion, a question would be asked about Paige's academic career, and she would answer as politely and properly as she could.

Caroline did not have to know that Paige did most of her schoolwork on the office computer within the premises.

Once all four of them were finished, Peyton stood from the table and collected the plates. He brought them over to the counter and began putting them in the dishwasher. Paige stacked up all of the cups on the kitchen table before she could be stopped and marched over to Peyton. She extended the top rack of the dishwasher and placed each glass delicately where it was supposed to go after ensuring each one was free of water.

"You didn't have to do that," Peyton protested once Paige caught his eye.

Paige shrugged and pushed the rack back in. "I wanted to."

The boy lowered his voice so his parents were out of earshot. "I'm sorry about Mom and Dad being so nosy."

This caught Paige off-guard. Instead of questioning it, she

smiled. "What are you talking about?" she probed gently. "I'm having a nice time."

"Well, Dad keeps picking fun at me. I know it's all play, but it can be embarrassing."

"Have you told him to stop?"

"He's my dad," Peyton deadpanned so seriously it took all Paige had not to burst out into laughter. "It's his job."

Paige shook her head, leaning against the counter. "I've noticed."

"So, uh," Peyton paused when he realized he had no idea where his next words were going. "What'd you want to do now? It's only like a quarter to eight."

Paige had to consider his words for a moment. What *did* she want to do now? She had already witnessed Peyton endure forty-five minutes of nothing but his parents, himself, and a guest. In her authentic opinion, he handled it quite well. It looked as if Peyton had passed the first portion of her test. She had yet to come up with a second portion...until she began to hear the rumbling of music in the distance.

"What is that?" Peyton inquired once he noticed it as well.

"It's that stupid fraternity house again," Lucas grumbled with annoyance. "They have their dumb parties even on weekdays. Don't they realize some of us need to sleep?"

Paige turned to Peyton. "Fraternity house?"

"Yeah," he replied. "There's the Theta Cho fraternity house a few streets over from us. They usually start throwing their parties around this time of year. We've been dealing with it since forever. This must be their first one of the semester."

Paige watched as Lucas deflated like a balloon. He stiffly stormed over towards the front door and opened it. Sure enough, the music grew louder, which caused Lucas to hurriedly shut the door.

"Kids," he mumbled while Caroline approached to soothe her husband's anger.

This gave Paige an idea. Despite the idea of a party being the last thing normally on her mind, maybe it would be the perfect solution for the second portion of Paige's test. How would Peyton act around an individual at a party? Paige needed to be inconspicuous about this whole endeavor. That was a word she liked a lot. With a sharp inhale and then a slow exhale, her attention was brought to Peyton.

"I know *just* what we should do."

"What's that?" Peyton shut the dishwasher with a small slam.

Paige's lips curled upwards in a spirited smirk. "Let's have some fun."

Chapter Eighteen

WHISKEY

Peyton had no idea where the curly-haired girl was taking him. One minute, the two of them were seated at the dinner table with the former's parents drilling questions in the poor girl's way while Peyton watched in near silence. On occasion, his father would begin a brief bickering battle with his son, but he figured that was because he did not want his "little boy" to be left out.

Either way, a crimson flush flooded his complexion, only to be cured by the escape Paige was offering him. Despite the secrecy of the situation, he was eager to be on the latter end of the awkward encounter. Paige smoothed out her fluffy sweater and waited patiently at the base of the stairwell, which was placed at a modest distance from the front door. Peyton was busy enough yanking a jacket over his shoulders to prepare for whatever adventure laid ahead.

"You ready?" Peyton inquired despite the answer being obvious.

Paige raised and lowered her head in a graceful nod,

attempting to hide her enthusiasm at least while his parents were in earshot.

Peyton yelled over his shoulder, "Okay, we're going out, now

"Have fun, Pey!" Caroline called after them. "It was a pleasure meeting you, Penny."

Paige peered around the corner of the stairwell to meet Caroline's warm, friendly brown gaze. "You too."

"Don't get into too much trouble," Lucas added on to their dismissal.

"We won't," replied his son.

Mr. Finlay was in a joking mood. "I was talking about you. Penny, keep him in line."

"Yes, Sir." Paige teasingly saluted the middle-aged man.

"I like her." Lucas prodded his wife.

Caroline just shook her head with amusement. To Peyton, that was their cue to leave. He unlocked the front door and held it open for Paige to walk through first, which was what she did. Peyton secretly adored the way Paige hopped down the steps like a foal ready to gallop freely in a pasture. He hid his expression of enjoyment, though, once Paige expectantly looked his way. He silently composed himself, adjusted the collar of his band t-shirt, and followed behind.

"Where are we going?" Peyton questioned the girl who suddenly stopped at the end of the driveway once she realized she didn't know either.

"Somewhere fun, and I want you to take me."

Peyton was skeptical. "And what is this "fun" place?"

Paige turned on her heel and proposed with nothing but confidence: "I would like you to take me to that fraternity party."

"Excuse me?" His eyebrows shot up.

"Oh. Maybe I didn't ask nicely enough?" Paige tried again. "Please?"

"Don't you realize how dangerous those are? Are you out of your mind?"

"Oh." Paige brushed her ebony curls out of her face, arguing, "Well, have you ever been to one?"

"Well, yeah, but-"

"So, you know what to expect."

"My dad told me to stay out of trouble," Peyton countered worriedly.

Her lips curved upwards. "He didn't tell me to do that, now did he? I'll go and you supervise."

"This is a bad idea."

"I think it'll be fun."

"Do you even know what to expect at these parties?" Peyton began pacing around Paige in a circle, beginning to rant, "There's alcohol. There's *that* kind of dancing. There're idiots. There're drunks. There're stupid people. Do you really want to be around them?"

"I've never experienced a party," Paige informed him. "And besides, if they weren't fun, then why would so many people go to them?"

"Hm." Peyton had to think about it. Then, he caved and realized her logic was starting to make a bit of sense. "Touché"

"So, are you taking me or what?"

"I guess so," he shrugged.

Paige offered him a satisfied smile. "Thank you. Let's go, then."

"I'm only taking you if you know how to be safe at one of these things," Peyton asserted as he started walking towards the sound of the muffled music. "Firstly, don't take any drinks that don't come from a can or an unopened bottle."

Paige eagerly walked beside him on the concrete sidewalk.

"Well, duh."

"I'm just saying." He held up his hands in mock surrender. "Just don't be an idiot. Do you have a phone?"

"No."

"Okay, then..." Peyton racked his brain for a solution. "Just don't get separated from me."

"So, you're my chaperone?" One of Paige's eyebrows lifted comedically.

"If that *helps* you, yes."

"Got it."

Paige stayed true to her word, walking directly next to Peyton even though the two of them were still several meters from the fraternity house a few streets down. Once Paige and Peyton turned the corner, though, the former had no idea how she had never noticed this building before. It was massive, with at least three floors and pillars lining the entrance. The gray, neatly shingled roof looked taller than life itself. Paige would have mistaken it for some sort of castle if she hadn't known better. The brick fraternity house stood out like a sore thumb, but was somehow even more elegant than the simple, but well-taken care of homes in the "regular" portion of Peyton's neighborhood.

"Damn," Paige whistled once she took the scene in.

Peyton did not like the way the loud music created vibrations under their shoes. "Are you sure about this?" he asked her.

"I'm sure." Paige offered him an encouraging expression. "Now, come on."

Peyton bit back a certain remark when Penny grasped onto his hand and practically dragged him up the exterior marble stairs. He hated the way his ears were full of nothing but noise. Oh, how he missed the silence of his four room walls safely crowded around him. Paige felt the same, as if she was severely out of place. When the right-hand door of the fraternity building was opened by Paige's enthusiastic free hand, overstimulation wafted through both of them.

To put it simply, everyone was everywhere. The vast lobby of the building was where the party truly was. Several college students, both young and old danced in the middle of the room and even on the second floor up two more decorative flights of marble stairs. Multicolored lights flooded the lobby and released a rainbow over the dance floor. Paige quickly discovered the source of the loud music: a disc jockey in his mid-twenties with his turntable, speakers, and several different forms of equipment Paige did not know the name of.

The temperature of the lobby and the misty outdoor air was significantly different. At least a hundred sweaty bodies danced among each other while the DJ played some peppy song Paige had heard on the radio at least once. The bass rumbled the floor underneath her feet. It was almost too much to be uncomfortable, but Paige pressed forward, dragging Peyton behind her.

"Where are we going?" Peyton inquired just over the music.

Paige had to shout in order for him to hear her. "Away from this huge crowd."

"Then why are we even here?!"

"Because I wanted to check it out," she replied once the two left the lobby to enter another, quieter, and smaller room. "What do you think?"

"What do I think? What do I *think*?" Peyton didn't realize he was still grasping onto her hand. "I don't like this, Penny. I don't think it's safe, and I think we should do something else."

Paige feigned a pout. In reality, she wanted to leave too, but she also wanted to test him. Little did she know she was actually testing herself. "Can we stay for a few minutes?" she asked him politely.

"Why? It's not safe," he persisted with concern, "especially for y-"

"Why especially for me?"

Peyton fumbled over his response. "...Because you're... You're a...um..."

"I'm a girl?" Paige sharply finished for him. Peyton gulped and nodded when she elaborated: "Look. I'm not mad, but girls can defend themselves too."

"Well, I know that, but-"

"So, let's explore."

Peyton appeared as if he was about to retort, even lifting his index finger to make a point, but once he realized how insistent the black-haired girl was, he lowered that appendage. Once Peyton grounded himself, his eyes darted downward to realize he was still clinging onto Paige's hand, which was loosely around his. To make the situation less awkward, he discreetly let go and shoved his hand into his pocket.

He missed the way Paige's lips contorted into a miniscule frown for a fraction of a second.

Paige watched as the multiple scenes in the room unfolded. There was a pool table in the middle of the area with at least four people playing pool. Red solo cups were placed in almost every direction, whether they be on tables, arms of chairs that lined the walls, and even windowsills on the two walls overlooking the outside. The atmosphere in this room off to the right was much calmer than the lobby, but it was still the slightest bit overwhelming. Paige knew Peyton was uncomfortable, so she led him over to the back corner where a half-empty sectional sofa laid and a television was playing a local sports game.

"Better?" Paige asked him once the two sat down on the opposite side of the couch than another person on their phone.

Peyton nodded and took his phone out of his pocket. "Yeah.

CHAPTER EIGHTEEN

Thanks."

Paige frowned once again when Peyton started looking at his phone rather than at the party around him. All at once, the feeling of guilt shrouded every inch of her body. Over the past few weeks of knowing Peyton, she had noticed him retreat to his phone when in uncomfortable or unsettling settings. She had brought him here. No...she had *forced* him here. What kind of person was she, disguising herself as someone completely different and not being her authentic self in front of someone who looked scared to death? Her brown eyes darted around desperately for a solution to her problem. Then, she noticed the baseball game on the television.

"Who's playing?" she questioned to make casual conversation.

Peyton's eyes unglued themselves from his phone and looked at the screen. "Oh, um...the Arkford Blue Warriors and the Cambridge Knights."

"Which one's our team?"

"Uh..." Peyton trailed off, unsure if she was joking or not.

"Relax. I'm teasing."

"Oh," he chuckled away his embarrassment. "Have you never seen the Blue Warriors play before on TV?"

Paige shook her head.

"Wait, really?"

Once again, Paige did the opposite motion of a nod.

"One of these days, I'm going to take you to a game. They play right around Azure's campus. I'm surprised you've never seen them at all."

"I'm not a sports person," Paige squeaked, remembering she needed to keep up her persona.

Peyton shrugged and put his phone down. Success! "Do you know how baseball works? I'm guessing not, so I'll explain it."

"You're correct."

"So, basically, the away team bats first. The other team consists of the pitcher, who throws the ball, the catcher, who catches the ball if it goes past the batter, several basemen, which are players, at each base, and outfielders, who can get the ball if it goes out to the furthest part of the field. Each player gets three strikes. If they hit a foul ball, which is a hit out of bounds, that counts as a strike, but can't count as an out. If the batter can't hit the ball but it passes them and the catcher gets it, that counts as a strike and can get them out. If the player swings and the ball hits the plate or is outside of the batters' box, which I'll show you in a second, that counts as a ball instead of a strike. Four balls mean the batter walks to first base. Batters can also get singles, doubles, triples, and home runs. Am I making sense?"

Paige hardly heard a word he just said, but nodded anyway, which earned her a wide grin.

"There's nine innings in each game, and if both teams are tied at the end of nine, they can go into extra innings," Peyton explained rather enthusiastically. "In each inning, each team gets three outs. You can get out by three strikes or if an outfielder catches the ball before it hits the ground. You can get home runs by hitting the ball into the bleachers still in bounds or if you get a single, double, or triple while someone else is on a plate that is in scoring range."

"Oh, I see," Paige exhaled dramatically while taking in all of the information.

Peyton's whole face seemed to light up. "You do?"

"No."

Paige's response was so blunt that Peyton could not help but burst into laughter. This was the first time that night that Paige had seen Peyton so cheerful and open with everything around him. The dinner with his parents was awkward. Going to the party was overwhelming. Now, a simple conversation containing Peyton teaching Paige - Penny, to him - about the rules and regulations of baseball put him in an overall good mood. Paige smiled at the fact she had done *something* right that evening.

That smile in the midst of a blissful moment that neither of them could get back did not last for long, though. A shrill, nasally voice seared through Paige and Peyton's happiness like magma burning everything in its path.

"What's so funny over here?"

Both Peyton and Paige were ripped from the positivity the two of them gave each other. Paige recognized that voice at once. Every aspect of it had been engraved in her mind ever since the incident in the hallway. Paige had not forgotten what the brunette did to her, posting embarrassing videos on social media of her early experiences at Azure University. She thought nobody cared about that sort of stuff in college. Why were young adults so...juvenile?

"What do you want, Hannah?" Paige answered her question with one of her own.

"I just thought I'd check on how you're doing," Hannah sarcastically replied, and then looked at Peyton. Her lips feigned a pout. "I'm so sorry you have to deal with this pig."

"Knock it off," Peyton growled as if he was a cat and she was a mouse.

"You pity her. Is that right?"

Paige's black eyebrows lowered into a scowl. "He doesn't pity me."

"Well, someone has to," Hannah snorted like she couldn't believe her eyes. "What's your problem, anyway? Ever since I saw you typing with two fingers, I thought you were mentally challenged."

"Okay, you need to leave her al-" Peyton started, but Paige

stopped him.

"I can handle this," she mumbled to him. She sat up straight and eyed Hannah viciously, but with a sense of tranquility. "I'm not sure what makes you feel so entitled, but you need to stop. College is supposed to be a learning opportunity, to receive an education and to be your own true self. Why do you seem to care about others who are in a different stage of their learning experience?"

Hannah's mouth opened and closed; she had not expected Paige to speak so eloquently, but she did not let that stop her. Paige took this opportunity to look her directly in her electric blue eyes. She had seen those before...then, it clicked as easily as a pen. The Dairy King cashier, who Paige believed was named Danny...or Dylan...or something...had the same strange glint to his abnormally azure gaze.

There was something aloof about that icy glare.

"What makes you so great?" Hannah spat in her direction. "Why are *you* so special?"

"If you like Peyton or something, just say it," Paige deadpanned. "It must take a desperate girl to be so rude for no reason."

"I'm not talking about him. I'm talking about *you*."

"What about me?"

Hannah put one hand on her hip. "What makes you think that you can actually do proficiently here? You're just a pig who can't do anything right. Everyone else believes it too."

"Literally nobody cares in college," Peyton piped up angrily.

"Literally nobody cares about your opinion."

Paige lurched to her feet. Despite Hannah towering over her in stature, she jumped back at the sudden movement. "You leave him *out* of this," she snarled with a voice louder than she thought possible. "You hear me?!"

That caused most of the room's occupants to look in their direction. Despite the music pounding in the background, the television by the couch whirring play after play, and Paige's heart in her throat, everything was silent. Even the person who was obviously drunk and was about to hit a ball into the corner pocket of the pool table stopped what he was doing to receive all of the latest gossip. Ever since the video, everyone was aware of Penny. They just did not seem to care as much as Hannah. Paige thought she was just plain crazy, especially when she began to laugh. It was soft at first, but then grew manically louder.

"Oh, Honey," she drawled cockily, "This is between you and me. Let's put that to the test, shall we?"

"Excuse me?" Paige was too deep in her anger to realize how ridiculous this whole situation sounded.

"You want to fit in?" Hannah grabbed a half-empty shot glass from the table next to them and chugged the rest of its golden contents. She then slammed it on the table's wooden surface when she proposed, "See if you can beat me at an old fashioned. Last one upright wins."

Paige eyed the shot glass on the table, Hannah's smug expression, and then her outstretched hand. How was she supposed to get out of this one? The answer was simple:

She didn't.

"Deal."

Before Peyton could stop her, Paige firmly clasped onto Hannah's right hand and shook it. The brunette yanked her hand out of Paige's and attempted to hide the fact her knuckles were burning from the iron grip the girl gave her. Once their hands had left each other, both of Hannah's hands collided in several sharp claps.

"Eric!" she screeched over the sound of nothingness. A portly man with acne all over his face and brown, greasy hair down past his shoulders burst into the room when she called. "We have a Code Seven!"

"Code Seven?" Eric fingered through all of the codes in his mind before snapping his fingers. "Oh, right! An old-fashioned drinking game."

Peyton leaned over to Paige's ear, hissing, "This is a *really* bad idea."

"I can handle it," Paige whispered back.

"Don't you realize what you're getting yourself into?"

"It's just a couple drinks. I'll be fine."

"Penny, I-"

Eric grabbed both Hannah and Paige by the hand and dragged the two of them into the back portion of the lobby. Paige failed to notice the large bar with countless alcoholic drinks upon racks behind the counter. Eric led the two girls with Peyton in tow to a table near the bar with two seats across from each other. Hannah sat in one and Paige sat in the other. The former looked much more confident than the latter, but Paige sat up straight. Her lips became a thin line once a shot glass was placed in front of each of them and more of the golden liquid from a bottle was poured into each glass. Paige snuck Peyton a proud look; it had come from a bottle.

"First to five shots wins," Eric instructed with an almost flirtatious grin on his face. "Ready?"

Hannah nodded, smirking deviously, while Paige offered him a curt variation of the same gesture. Paige tried to ignore the anxious look Peyton had been giving her ever since she shook Hannah's hand.

Eric then smacked the table. "Go!"

Hannah snatched up the shot glass, almost spilling the alcohol all over herself, and downed it in one gulp. She wiped her mouth off with the back of her hand and slammed the shot glass down on the table. She snapped her fingers, and another glass was set in front of her being poured with whiskey. Paige had no idea what to do. She had zoned out once Hannah asserted her dominance.

That was when Paige decided to get it back. She grabbed her shot glass and did the same as Hannah. Her taste buds instantaneously tried to reject the odd taste. It was spicy, but sweet at the same time. Paige similarly compared it to the caramel in her favorite drink: a caramel hot chocolate. She placed the shot glass back on the table in a gentler fashion, which provoked Eric to pour her another glass. She did the same with the second glass. The taste began to get more familiar with this one. She missed the way Peyton sighed and covered his eyes with his right hand only to peek through a gap in his fingers.

Hannah was on her third shot, and she did not look like she was backing down anytime soon. This caused Paige to hurry up. Once she received the second shot, she practically tossed it in her mouth like a piece of candy and silently demanded another with her left-hand gesture. The two were tied once it reached four shots apiece, and Paige was slightly ahead when the two of them obtained five shots each in their system. Despite Hannah's slightly woozy composure, she demanded more.

"Let's go to ten," she told Eric when she realized Paige was a split second in front of her.

Eric's eyes widened. "Are you sure? You look a little tip-"

"Just do it!"

The bartender did not complain. Instead, he grabbed another two shot glasses from behind the counter and placed one in front of each girl. At this point, a few partygoers began watching the contest between Paige and Hannah. A few were followed by at least fifteen, then twenty, and then thirty. The amount of college students watching increased with the number of shots each girl consumed. Paige noticed Hannah become visibly tipsy, especially after the sixth and seventh shots, but oddly, she felt completely normal other than a small buzz in her imagination.

Hannah was a silent disaster when the two reached ten shots each and a second bottle of whiskey opened. Paige had finished first once again with no apparent cost. It took several seconds for Hannah to realize Paige had won the contest. It was only when Eric began to announce "We have a winner!" when she yelled once more.

"Fifteen!"

"What the hell?!" Paige snapped from over the table. "I won!"

"We're going to fifteen!" Hannah insisted.

Eric knew better not to question her at this point. Instead, he popped open a third bottle of whiskey and filled up two more shot glasses. It was then that Peyton rushed over to Paige and tried to convince her to quit.

"Penny, this is getting insane," he pleaded with her. "Aren't you getting tipsy?"

"No," she shrugged. "I feel fine."

"Apparently so, but you won't later. Just stop this whole thing and I'll take you home."

"No, I have to win."

"Why?"

"I want to fit in." Paige grabbed her full shotglass and chugged its contents without a single hesitation.

Peyton exhaled and backed away. He knew there was no stopping this in time before something horrible would happen. Thankfully, Hannah downed three of her shots quicker than Paige could with two. She understood she needed to outsmart the powerhouse rather than beat her physically and with the required speed. At her fifteenth shot, Paige suddenly stopped once the glass reached her lips. She let out a loud groan and clutched her stomach with her free hand.

"Oh, God...," she slurred while shakily putting her glass on the table and bending over to hug herself.

As she expected, Peyton once again rushed over in case he needed to keep her from hitting the floor. "Penny! Are you alright?"

"N-..."

Hannah jumped out of her seat once she put her next full shot glass down and raised both hands in the air. "Yes! I won!" she exclaimed.

Her enthusiasm did not last for long, though. Once she stood upright, her head felt as heavy as a pile of bricks and as light as a feather at the same time. Her eyes rolled back in her head and she collapsed to the floor. Peyton watched Eric pick her up off the floor and begin to drag her over to a more comfortable seating area. He did not envy the poor man, especially when Paige sat upright with a wide grin and picked up her shot glass, downing the liquid.

"I am now," she cheekily chirped, pushing her glasses back into place.

Peyton's lips matched her own as he engulfed her in a hug. "Oh, my God, Penny. You had me worried. Are you feeling okay?"

"Uh, a little wobbly, but I'm fine," Paige giggled. *Giggled?* She was not feeling right.

Peyton knew that too, especially when he tried to ease her up. As the crowd that had gathered applauded Paige's victory over Hannah, who nobody seemed to like right then and there, Paige kept almost her entire body weight against Peyton. She knew she could hardly stand up straight. This much vulnerability was new to her, but Paige had too much alcohol in her system to care. Instead, she leaned against the taller boy willingly and dug her nails into his arm as he led her towards the front door of the Theta Cho fraternity building.

"Where are we going?" she murmured as soon as the cool evening breeze hit her face.

Peyton straightened her posture just a little bit to keep her steady as can be as she walked down the stairs. "I'm taking you home. What's your address?"

"What?!" Paige stiffened but could not stop in her tracks. "I can't go back, I-...," she stopped, fumbling for an excuse. "My parents will kill me."

"Well, so will mine," Peyton worried. Then, he got an idea. "Wait a minute..."

Paige fought through her sleepy eyelids to look up at him. "What?"

"You've met Leo, right?"

"Mhm...I think so... Why?"

"Hold on."

Peyton slowed the two of them to a halt on the sidewalk. He removed one hand from around Paige's petite frame and removed his phone from his pocket. He clicked on his most frequent contact and held his phone between his shoulder and his ear so he could use both arms to steady Paige as the two of them walked. It took just over one ring for Leo to answer.

"*Hey, man! What's up?*"

"Hey, Leo!" Peyton exclaimed. When Paige groaned something about a headache from under him, he lowered his voice. "Listen, I need to stay at your place tonight."

"*Did it go that bad?*"

"What? No. I actually have Penny with me and she's *destroyed*. She can't go back home because her parents will be really mad at her and I can't go home because my parents will kill me. Can we stay with you?"

"Uh, yeah. *Just text when you get here and I'll sneak you two into the guest room.*"

Peyton sighed in relief. "Alright. Thanks, Leo."

"*No problem. See you in a few.*"

"I'm sorry," Paige muttered just loud enough to be audible.

Peyton put his phone away. "Why?"

"I'm...how'd you say it?" Her voice was whinier than she remembered. "Destroyed?"

The boy chuckled at that. "Yeah, you are, but hey, it could be worse. You're upright, and-"

Paige stumbled and had to latch onto Peyton before she hit the sidewalk. Luckily for her, he caught her before her knees made contact with the concrete.

"Well...not anymore," he finished breathily. Paige wondered why his arms tensed around her until her feet left the ground and she was being carried bridal style. "C'mon. Let's get you to Leo's before I have to drag you."

"You can put me do-"

"And let you faceplant into the pavement? Not on my watch."

"But-"

"No buts."

For some reason, a giggling fit surprised the both of them. "You're funny," Paige laughed.

"Oh, I know." Peyton grinned gently down at her. "You're pretty amusing when you're drunk too."

"I'm not-" she retorted, suddenly angry.

"You had fifteen shots. You're loaded. What else would you call it?"

Paige smiled up at him. "Not drunk. *Destroyed*."

"Oh," Peyton exhaled dramatically. "Pardon me."

That got Paige giggling again. Peyton had never seen his classmate so loosened up, but there was something about the whole situation that made him uncomfortable. The two of them were making their way through a dark neighborhood with nobody around. For a split second, Peyton thought the two would be getting mugged, but then, he remembered the patriarchy existed. Men were much less likely to get attacked in the middle of the night, but women were prone to it at nearly every instance. Peyton hated the way that the only reason why Paige was not in grave danger was because he was there.

Smash the patriarchy.

Thankfully, the corner of York Street and London Place appeared before he knew it. Rather than approaching his own house, he walked up the porch steps of Leo's. He carefully set Paige down next to him and sent a quick *"We're here"* text to Leo. Peyton figured he would deal with his parents at a later date. They trusted him. He was just doing what was best for Penny without getting himself caught in the crossfire.

Speaking of the girl beside him, his gaze jerked downwards when he felt a head rest on his shoulder. Her black curls nearly made him sneeze, but he managed to swallow the tickling sensation down just as Leo opened the door. His red hair was sticking up in tufts every which way and there were dark circles underneath his eyes. Peyton hadn't realized how late it was and how long it took for the two of them to get back to their neighborhood. When Leo realized there was a girl struggling to stand up and leaning desperately against Peyton's strong - ish - frame, all of the fatigue was washed right out of him.

"Peyton, she's…she's *smashed.*"

Those were the last words Paige heard before she let the exhaustion of the alcohol in her stomach get a hold of her and she slipped - metaphorically and literally - into a state of much needed, but unwanted slumber.

Chapter Nineteen

HONEY

Natural disasters were no joke. If a hurricane was about to blow through a town, every single civilian would be flooding the local grocery stores, buying out every single item imaginable for their extended time of shelter. Trees would collapse, power lines would snap, and wind would burst through every nook and cranny of the town. Some houses would stand tall; others would become devastated, dusty piles of rubble, flattened from the tall structure they were before.

Natural disasters occur everywhere, within weather or humankind. This natural disaster, however, was different from all the rest. It was foreign, something that was unheard of. Somehow, though, it was the worst of them all. It was so terrible that it could hardly be considered "natural" at all.

What *was* this natural disaster anyway?

Paige was experiencing the brutal aftereffects of spending her golden years like her fellow college students.

The pillow her head rested against felt like a brick against her throbbing forehead. Pain seared through every inch of her face. Paige's entire body felt heavier than it truly was, and she consisted of an almost unhealthily lightweight figure. Droplets of sweat dotted her forehead, her back, and her curls that she did not recognize. In fact, she did not recognize anything about the situation she was somehow in.

With a frantic burst of energy, Paige sat up straight in the unfamiliar bed. The room spun around her like a rogue carousel. Paige bit back a groan as her surroundings slowly fell like pieces into place. All at once, the white horses screeched to a stop, the sound being like nails on a chalkboard. Reality came like a slap to the face. Paige's hands looked the same. Her black knit sweater looked the same. What did not look the same were her black locks and the pair of square glasses folded neatly atop the nightstand next to the bed.

Despite the lenses having no prescription, Paige knew playing the persona of Penny Hamilton was necessary. She unfolded the pair of glasses and placed them on her face. Despite this, nothing became clearer. For a moment, Paige thought she was going blind. Her heart beat like a snare in her chest, threatening to break free. Her wobbly legs staggered to stand, but they did anyway. Unbeknownst to Paige, lilac energy sparked around the fingers of her dominant hand as she sauntered towards the door.

Once the door opened, though, the fact that she was in an unfamiliar house hit her like a ton of bricks. She found herself in the middle of a hallway that was not Peyton's. It looked similar, but instead of her room being on the opposite side of the upstairs bathroom, it was right next to it. That was the first clue. The next was the small ball of orange fluff approaching her.

Paige froze. What in the world was this...*thing* approaching her? The creature had four legs, glistening white paws, and a long, striped tail covered in a burnt, fiery orange topped with peach fuzz. It possessed striking green eyes with flecks of brown just over a pink nose and countless white whiskers. Two pointed ears topped its head with tufts of white splaying off of them. What made the whole situation worse was the noise this animal made.

Meow!

"*Did that thing just yell at me?*" Paige fought the urge to dropkick the creature across the room, especially when the jingling of a doorknob turning caught her ears. "*Oh, God. My cover's been blown!*"

Thankfully, no sparks flew when the door opened and Paige turned to view a very sleepy Peyton standing in the middle of the frame. He rubbed his tired eyes with his palms and had to do a double take when he realized Penny was in the hallway having a staredown with his best friend's cat. He forced a chuckle back down his throat.

"Morning, Penny" he mumbled directly before another yawn.

Instead of replying, Paige pointed at the feline and asked, "What is...*that?*"

Peyton did not eye the creature with disdain like Paige did. He smiled. "*That*, as you so graciously call Ollie, is Leo's cat."

"A...cat?" Paige looked at the cat. "Ollie," Peyton had called him,

"Yes." To her surprise, Peyton scooped up the feline, who seemed more than happy to oblige. "He won't bite. Have you ever met a cat before?"

"No."

"Seriously?" The boy gently scratched Ollie's head. The creature began emitting a loud, rumbling noise from the back of its throat. At first, Paige thought it was a growl but then, Peyton elaborated, "Would you like to pet him? He's purring, so he's in a good mood."

Paige gazed into the green eyes of the fluffy animal staring back at her. "Shouldn't we be asking his guardian?"

"Leo's like my brother," Peyton explained, and Ollie seemed to agree. "I stay over at his place all the time and his cat loves me."

"But I don't."

"Oh, well...I guess that's true."

"I'm not supposed to be here." Paige's anxiety levels rose to an untimely high. "I need to leave."

Peyton frowned despite two fluffy white paws batting at his overgrown bangs. "Want me to help sneak you out?"

"I should at least thank Leo for letting me stay...apparently." Paige shoved as many of her ebony curls out of her face as she could mid-yawn. "What...what even happened last night?"

"How about we start with this: what do you remember?"

Paige tentatively reached out to pet the fluffball in Peyton's arms in order to distract herself. Once she realized Ollie leaned into her touch, she continued scratching him behind the ears. "I remember everything up to Hannah challenging me to that drinking contest," she shrugged monotonously. "After about the tenth shot, it was Happy New Year."

"Yeah, you were out of it," Peyton humorously agreed. "I'm surprised it took you that many before you even got tipsy."

"And I was stupid. Humonguously stupid." Paige refused to meet his eyes.

"And you made Hannah look even stupider." He placed one of his index fingers - the other arm cradling the tiny orange cat - and softly lifted her chin. "Welcome to college, Penny. A bunch of stupid people do stupid things."

"I'm supposed to be thinking of my studies." That one realization instilled another sense of panic into her brain. "Wait," she stammered, even halting petting the cat. "What time is it? Am I late for class? I can't skip."

Peyton's eyebrows furrowed. It was becoming an annoyingly predictable habit of his. "How many skips do you have left?"

"Three."

"How many classes do you have today?"

"One."

"Then skip." His shoulders casually raised and lowered. "It's not the end of the world if you do, and besides, the semester's almost halfway over anyway."

Paige blinked at that. "Is it really?"

"It's October, so, yeah."

"I still should go, though," Paige reasoned between two labored yawns. "I have Quantitative Reasoning today."

Peyton's brows shot up. "What the hell is Quantitative Reasoning?"

"Exactly."

"Would you like me to sneak you out?" He repeated his offer.

Paige's mind wanted her to say "Yes! I would," for a split second, but instead, she shook her head. "No thanks. I got it, and besides, doesn't your class start later than mine?"

"Uh, yeah, actually," Peyton fumbled at the sudden information. "How'd you know?"

"*Oh, shi-*" Paige realized she almost blew her cover. She knotted her hands together, cleared her throat, and then made up yet another excuse. "I just never see you when I'm heading to or leaving class. It's a small campus."

"*I'm so sick of making excuses...*"

Peyton's train of quizzical thought was interrupted when Ollie meowed for more pets, which were immediately given. "That makes sense. I have Advanced Chemistry with Leo at twelve forty-five on Tuesdays and Thursdays."

"Wow, that sounds...," Paige trailed off at the awful idea of needing to take an advanced science class, "...fun."

"I actually like it. I'm studying to be a doctor, so I guess I need it."

Paige shifted her weight from one foot to the other. "Good luck with that," she encouraged him with a lowered voice.

"Thanks." Ah, there was Peyton's grin that she somehow grew to love seeing. "I'll need it."

Paige caught herself soaking in every drop of sunlight from Peyton's beaming, yet timid expression. He had grown quite fond of Penny, and she was the same with him. Despite seeing it every day, his smile was nothing she could fully get used to. The gesture seemed like a brand-new experience every time, and more recently, it had started truly making Paige feel better about the situation she was thrown into.

"I should get going." She snapped out of it and genuinely expressed her gratitude, "Thank you for taking care of me. I mean it."

Paige barely heard the soft, pleased exhale escaping Peyton's lips. "You're welcome."

"I'll see you later."

She turned around without waiting for a response. Paige was about halfway down the hallway approaching the stairs when a sharp, electrifying sensation bolted throughout her system. Paige let out a startled gasp and needed to lean against the wall to keep herself from collapsing entirely. She staggered when the tingling in her body reached every inch of her frame, from the back of her neck all the way to her fingertips.

"Woah! Hey-" Peyton put Ollie on the carpet, dashed down the hall, and gave her a steady figure to cling onto. "Are you alright?"

"Yeah," Paige breathed. To her relief, the burning stopped and she stood upright. "I'm fine."

"What *was* that?"

"I, uh...I-...I tripped," she lied through her teeth. "I'm really tired from last night and I should *really* get going if I want to make it to class."

Peyton held a study arm out in her way. "You don't look like you feel well. You should at least rest some."

"I'm in a *stranger's* house," she argued just above a whisper. "I need to leave and attend class like a good student would."

"Nobody's perfect, Penny," he defended his reasoning to protect her well-being. "I just want you to be okay. It doesn't look like you can even stand up straight. Can I get you anything?"

Paige almost screamed with relief. She had figured out her plan! "Actually, yeah," she replied to Peyton's surprise. "Are there any painkillers I could take with a glass of water?"

"Yeah, of course." Peyton walked past her. "Stay here. I'll be right back."

The boy took one last look over his shoulder before he pranced down the stairs. Paige turned towards Ollie, who was sitting innocently on the carpet watching her with his huge green eyes. She placed a finger to her lips and made a silent shushing noise before disappearing completely.

Mrrow!

Ollie surely had a lot to say about that.

Paige followed Peyton downstairs and stayed on the second to last step to the bottom. There was a woman and her husband seated on the couch in the living room to her right. In fact, the Rhys' household looked a lot like the Finlays'. At least the design did. Leo's parents seemed to be like the Finlays as well, especially by the way they greeted Peyton like he was their own son.

"Oh, hello, Peyton!" Mrs. Rhys exclaimed once he made his debut in the kitchen.

Peyton fished through the cabinets and replied cheerily, "Morning, Rebekah! Hi, Dan!"

"Hey!" Dan gave a friendly wave to the blond boy.

It did not take a rocket scientist to determine that Leo's parents looked vastly different from the redhead himself. In fact, Leo looked like he belonged in a completely different house. His pale skin was the exact opposite of Mr. and Mrs. Rhys, both possessing smooth, elegant melanin within their pores. Then, the concept of Leo being adopted reached her mind. That must have been the situation, but it was not like an invisible figure could ask such a blatant question.

Leo was dearly loved, and that was all that mattered.

"Do you need something, Dearie?" Rebekah, Leo's mom, inquired with a friendly tone.

"Oh, I just needed some painkillers," Peyton explained. Paige was shocked to discover him lying just a second later. "I have a headache. Top drawer, right?"

"Exactly! Would you like some breakfast, Sweetheart?"

"Sweetheart...," Paige's mind stuttered. *"Where have I heard that before?"*

"I'm okay for now, but when I drag Leo out of bed, I might take you up on that offer." Peyton grabbed a bottle of painkillers and shook a few out. "Thank you."

Rebekah smiled authentically. "Not a problem! Leo would certainly be late if he didn't have you."

"That's why I'm here." Peyton filled up a glass of water. "And your company's pretty cool too," he teased.

Paige blinked. How in the world could Peyton be so friendly with everyone around him?

Dan chuckled, "We appreciate that, Sport."

"Not a problem."

Peyton held the two painkillers in his right hand and a glass of cold water in the other. He trotted back up the stairs

CHAPTER NINETEEN

without a second thought other than the fact he truly loved Leo Rhys' parents like they were his own. He was like a brother to Leo and a son to Dan and Rebekah. The fact that Leo was adopted made no difference: they were a family through and through.

"Penny, I got you some pain...," Peyton abruptly closed his mouth when he noticed one crucial detail about the task at hand.

Penny was long gone.

"...killers."

Without hesitation, Peyton popped the painkillers into his mouth and chugged the glass of water. It was then that he realized it was going to be a *long* day.

Meanwhile, Paige dashed down the sidewalk outside of the Rhys' household and then past the Finlays'. Despite the dizziness flooding her system, she was a true powerhouse, sprinting down the concrete tiles without a look back. Paige raced away from the neighborhood and towards the urban jungle she was used to. Only one thought crossed her mind.

She had screwed up.

Paige *knew* she had recognized Rebekah and Dan from somewhere. It was then that she remembered where.

"How about we get you someplace warm," she suggested. The child failed to respond, which prompted her to ask, "Are you able to speak?"

"My mommy told me not to speak to strangers," a small voice retaliated.

The woman was taken aback. So, this child did have a guardian...or so she thought. "Where's your mommy, Sweetheart?"

"I-...I don't know," mumbled the girl in defeat.

Paige blinked back the guilt budding into a garden in her stomach. That was *Rebekah*. Then, she encountered Dan on the following day...

"I-...I'm so sorry, Sir, but I don't have any money." Paige's bottom lip trembled.

"Then, I'm sorry."

Paige tried one more time to receive pity with her ginormous, pleading eyes. "Okay, then," she mumbled tearily. "Thanks anyway."

The little girl was about to walk away and out of the store when the man behind her in line spoke up before she could take a step. "Don't go! I got it."

"Are you sure?" the small child could not help but ask.

"Of course," the man replied cheerily. He inserted his card into the chip reader and paid for her meal without a second thought.

As soon as the transaction was completed, Paige whispered, "Thank you."

"Not a problem! Now, enjoy." He smiled at her.

Paige could have slapped herself directly across the face when she realized what exactly she had done to two such kind souls. "God, I'm such an asshole."

Instead of doing just that, she kept going down the sidewalk. That did not last for long, though, because the chilling electric shock returned with a pang. Paige's dominant clutched her chest as she stumbled forward. Her shoes pedaled forward to catch herself just before the rest of her body hit the ground. The tingling current buzzed through her head all the way down to her toes before vanishing like it was never there.

Paige took a deep breath and pushed forward. This was not what she should be worried about right then and there. Instead, she needed to focus on her studies along with...some moral obligations she needed to address. That was on the back burner for now, though. Getting to class on time without another tardy was crucial, at least for her.

Her imagination blurred together when she entered the familiar double doors that belonged to Azure University. Her conscience was grateful to leave the hustle and bustle of Arkford's metropolis behind to make way for a slightly less overwhelming enclosure. Despite the fact Paige was visible to the public, she felt trapped in her own body. She had the ability to disappear right then and there, but society kept her from doing so. Her *studies* kept her from doing so. Paige felt like she was in an endless loop–class, homework, eating, sleeping, and then doing it all over again.

Was this how other university students felt?

Paige tried to pay her struggles no mind as she entered her Quantitative Reasoning classroom and sat in the front row of tables like she always did. This room seemed different from the others, more specifically her United States History classroom. Instead of blank separate desks, there were long tables with a computer monitor at every seat, which had wheels at the bottom. This room reminded Paige a lot of the computer lab on the other side of the building.

She rolled her chair forward and turned on the computer just like she always did. Paige wiggled the mouse and clicked on one of the icons at the bottom of the screen that she learned was called "Google Chrome." The university's website was thankfully the homepage - Paige had not discovered how to properly search for that on the internet - and she eagerly logged in, having memorized her student number.

The rest of the class filed in behind her and retrieved their seats. Paige opened up something else that she discovered on the internet called "Google Docs." She had no idea what a "doc" was, but all she knew was that she could type to her heart's content on one computer and then log into her student email address on another computer and access what she wrote. Paige found that to be much easier than carrying a notebook around.

Her tall, female professor with long hair as straight as a pin elegantly entered the room after the rest of the class. She wore a black pencil skirt and a loose floral top. Paige wondered why this woman felt the need to wear heels when she was easily over six feet tall without them. Nevertheless, this woman was not intimidating. In fact, Professor Esther Springfield was a kind, gentle soul that merely wanted to teach her students what they needed to learn.

"Good morning, class," Professor Springfield exclaimed in her usual soft demeanor. "I hope you all are doing well."

Murmurs that Paige could hardly understand were a response to the professor's exclamation. She was tempted to join in to be polite, but just as she was about to speak up, that dreadful prickling sensation spurred from the back of her neck. Before it could spread anywhere else, Paige smacked the back of her neck. The tingling stopped, to her relief, and she focused her attention to the front of the class.

"Today, we will be reviewing the Quadratic Formula, which can be used to solve *every* quadratic equation. Isn't that amazing?" The professor booted up her computer and projected the screen onto the whiteboard in front of the class. "I know most of you have learned about this in high school, but we're all in different stages of life here. This formula will help you all immensely in the world of mathematics."

Paige stared at the blinking line that indicated where she would type next. All she had in her notes was "Quadratic Formula - IMPORTANT."

Brilliant. This was getting somewhere.

Sarcasm.

"Now, if everyone could copy down this formula somewhere in your notes, that would be great." Professor Springfield inserted a photo of said formula on the whiteboard. "I'll read it out as well. X equals negative B plus-minus the square root of B squared minus four A C all over two A."

CHAPTER NINETEEN

"What the hell is this? Gibberish?"

Paige typed out the formula as quickly as she could despite not understanding it. She knew as much as the letter X needed to be solved for at all costs. She also guessed that in order to solve for X, the numbers correlating with the letters A, B, or C needed to be solved for and plugged in. That was as far as she had gotten in this class. For only knowing basic math from her early childhood, she thought she was progressing well.

She was about to feel proud of herself when the buzzing feeling returned in the back of her neck. Paige slapped it and it stopped for a second time. This let Professor Springfield gain her attention just enough for her to continue explaining the concept to the class.

"To get to this formula in the first place, we need to understand which coefficient is which. First, we bring the equation to the form of A X squared plus B X plus C equals zero. Then, we plug each coefficient into the formula."

Paige typed every single bit of information into her document. Instead of using just her index fingers like she used to, she tried implementing the rest of her fingers as well. Paige found this to be much more efficient in a short period of time.

She could thank Hannah for that.

"How about we try an example problem to make sure we're grasping this." Professor Springfield progressed to the next slide of her presentation. "Six plus two X squared minus three X equals eight X squared. If any of you get the answer, please raise your hand."

"What is this?! Some sort of joke?"

Paige looked around frantically at her peers using sheets of paper and pencils to solve the problem at hand. All she had was a computer. She could indeed ask one of her classmates for one of each, but she decided against it. After all, *nobody cared in college*. She had learned that for a fact...once again, except for

Hannah, whom Peyton compared to a "Queen Bee" from some sort of fictional high school scenario.

She decided to try a different approach. Paige opened a new tab on the internet. She clicked on the search bar at the top and typed out "Quadratic formula." One of the options she could search for that popped up consisted of the two words she typed followed by the word "generator." Paige wondered what that was. Generators...generated things, right? She had to try.

One click later, and she was plugging in the problem to a generator at the top of the search results.

When an educated response came in a matter of seconds, Paige bit back the urge to screech in joy. She had worked and solved the problem all on her own, and it felt *amazing*. She looked around at the class once more. The only sound was of pencils scribbling on paper. This was it. She was going to take a stab at it.

This was her moment.

Paige's hand shot up in the air and instantly caught the attention of the professor.

"Yes, Miss Hamilton?" Professor Springfield smiled at her normally silent student in the front row.

"The answer is one plus-minus the square root of seventeen over negative-"

The confident and correct answer was quickly drowned out by an intense shockwave radiating throughout Paige's body. Her lips opened to complete the answer, but instead stuttered into nothingness. Her teeth chattered as her entire frame began to shake.

"Penny!" At once, the worried professor was right by her side, which was a feat in itself–running in high heels should have been considered a sport. "Is everything alright? Can you hear me?"

This caught the attention of the whole class. Everyone

turned to view a violently trembling Penny Hamilton barely held upright by Professor Springfield. A tiny trail of blood began to cascade from Paige's lip where she must have bitten it in the midst of her tremors. At that moment, no one knew what to do, including the professor.

"Should I call Nine-one-one?" a male student inquired.

No! They cannot do that!

Professor Springfield nodded promptly. "Yes. She looks like she's having a seizure."

"*No! I'm not having a seizure!*" Paige wanted to scream out, but nothing - not even a whimper - left her lips.

Paige began to panic once more when she saw her classmate dial the three numbers to contact much more "guidance" to her aid. Her brown eyes frantically scanned the room as she considered what she should do. Her consciousness faded away from her with each second. She hardly realized she had collapsed from her seat in her rolling chair to the hard, tiled floor, sending the piece of furniture at least a yard away. She felt hot and cold at the same time. When Paige tried to move her legs to stand, they refused to cooperate.

Professor Springfield snapped her fingers in front of Paige's face. She attempted to redirect her gaze, but it was to no avail as the numbness began to take over.

"Penny, help is on the way. Can you take some deep breaths for me?" the tall woman desperately asked of her.

She was indeed doing that as Dr Kelley's repetitive words rang through her ears:

"*No matter what, don't let yourself be publicized. You know what will happen if you do.*"

Paige only had one option left.

She allowed herself to vanish into thin air.

Chapter Twenty

OLIVE

"Wake up!"

No matter what Peyton did, there was absolutely no way that he could wake up his best friend in one attempt. He had tapped his cheek, ruffled his hair, and even threw a pillow at his face, but it was to no avail. The redhead was sound asleep just like he was every night. It had become a ritual for the two of them. Despite their class not starting until the early afternoon, Leo somehow found a way to sleep in just enough to make them have to rush to arrive on time.

Peyton eyed the petite orange cat that was snuggled against Leo's cocoon of a body. He snored softly with his head sunken deep into one of the many pillows on his bed. The poor feline was awakened from his light slumber when Peyton gently grabbed hold of him. Ollie rested his head right under Peyton's chin. This could be a problem—a loophole in Peyton's web of planning.

"Okay, Ollie," Peyton tried to reason with the car in his

CHAPTER TWENTY

arms. "On the count of three, you're going to wake up your stupid brother. Okay?"

Ollie did some sort of a chirp-meow in response.

"That'll have to do. Three," he started counting down.

The cat shut his eyes.

"Two."

Ollie nuzzled Peyton's chest lovingly.

"O-"

Peyton stopped mid-word when a soft, purring sound emitted from the small animal. He looked down at the sleeping Ollie. He snickered at how his tail drooped down and twitched contently with each passing second. Peyton had never heard of such a calm, kind, *clingy* cat. He wished so much that he could stay in Leo's room and hold the bundle of fluff for the rest of the day. Unfortunately, that could not happen.

The two of them had a class.

"Oh, what the hell." Peyton flipped Ollie around so his paws were facing downward and dropped him directly on Leo's head.

"Jesus!" Leo lurched upright at the same time Ollie let out a loud *mrrow*!

"I think he heard you," deadpanned Peyton with a smirk. "Now, get up. We have class."

Leo rubbed his sleepy brown eyes. "Is it noon already?" he yawned out.

"Yup."

"I need to start setting an alarm."

Peyton blinked puzzledly. "You haven't before? No wonder you sleep so late!"

"Nope."

"Why not?!"

"You're my alarm." A fatigued, almost loopy grin grew on Leo's face.

Peyton's lips flattened. He grabbed a pillow and smacked Leo directly in the face. His friend fell backward onto the bed and retaliated by simply pulling the comforter over his head. Peyton had enough of this. He reached under the blanket, took a firm hold of Leo's arm, and began dragging him out of bed. He mustered up all of his strength and groaned at the effort. Thirty seconds later, Leo was only halfway on the floor.

The ginger had a smug look on his face. "Nice try, Noodle-Arms."

"Shut up," Peyton whined desperately. "You're so lazy!"

"I'm not the one who crashed at my friend's place when they literally live next door," he teased, and Peyton was well aware of it.

"That was Penny's request and you know it."

"Oh, yeah," Leo recalled thoughtfully. "Damn, she was *hammered*. Where is she even? Still asleep?"

Peyton shrugged his shoulders. "She insisted on going to class even though she had all of her skips left."

"Nerd."

"Pretty much."

"Seriously, though, is she okay?"

"Other than a massive hangover, she should be fine."

"You're one to talk after your ginormous one last semester," Leo bit back jokingly.

"Excuse me?" Peyton whacked him with a pillow. "That was because Mr. Hutchinson and Mrs. Cullen made me want to forget their classes even existed."

"True."

Peyton was well aware that he was dressed in the clothes he wore the previous day, so while Leo finally made his way out of bed, he dashed over to his house and prepared himself for the long day ahead. It was a Thursday, which meant he had a lab that ran until the evening. Oh, how he wished he lived less than a twenty-minute bike ride away from Azure's campus. A quick shower, a new change of clothes, and even a small pep talk in the mirror later, Peyton was rolling out from his garage on his electric blue bicycle. Leo was close behind on his red bike as the two of them rode off towards the urban skyline together.

Leo yawned dramatically to Peyton's left. "I could fall asleep right now."

"Do it," the blond teasingly dared him. "You'll probably end up head over heels in the street somewhere, but it'd be funny."

"Or I could sleep in class."

"That too."

"I'm surprised you haven't been caught yet."

"They're college professors, remember?" Leo reminded him with a smirk as he dodged a pebble on the street. "They don't give a-"

The redhead was cut off by Peyton's phone ringing. Without losing his momentum, Peyton removed his phone from the front pocket of his jeans and studied the number, all the while holding onto the handlebars with one hand. He recognized the contact because it blatantly said "Home phone." That was odd. Both of his parents were at work by that point. Who could be calling at this hour-

Oh.

Peyton remembered Paige with a pang. He had been so caught up with Penny for the past day that he had completely forgotten about the fact he had a young woman secretly residing in his family's guest room. Guilt was the only emotion to describe him because of his negligence towards her. Paige probably had no idea what happened. She had been shut in her room ever since the family dinner the previous night. Peyton felt horrible about not inviting her to dinner as well. Worry clogged Peyton's throat as well as his senses.

What if Paige was mad at him and calling him to chew him out?

What if Paige was calling him because she felt left out and wanted to explain her feelings?

What if-

"Good God, Peyton–answer the phone!" Leo slammed into his cellar of thoughts without a key–he broke down the whole door.

Peyton had no time for what-ifs. He did just what Leo suggested and accepted the call, held his phone up to his ear, and began to speak.

"Hel-"

"*Peyton!*"

Paige's unfamiliar tone containing nothing but fear screamed in his ear so vibrantly that Peyton nearly dropped his phone on the asphalt. He caught his device firmly in his hand despite wobbling desperately on his two-wheeler. Albeit hesitantly, Peyton placed his phone next to his ear once again.

"Pai-...what's wrong?"

"*Peyton, I need you!*" she shrieked hurriedly. "*Come home! Please! I-I can't do this! It won't stop! I-*"

The electric blue bicycle skidded on the dark pavement so much that it burnt rubber. Leo stopped his own bike a few feet ahead. He had no idea what was going on, but the way Peyton whirled the front wheel of his bicycle around and began pedaling as fast as his legs could carry him, he knew something was wrong.

"I'm coming, Paige–don't worry!" he wheezed from the sudden burst of adrenaline. "Can you breathe for me? What's going on?"

"*I can't! Peyton, I can't! It's too...it's too...*"

Her voice was cut off by a high-pitched wail that exploded from her mouth. That only caused Peyton to pedal quicker. "I'm two minutes away. *Please* try to stay calm. Are you hurt?"

He was only answered by another scream that wrenched his heart right out of its place in his ribcage. Leo struggled to keep up with him.

"What's going on?!" Leo puffed tiredly, but somehow remained by his side. "Who's Paige?"

"It's a long story, but she's in trouble." He redirected his attention to the phone. "Paige, stay where you are. I'll be there really soon. Where are you?"

"*I'm on the kitchen floor. I can't move...I-*"

"Shh," Peyton tried to soothe her to the best of his ability. "Keep your joints loose. If you tense them, it could increase the pain. Try to relax."

"*Peyton, you don't understand; I-*"

"Easy... Can you breathe for me? In through your nose and out through your mouth?"

Peyton stopped only to hear a deep inhale on the other end of the line followed by what seemed to be a proper exhale, but it was cut off by a wheeze and yet another yelp. He guessed a bit of saliva caught in her throat since she was sent spiraling into a coughing fit. The sensation of ribs tightening and a throat closing only worried Peyton further.

"I'm coming, Paige. I'm right down the street. Hang on."

There was no answer on the other end of the line other than...heavy breathing. Peyton thought he heard her begin to gently break into tears, but he thought it was merely his imagination. After he tossed his bike to the side in the driveway rather than wheeling it into the garage, ran up to the porch, and unlocked and slammed the front door open, he realized it was not just in his thoughts–it was reality.

The sight of Paige trembling like a meek chihuahua on the

kitchen floor unnerved him more than he expected it to. The home phone rested on the hardwood next to her outstretched right hand, which he guessed was holding it. The whites of her eyes were the most prevalent—even more so than her pupils. How she was not unconscious by then, Peyton had no idea.

"Oh, *God*..." Peyton knelt down and cautiously lifted Paige's upper half into his lap. The fact she made no move to squirm out of his reach or, in fact, vanish through a wormhole, was concerning. He lightly smacked the side of her cheek to try to get her attention. "Paige? Paige! Can you hear me?"

A fatigued groan was all he received in response.

He started to shake her, softly at first, but when she failed to answer, he increased his momentum. "God dammit, *Paige*!" he raised his voice more. "Please!"

"Huh? What?" a groggy voice wavered from below.

A pair of hazel eyes flickered open to the relieving sight of Peyton keeping the upper half of her body from the cold, hard ground. She was absentmindedly leaning against him while trying to catch her breath, which came in sharp, soft puffs. Paige would never admit it out loud, but the feel of Peyton's arms, despite not being much bigger than hers, around her body was calming, maybe even safe.

"Oh, praise Jesus," Peyton sighed in relief when they made eye contact. "What happened? What are your symptoms?"

"I'm fine, I just...," Paige stammered in an attempt to speak. "You need to help me."

"Anything. What can I do?"

"I need you to cut something out of me."

Peyton felt like he was going to get whiplash from how hard that statement hit him. "Excuse me?"

He stopped himself from questioning further when he realized Paige was dead serious. "You're studying to be a doctor, right?" she inquisitively asked.

"Well, yeah, but–wait. How'd you know?"

Paige had no time to worry about lying to his face anymore. "You told me before. I will tell you everything if you do this for me. Now."

"Uh, okay, but..." Peyton struggled to find words through his uncertainty. "What am I cutting out? I don't have any anesthetics or anything except my dad's first aid kit and supplies upstairs. I'm not a real doctor."

She looked him dead in the eyes and elaborated, "This might sound crazy, but I have a microchip under my skin on the back of my neck." Paige carefully calculated that the gears were spinning in Peyton's brain. She had no time for that. "It's malfunctioning and could very likely kill me if you don't get it out."

Peyton struggled to keep his eyes from falling out of the sockets. "You can't *possibly* expect that from me." He held his hand out in front of him.

"I need you to do this for me."

"Paige, I-"

"Now."

"Listen-"

"*Please.*"

The tone of Paige's voice became a desperate plea. She grasped onto the collar of his shirt only to slowly let go when she realized what situation she had put herself in. Paige was unaware of the lone tear cascading delicately down her cheek and onto her lap. She had no idea what else to do than to trust in the one person she could on this planet.

That was when Peyton realized...he needed to do the same.

"Come on, then," he muttered with a newfound determination. "Let's get you on the couch so I can try not to screw this up."

Paige was too exhausted to express her gratitude. She

clung onto Peyton like a koala to a tree as he lifted her to her feet and guided her over to the living room couch. She laid down on her stomach and rested the side of her head on her folded arms. Her body quivered periodically, which caused her jaw to be wired shut in hopes to lessen the pain. Paige remained in the same position while Peyton went upstairs to retrieve his father's doctors' kit. When he came back into view, Paige noticed he was holding a briefcase that he set down on the table across from her.

"Okay, what the hell is going on?!" Leo was tired of waiting outside the front door and stormed inside without any type of warning. He stopped in his tracks when he saw Paige face down on the couch. "Who's that? Is that Paige?"

Peyton sighed, rummaging through the leather briefcase. "Just stay quiet. You might need to hold her down in a minute, though."

"Hold me dow–*no!*" Paige protested, beginning to get up from her position.

"It's going to hurt," retorted Peyton with a stern look.

That was enough for Paige to lay back down.

He turned to Leo, who padded his way into the living room at that point. "I'm removing something from the back of her neck and you need to hold her shoulders down while I'm doing so."

"What?!" Leo was dumbstruck. "Are you crazy?! You're not a real-"

"I know, I know," Peyton fretted as he tugged a blue rubber glove onto each hand with quite a struggle. "But this is the situation we're dealing with, so, hold her down."

"I don't know about this."

"Just *do it!*"

Leo scooted his body over to the couch and plopped his bottom down next to Paige's abdomen. He reached down, but almost recoiled when he touched each of her shoulders, like they were covered in slime or something else that was gross. Nevertheless, the stern glare he got from Peyton made him obedient. The same occurred with Paige, who tried her hardest to lay still as Peyton grasped onto a clean, sterilized scalpel from his doctors' kit.

"Am I going to throw up?" Leo squeaked right when Peyton leaned down over Paige's upper half and adjusted his grip on the surgical knife and a cotton ball soaked in saline solution.

Peyton just stared at him like he had seen a ghost.

"I guess I'll have to hold it," the redhead swallowed. "Speaking of holding it, I may or may not have to pee."

The blond ignored him, keeping his eyes only on the back of Paige's neck. "Are you ready? Is it the bump on the back of your neck?"

"Yes, and yes." Paige's voice was muffled from being against the couch cushion.

"Okay. You're going to feel coldness from the saline solution. This is to clean the area before I start an incision. I'll make it as small as I can, but I don't know how big the thing is, so I might have to make it bigger."

"It's small."

"I knew that." Peyton carefully brushed her hair out of the way. "It has "micro" in the name."

Paige stifled a smile, but her expression quickly turned cold when the icy fingers of the saline solution caressed the back of her neck. After several smooth strokes, the source of the flurries crawling down her spine was removed. Peyton asked her one more time if she was ready, which she answered with a curt nod.

Her breath hitched in her throat once the sharpest point of the medical scalpel made contact with her skin and dug through the first layer. She compared it to a small bug bite or a zit she had just rubbed her finger over. The knife was lowered through the epidermis. Paige's teeth clung onto her bottom lip for dear life once the scalpel began tearing a small gash in the skin. The sensation of metal feeling around under her skin was not quite ticklish, but it made her nerves tighten and tense. Leo must have tightened his grip on her shoulders since she could not move even if she wanted to.

"Holy shit, this thing is small," Peyton muttered after a few more seconds of digging.

Leo peered inside despite the warm crimson blood bubbling up through the small incision. "Is that a microchip?"

"Yes," Paige gritted in annoyance. "Now, get it out. *Please.*"

"Leo," Peyton ordered without hesitation. "Get her a dish towel or something to bite down on. This is going to hurt."

The poor redhead let go of Paige instantly and dashed into the kitchen, only to return ten seconds later with a large assortment of colored washcloths. He had not a clue where to put them, so he tossed them all on the coffee table. Peyton's eyebrows furrowed; he clearly had his hands full with an open wound on someone he cared about. The fact *he* made it in the first place sprouted the first bud of guilt.

The second came when he instructed Leo: "Give it to her. I need to get this out."

The way Leo stuffed a red washcloth in Paige's mouth was almost laughable if the situation around them feigned to exist.

"I need the forceps from the kit," Peyton notified his friend.

"The *what*?"

Peyton let out a long exhale. "The tweezer-looking things with handles like scissors. They're basically scissors, but instead of using them to cut, they grab stuff."

"This?" Leo thankfully picked up the correct tool and handed it to Peyton.

"Yup. Thanks." Peyton leaned over closer to the wound. "Hold onto her."

The ginger did not hesitate. He assumed his former position once again and waited for Peyton's signal, which came as a question for Paige.

"I'm going to get it out. If it hurts, bite the washcloth. Try not to struggle. Okay?"

"Fine, just *get it out!*" Paige demanded. She did not mean to be harsh, but the position she was in, both mentally and physically, was uncomfortable.

As soon as he made sure everyone was ready, Peyton took a deep breath, pried, and held the gash open with his left gloved hand. With the other, he guided the forceps into the opening. He latched them onto the silicone object just under the skin. After a moment of thought, Peyton began to pull at it. It was gentle to begin with but grew to be more difficult than he assumed.

Paige bit down on the washcloth in her mouth as Peyton pulled harder. He tightened the forceps' grip on the microchip and increased the velocity of his actions while somehow still being just as gentle and cautious as before. Leo tightened his hold on Paige's upper body when she began to squirm and her frame started trembling. A small noise began emitting from the back of her throat. At first, it was a low moan, but then it grew to be more of a shrill whine. It reminded Leo of a time Ollie had fallen from the kitchen counter and hurt himself.

"Hold on, Paige," Peyton mumbled just loud enough for her to hear. "I've almost got it."

Her body continued to shake, harder this time. Paige was transported back to the classroom just over an hour before. One of the students said she was having a seizure. Was this happening again? Her heart throbbed against her ribcage as the world around her shrunk into a glass box. The whine she was concealing became a fearful, ear-piercing wail when a sharp electrical current rocketed its way through her system. The numbness grew stronger and stronger, much more difficult to bear until...

...it stopped.

Paige flopped like a wet autumn leaf onto the couch. Sweat drowned her forehead just like the unknown tears to her cheeks. The washcloth fell out of her mouth as she began gasping, coughing, and wheezing for breath that she never knew she needed until that very second. Her entire body became limp. Leo's hold on her shoulders was released and he made a dash for the nearest restroom; for number one or to empty his stomach, Peyton did not know.

Her eyes fluttered open to a hand waving in front of her face. Paige's hazel irises floated upwards to meet Peyton. Then, they focused on the red ends of the forceps that were clinging onto a silicon wafer. Peyton shot her a cheesy grin when he revealed his prize.

"Got it."

"Oh, thank Heaven." Paige's eyelids slammed shut.

The rest of the following ten minutes were much more of a breeze. Peyton decided against using stitches to suture the incision since it was so small. Instead, he cleaned the area with an alcohol wipe once he got the bleeding to cease and placed a firm bandage overtop. Just before that decision was made, a toilet flushing distracted the both of them. Leo wobbled out of the bathroom with an olive tint to his cheeks, hinting that the second possibility of why he dashed off became reality. Or maybe both occurred.

"Are both of you alright?" Peyton asked stiffly, as if one sudden movement would mess everything up.

"Just peachy," Leo blabbered from between the open concept living room and kitchen.

CHAPTER TWENTY

The blond turned to the girl on his sofa. "Paige?"

The room was silent. Paige slowly pushed herself upward so she was not completely laying down on the comfortable gray cushions. Her vision cleared once her eyes got used to the light after several minutes being shrouded in darkness. Peyton was sitting awkwardly on the coffee table tugging his rubber gloves off of his hands. He had set the bloody microchip and forceps on one of the washcloths Leo tossed on the wooden surface.

The last thing Peyton expected was for Paige to fling her arms around him and nearly squeeze the life out of him in the form of one of the biggest hugs he had ever received. Peyton was not anticipating Paige to be a hugger, especially after everything the two of them had been through together. Peyton could only return the gesture, burying his face in her long, smooth hair while she did the same with the crook of his neck.

"How are you feeling?" he inquired against her shoulder.

"I feel..." The next word out of Paige's mouth pleasantly surprised him, "free."

Peyton could only smile at that. He did not know what exactly she was free from, or what was caging her in the first place, but he could take a solid guess, which he was about to do before Leo interrupted obliviously.

"So, uh, can someone *please* tell me what's going on?"

Paige removed herself from the embrace she and Peyton shared. The vulnerability in her eyes was worrying. "Can we trust him?" she lowered her voice.

"He's like my brother," Peyton assured her. "We can trust him more than his cat."

"Hey!" Leo retaliated defensively. "Ollie is very trustworthy!"

"He seemed a bit manipulative when I saw him," Paige casually noted.

Peyton struggled to connect the dots. "Wait...when did you meet Ollie? I didn't think you went over to Leo's with me."

"Peyton," she breathed out and rose to her feet. "I don't know how you haven't figured it out yet."

"Figured out what yet?"

"There's one ability of mine that I've been keeping from you for a while now." Paige took two steps back, to which Peyton was tempted to pull her back from. "I need you to promise me you won't freak out."

"Last time you said something along the lines of "freaking out," I ended up puking all over someone's yard."

"Wait." Leo questioned, still oblivious. "That *wasn't* a dream?"

"Leo!" Peyton hissed. "Not now!"

"Sorry."

"Promise me," Paige insisted, her eyes like balls of fire.

Peyton knew he was not getting out of this unless he obliged. "I promise."

The girl knew something was amiss, but she had no choice but to follow up with her word. She promised Peyton that she would tell him everything, which was exactly what she was about to do. First, she looked at Leo, who was still awkwardly standing halfway between the kitchen and the living room. Then, her gaze landed on Peyton, and remained there. Paige felt her heart yearn to leap out from her throat when she performed the familiar ritual of morphing her body into something it was not.

Penny Hamilton's black curls cascaded down the back of her knit sweater all the way down to the ebony flats she wore on her very first day at Azure University. Her school tote bag was hidden in the guest bedroom upstairs. Obviously, Peyton had not a clue about Paige's secret identity, because once her transformation concluded, his lips parted and attached like a misplaced goldfish in the middle of the ocean.

"What the...you're...but...you...you're... *Penny?*" Peyton stuttered out almost inaudibly. "That was *you* the whole time...?"

Paige was most certainly a deer in headlights...until the beams, which were actually Peyton's widened brown eyes, rolled back in his head and he collapsed onto the floor.

Paige and Leo looked at each other in shock.

He really fainted.

Chapter Twenty-One

WISTERIA

"Okay, you get the legs and I'll get the arms."

"Who says I can't get the arms?"

"Because the torso is heavier."

Paige folded her arms over her chest and shot an expression of accusation in Leo's direction. She eyed Peyton's unconscious body on the floor and then looked back up at him, noting, "He's a twig. I can lift him."

"But you're-"

"A girl?" Paige interrupted him and brushed her blonde hair behind her shoulders. "Just because I'm a girl doesn't mean I'm weak."

"I wasn't going to say that!" Leo shook his hands out in front of him. "I was just going to say that you're smaller and might feel better getting his legs."

"If anyone's going to drop him, it's you."

"Okay, well–that's true."

"I have a better idea."

Prior to Leo reacting in any sort of way, Paige opened a vortex just large enough to fit Peyton's body through. He disappeared through the portal and fell through another one, landing on the living room sofa. Peyton's head was resting on a pillow and by the looks of it, he was quite comfortable in his slumber. Leo had to do a double take, his pupils darting from Peyton on the couch to Paige cracking her knuckles in the middle of the room. The entire process seemed easier all of a sudden.

"Why didn't you do that before?" was Leo's question.

Paige's response never failed to be brief. "I didn't want you to throw up again."

"It was from the blood, not...that. What *was* that?" Leo's eyes visibly lit up. "That was so cool! Have you always been able to do that?"

"Not exactly."

"So, you learned?"

"You could say that." Paige averted eye contact, ignoring the fact she hardly knew Leo. "How come you aren't as surprised as Peyton?"

To her surprise, Leo smirked. "You're not the only one living a double life."

"Excuse me?" His revelation surprised Paige.

"Only Peyton knows this, but you're cool, so I'll tell you too." Leo leaned into her face to whisper in her ear. "I'm secretly a computer and technology nerd. Don't tell him I told you or he'll be teasing me about it for *months*."

Paige smacked him upside the head.

"Ow!"

"How does he deal with you?" she muttered under her breath.

"Honestly, I don't know, but it's been almost ten years at this point." Leo shrugged and leaned over Peyton, who was still unconscious on the sofa. He snapped his fingers in front of his face. "Anywho...hey, Peyton! Wake up, Loser!"

Paige sat down on the coffee table - which she only deemed okay since Peyton did the same thing - and watched the show.

"Peyton!" Leo continued snapping his fingers and ruffling his hair. "Wake up, you jerk!"

"Do you *really* think that's going to work?"

"No."

"Then quit it."

Leo then snapped his fingers one more time. "Hey, wait. I got an idea."

Paige's gaze followed Leo into the kitchen. He opened a cabinet next to the refrigerator and removed a glass, dashing over to the sink and filling it up nearly to the brim with water. Paige still struggled to put the pieces together until the scene unfolded right in front of her. Leo pranced back into the living room, shot Paige a wink, and proceeded to dump the entire glass onto Peyton's head.

The blond boy flew into reality with a jerk. He spluttered and coughed with freezing cold water dripping down his flushed cheeks. Peyton blinked his eyes open to glare at the culprit chortling and snorting right above him. He grabbed the empty glass and shoved it in Leo's face, causing him to fumble and practically juggle it until he caught it. Paige glanced between the two of them innocently. Huh. Leo and Peyton truly were brothers.

"What?" Leo asked in a childlike tone. "What else were we supposed to do when you were passed out on the floor?"

Paige's eyebrows lowered. "Leave me out of this, you oaf."

"Oaf? What's an oaf?"

"An idiot," Peyton grumbled, rubbing the sleep from his eyes.

"Hey!" Leo's face suddenly became concerned. "Seriously, are you okay, though?"

"I'm fine. That just...threw me for a loop."

"Well, now you have two friends living double lives."

Peyton rolled his eyes at that. "Nerd."

"How come you told me not to bring it up, but then you did the job yourself?" Paige inquisitively questioned Leo, who was about to bite back.

"Because he's stupid."

"No, I'm not!"

"You threw up after seeing a couple drops of blood."

"My stomach didn't like seeing a pair of tweezers in someone's neck."

"Stop it!" Paige raised her voice and successfully got the boys' attention. "This is a serious matter. Peyton, I need you to understand why I've been doing this."

Peyton adjusted his position on the couch to be more comfortable. "I'm listening, Paige," he teased with a hint of remorse, "or, should I call you "Penny?""

"Look. I'm sorry." Paige stared at her worn high-top shoes.

"Would it be too much to ask why you did this?" Peyton squeaked out nervously. Nervous? Why was he nervous?

"I told you I would explain everything if you did what you've already done. I owe it to you."

Peyton patted the cushion next to him and looked at Leo. The redhead obediently obliged and sat down next to his best friend on the couch. Paige swung her short legs back and forth, formulating exactly how she was going to disclose her deepest secret to two boys—one she had grown to trust and the other... well...it was complicated. If Peyton said she could trust him, though, she would at least give him a chance.

"I have been bound to a governmental organization since I was a little girl." The dark hardwood floor was very interesting to her. "I never truly knew my parents like I thought I did. This organization wants nothing but utmost power and control. So, they started with me."

"Let me go!" the three-year-old girl screamed at the man in dark clothing dragging her away from her parents who were holding her hand on either side of them.

"Come here, you little brat!" The man's hood was over his eyes, which made him even more frightening to the small child. He reminded her of a character from a scary movie.

Paige fought back a shudder from the memory she had blocked out for years. "This...*man* took me from my mom and dad. They could've stopped him. It was two against one, but... they didn't."

"Mommy! Daddy! Help me! Please"

The raven-haired father and the brunette mother looked at each other and then at the dark man. They both appeared as if they had been hiding something from the child and had no idea how to explain it to her. The mother was unsure, but when the father nodded, the two of them turned to Paige.

"It's for your own good," her mother stoically said.

"I screamed and cried for them to come back and to take me home, but they left me with him and he took me back to the same warehouse that you were imprisoned in, Peyton. I continued to be told that this was "for my own good," but it was not. It was *theirs*."

"Please let me go!" The toddler begged and kicked at the man who was carrying her away from her mommy and daddy.

"No, Sweetie," the man rejected her plea. "This is for your own good. Soon, you'll learn what it means to be the most special girl in the world."

She watched her parents fade into the concrete jungle of Arkford. Paige never saw them again.

"It turns out my parents signed a deal with the organization that would permit them to have experiments done on me without my consent. I was too little for that."

"No, stop it! What are you doing to me?"

CHAPTER TWENTY-ONE

The man whom the child still could not make out an appearance to smiled a yellow, toothy smile from underneath his hood. "Something you will not come to regret."

The toddler struggled and tugged at her restraints that confined her to a metal chair until a sharp prick entered her arm. She let out a wail before going silent with fatigue.

"Over the years, I was injected with serums I never knew the names of, tortured many times over with different devices," Paige concluded her explanation without removing her eyes from her Converse. "Eventually, I discovered these... cognitive abilities that have developed became external. The organization suddenly became afraid of me, so...they imprisoned me further."

"I promise I won't run away!" a ten-year-old begged on her knees. "Just don't put that in me! I don't know what it does!"

"It will simply keep you in line." The yellow-toothed man who the girl soon learned was named Dr. Kelley. "This will ensure you won't."

"No, stop!"

"The microchip was programmed to keep me under control. I had no rights. Eventually, I started to get on their good side when I finally gave up fighting. I would let them do these experiments on me and to try new things with me and would pay me little and house me in return. I was getting my own life back, but then, the bus incident occurred."

"That was *you?!*" Leo would have spit out his drink if he was consuming one.

Peyton whacked Leo on the upper back. "You idiot! *That's* what you're getting from this?" He apologetically looked at Paige when Leo yelped at him. "I'm so sorry. Continue."

"No, no. I'm done." The emotionless look returned to Paige's face. "I didn't mean to bore you with my sob story."

"Oh, my God. Absolutely not." Peyton took Paige by

surprise and engulfed her in his arms, to which she did not pull away from. "I'm glad you're here now, and...alive. Nobody deserves that kind of torture. I'm so sorry."

"It's not like it's your fault."

"I know, but you've been through so much that I don't know what to say."

"You don't need to say anything."

So, that was exactly what he did. Peyton kept Paige in his embrace and was nowhere close to letting her go. He was afraid she would slip through his fingers if he did so. After all, with everything that had been going on lately, he had no idea who to trust. Paige, Penny... Hell, two girls who he thought were his separate friends ended up being the same person. What if she was hiding something else from him too?

No.

That was insensitive and cruel. Paige was pouring her heart out to him. He had no right to question whether she was being truthful or not. She was nothing less than a friend, sticking by his side no matter which identity she presumed at the time. Despite Peyton being on the outside, he peered through the window that was no longer fogged up. *This* was who the girl in his arms really was: a vulnerable, broken girl trying to pick up the shards of glass only to cut her hands on them.

Leo scanned the two of them from the other side of the couch. Clearing his throat, he slowly inquired, "Should I join the hug or..."

He was met by two faces scowling at him.

"What?!" Leo's fringe flopped when his body tilted forward with the force of his inquiry. "Sorry I'm being a third wheel here. I just don't know how to handle emotional situations."

Peyton made the wise decision to ignore him. Instead, he changed the subject. "Leo, since you're oh-so good with tech, how about you examine that microchip, do some research, and see what you can find on it?"

"As long as you get the blood off of it."

"Deal."

Paige neglected to notice she had been watching Peyton this whole time. The two of them were seated next to each other on the coffee table, one of his legs over hers to minimize the distance between them. The two of them had their arms loosely around each other without their knowledge. When Paige tried to retract her limbs from his frame, Peyton's eyes met hers.

It was safe to say that both of their complexions turned red as they shuffled away from one another.

Leo smirked.

"Idiot." Peyton definitely saw that.

"Oh, right!" The redhead noticed his best friend shooting him a suspicious look. "The microchip! Can you get the blood off of it?"

A wisp of air left Peyton's lips as he grabbed the microchip on the table along with a clean washcloth. He lazily wiped it off and handed it to Leo. The latter was not pleased by how Peyton went about with this matter. He daintily pinched the object with his fingers and ventured into the kitchen. One drawer opening and closing later, he came back with a sandwich bag, dropping the microchip inside and sealing it shut.

"I'll take a look at it. Is there anything I should know about this thing before I start doing research and such?"

Paige shrugged. "You know just as much as I do."

"That's reassuring."

"Glad I could help," she sarcastically mused.

Leo lingered in the living room for just a few minutes more. Paige sat quietly on the couch while regaining her strength from such an emotional, exhausting ordeal. Sweat occasionally dribbled from her forehead and dampened her hair. Her jaw ebbed with soreness consequent to clamping down on the washcloth in order to prevent a scream. Paige rubbed her cheek, trying to push that memory deeper into her mind.

The redhead did not remain for too much longer. After giving each of them a hug, which Peyton accepted willingly but Paige was wary of, he paraded through the front door to his home next door, dragging his red bike behind him. Peyton took the time that Leo was using to do research on and investigate the microchip to ensure that the girl he was housing was, in fact, in a better state of mind than she was about ten minutes earlier.

"Are you feeling any better?" Peyton's tone was nothing but authentic.

Paige shrugged, sitting cross-legged on the couch. "I guess so."

"You said you felt free. I wonder if that's the case literally."

"What...what do you mean?"

"Like," Peyton concluded, his eyes gazing at the ceiling and then back at her, "if you feel free now, then you must've been limited before. If I may, how so?"

Paige needed to think about it for a moment. "It's always seemed as if there's been some sort of barrier. For example, when it comes to my...powers as you'd call them. I feel like I could do more, but something's not letting me."

"Do you think you could try it now?"

"Now? Try what now?"

"What have you tried before that the microchip stopped you from doing?"

"Um, well...," she almost seemed nervous when it came to this subject. "I've never been able to shift into animals. Just other humans."

Peyton was suddenly ecstatic. "Can you turn into Leo's cat? Please, please, please?!"

"I, uh...I can try..."

Paige rose to her feet and stood in the middle of the room. Peyton's eyes never left her as a bright, purple hue enveloped her body. It grew smaller within the second, and when the small puff of wisteria smoke and sparks vanished, an exact replica of Ollie was seated on the rug. Peyton blinked, then rubbed his eyes. Then, a wide grin crowded his face.

"What the hell–that is so *cool*!"

"Oh, for the love of God," the cat grumbled in annoyance.

Peyton was gobsmacked. "You can talk as a cat?"

"Yes."

"Can I pet you?"

"Okay, we're done experimenting."

Before Peyton could say another word, Paige's human form popped into view. "Aw," he pouted dramatically, "I wanted to pet you. You looked fluffy."

"Too bad," dismissed Paige, leaving no room for argument.

"Can you try something else cool?" he politely questioned.

"Like what?"

"Can you read minds? Or do telekinesis? Or teleport longer distances?" Peyton's enthusiasm, along with his voice, rose along with each question.

"I couldn't read minds to begin with and I'm not sure about the other two." Paige was curious, though, tucking a strand of her long hair behind her ear.

Peyton's field of vision drifted to the coffee table. "Can you try to move that cup?" He pointed to the glass Leo used to dump water on his head.

"...We'll see."

Paige failed to remember the last time she had concentrated so hard. She felt like an idiot due to the way her right hand was splayed out in front of her. Her fingers began to twitch from the tension she was putting on the poor appendage. Paige's eyelids shut and her whole face screwed up for at least ten seconds while she stood there and waited for something to happen. Then, she opened her eyes.

Nothing happened.

She tried to hide the disappointment on her face when she lowered her hand. Still, she could not avoid Peyton's dominant presence in the room, which was why her eyes landed upon him. Rather than benign filled with dismay, Peyton had an aura of encouragement around him.

"Try not to try so much," he suggested.

Paige's eyebrows lowered. "And what is that supposed to mean?"

"If you try too hard, you'll get too stressed out and won't be able to reach your goal," Peyton explained as if it was the simplest concept in the world. In a way, it *was*. "Just let your mind do the work and relax."

"It's not that easy."

"Just do your best."

Paige knelt down in front of the table and focused her gaze on the glass. Instead of slamming them shut, her eyes closed on their own. Her hand extended from the side of her body. This time, instead of trying to concentrate, she held it out loosely. Once more, her fingers began to twitch, but not from tension this time. Alternatively, the same lilac sparks that extracted from the energy fields she had been conjuring for years at that point misted around the cup.

Peyton watched with wide eyes as the object rose off the table and began floating in the middle of the room. He tapped Paige on the shoulder, to which she opened her eyes. The glass faltered once she realized what she was doing and nearly hit the table, but just before it did, Paige raised her hand and redi-

CHAPTER TWENTY-ONE

rected it upward. Paige's entire body lit up and she rose to her feet when she made this new discovery. Her left hand flew into the mix. She began to juggle the glass left and right and spin it in circles. Peyton's chocolate irises followed the glass as it leapt and spun through the air. Then, he looked at Paige.

She was truly...free.

At least, that was until she lost the comprehension of how high the glass was soaring. It hit the ceiling and then crashed onto the floor once Paige lost control. It shattered into thousands of tiny rainbow shards. The floor looked like a stained-glass window or a kaleidoscope of sorts.

Paige and Peyton looked at each other with wide eyes. To both of their surprise, Paige spoke first with an offer Peyton could not dismiss.

"If you clean that up, I'll try to teleport us both to school tomorrow."

"Deal."

Chapter Twenty-Two

CHAMOMILE

For years, Paige O'Connell wished freedom upon herself. Every second of every day, there was nothing but control. The young girl who had just become a teenager that very day was unable to make a single decision for her life. She needed to get some rest to prepare for another mundane day? Permission had to be granted. She needed to eat for the first time in days? Permission had to be granted.

She was visibly sick of the life she had been forced into from an early age. Most hours of sunlight, Paige occupied herself in the cell she was confined in. Often, she bounced an energy ball of her own creation off the walls, caught it, and repeated the process until she got bored of it. This happened rather quickly, so she would usually resort to lying on the floor - no, she did not have a bed, either - and staring up at the ceiling. Most days were like this.

Others...were torture.

Today was one of the latter.

The usual routine occurred just like it did every day before. Paige awoke sometime when the sun was reaching its highest point in the sky - this was due to the dark being difficult to sleep in - and began her daily ritual of staring at the ceiling. Eventually, she generated an energy ball that ricocheted off the gray brick wall across from her until she bounced it back. Then, the scenario repeated itself over and over...

...until a key inserted itself into her metal barred cell door, which swung open with a clang.

Paige jumped to her feet. The energy ball she was playing with shattered into millions of lavender sparkles that vanished once the guard in black stepped into view.

"You are needed for more chemical testing," his stoic voice announced.

The newly teenage girl fought the urge to roll her eyes. "Can I do it later? I was just about to beat a high score by counting how many bricks are on the ceiling."

"That was not a request."

"Can I still do it later?"

Paige felt the guard dressed in nothing but raven's glare through his goggles despite being unable to see his eyes.

"I'll take that as a no."

Blonde hair trailed behind Paige as the guard grabbed her by the arm with his gloved hand so tightly that she was expecting a bruise the next morning. Paige followed him through the familiar halls of the warehouse she yearned to escape from on the daily. Everything was the same, from the walls to the floors to even the people passing by the halls. They all had the same black uniform, goggles, and an assortment of weapons on their belts.

There was no escape.

Paige gave up on that years ago.

"So...," the girl awkwardly spoke to the guard dragging her along, "what are you guys doing to me this time? Didn't you inject me with heroin last time?"

The guard did not answer.

"I'm just curious. I'm not going to fight back. Will you not tell me?"

This time, Paige's head snapped to the right when a gloved hand made contact with her cheek. The young girl yelped and grasped the side of her face where a pink handprint was already starting to form. She stared pleadingly at the man next to her, but he shook his head dismissively and led her into the room straight ahead.

Less than five minutes later, behind that closed door, a scream ripped out that could be heard throughout the whole warehouse. Restraints were placed upon Paige as she was lowered onto a table. Needles penetrated the skin on her arms, legs, and stomach. It was not the physical pain that projected her hollering, choking sobs through the building; it was on the emotional side. The organization was getting exactly what they wanted:

Control.

Paige had no idea it was even her birthday that day. She had forgotten years ago. The ebbing pain, no matter how stale or numbing it had become, however, was never forgotten.

It never would be.

Droplets of warm water cascaded down the naked frame of said girl several years later. Steam floated from the tiled floor beneath her feet to the ceiling before it evaporated entirely and allowed the process to rewind and play from the beginning. Paige pressed down on the soap dispenser on a shelf in the shower and scrubbed her arms with the foam it deposited. It was not too terribly often that Paige had this opportunity, so she took advantage of every instance she was blessed with the luxury.

After rinsing off every crook and crevice of her bony body, she leaned forward and allowed her straight hair to fall in front of her. She brushed her fingers through the strands which smoothed with each comb. The showerhead above produced the only element that prevented her frame from feeling

CHAPTER TWENTY-TWO

nothing at all. Once all of the chamomile soap withered its way down the drain, Paige turned the faucet to the right and shut off the shower. She reached out from the curtain and grabbed the nearest towel off the rack.

Paige stepped out of the shower into the breeze that nipped at every inch of her skin. She wasted no time drying herself off wherever she could. She watched as cool water dripped from her hair onto the matt beneath her toes. Once more, she flipped her hair in front of her and began drying it off so she would not track it all over the house. That would have been suspicious, but then again, she did not know what to expect other than the beads soaking into the carpet.

She certainly did not expect a sleepy Peyton to waltz into the bathroom without knocking.

Paige was not one to scream, but she surely was one to be startled. At an instant, she turned away from him and wrapped the towel snugly around herself. Tentatively, she looked over her shoulder and through her drenched hair at Peyton. He was still wearing an oversized t-shirt and a pair of fluffy pajama pants from the previous night. Peyton still neglected to realize another person was in the room while brushing his teeth thoroughly with his blue toothbrush.

That was...until Paige turned all the way around and cleared her throat.

Peyton dropped his toothbrush into the sink. "What the hell?!" he blubbered through a mouthful of spearmint toothpaste.

"I believe you interrupted me," Paige explained the obvious.

"You were being so quiet that I didn't even notice you." He spat a mixture of saliva and toothpaste into the sink and hurriedly cleaned up after himself.

"You should've knocked."

"I'm sorry. I was half asleep and wasn't expecting someone to be in my bathroom."

"I've been staying here for what? Two weeks now?"

Peyton filled up the Star Wars cup that lived in his bathroom with water and gurgled it in his mouth, spitting it out a moment later. "To be honest, I haven't been keeping track."

"Can I have some privacy?" Paige changed the subject. "Please?"

"Yeah, just give me a minute." Peyton retracted his arms through his sleeves and pulled his shirt off from his body.

The blonde girl blinked at him. "...What are you doing?"

"Getting ready for a shower." He tossed his shirt in the sink. "Do you mind?"

"No."

"Then why are you looking?"

Paige could not help it. She had never really seen a boy her age without the upper half of his body covered. He was not one of those individuals in novels she had overheard civilians and college students speaking about who had six-packs and muscles all over. Instead, Peyton looked like a regular healthy boy, perhaps the slightest bit underweight, but she figured that was due to genetics since Lucas Finlay was small as well. Still, something unknown compelled her to take more than just a sneak peek of Peyton's figure. There was nothing special about him...

...or was there?

That was when she realized she was *truly* staring.

"Uh, oh." Paige blinked away from him.

The next thing Peyton was aware of was Paige disappearing through a self-created vortex in the floor that closed a second later.

Peyton scratched his head, pausing for a second or two before he continued to undress himself to prepare for a shower.

"*Huh. That's new. At least we're even now,*" he thought with a chuckle, remembering not too long ago when Paige walked in on him taking a shower.

Paige reappeared in the guest room-turned-her room and continued drying herself off. She wore nothing but a crimson blush until she yanked on a pair of ripped jeans she wore almost every day and a band t-shirt. Lastly, she pulled her black sweater over her arms and yanked it tight around her back. Paige opened the drawer in the nightstand next to her bed and began brushing her wet hair out with a brush she discovered inside it. Peyton must have put it there for her to use.

Her mind never left Peyton throughout the whole time she was getting dressed in the confines of her room. How, after at least two weeks, maybe three at this point, has he managed to be nothing but kind to her? First, Paige broke into his house, began living there, and was taking advantage of everything in it. Still, she did not feel guiltier than she needed to.

Why?

Because Peyton *gave* it to her.

Where she was before, nothing was given to her but torture, isolation, and most of all, overbearing control. The absence of such was something she was still getting used to. Other than hiding herself from Peyton's parents, who were already as sweet as pie - which she had yet to try; Caroline made wonderful dinners and desserts that Peyton snuck up to her - Paige had free reign of the house. Now that Peyton knew about her secret identity, she could freely complete her homework on the office computer while he was present rather than sneaking out in the middle of the night.

Secrets being revealed were terrifying but simultaneously liberating.

By the time Peyton took a shower, got dressed, and

ventured into the kitchen to grab breakfast - plus an extra serving for Paige; his mother thought he was very hungry because of the fact he took four slices of cinnamon toast that he stuffed in his backpack - the girl herself was already outside. She had her tote bag slung over her shoulder and her sweater wrapped snugly around her frame, which still was too oversized to do the job correctly. Apparently, the way Paige was leaning against the edge of the garage door frame when Peyton opened it from the inside and rolled his bike out was startling.

"Holy–uh, hey, Paige," he faltered and shut the door behind him. "What are you doing out here?"

"We have school. Remember?"

"You, uh, what? I thought...*oh*. That's right."

Paige fought back a smile and lost the battle. "You forgot already?"

"No, I just..." Peyton's attempt to explain drastically failed. "It's going to take a bit to get used to. It's not every day that two people merge into one."

"Very true." She pointed at the electric blue bicycle. "You aren't going to need that, are you?"

"If you can't teleport us that far, then yes."

"What do you expect me to do, then–ride in the basket?"

"Yes."

Paige glared at him, which made him elaborate, "I'm joking. Now, put the bike back so we can try this."

"What if it doesn't-"

"You were so supportive of me yesterday," Paige mused jokingly. "Put it back."

Peyton knew better than to disobey. He wheeled his bike back into the garage and dashed out. Instead of typing in the passcode on the keypad on the door frame opposite of which Paige was still leaning against, he mashed in the "enter" button, signaling the garage door to lower itself. Paige stood up straight and approached Peyton with one hand outstretched. When he did not immediately take it, she cocked her head to the side.

"What are you waiting for?" she inquired with anticipation.

"Nothing." Peyton was oblivious, gesturing to her hand. "What am I supposed to do with that?"

"Insufferable idiot," Paige playfully thought. She then clasped onto his hand herself. "Hold on, and don't scream like last time."

"You gave me no warning last time."

"Well, here's your warning. Three, two-"

Paige did not even get to one when she opened a wormhole-like passageway beneath her worn down shoes. Peyton bit back the urge to scream. The adrenaline rushing through his lungs reminded him of a roller coaster catapulting down the first massive drop. That was the only thing he could compare this sensation to. Even though it only lasted a couple of seconds, it felt like forever, falling down a rabbit hole.

When his feet touched the ground again, Peyton breathed out a sigh of relief. He opened his eyes, which had been slammed shut for the past few seconds to view Azure University's campus directly in front of him. He looked to his right and instead of Paige standing next to him, it was Penny, or at least how Peyton knew her. He rubbed his eyes, which darted between the building in front of him where several students poured in through the doors and Penny–no, *Paige*.

"Woah. That's freaky," he stammered, thankful the two were behind a tree in the yard surrounding the campus. "When did you-...you know, do that?"

"While you were busy clamping your lips shut," Paige teased him.

"How are you so *calm* during all of that?"

"Years of practice." Paige pushed her tote bag further up her shoulder. "Now, c'mon. We're going to be late."

Peyton watched Paige as she strutted forward. He had so many questions to ask her, so he needed to pick up his pace in order to do so.

He was huffing and puffing by the time he caught up to her, "So, uh...I get the fact you're the same person shapeshifted, but...when'd you find the time to do homework? I mean, you've lived with me for a while and I've never seen you do one assignment"

"I either did it in the computer lab and stayed up late or woke up in the middle of the night to use the computer in your home office."

"So *that's* what you needed the password for."

"I still don't know why your password is ButtKicking-Chicken."

"Because that's my mom for you. You've met her."

"True, but I've had to avoid them most of the time," Paige reasoned with him.

"I guess that's true, but-"

"Well, well, well. What do we have here?"

An unfamiliar voice vaguely cut Peyton and Paige's conversation directly in half. Paige stopped in her tracks just a tad before Peyton, which caused him to tread on his own toes in order not to slam into her. At first, she thought it was Hannah, but since when did she get a deeper voice and sound like she actually went through puberty? Paige looked to her left, adjusted her glasses, and assessed the boy who had just addressed the both of them.

If it were not for the icy, unnatural hue to his eyes, Paige would not have immediately recognized the brunet young man as the emotionless Dylan from Dairy King two weeks prior.

CHAPTER TWENTY-TWO

Paige made the wise decision to be quiet, but, to her horror, Peyton did not. "Who the hell are you?" he questioned suspiciously.

"So, you're the girl who had the seizure in class yesterday," Dylan blatantly ignored and pushed past him to get to Paige. "What the hell was that?"

Peyton inserted himself between the two and shoved him away. "Back off. It's none of your business."

"Why not?" he maliciously argued. "Don't you think it's weird that she's not in the hospital after such an awful thing? An ambulance came to the school and everything, but, lo and behold, you weren't there."

"It's none of your business."

Paige took a firm hold of Peyton's hand and started dragging him away from Dylan. "Come on. We need to get to class," she reminded him through gritted teeth.

"I just want to know what happened." A devious smile began to dance on Dylan's lips. "I worry about my fellow classmates, you know."

"I didn't even see you in my class," Paige retorted with a growl, "if I did, I would've noticed your blatant stupidity and low regard for others' personal matters."

"Oh ho!" he dragged out his exclamation. "Damn, Baby. You've got a mouth on you. Tell you what—I'll put that to good use, yeah?"

Peyton wrenched his hand out of Paige's and stormed towards him. "Listen here, you-"

"Come *on*!" Paige urged him along.

"But he-"

"Retaliation is what he wants. *I* would know." She dropped her voice to a whisper.

"How would you-"

Paige interrupted him with a jerk on his arm in the opposite direction. She dragged Peyton away from Dylan, the former willing to get himself into a fight with the cocky latter. Despite acting odd as the Dairy King cashier the last time the two of them got semi-acquainted, there was something different about Dylan. It was as if he was only meant to provoke, which only meant one thing:

The organization was catching on to Paige's secrecy.

"Babe, come back here!" Dylan speedwalked behind them and then wolf whistled. "Ooh, damn. That's a nice a-"

He couldn't finish his unfortunately timed catcall due to the thin rope of energy at his ankles Paige conjured at the tip of her fingers tripping him with his next step.

Peyton stifled a laugh when Dylan's face hit the floor. "Okay, that was good." He offered Paige a true compliment. "He's an asshole."

"Takes one to know one." Paige did not hide the small smirk ebbing on her face.

"Are you *mocking* me?"

"Yes. Yes, I am."

Once the two of them rounded the corner, though, Peyton's thought process became serious. "Can I ask you one thing?"

"Shoot," she replied casually.

"Do you know anything about his eyes being a weird color? That's not normal."

Paige halted next to a closed door that had a label on it: "Janitor's closet." Once again, she grasped onto Peyton's arm, opened the door halfway, and shoved Peyton inside of it. He attempted to fight back with a yelp and flailing arms, but before he could win the battle - which there was a low chance of him doing so anyway - Paige interrupted him.

"Sorry." She shut the door behind them and illuminated the darkness-filled room with an energy field above both of their heads. "I need to tell you in someplace private."

CHAPTER TWENTY-TWO

"I'm listening." Peyton's eyes flickered between her face and the lilac star-like object in between them.

"The organization is behind it. I've seen it before in their tests and experiments," Paige explained in a hushed tone. "The only reason they didn't do it to me was because they had implanted the microchip once they developed the technology to alter the brain itself."

"Alter the br–excuse me?!" he spluttered prior to Paige slamming her hand over his mouth.

"I need you to be quiet. The organization is everywhere. They, along with every local news source, are looking for me: Paige O'Connell. Not Penny Hamilton. I *can't* have publicity either way. Do you understand?"

Peyton nodded eagerly at that.

"My theory is that Dylan, along with Hannah and her two friends, have all become brainwashed by the organization," she expressed breathily, her eyes darting around as if she would be found at any second. "Ever since I escaped my apartment and from an assassination attempt on me, the organization has been on red alert. The alcohol I consumed at the fraternity party on Wednesday made the microchip malfunction and caused something similar to a seizure in the middle of class yesterday. That's what Dylan is talking about. I *can't* let him know the microchip is out of my body or he will tell the organization and they will come after me. They think I'm dead."

Peyton pried her hand from his mouth. "Wouldn't they know you're still alive from the microchip's functionality?"

"That's where the experimentality comes in. They don't know what would happen if I died with it in me. They probably won't question the fact it was shut off when you removed it because it's all part of their experiments; they don't know if it would take a while to shut off after its host had been terminated."

"So, hang on." Peyton's eyebrows furrowed with thought. "You mean to tell me that there are quite possibly four people under the organization's control who think you're dead but are patrolling the school to terrorize you? Do we know if *they* have microchips too?"

"This is where I don't know." Paige averted her eyes from Peyton and watched the floating orb. She flicked the fingers of her right hand and studied it as it began to spin. "If they are under their control, then it would be under newer technology, which I don't know much about. I hope that's where your friend, Leo, will help us."

Peyton placed a comforting hand on her shoulder. "He's good with tech stuff and I'd hope I'm good with doctor stuff, including brain stuff. I'll do my best to research with him."

"Are you sure?"

"Positive." Peyton tried to pop the energy orb with his finger, but it remained intact. "How do you pop it?"

Thankfully, Paige smiled. "Like this?" She poked the ball with her index finger and darkness shrouded the room once more so she could not see Peyton's reaction. "Come on. I don't have anything else I can tell you, so we might as well get to class."

"Sounds like a plan."

Peyton followed Paige out of the janitor's closet and into the busy hallway of the university. The two of them continued on their route to their United States History classroom, which was no more than a hop, skip, and a jump away–not literally, of course. The fact the classroom was less than half full despite them being at least a minute or two late was promising. Even the professor had not arrived yet. Instead of sitting behind

Paige this time, Peyton sat to her side, which the former appreciated very much.

Paige removed her notebook from her tote bag and placed it on her desk along with her pouch of pencils, pens, and other stationery supplies she might need for a school day. She flipped open the notebook to a fresh page and wrote the date on top along with her class' title. She could hardly believe that the end of September was nearing quicker than her mind could grasp.

"Hey, Pai—I mean, *Penny*," a voice from next to her hissed.

The girl snapped her head to the right to view Peyton awkwardly holding what looked to be a bag of bread out towards her. "I brought cinnamon toast for us to share. Mom made breakfast...I forgot."

This time, Paige could not conceal her smile. "I'll save mine for lunch," she replied, pushing the bag delicately towards him with her fingertips. "Thank you, though."

"You're welcome." Peyton returned the gesture.

Some sort of magnetic force seemed to have pulled the two of them closer together over the past couple of weeks. Peyton noticed this was occurring when he could not take his eyes off of her for most of the seventy-five minutes of class. Somehow, the way Penny - no, *Paige* - scribbled down notes and looking in between the whiteboard and her work was alluring. Every so often, she adjusted her glasses to keep them from falling off her face. Peyton knew she didn't need them, but he thought they were endearing anyway.

Then, Peyton realized he was taking absolutely no notes of his own. The document that was open on his laptop consisted of nothing but the date at the top.

Eighty-five minutes came and went, and eventually, the two of them left Dr. Mike's class. Like clockwork, the duo approached the university's café. It was then that Paige finally looked at the sign above at the name:

"The Usual."

"The usual what?" Paige thought to herself. *"That's a dumb name."*

It was only when Peyton and Paige stopped at the end of the line leading into the buffet when the latter understood the meaning from the former. "The usual?" Peyton inquired.

"Uh, sure."

Peyton put a cheeseburger and a container of fries on his tray for Paige. He left room to place a chicken wrap and another fry container for himself on the other half of the tray.

"Thank you."

"No problem. Lunch is on me."

"You don't have to pay for me," Paige assured him. "I have...money."

"I can get it," countered Peyton, grinning like Paige was enamored by. "It really is no trouble. The food is cheap here."

"And surprisingly good."

Paige bit her tongue when they reached the register and Peyton instantly paid for both of their meals with his credit card. He did not even bat an eye when the price popped up on the screen. Paige tried not to look at it, but she did anyway. Peyton might have thought the food was inexpensive, but to Paige, he lived like royalty.

"Thank you, Peyton," she genuinely expressed her gratitude.

Peyton could not hide his smile. There was something about the way she said his name... "You're welcome."

Paige's stomach rumbled with the promise of food. She was blessed with the luxury of Peyton treating her to lunch at the university - no, "The Usual" - café most days the two of them saw each other. Now that Peyton knew she and Penny were the same, the two were even more inseparable than they were before. Paige hardly remembered the times where she had to sit on city streets posing as a little girl strapped for cash to have a bite to eat from a kind stranger.

Her heart sank with the reminder that Leo's parents were two instances of kind strangers.

There was something off about the entire situation. It was *wrong*.

Just as the two of them were about to sit down, Paige paused and mumbled almost incoherently, "I'll be back. There's something I need to do."

"What?" Peyton already had at least three fries in his mouth. "Your food will get cold...and eaten."

Paige rolled her eyes. "Then guard it." Her lips twitched upward just a tad, knowing Peyton would merely be guarding her food from himself...which most likely would not end well.

"Yes, Ma'am."

"Block for me."

Despite not understanding, Peyton did as he was told and stood in front of Paige. Thankfully, the wall was on the other side because she vanished through another vortex at Peyton's feet. Peyton did not want to look strange, standing next to a table staring at the wall when he had a tray of food in front of him. The rest of the café's customers were either waiting in line for their lunches or consuming what they bought. Peyton decided to do the same.

After a few minutes of scrolling on his phone, Paige reappeared in the seat between him and the wall. Peyton could not conceal his flinch when she suddenly made her presence known by stealing one of his fries.

"Hey!" He swatted at her hand. "You have your own!"

"Like you said, they might be cold right now," Paige retorted playfully.

"You were hardly gone for five minutes. It's not cold."

Paige popped a fry in her mouth and began unwrapping her burger. "True."

"Where did you even go?"

"Oh, uh," Paige stammered in between two hurried bites of her cheeseburger, which she swallowed down to elaborate, "I was just taking care of some loose ends."

Peyton did not need to know about the red and yellow paper bag sitting at the Rhys' front door along with two caramel hot chocolates.

Not now, at least.

Chapter Twenty-Three

BLUE

"No, no, *no*! I don't want to die! Not yet! Not now!"

"*Oh, stop being so dramatic!*" Peyton retorted over the phone. "*It's not my fault you suck at Crush Bros!*"

Leo smashed buttons on his controller as quickly as he could–it was at lightning speed to him. "All it is is spamming buttons. I don't understand why I suck at that!"

"*You're too dainty with the controller. It's called "Crush" for a reason.*"

"What do you think I'm doing?!"

"*Delicately pressing each button waiting for something to happen?*"

"I'm *smashing* them."

"*Okay, then. I'm just better than you.*"

"Hey!"

Leo frowned at his television screen. His room was comfortable and neater than the average teenager's. Take Peyton's for example. He rarely made his bed, clothes covered most of the carpeted floor, and let us just say he hardly took time to dust off most surfaces. He was too busy for that. Leo, on the other hand, possessed a greater appreciation for cleanliness. His room was as neat as a pin. His bed was made, the carpet was recently vacuumed, and his clothes were all neatly folded and organized in his dresser drawers. Even the top of the television mounted on the wall had been recently wiped clean.

Everything around Leo was neat, from the living room and kitchen on the downstairs floor all the way to the closets connected to bedrooms and the perfectly trimmed yard around the house. Next to Peyton's house, the Rhys' home appeared to be perfect. Of course, there was nothing wrong with the Finlays' household. Leo's parents along with himself enjoy keeping the house as tidy as possible.

The large, bold letters reading "Game over" flashed in Leo's face. He fought the urge to toss his controller on the floor when Peyton started chanting over the phone.

"I won! I won! In your face, Leo!"

Leo just shook his head. "I hear you, Moron."

"You're the one who lost."

"Yeah, yeah. Very funny."

There was silence on the other end of the line. If Leo leaned into the phone, which was on speaker anyway, he could hear Peyton and another voice murmuring about something incoherent and inaudible. He was not trying to snoop, but he was very curious about what was occurring in the house next door. Ever since the miniature surgery that Peyton performed on Paige yesterday - and Leo's frequent trips to the restroom even after he left - everything had been...different.

Weird was the only word Leo could use to describe it.

First of all, Peyton had *never* been around a girl in his life. Suddenly, he had one living with him.

Secondly, this girl had a microchip in her neck that he was investigating.

Last, but certainly not least, this girl had...superpowers? Shapeshifting was the only one he had witnessed so far. He wondered how many more that she had.

Once again, weird...but cool too.

Definitely cool.

Peyton's voice paraded its way through the speaker, nearly making Leo drop his phone since he was holding it so close. *"Sorry about that. Paige just walked in and was wondering if you had any status updates on the chip."*

"Well, uh," Leo really had to scratch his head to think about his progress, "I'm taking a break right now, obviously, but I haven't found out anything yet."

"I didn't see you at school today," Peyton commented. *"Neither did Paige. Don't tell me you stayed home just to do research."*

Leo cleared his throat awkwardly. "Okay, then. I won't tell you."

"Leo!"

"What?!"

"You shouldn't waste absences like that!"

"It's not a waste if it's for something important." Leo picked up his phone off the bed and collapsed onto the mattress. "It sounds like whatever this microchip is for is important."

There were more mumbles on Peyton's end. Then, Paige's voice took over the phone and began to speak. *"Hi, Leo. The microchip was used to regulate whatever abilities I had. The organization was unsure of what I was capable of, so they chipped me to keep me stable."*

"Wait, wait. Hold on." Leo rolled over onto his feet, dashed across the room, and yanked a notebook as well as a pencil off of his desk that he used for school. "So, it was used generally to control and stabilize you and your abilities. Did it do anything when you challenged that control?"

"*Um...*" There was a pause on Peyton and Paige's end. The latter knew the answer, but she was hesitant in revealing it. "Compare it to a shock collar on a dog. Basically, it did the same thing to me if I disobeyed or went too far. Or...if it was manually set off."

Peyton was quick to begin interrogating. "*You mean to tell me someone set it off on purpose? How many times has this happened?*"

"More than I can count. The person in charge of me, Dr. Kelley, did it a lot when I had a "smart" attitude towards him. He basically considered me his pet and I had to do whatever he said."

"*Can I kill him? Please? I want to kill this bast-*"

"No. That's my job."

Leo quietly intervened, "Neither of you will until I figure out this chip and make sure whatever you two end up doing is safe."

"We don't have anything planned," Paige asserted in a neutral tone. "Yet."

"*Yet?! Are we going to go on another mission to that crackhouse?!*"

"Enough, Peyton."

"*What? I'm just asking the logical questions here.*"

"I don't believe that's in your existence description."

"*Excuse me?!*"

"You two act like an old married couple," Leo observed passively from the sidelines.

"*Shut up,*" the both of them chorused in unison.

The redhead pouted. "*Why are you two so mean to me?!*"

"Because it's fun," Peyton replied at the same time Paige did: "Because it's simple."

Leo was once again about to retort when there was a knock

at his door. "Hold up," he instructed his two friends on the phone and redirected his attention to whoever was on the other side of his bedroom door. "Yeah?"

"It's Mom!" Rebekah's sweet voice rang through the wood like a crystal doorbell against the wind–fragile, but melodious.

"Sorry, you two, but I've got to go," Leo picked up the phone and turned it off of speaker mode. "I'll be back later. I'm pretty sure it's dinnertime."

"Okay, see you later!" Peyton exclaimed in his usual optimistic tone.

Paige was second to politely respond, *"See you, and thank you for your help."*

"No problem. Call you later." He hung up the phone and slid it into his pocket.

Suddenly, Leo felt truly useful. He knew Peyton and Paige were merely joking on him, but being helpful was wonderful for his self-esteem. He rose to his feet and put his notebook back on his desk before walking to the door and opening it. There was his mother, with the same black curls she wore every single day, but she still managed to make her husband's jaw drop every morning at the break of dawn. Her pearly smile was evident. Despite the fact Leo was almost always greeted with that expression, it spurred a growth of joy in his chest.

"Hey, Mom." He stood in the doorway. "What's up?"

"I was going to call you down for dinner. Your father just got home and found a bag from McDanny's on our front porch. He has no idea where they came from."

"You mean someone got us food?" Leo perked up at the promise of supper.

"I can't think of any other reason why there would be food on the front porch." Rebekah shrugged, ushering her son out of the doorway and towards the stairs. "Now, come on. Your dad said there's three meals in it, so I guess dinner is taken care of."

"What are they?" The ginger dashed down the stairs and landed on the bottom floor with a thud.

"Looks like three cheeseburgers with fries," Dan, Leo's father, replied from the kitchen. "Whoever got this for us has taste. Gotta love a good cheeseburger every now and then."

"But *who* got us dinner?"

"We don't know," Rebekah and Dan confirmed at the same time.

Leo took his phone out of his pocket and texted the most recent contact on his messages app. *"Hey, Dude, did you get us dinner from McDanny's? Because you totally didn't have to."*

He totally expected his best friend next door to have bought them food. The Finlays were very kind, generous people who were like a mule with a spinning wheel; they had a whole lot of money and no clue what to do with it. Sometimes, the two families treated each other to meals, but such planned occasions would occur at restaurants, not out of the blue. This was why Leo was less surprised than he thought when Peyton texted back.

"No? I didn't buy you dinner."

"Oh. Do you know who could've?"

"Not a clue."

"Very helpful. Thanks." Leo sent a sarcastic emoji, to which Peyton responded with a couple of crying laughing ones.

"Well, who cares who got it for us? I'm starving!" Dan announced to pretty much the whole neighborhood.

Rebekah started putting the meals out onto plates. "Sounds good to me." She handed one to Leo. "Here you are, Sweetheart."

"Thanks, Mom." Leo took the plate from her and headed towards the living room.

"Honey, you know most families sit down at the kitchen

CHAPTER TWENTY-THREE

table for dinner," Rebekah commented, slowly raising her voice when her husband followed their son.

"I wanted to watch the baseball game!" Dan pouted like he was three years old. "Can we eat in the living room just this once?"

The middle-aged woman exhaled animatedly, "You've said that every night for the past three years, Dan. We never sit at the kitchen table anymore."

"But I want to watch the game and spend time with you two," protested her husband. "It's not every day that a game is on TV."

"We can spend time together at the table."

"And in the living room," Leo piped up helpfully.

Rebekah did not think her son was contributing to the correct side, though. "Okay, who votes to sit in the living room and watch the game?"

Both Dan and Leo raised their hands.

"I guess I shouldn't bother asking for votes on the other option unless Ollie learns how to raise his paw."

"Yes!" The father and son duo chanted and gave each other a fist bump.

With an amused roll to her eyes, Rebekah turned off the kitchen light and followed her husband and son into the living room. She and Leo sat down on the couch while Dan made himself comfortable in his recliner. The Arkford Blue Warriors away baseball game was already on the television and seemed to be in the top of the third inning.

"Wait a second," Rebekah interrupted both Leo and Dan before they were about to take their first bites of food.

"What?" the two of them questioned.

"We need to say grace."

"Oh. Whoops."

"Leo, would you like to bless the food?" Rebekah smiled at

her son while her husband muted the television with the remote on the arm of his chair.

"Sure." All three of them bowed their heads and closed their eyes. "Lord, thank you for the food in front of us that some random stranger bought for us, which was really nice. Please bless it to our bodies and let us have a great rest of our night. Amen."

The family opened their eyes in unison. Rebekah's face gleamed with pride. "That was lovely, Honey."

"Thanks, Mom," Leo replied with his mouth full.

"Leo! Manners."

"Sorry." He swallowed down a rather large bite of cheeseburger before apologizing.

Dan unmuted the television and started watching the game along with digging into his fries. "Man, McDanny's never fails to make a hell of a good cheeseburger."

"Yup," Leo agreed, suddenly objecting to a play on the TV. "Oh, come on! That was out!"

"The umpire made a bad call," Dan explained to his son.

"That was absolute BS."

Rebekah shook her head, daintily picking at her food like she was some sort of bird. "It's so wonderful having the family together for dinner."

It surely was. Even though none of them knew Paige was the mysterious donor, all of them were sincerely grateful. An invisible lesson was learned:

Good deeds possessed good karma.

Chapter Twenty-Four

GLAZED

Hope was a complicated subject that Paige had clung onto her whole life. What would happen when it eventually slips through her fingers?
She was about to find out.

Grasping onto someone's promise for just over two weeks now was becoming overwhelming. At first, it was easy. Her mind was an analog clock, ticking slowly and steadily, but relying on a battery to keep itself going. The tick-tock of the clock resembled her heartbeat throughout these two weeks. With each passing day, it became slower and slower until it kept her up at night. It was as if she could feel time moving. At first, she thought she knew everything. Now, without the aid of a much-needed answer, her reality was forgetting everything she had ever learned about herself and the world around her.

There was something occurring behind the walls of the warehouse the organization owned. Paige knew that fact by heart. That did not keep the clock in her chest from gradually declining and eventually needing a new battery. Paige was at that point right then and there. At first, she blamed her mistrusting nature on her youth, but then, when she discussed this matter with Peyton, she was reassured that she was, in fact, not being "youthful" at all.

"I wish I wasn't so impatient," Paige muttered in the midst of playing a racing game with Peyton on his room's television.

"What do you mean?" he inquired, keeping his eyes on the screen.

"It's just that...," she paused to consider her wording, "I wish I knew what was going on. It hasn't been long, but I really want Leo to hurry up with his research. How long does that take?"

"Honestly, I don't know. It should be soon, though."

"You said that three days ago."

Peyton subconsciously shifted his body to make a wide turn in the game, accidentally leaning against Paige's frame before scooting away, red in the face. "I know, but I trust Leo. He will let us know what he knows as soon as he gets the information."

"How do you know for sure?" Paige's eyes were larger than she wanted them to be.

"Because he's my brother and I know he won't let us down. He won't let you down."

Paige, albeit hesitant, nodded. "Thank you," she acknowledged.

"You're welcome."

Despite how many times Peyton had assured her of Leo's diligence to the task, Paige thought he had simply given up by that point. It reminded her of herself, spending years upon years in a cell with nothing but the mortar between the bricks and the occasional ball of energy she created to entertain her. Even though she had been avoiding that environment for quite some time now, her mind never took the leap and joined her on the greener side.

Being disappointed and feeling hopeless was merely... nothing new.

Paige glared at her notebook like it had done something terrible to her, as if it had betrayed her in some drastic way. In a way, it had, due to the blank page in front of her filled only with the date at the top and scribbles since she had no idea how to draw anything other than a smiley face. Instead of watching Dr. Mike animatedly discuss the Patriots versus the British Redcoats, she caught herself drifting off into thought. Every so often, she would shake her head in order to snap out of whatever trance her mind hypnotized her with and return to reality.

From next to her, Peyton would pitch a little smirk every time she did so. He would never say anything, but he found Paige's way of paying attention to be adorable...and funny.

"Okay, class," Dr. Mike exclaimed to the jam-packed room in front of him, "who can name at least one of the unalienable rights from the Declaration of Independence?"

Peyton's hand shot up in the air.

The professor smiled at such enthusiasm. "Yes, Peyton?"

"The three certain unalienable rights listed in the Declaration are life, liberty, and the pursuit of happiness," he answered confidently.

"Very good!" Dr. Mike shot him a smile and clicked onto the next slide in his presentation. "Now, these rights are unarguably the most important part of the Declaration of Independence. Without these three rights explicitly stated, we would not be the country we are today."

Peyton blinked at the notebook that Paige had passed him. The page she was staring at was not practically blank anymore. Instead, delicately written letters spelling out "Kiss-ass" looked right up at him. He whirled his head towards Paige, who he was still getting used to being in class with him, and just sighed with a little grin on his face, passing the notebook back to her.

Paige was getting used to pulling "pranks," as Peyton called them. She thought back to when Peyton mentioned the time when he poured an entire glass of water on Leo's head to wake him up as well as dropping his cat, Ollie, on him. Ever since the two started living in the same house, Paige noticed she had begun picking up on some of his habits, especially teasing.

Of course, Peyton did not mind. He found it to be quite endearing.

There he was, sitting up as stiff as a board while typing in every possible word he could fit into his document relating to Dr. Mike's lecture. Paige looked down at her own paper and erased the remark towards Peyton before inserting the tip of the eraser between her teeth and twiddling the pencil around. Her professor sounded like a radio station that was out of range. Nothing was intelligible.

At least, Paige thought that was the case when Peyton's phone started vibrating from on top of his desk.

Peyton took one look at the caller identification on his phone and rose to his feet. Paige watched him as he abruptly strutted across the classroom, swung open the door, and closed it quietly behind him. Even when the doorknob stopped moving, Paige's eyes were glued on the door. A small window separated the two of them that Paige could barely see through, but she could just make out Peyton pacing around in the hallway.

"Hey, Leo. What's up?" he inquired in a soft tone as to not disturb his classmates.

"I just found out something huge about the chip!" Leo yelled enthusiastically through the phone. *"Is Paige there? She'll want to know this."*

Peyton leaned over to peer through the small window in the door. He caught Paige's attention instantaneously, espe-

CHAPTER TWENTY-FOUR

cially since she was already watching in that direction. He gestured with his free hand for her to join him, which she did. Paige erupted from her seat and half-walked, half-jogged to the door while the professor continued to ramble about the Declaration of Independence. She understood the importance of the lesson, but she could learn about it anytime via the internet.

"What's going on?" Paige demanded to know once she shut the door behind her.

"Leo found something," explained Peyton, setting his phone to speaker mode. "What'd you find, Leo?"

"*This chip has a connection to a confidential database regarding the organization you were aligned with, Paige,*" Leo spoke hurriedly. "*It's all here on my screen. Using the chip, I was able to hack into the organization's files. Everything's here. Everything. I wish I could show you because it's too much to explain over the phone.*"

"We'll be there in ten," Paige took the phone from Peyton and then handed it back to him.

Peyton simply stood there, frozen, while Paige returned to the classroom and scooped up Peyton's laptop and backpack along with her notebook, pencil case, and tote bag. She started towards the door, unaware of the entire classroom's eyes on her. Dr. Mike had stopped mid-sentence. The room was so quiet a pin dropping would be audible. Paige stopped in her tracks with her arms full of she and Peyton's belongings.

Dr. Mike cleared his throat. "Um, Penny, is everything okay?"

"I-...um...*yes*," she stuttered out, trying to think of a lie. "Family emergency. Peyton offered to drive me home."

"Oh, alright, then." Dr. Mike scratched the back of his head with visible concern. "I hope everyone is okay. Please update me on the situation."

Paige nodded, a polite smile on her face. "I will."

Without waiting for a response, Paige burst through the door by kicking it open. She tossed Peyton his things, which he caught not before they bounced in his hands several times. Paige grabbed a hold of his arm and led him down the numerous hallways. Despite them being clear of their peers, there was nothing wrong with taking precautions. Once the two of them were out of sight of any possible person, even a student merely walking to the restroom, Paige made the two of them vanish through a vortex beneath their feet.

The scene in front of them when their teleportation was complete. Paige and Peyton were now standing in the middle of Leo's room where the boy had slowly wheeled his chair around from his laptop screen. His jaw was on the floor as well as his phone, which had slipped through his fingers once the two of them appeared. Paige still had a firm grip on Peyton's arm, but she quickly let go when she realized what situation they were in.

"Hey, you didn't scream this time," Paige noted teasingly.

"Oh." Peyton's complexion flushed. "I guess I didn't."

"You mean...," Leo stammered, looking between the two of them. "This is *normal*? I thought you meant ten minutes–not ten seconds!"

"Well, this one is full of surprises." The blond boy patted her shoulder.

Paige tentatively brushed it off. "Now, what did you find?" she directed towards Leo.

Leo turned his chair around to his computer screen. "Everything," he replied wistfully. "Simply everything. I don't know where to start."

"The beginning would be helpful," Peyton commented.

"Not helpful."

Paige fought back a flicker of a smile, pressing her lips

together into a thin line. "The beginning would be a great place to start."

"So, that's where we'll begin." Leo backspaced a couple of times on his laptop and began to explain. "It took a while to actually get into the chip's database, but once I did, I uncovered many strategies and experimental data leading to one common goal." He turned to look at Paige. "Control, which is *exactly* what they used this chip for–as you said."

"That's nothing new."

Leo whirled around and typed into his computer. "I'm aware of that, which is why I dug deeper to figure out how exactly they would get this control. It turns out that the base of this microchip contains elements of Endiridium, which is a mostly unknown chemical that can be altered to the user's needs. As the name suggests, it has endless possibilities. Have you ever heard this word before?"

"No," Paige admitted almost hesitantly.

"The organization has been using this...Endiridium to control you with a light dosage," Leo elaborated on the element. "From this database and the research done on this chemical compound, a higher dosage would mean more control. This is just common sense. It says here-" Leo pointed to a small grouping of text aligned by bullet points on his screen. "-that four individuals have been given said dosage through a vaccine rather than a microchip. Since it is in their bloodstream, it will obtain better results."

Peyton rested his elbows on the desk and stared at the laptop. "So, like a lobotomy of sorts?"

"Exactly. These four people still have the Endiridium in their system, as far as we know." Leo clicked on a folder. "Visible symptoms of this affecting a person include blue, glazed eyes, almost zombie-like movements, and behavior significantly different than their own. This element brings out the worst in them for the organization's gain."

"My God..." The dots connected like a puzzle piece falling into place. She tried snapping her fingers like Peyton did when he had an idea, but miserably failed. She ignored the amused look Peyton was giving her. "I know who the four are."

"That quickly?" Peyton blubbered out like he was some sort of drowning goldfish.

"It's Hannah, her two friends, and Dylan."

"Dylan?" Leo inquired obliviously.

"Some weird guy from Dairy King who harassed Paige in the hallway at school," Peyton grumbled.

"How did you not figure it out before?" Paige exhaled a long sigh. "I explained it to you in the janitor's closet on Friday."

"Friday?" Leo looked between the two of them. "Janitor's closet? Are you two not telling me something?"

"No!" Peyton and Paige fussed at him.

"Okay, okay. Carry on."

Paige stood up straight and began to pace around Leo's irritatingly spotless room. "The Endiridium being in their bloodstream is obviously causing the brainwashing. Leo, did the database say anything about a reversal?"

"No." Leo scanned the screen desperately. "I've looked for at least three hours now."

"We need to figure out a way to reverse the effect from these four innocent people."

"Innocent?" Peyton questioned her. "But Hannah's a bi-"

"Don't you remember what Leo said a minute ago?" Paige was exasperated by Peyton's naïvity. "This chemical causes behavior that is almost, if not, *exactly*, the opposite behavior than normal. If Hannah acts like this under the influence of Endiridium, then she's probably one of the sweetest people on this planet, which is why we *have* to save her, her friends, and Dylan."

"But how are we going to do that?"

"We need to think of a plan." Paige stopped short when an idea floated into her mind. "Leo. How good are your hacking capabilities?"

"I'd say pretty good after being able to hack into a microchip." Leo shrugged.

Peyton agreed, elbowing his best friend in the upper arm, "Yeah. He's freakishly good."

"Very well, then." Paige lifted her tone to be one of authority. "Leo, I would like for you to try to hack into the organization's system to see if they have any Endiridium on hand. If they do, and if you can, try to find the room number and floor where it's stashed. I'll have it back by the next morning. *Please.*"

"Woah, woah, woah," Peyton hurriedly interrupted. "You're going to go in there and steal some of the precious chemicals they're using to control people? This is crazy!"

"There's no other way."

"Yes, there is." The boy stood tall next to her. "You're not doing it alone because I'm going to help you."

"Absolutely not," Paige dismissed his offer.

"Absolutely yes, and you can't say no to us because we're all in this together."

Leo held his head in his hands. "No not a *High School Musical* moment."

"Please let us help, Paige," Peyton ignored Leo, who looked as if he wanted to disappear. "I promise I won't ask any questions and I'll be inconspicuous. I just want to be able to watch your back and make sure we both get out of there in one piece."

"I'll help too." Leo rose his head from his hands with a confident expression. "I can try to hack into security cameras if they have them and give you guys headphones and stuff. It'll be like something out of *James Bond!*"

Paige paused before finally caving, "Just don't take this too lightly. Either of you."

"I promise," the both of them swore.

The blonde girl's hazel irises had a different glint in them right then and there. For years, she had been on her own. Hope unraveled from her blanket of dignity with each passing second, which became minutes, hours, days, and eventually... years. Now, the two boys in front of her had taken hold of a needle and were slowly beginning to sew her confidence back together stitch by stitch.

Ultimately, relief glided its way into her lungs.

Leo then timidly brought up: "I do have one question, though."

"What's that?" Paige snapped out of her imagination.

"Does the organization have a name, or is it just called "the organization?"" Leo asked between air quotes. "Because if it's the latter, that's a really dumb name."

"Yeah. It's even worse than the O.W.C.A.," Peyton agreed with him. "It literally stands for "Organization Without a Cool Acronym."

Leo smacked Peyton upside the head. "You moron. Perry the Platypus is their top employee, which automatically makes them cool. This one has some weird scientist dudes who want to control college students. That's weird."

"Agreed," both Paige and Peyton nodded, despite the former having no clue what O.W.C.A. was in the first place...or what a platypus was.

"So," Paige inquired after a moment or two of silence. "Shall we begin?"

Leo stood up from his chair, picked up his laptop, and moved over to his bed. He sat down in the middle of it and motioned for the both of them to join him. Paige sat on Leo's left and Peyton was on his right as he opened up a new document—a blank page full of new opportunities.

His eyes landed on Peyton, and then on Paige. He smiled brighter than before. "Let's do it."

Chapter Twenty-Five

PERIWINKLE

Paige pulled the hood of a navy-blue sweatshirt that Peyton pretty much gave up on letting her "borrow" and cracked her knuckles. Her hazel eyes scanned the screen of Leo's laptop as if her life depended on it. The redhead was typing in some sort of coding language that Paige could not even begin to comprehend. Peyton did not try to look over his shoulder, instead resorting to pacing around the room shrouded in worry.

His footsteps were like a ticking time bomb, simply waiting to go off at any second. The rhythmic beating against the carpet of Peyton's bedroom. Paige sat on Peyton's desk, which he protested to for at least two seconds, but once he realized how comfortable she looked and how her legs were swinging back and forth with content, he caved and figured she was too lightweight to break the desk.

He learned that particular "breaking the desk" lesson the hard way.

"Are you going to be done with that sometime today?" Peyton asked impatiently without breaking his stride.

"I told you," Leo countered calmly, not missing a beat in his typing marathon, "I'll be done before noon."

"We have enough absences to skip, though."

"I only use mine in case of emergencies."

"I'd say this is considered an emergency."

"Neither of you will need to use one-" Paige hopped down from the desk and adjusted the hood on her head, "-because I'll be back with plenty of time to spare. Leo, what's the progress on those security cameras you're working on?"

"I'm calibrating my incognito user broadcast with each security camera that will be pointing in your direction during the route you will take. It's about ninety percent completed."

"Already?" Peyton blubbered out. "I thought you've only been here for twenty minutes."

Leo continued typing at a flawless tempo. "More like two hours. I'm making phenomenal time."

"I don't understand any of this technical stuff, so I'm going to say...*great job?*"

"Thank you."

"You're welcome."

Paige rolled her eyes at the obvious sarcasm that Peyton neglected to catch as he continued to circle the room. "Can you stop pacing?"

"I will when you stop kicking my desk," Peyton retorted.

The girl looked down at her bare feet and the fact they continued kicking the vertical wooden surface containing three drawers. Paige's cheeks heated into a flowery pink. At once, and to Peyton's amusement, she became still.

"I was joking," clarified a grinning Peyton. "Just don't dent it."

Paige felt as if her head was about to explode from embarrassment. "Oh."

Peyton chuckled at her reaction, "I hope you know I'm just teasing, Paige."

"There's something about the way he says...my name..." Paige's inner voice was as fluttery as her chest—a foreign feeling, really. She cleared her throat and composed herself. "Right."

She did not miss the lingering smirk on Leo's face while his eyes were still on the screen. He had never stopped typing during their few minutes of conversation, but provided a listening ear and his two cents every so often. That was what Peyton was used to, and he would not have it any other way. On the other hand, Paige was still becoming accustomed to Leo's mannerisms. She had only gotten used to Peyton's recently.

Leo watched intently with Paige's eyes over his shoulder as the bar commemorating his progress slowly filled to ninety-nine percent. That was a moment that lasted until eternity. Neither Paige, nor Leo blinked while waiting for the two-digit number to increase to three. Slowly, the pink bar crawled along. Their eyes began to burn from an extended period of time being exposed to oxygen. Then, a miracle happened.

The bar hit a hundred percent.

Paige and Leo blinked repeatedly in unison. "Thank God," the latter exclaimed, rubbing his stinging eyes. "Everything's calibrated. There are sixteen security cameras on your route."

"Perfect. Where are they?" Paige hopped down from the desk.

"Five of them are in the downstairs lobby, four are in the hallway, one is in the elevator, four are in the next hallway, and two of them are in the storage room," Leo explained, clicking on a folder that opened an overhead view of the warehouse. "This is room 378, which is on the third floor down the furthest hallway."

"You know, since I can teleport pretty much anywhere

CHAPTER TWENTY-FIVE

now, I could just go into the storage room, take the Endiridium sample, and then pop up back here."

Leo's brows furrowed while Peyton was stifling a laugh. "Okay. Well...then, you only have two security cameras to worry about."

"Exactly."

"...Then why'd you have me proof the hallways?"

Paige's mind was as blank as her response. "I don't know. Maybe just in case I can't make the wormhole into the building or something malfunctions?"

"Good idea," Leo agreed and fished through the top drawer of Peyton's desk. He revealed two headsets, one of which he handed to Paige.

"Um." Paige tentatively held the headset with both hands and studied it. "What are these?"

"They're gaming headsets. Peyton and I used to use them to whisper to each other when we were embarrassed of how late we stayed up playing video games together. Now, our parents don't care, and we can yell at each other over the phone as much as we want."

Paige cocked her head to the side. "What is with boys?"

Peyton and Leo shrugged at the same time. "We don't know."

"Anyway," the redhead continued, "wear that while you're in the warehouse. I can hack into each security camera and replace the current footage with old footage. That way, the cameras won't be able to see you as you make your way through."

"I can literally disappear," Paige deadpanned.

"Right, but it doesn't hurt to be careful."

"This is some *National Treasure* type stuff." Peyton had an epiphany.

Leo powered his headset on and placed it on his head. "Did Nicholas Cage get the Declaration or not?"

"Well, he did, but-"

"There you have it." Leo tapped the mic, testing its reliability. "Are you ready, Paige?"

Paige fit her headset underneath her hood and tugged it tight. She powered it on and was unpleasantly met with the buzzing of discreet static. "Ready."

"Wait, you're going *now*?" Peyton blubbered when he realized what was going on.

"Yes, Peyton," Paige exhaled impatiently, "try to keep up."

"Sorry."

The girl stood in the middle of the room and eyed them both neutrally. "Are you both ready?"

"Ready." Leo turned around to face the computer.

"I'm ready to provide emotional support," Peyton added cheekily.

"Right. I'll see you both later."

"Wait!"

Paige stopped despite not starting to do anything yet. "What is it?"

"Be careful." Either Peyton was very talented with different facial expressions or Paige did not notice the authentic concern in his eyes. "Please."

"I will. I promise."

Paige felt a sudden urge to lurch forward in Peyton's direction. It was a sensation she was nowhere close to understanding, much less acting upon. What had her mind been corrupting her with for the past couple of weeks? This feeling was intoxicating, putting the fifteen shots of whiskey from that fraternity party to shame. Why was her stomach floating around like a kaleidoscope of butterflies was carrying it around?

CHAPTER TWENTY-FIVE

No matter. She had yet another mission to attend to.

Without any more contemplation about the instance at hand, Paige opened a vortex beneath her worn black Converse. She fell through it, neglecting to blink. It was something she had thoroughly gotten used to over the years–leaving one location to enter a completely different one. What she did not expect, though, was a detour in her portal's route.

Instead of reappearing on the interior of the organization's warehouse, she ended up on the outside premises. Paige knew exactly where she was, but it was simply not where she wanted to go. This "easy" mission had suddenly become an issue. Paige tapped the mic on her headset and started urgently whispering into it.

"Leo, can you hear me?"

A couple of seconds passed, then a crackling noise ensued followed by his voice, *"Yes, I can hear you. Did you get there okay?"*

"I did, but there's one problem."

"What's that?"

"I think the warehouse has perfected a security system that protects against my cloaking devices and entry maneuvers," Paige hurriedly elaborated.

"Your what now?"

Paige's forehead dropped into her palm. "Can you *please* start your hacking and guide me up to the room?"

"Affirmative," Leo confirmed with a confident tone to his voice. *"Lobby cameras will be all set right about..."*

She crept towards the front entrance of the warehouse and waited for Leo's signal. Once she received it in the form of *"Now!"* Paige opened up the front doors leading to the main lobby of the organization's warehouse. It was just as she remembered: plain and drab without a hint of character. It was somehow nostalgic and unfamiliar at the same time.

Not even a receptionist inhabited the front desk. Paige ignored the uneasy feeling in her stomach and pressed forward.

"*Hallway and elevator cameras are deactivated...now.*"

Paige followed Leo's lead and visibly - since the security system made concealment impossible - made her way to the nearby elevator. She pressed a button next to an arrow facing upwards and waited for the machinery to catch up with her intentions. She tapped her foot impatiently until the doors smoothly opened and she stepped inside.

"*Third floor cameras are deactivated,*" Leo informed her.

"Got it. I'm in the elevator."

"*How's it going?*" Peyton's worried voice sounded through the mic. He must have taken it from Leo, which she undoubtedly saw him doing.

That thought brought a smile to her face. "As good as it can be," she affirmed breathily.

Leo took the mic back. "*The two cameras in the storage room should be deactivated and replaced with old footage. I can see you in the elevator. You're doing great.*"

"Wait. You can see me?"

"*Yeah. Through the camera.*"

Paige looked up into the back left corner and noticed a small camera mounted to the ceiling. She plastered a smile - small, but genuine - on her face and waved delicately. Even though she could not see them, she pictured two goofy boys around her age, one blond and one ginger, waving back with dorky smiles on their faces. That mental image appeared to put her at ease until the elevator doors opened.

Once more, she cracked her knuckles and strutted down the hallway, keeping account of the room numbers as she went. One hand sweated uncontrollably in the pocket of Peyton's hoodie that she had silently refused to give back while the other outstretched a pointed index finger to deliberate each number on the wall.

"370... 372... 374... 376... 378. Found it," she spoke out loud to herself.

"*Nice!*" Leo exclaimed. Paige could hear him hastily typing on the other end. "*Okay, I just double checked, and you should be good to go in there. The Endiridium vial is on one of the shelves in the back corner encased by glass. I'll try to disarm any sort of alarm system, but it might take me a little while.*"

"Well, please try to hurry because I don't know how long these hallways will be empty."

"*I'm doing my best. Just sit tight.*"

Just like in the elevator, Paige waited outside the storage room hallway until she couldn't anymore. A pair of footsteps began thumping in her direction. Paige's heart quickened at the fact a guard was heading towards her, but thankfully had not turned the corner yet. Paige turned the handle and was very thankful that the storage room's door was unlocked. She cracked the door open halfway and slunk inside, shutting and locking it behind her from the interior.

"Any luck with the security system?" Paige inquired just above a whisper as she moved away from the door and towards the poorly concealed equipment. "I just heard a guard pass by. I need to get out of here."

"*I'm trying to deactivate it, but there's a firewall I can't breach.*" Leo's response was the exact opposite of what Paige was hoping for. "*It keeps coming up with an error message or it closes the folder completely.*"

"*Paige, get out of there.*" Peyton took over the mic and spoke firmly. "*The chemical doesn't matter. You do.*"

"God dammit, Peyton," Paige thought to herself. That alone was almost enough for her to turn back. Her imagination, on the contrary, had other plans.

"*You can't leave without it.*"

"*What's the point of a mission if it ends in failure?*"

"*You're a failure if you can't complete this simple task.*"

"*You are just as you thought you were without your powers: nothing.*"

Paige desperately shook her mind's voice out of focus and trained her eyes on the small vial of glowing blue liquid Endiridium encased by a glass box. She felt like some sort of American explorer as she approached it with careful hands. Unfortunately, she did not have a counter weight to place on the pedestal in the vial's stead. It did not matter anyways, because there was already a barrier separating her from the precious Endiridium.

Not for much longer, however.

She clenched her fist together, her thumb to the side of her fingers, and throttled her stone hard hand into the glass—not in the center, but beside one of the most fragile areas: the edges.

Paige ignored the stinging pain in her knuckles and beads of crimson blood bubbling from her fist. She grabbed the vial of Endiridium with her wounded hand and shoved it in the middle pouch of her sweatshirt. She hardly noticed the sickeningly loud alarms beginning to blare throughout the whole building. Paige had a decision to make, and she needed to make it fast.

She did the only thing she could:

Run.

"*Paige? What's going on over there? Come in!*" Leo's voice rose over the siren.

"I smashed the glass and have the vial. Alarms are going off," Paige reported in between strides that her short legs tried to make larger. She burst through the storage room door and picked a random direction to sprint in. "Where's the nearest stairwell?"

"*Oh, fu–uh...let me look.*" Leo typed furiously into his computer. "*At the next intersection, turn right and the second door on your right will be the stairwell.*"

"On it."

Paige pushed herself to run faster. The footsteps behind her grew more voluminous, meaning there were more guards in black on her tail. She turned the corner and flung open the second door on her right. It was indeed a stairwell, where the siren sound of the alarms echoed loud enough for her to almost want to slam both of her hands over her ears.

Paige climbed flight after flight until she reached the final door at the top. She shoved it open with her free hand and found herself on top of the multi-storied warehouse in a menagerie of fog. Paige felt as if she was about to tip over from an intense bout of wind. The higher altitude caught her off guard, especially when the storm clouds overhead began to precipitate upon her. She backed away from the doorway and towards the edge of the roof.

"*Wait. Why are you going to the roof?*" Leo inquired as she stepped backward. "*Do you need us to come get you?*"

"No!" Paige yelled over the gusts. "I'll think of something. They're coming."

"*Who's coming?!*" screeched Peyton. "*Paige!*"

For the second time in less than a minute, the door burst open to reveal a countless number of Dr. Kelley's men dressed in all black. Each one of them held a semi-automatic rifle, which were all cocked in unison and pointed in her direction. Instinctively, Paige held up her free hand, but left the other in her pocket in order to cushion the freely bleeding incisions.

"Freeze!" One of the men shouted. "Raise your other hand too!"

Paige refused to answer, instead slowly backing away from them. The wall of men parted to make way for the "doctor" himself. He wore a sorry excuse for gray hair on top of his head, but the perfectly creased black suit that covered his decrepit, wrinkly body underneath. His lips parted in a crooked, yellow smile that Paige adored to despise. Her own pearly whites gritted together at the thought of seeing this awful man again.

"Well, well, well," Dr. Kelley mused in the midst of toned-down laughter. "What have we here? Should've known that you'd be slinking around these parts. You just can't function without us, now, can you?"

She neglected to respond despite Leo and Peyton's constant questions in her ears. *"Paige! Are you alright?"* Static clouded the earpieces more than Leo's demands and Peyton's concern. *"Come in, Paige!"*

Unfortunately, Paige was forced to ignore them. She stuffed the mic piece under her hood so it was intelligible. "What do *you* want?" she questioned the man several yards away.

"Right now, the entertainment you're providing is more than enough." The sickly old man was elated. "Do I even need to ask what brought you here? The Endiridium, perhaps?"

"Fuck you and the hell hole you imprisoned me in," Paige dodged the question, spitting, quite literally, at his feet. She stepped back more and abruptly stopped when her heels hit a ledge. "I've gotten my freedom and there's no way in hell you're going to take it away from me."

To her disgust, the pathetic excuse for a human being's smile grew wider. "Maybe not now, but very soon. Men, if you will..."

The very second that Dr. Kelley gestured towards his men, Paige gave him and the rest of his guards an explicit view of her left hand's middle finger. She glanced down to the concrete five stories below. Then, Paige turned her stone-cold eyes towards the men. Emotionlessly, she stepped onto the ledge,

CHAPTER TWENTY-FIVE

gave them a salute, and fell backwards. If she could survive twenty-six floors, she could definitely endure five.

Bullets mixed with the rain pouring down onto the scene. Since Paige was out of the warehouse's jurisdiction, she opened a portal underneath her falling body. It swallowed her up and guided her through a wormhole leading directly to Peyton's room. Paige groaned when she realized she misjudged the exact location of his bed, seeing as she fell from the ceiling and landed in the middle of the room on her bum.

"Paige!" Peyton and Leo yelled in unison. The latter threw his headset to the side and followed the former as he ran to help her up.

"Good Lord, you're soaked," Peyton stated the obvious, outstretching his hand.

Unlike previous instances, Paige did not hesitate to grab his hand and let him pull her to her feet. "Roof," she bluntly explained, tugging off her headset and hood.

"Leo, get a towel," the blond boy requested. "You know where they are."

"Got it." Leo dashed out of Peyton's room and came back literally five seconds later with a towel from the hall closet.

The redhead tossed Peyton the towel, which he caught, and placed over Paige's shoulders. "Are you okay?"

"I'm fine," Paige mumbled. She had not realized she was trembling from both the cold and possibly another reason.

Was it fear?

It *couldn't* have been.

"So...how'd it go?" Leo inquired while spinning around in the wheeled chair.

Paige reached into her pocket and disclosed the full vile.

"Yes!" He stood from his chair with enthusiasm.

Peyton, however, had a different response, taking a hold of

the wrist connected to her injured hand. "You're hurt. Holy *shit*, that's a lot of blood. Are you alright? Lightheaded?"

"Yes, and maybe."

Paige tried not to appear puzzled by Peyton's behavior. The fact that he cared about her more than anyone else in her life combined was still an unnatural phenomenon. It was something that she would never get used to, but this sort of affection was most definitely a characteristic of Peyton's that she could get comfortable with. It was as if a magnet pulled the two of them together, and not just in a protective way.

"I'll be right back."

Peyton promptly let go of Paige's hand and disappeared down the hallway. He came back with his father's doctor's kit that Paige recognized from the last time she needed it. Peyton undid the latches on the briefcase and searched through it until he found a pack of gauze and an ace bandage. He unwrapped both of them and sat down on the bed next to Paige. He took a tender hold of her hand and began carefully placing the gauze along the miniscule cuts on her knuckles and top of her hand.

"Oh, sorry." Peyton offered her an apologetic look. "I should've asked first. Are you okay with me doing this?"

Paige was dumbfounded. She numbly nodded and couldn't keep her eyes off of him nor how he was delicately tending to her injury. She could not ignore the fact her heart was beating like a kettle drum against her rib cage. Paige instead tightened the towel around her shoulders with her free hand to conceal her anxiety. Where was this coming from? This was a foreign feeling to her, but it was also one that she somehow wanted to remain embedded within her.

It made her feel more *alive*, as if she was a human being just like Leo and Peyton.

Speaking of Leo, Paige did not notice the amused smirk

residing on his face while Peyton was wrapping up Paige's hand. He knew exactly what was going on, but he did not want to ruin the mood for them both, so, instead, he focused on the vial that Paige had delicately placed on Peyton's bed.

"Can I take a look at this?" Leo pointed at the chemical.

"Yeah, go ahead." Paige did not even look in Leo's direction. She did not even care about the vial at that particular second. Her attention was completely on Peyton whether she liked it or not.

She did, in fact, like it.

Leo picked up the vial and inspected the glowing blue liquid inside it. He squinted to see clearer before bringing it to the desk. He shone a tabletop light on the glass tube to get a better look. Leo held it up to the lamp and continued to take a look until Peyton finished up with Paige's hand.

"There," the blond concluded, patting the top of her hand. "Better?"

Paige did not have to force a smile this time. "Much better. Thank you."

"You're welcome."

Unfortunately for the both of them, Leo interrupted their small moment of gazing into each other's eyes as if time failed to exist.

"Wait a minute. I think I have an idea." He had a sudden epiphany, which caught their attention. "Paige, if I get this open, could you see if your purple sparkle things do anything to a small portion of the chemical?"

"Uh, I guess," Paige stood from her seat and cracked her knuckles. "Let me know when you're ready."

"Take these." Peyton tossed a pair of blue rubber medical gloves to Leo.

Leo caught them in midair and struggled to tug them on. "Thanks."

When he finally succeeded, he began to work on unscrewing the vial's cap. Thankfully, there was no method of extra security–just the cap. Leo slowly opened up the vial and held it out towards Paige.

"I'm ready when you are," Leo informed her.

Paige held her hands out in front of her and did what she always did. Instead of creating an entire energy field, though, small purple sparks were conjured around the vial. They carried a small portion - about one fifth, to be precise - of the Endiridium out of the glass container. It floated towards the center of the room as a small speck of blue surrounded by purple. This was when Paige began to concentrate on a higher level. The periwinkle dust began spinning, slowly at first, but it slowly increased in speed. It did not take long until a miniature purple tornado surrounded the ball for at least five seconds before it died down with a small pop. The azure was gone, leaving only a gray sphere.

Peyton handed Leo a pair of tweezers from the doctor's kit, which the latter used to pick up the spark. He dashed over to the desk lamp and looked at it under the light.

"Remarkable!" Leo studied the colorless spark. "Simply remarkable!"

"What is?" Paige twiddled her fingers and small lilac dust swirled around them.

"Don't you know what this means?"

"No?"

Leo dashed across the room, leaving the spark on the desk. "You drained it of its power," he explained, shaking her shoulders gently. "You could literally take all of the harmful qualities out of this chemical."

"Oh, my God," Peyton exclaimed in a squeakier voice than he would have liked to admit. "Paige! You know how all of the corrupted people have blue glowing eyes? That's from the chemical! If it works on this thing, it should work on them and turn them back to normal."

Paige hesitated to ponder the matter. "Wait a minute... You're right. You're *right*!"

"Now, all we have to do is find all of the corrupted people and have you rip the evil right out of them!"

"I think that could work. How would we find all of them, though?"

Leo cut his way into the conversation. "I can do some more research on the organization's database. If they plan on spreading this tactic to other people, there *has* to be something in there."

"Good idea," Paige agreed. "For now, though, we need to figure out a plan if it comes to us against the organization."

"Honestly, if it comes to that, I'd probably be stuck on the toilet," Peyton admitted sheepishly.

Paige and Leo gave him an odd look.

"What?! I have IBS!"

"Okay, that's too much information." Paige exhaled and looked away from him while Leo stifled a bout of laughter.

"Okay...," Leo abruptly changed the subject. "I think it's about time we all get ready for class, isn't it?"

"I'm already late, but I don't care. I can just teleport there now."

"Can you teleport us there too?"

"Sure. I don't see why not."

Leo appeared to be thoughtful, looking at Peyton. "Hey, can I borrow her whenever I need to go to the store for my mom?"

"You'd have to ask her," Peyton chuckled–a nice sound for Paige.

"Hello? I'm right here," she reminded the both of them.

"Oh, right." Leo stuffed his laptop into his backpack that

was next to Peyton's desk and his own backpack which was already packed. "Are we all ready to go?"

"Wait."

Paige dashed into the guest bedroom to grab her tote bag, which she slung over her shoulder. On her way back, she diligently morphed into the body of Penny Hamilton, something she had slowly gotten used to over the past two and a half months of school. Her new appearance caused both Peyton and Leo to do a double take.

"Woah." Peyton backed away for a second before realizing. "Sorry, I forgot you could do that for a hot second."

Paige almost grinned at him. "It's a common misconception."

"Okay. Are we ready now?" Leo inquired almost impatiently.

"Yup, and one thing."

"What?"

"Try not to scream."

"What are you talking abou–*ah!*"

Leo broke his unspoken promise once the three of them disappeared through a wormhole in the floor. He clung onto Peyton's arm since he was the closest person to him while Peyton, despite having gotten used to the sensation, took a hold of Paige's hand. His mental excuse was "for them to stick together," but he was well aware that Paige would think that was a load of nonsense.

It was.

Once the three pairs of shoes hit the ground behind a tree on Azure's campus, Leo let go of Peyton, his face screwing up in faux disgust. "Ew!" he whined like a child, wiping his hands on his maroon jacket.

"Oh, come on." Peyton rolled his eyes. "I hug you all the time."

CHAPTER TWENTY-FIVE

"Whatever. That's different."

Leo started towards the familiar double doors of Azure University's main building. Peyton and Paige trailed behind, side by side. The former's hand ached to hold the latter's, but Peyton refused to give in to the urge, knowing that it would possibly make Paige uncomfortable. Instead, however, a more positive, calming thought came to mind.

He decided to put it into action. "I told you."

He would never get fully accustomed to Paige's delicate, but worn, eyes that had seen it all meeting his. "Told me what?" she innocently asked.

"I told you you were a superhero."

The smile on Paige's face was as prevalent as the blush on her cheeks. Peyton was more than happy with that.

Chapter Twenty-Six

NAVY

"Tell me again how you think this is a good idea."

"I never said that," Paige argued with the boy sitting behind her. "I said that it would be a good idea for you to practice for when we actually go through with our plan."

Peyton leaned over to view Paige in the passenger seat. "Practice what?"

"It's a surprise," Leo and Paige concluded at the same time, the latter elbowing the former.

Peyton sat in the back of Leo's vehicle–a tan Nissan that looked like it had seen better days. Every time Leo pressed down on the brakes, they squeaked in just the slightest. He needed to turn his steering wheel an barely longer amount of time to make a turn than regular cars around them. Still, though, Leo loved his car like it was his own son. It was obvious by the way he cherished the vehicle. It did not have a single dent on it that was not from the curb, nor did he possess a single ticket to his record.

Peyton ignored the fact he was looking and acting like a

five-year-old on the way to his birthday party that he had no idea about. "Why won't either of you tell me?"

"Because you'll laugh," Leo remarked with a simple shrug.

"I won't. I promise." Peyton held out his pinky like he was about to make a promise. He leaned forward even more. "If I do happen to laugh, it'll be at Paige's outfit."

Paige glared at him from under the Arkford Blue Warriors baseball cap and hood of an oversized navy sweatshirt she was wearing. "It's not my fault I have to wear a disguise."

"You know, I think it would be less funny if you wore a pair of those disguise glasses with bushy eyebrows, a big nose, and a mustache."

"Idiot." She watched the road in front of her.

Leo fought back a smile while he directed his tan Nissan straight ahead. Peyton leaned back in his seat and looked out the window to view a building larger than life slowly appearing over the midday horizon. Peyton knew this massive building by heart. He and his parents used to drive this way every single weekend as a family event. How had he not caught on before? First, the long drive through the suburbs, the quick merge and coast on the interstate for just a couple of minutes, and then the familiar exit?

Peyton truly agreed with the fact Paige called him an idiot, albeit jokingly.

"Wait," he deduced enthusiastically. "We're going to the mall! I love the mall!"

Leo shook his head and chuckled, nudging Paige, "See? I told you he'd be excited."

Paige returned the gesture. "I figured."

"What's that supposed to mean?" Peyton questioned with his arms lazily, but tightly, folded over his chest.

"Nothing of importance."

Peyton did not miss the amused look that both Paige and

Leo were sharing as they turned into the familiar mall parking lot. Leo expertly weaved through the overwhelming amount of cars, trucks, and pedestrians walking in the middle of the road for some reason. Paige often wondered how civilians could be so careless. Then again, everyone was careless in their own sort of way. Paige knew she was, especially when she got out of the car as soon as Leo put the vehicle in park near the entrance of the mall.

Paige tightened the hood over her head, lowered the brim of her baseball cap, and slid a pair of sunglasses over her face. "Ready?"

Peyton gave her one look and then burst out laughing, nearly falling out of the vehicle.

"What the hell are you wearing?!"

"I told you already: a disguise." Paige gestured to her... unusual outfit.

Her small frame was engulfed with a black Nirvana sweatshirt that nearly went down to her knees—it was over two sizes too big. What was not covered by the hoodie was concealed with a pair of loose black sweatpants held up with a drawstring. She wore her usual worn black Converse high tops. Paige preferred oversized clothes to regular ones, but this was a bit extreme. She had borrowed clothing from both Peyton and Leo's closets.

"You look like a vampire trying to hide from the sun."

"Your comments are unnecessary."

Leo shut the driver's side door of his Nissan and locked it. He pushed Peyton forward. "You heard her. Let's go."

"But-"

"Let's *go*, Peyton."

Paige fought back a smirk while leading the two of them towards the entrance of the mall. The double doors were larger than the imagination itself, gesturing towards a whole new universe for Paige. The ceilings were at least thirty feet high and consisted of skylights every few yards. The sunlight shone into the interior of the mall instead of fluorescent lights being installed. Paige had to stop to take it all in.

Stores lined the walkways as far as the eye could see. Electronic stores, video game stores - she thought Peyton and Leo would like those - even a tattoo parlor was in view. She could spot five clothing stores in one single dead end of the mall. Who even needed that much clothing? Still, out of all of these shopping centers, there was one place Paige had in mind.

"Okay, great. We're at the mall." Peyton stood awkwardly next to Paige. "Why exactly are we here? I want to stop by the GameGo store."

"We can do that later," Paige declined his request and began scanning the directory in front of her. "...How does this work?"

Leo stepped forward and tapped on the blue screen that viewed an entire map of the mall. He zoomed in on the opposite side of the mall with two of his fingers and pointed to a store at the far end of the metropolis.

"That's where we need to go," he explained to Paige.

"Wait." Peyton leaned towards the digital directory just as Leo put his hand over the location. "Where are we going?"

"If we told you, you'd chicken out," Paige deadpanned monotonously.

"What? No, I wouldn't!"

"You would if we told you, which is why it's a surprise. Now, come on. Leo, lead the way, please."

Leo did as he was told and was the brave line leader. Well, their formation was not much of a line–it was more of a triangle. Leo parted the sea of people walking the wrong way on the right pathway of the humongous building. The three of them weaved and wove around crowds of pedestrians who were either texting, in the midst of a conversation with a friend, or just plain clueless. Leo had lost count of how many times he had to dart out of the way of an oblivious individual.

Meanwhile, Paige struggled to keep up with the two of them. The Arkford Mall was a place she had never gotten around to going to. Being confined to a prison cell for the majority of her life was not how Paige wanted to spend her childhood years. Now that she was somewhat free, she could do whatever she wanted.

This was one of those instances. It was not necessarily just a want, but a need as well.

Peyton finally was starting to understand why the three of them were at the mall when they stopped in front of a BB gun store.

"Why exactly are we here?" Peyton asked anyway, gesturing to the large sign that said "The Bee's Knees BB Guns & Range."

"Since you'd literally kill yourself at a regular shooting range, we decided to practice with BB guns if we're going to go ahead with the plan," Paige explained with a pat on the shoulder.

"Who said that?" Peyton didn't even need to inquire. Leo's soft chuckling gave it away. "Quiet!" He smacked his friend.

"It's true, though," Leo argued jokingly while stepping back. "Ouch."

"Both of you, enough." Paige stood in between them and held her arms out. "We're all on the same team, so we need to work together if this idea is going to work."

"We are!" Peyton and Leo argued at the same time.

"I'm going in. You can either join me or go away because if you two aren't going to help, I'll do this alone."

"We're coming, but one thing first," Peyton insisted.

Paige turned around to take him in. "What?"

"I don't trust that bee with a rifle." Peyton pointed to the logo next to the name of the store.

All Paige did was roll her eyes and walk inside.

Peyton looked at Leo, who shrugged, and then the two of them followed behind Paige. The lobby around them was disappointing compared to the sign that gave the range a good name. Chips of green paint had fallen from at least half of the walls, leaving a spotted, starry look to a nuclear sky. The air conditioning whirred louder than the pedestrians in the mall's walkways. Then again, how welcoming was a bumblebee with a stinger *and* a rifle? Perhaps this place lived up to its sign after all.

Paige walked straight to the front desk where a man in his forties who looked like he had gotten nowhere in life sat snoring to his heart's content. An open newspaper was draped over his face and lifted up and down with his rhythmic breathing. Paige stood in front of the desk with both boys flanking her like a V-shaped gaggle of geese.

Paige cleared her throat. "Excuse me."

The man snored in response.

"*Excuse* me," she tried again a little louder.

Another snore.

"Oh, enough of this," Paige grumbled. She grabbed the newspaper from off the man's head, rolled it up, and then gently whacked him with it. "Excuse me!"

Finally, the man jumped up and nearly fell out of his rolling chair. Paige tossed the newspaper back down on the desk and tapped her foot while waiting for him. Eventually, he came to, rubbing his eyes, yawning lazily, and finally meeting the eyes of the three guests. From the look on his face, the three of them must have been the first customers that day, if not, of the entire week.

"Oh, sorry, folks," he apologized and wiped a string of

drool from the corner of his lip. "My name's Don. How are you all doing?"

Paige opened her mouth to speak, but Leo interrupted before she could snap, "We're doing well; thank you. We'd like to rent a target and BB guns for three."

"Got it." Don stood from his seat and typed into his computer for a second. "What type of gun would you like to rent?"

"Two pistols and a rifle," Leo requested politely.

Peyton gave Leo a sideways look. "Who's getting the rifle?"

"We'll switch out," elaborated Paige under her breath.

"Uh...okay?"

Don typed something else into his computer and then a total price popped up on the register's screen that Paige did not want to look at. She lowered the brim of her baseball cap while Leo removed his credit card from his wallet and paid for the three of them.

"Thank you." The scruffy man did not quite smile, but he seemed appreciative of their business. "I'll get those out for you."

"Are you sure this is a good idea?" Peyton questioned once Don made his way towards a glass display case full of nonfatal weapons behind the register.

"Better than a real shooting range," Leo countered.

"Hey!"

"There you are." Don set down two pistols and a rifle on the counter along with three pairs of safety goggles and gloves. "The targets are through those doors. Just don't hurt yourselves, now."

When Don leaned back in his chair once again "reading" the newspaper, Paige, Peyton, and Leo gave each other a puzzled sideways glance. Then, two pairs of brown eyes and one of hazel made their way back to the man who looked like he was hairier than a sasquatch. Was he truly not going to offer them any safety tips or even watch to see if they would leave the range with their BB guns and cause a massacre among little kids in the nearby play area? Either way, Paige did not care, because she picked up the BB rifle, slung it over her shoulder, and marched towards the double doors leading to the shooting alleys themselves. They all shoved their safety goggles on but ignored the gloves on the counter. Paige was the only exception, though, tugging them on and tossing her goggles aside to make way for her sunglasses.

"No way in hell I'm wearing these," she grumbled at the orange goggles on the floor.

All three of them were taken aback by how empty the place was. Not a single customer had a BB gun in their hand aiming for the target miles away. The room itself was nicer than the lobby, but it was far from having a fresh coat of paint. A thin layer of dust coated the floors. It seemed as if Don had not cleaned for weeks. Paige took a quick look at the walls, ceiling, and corners of the room to check for security cameras. When there were none applicable, she nodded in approval.

Paige ignored how Peyton and Leo were simply standing there and approached one of the aisles near the middle of the range. She swung her rifle back into her hands, cocked it without a strain, and held it into position. She closed one eye and focused on the sheet of paper with a silhouette of the upper half of a person. Without any warning, she fired off one shot to the middle left of the head. Then, after cocking again, another hit the right side. Then, five more BBs erupted from the gun's chamber towards the bottom of the face.

"Holy *shit!*" Peyton covered his ears despite the disappointing noise the gun made.

Leo squinted and noticed that the bullet holes that the BBs

made were in the shape of a smiley face. "Well done," he complimented genuinely. "When'd you learn to shoot?"

"Accuracy is a skill you need to develop. It doesn't come naturally." Paige swung the BB rifle over her shoulder again. "One of you–go."

"I'll go next," Leo exclaimed when Peyton took a step back.

The redhead held up his rifle with both hands and cocked it when Paige gave him room at the same alley. He hesitated for at least half a minute, focusing his eyesight on the target in front of him. Paige tapped her foot impatiently and Peyton waited quietly on the sidelines. When Leo did eventually take a shot, it was on target until a purple energy field appeared in front of it, causing the BB to ricochet off and land near Leo's foot.

"Woah–what the hell was that?!" Leo jumped back with an accusing look.

"You hesitated." Paige was insistent with her reasoning. "If you take too long, the enemy will be able to anticipate your next move and come up with a counterattack."

"What if I'm a sniper?"

"You're not invisible."

Peyton snorted at that, "But you could make him invisible."

"What if I'm not there?" The girl whirled around to face him with a snarl. "What's he going to do then, huh?"

"I thought he was going to be out of sight."

"What if his cover is blown?"

"It won't be."

"What if he's shot? I get that you know first aid, but-"

"*Paige*!" Leo raised his voice to get her attention. "Enough of the what-ifs. I don't think *any* of us know what we're doing, so you need to settle down a little bit. Please."

Paige's expression contorted from one that was originally angry, but then, it morphed into guilt. "I'm sorry," she apologized profusely. "I didn't mean to be...mean. I just want everyone to *survive*."

"We know," Peyton chipped in shyly. "I think we're all just... scared. And tired. We were up until like two in the morning planning stuff."

"I know." She shook her head and averted her gaze. "I'm just trying to protect you."

"But I don't think we need shooting lessons. We aren't even going to be shooting." Peyton looked between the three of them. "...Right?"

Both of them eyed Paige, who merely shrugged. "I don't think so, but you never know."

"Here's something I *do* know." Leo placed his pistol down on one of the railings. "If we stress ourselves out too much with this, then we won't be able to succeed since we'd be all worked up."

"That doesn't make sense, though."

"Training for stuff is good, yes, but who knows what we're going to do in the heat of the moment? All of that training could go to waste when we should've been doing something else, like strengthening the walls of our plan."

Paige's irises reached the ceiling thoughtfully. "I guess you're right."

"But I guess target practice would help us, especially if it puts your mind at ease," Peyton brought up to lift her mood.

Sure enough, it did. "Do you two really think so?"

"I know so."

Paige's field of vision landed on Leo, who nodded in agreement. A small smile tugged at her lips as she adjusted her rifle into position, cocked it, and aimed at the target in front of her.

"Sounds good to me."

The BB hit the target smack in the middle of the silhouette's forehead.

Chapter Twenty-Seven

CHARCOAL

The clicking of the buttons of a nearby keyboard scratched an itch in Paige's brain that she did not even know she had. A rolling chair reclined with a small creak that was the loudest noise in the entire room. Paige did not realize how fatigued she was until she finally sat down after an extensively long morning.

A small yawn left her lips while Peyton and Leo typed to her left. Peyton was in the middle of the three of them while Leo was on the far end. Both Peyton and Leo were using their laptops instead of the school computers. The more time that Paige spent with the two of them, the more she realized the devices in the computer lab were slow. Leo's laptop must have been suped up with some sort of intricate, futuristic technology to make it operate faster. Since Paige was nowhere near used to the internet, she had no idea how slow Azure University's student computers truly were.

Fatigue loomed over her like a bout of storm clouds ready to brew. She fought to prevent her eyelids from closing and for the realm of sleep to take over. Paige watched the tiled ceiling

CHAPTER TWENTY-SEVEN

boredly. One of the lights embedded in the mundane pattern flickered, a diamond in the rough. That fluorescent diamond, though, annoyed her, which brought her back to watching both of the boys type on their laptops.

She had no work to do; ever since Peyton discovered her secret identity, he made sure that the office computer was always available for her use to complete homework. In fact, none of them were truly working on homework. Leo intently typed through the database he had saved multiple copies of on his device just in case one of them became corrupted. Paige never would have thought of that—Leo was too smart for his own good.

"Peyton could surely take some pages out of Leo's book."

That was a joke, of course. Paige had been learning how to make jokes over the duration she had spent with the two boys. The two of them were partially a bad influence, but Paige could never think of them to be of the sort. In fact, they were the opposite of poor impact. Paige had accumulated knowledge of the internet, video games, school, humor, and even pranks ever since she encountered the duo. At the same time, she passed on the comprehension of existing outside the box, developing the supernatural, and expecting the unknown.

She would refuse to trade it for the world.

Peyton leaned over towards Leo's laptop and asked, "How's it going?"

"I'm still finalizing our plan," Leo explained just above a whisper since the trio were the only people in the computer lab. "Now, it's pretty simple. I'm trying to hack into the organization's computers and see if they have a certain plan for the future."

"Near future or far future?"

"I don't know." Leo never stopped clicking and typing. "That's what I'm trying to find out." He turned to Paige.

"You've been around these people for over half your life. What would you do if you were in their shoes and had this much power?"

Paige was taken aback by the question, but came up with an awkward, hesitant answer. "...Would the factor of me being threatened and almost murdered on top of the warehouse building while they knew the purpose of my trespassing be taken into account?"

Two pairs of eyes whipped towards her.

"What the hell?!" Peyton could not refrain from raising his voice. "Why didn't you tell us this a week ago?"

Paige shuffled uncomfortably in her seat. "I'm sorry. I didn't want to worry either of you."

"Paige, we've been worried regardless." His tone was laced with sincerity.

"I know. I'm sorry."

"You have nothing to apologize for."

Those words meant more to Paige than Peyton would ever know, at least for the time being. A hint of pink dotted her cheeks and it did not go unnoticed, at least by Leo. Peyton, on the other hand, pretended to be occupied with the lab report on his computer screen.

Leo removed his laptop from his lap and set it on the table in front of him. He turned his chair towards the rest of them. "In this case, if the organization has threatened you, whatever they want to do, they want to do it fast. From what I've detected in this database, the organization is planning on releasing large quantities of Endiridium among portions of the population. Now, I'm just trying to think of when and where that would happen. Everyone in this city is in different places at once."

"Are there any big events coming up soon?" Peyton inquired thoughtfully.

CHAPTER TWENTY-SEVEN

"Not that I know of. I've been so swamped with this that I haven't been keeping track of anything else."

"We all have," Peyton teased. "It's not just you."

Leo ensured his tone was nothing but sarcasm. "Oh, really? You're so full of it."

"No, *you* are."

"*You* are!"

Paige rolled her eyes as the two boys continued arguing like a pair of elementary schoolers fighting over the last glue stick. She decided to take matters into her own hands and logged into the slow, but functioning, computer directly in front of her. She scooted her chair forward. It took her a couple of seconds to find the internet, but once she did, she started typing with more than two fingers to get where she needed to go.

Blocking out the two boys that she had gotten accustomed to was never easy. She was used to being on her own, which her mind had reiterated time after time by this point. It was something she could not get out of her head. Why would these two boys want anything to do with her? She knew it was not for her abilities, although the joke Leo made about "borrowing" her did bring her a bit of unease. The concept of jokes was new to her. She would never get completely used to a "normal" civilian life.

Of course, normal civilians would not decide to shut down an organization's master plan to gain control over a metropolis.

Paige eyed the vertical line blinked at the far-left side of the search bar. Frankly, she had not a clue what to type in order to receive the information she wanted. Sure, there were several key words she could use, but none of them seemed to be a good fit. Paige decided on a simple "current events in Arkford City" and pressed enter to receive the results.

She was at a standstill when it came to one of the first headlines. Paige clicked on it and watched as a new page popped up on her screen titled "Sports Weekly." This information, albeit completely off topic, seemed to be perfect.

"Peyton. Leo." Paige snipped to get both of the boys' attention. "You two should look at this."

At once, Leo was on one side and Peyton was on the other. Despite both of their proximity being the same, Peyton's head lingering over her shoulder brought Paige to a slight state of unease. It was not an unsafe feeling, but one that was unfamiliar. She wanted him to go away or come closer at the same time. Now was not the moment for such thoughts, though.

"The Arkford Blue Warriors are set to battle the Cambridge Knights during Game Seven of the National Championship next Saturday, November second, at six P.M.," Peyton muttered as he read. "Thousands of fans from around the city are projected to parade into the stands to cheer on their home team. This is one of - if *the* - most anticipated events for minor league baseball fans around the country to gather together and...*oh my God*. Paige, you're a genius!"

"I'm a genius for looking up what big events are happening soon?" Paige questioned bluntly while Peyton shook her shoulders. "*My God... Say it again... Wait. What is going on with me?!*"

"Yes, because clearly, we're both idiots."

Leo looked to be offended. "Don't bring me into this."

"Seriously, though. This is perfect," Peyton asserted while scrolling through the webpage with the wired mouse. "Leo, you said that the organization is planning some sort of attack in the next couple of weeks where they can use the Endiridium on a ton of people. This *has* to be it."

"How do you know for sure?"

"What other event is going on in the next couple of weeks that's so important?"

"Halloween?" Leo genuinely asked.

"Oh, true. Candy is important."

Paige released a labored sigh when the two started arguing again. "Listen. We need to focus."

"You're right." The fact Peyton instantaneously took Paige's side made her heart swell. "Leo, keep doing research and if you find anything else, we'll figure out exactly what to do."

"But we already know what to do," Leo countered, turning his laptop to face them. "I have it all down in a Google Doc. I'll be hacking into the system like when Paige broke into the warehouse last week while she finds all four of the people affected: Dylan, Hannah, and her two friends: Ayla and Ivy. Then, she'll literally fry the brainwashing right out of them like she did with the chemical."

"But that was only one drop," Paige protested with a bit of concern. "How am I supposed to do that to a whole person?"

Peyton eyed her as if she was a complete and utter moron. "You don't know what you're capable of ever since that microchip was removed. Trust me. You'll know what to do when the time comes."

"Damn him." Paige caved with a start, cleared her throat, and then nodded. "I guess you're right. This could be really dangerous, though. What if someone gets seriously hurt...or worse?"

"Let's not think about that." Peyton's heart throbbed in his chest.

"No, I think we should," retorted Leo firmly. "If something happens to any of us, our families have the right to know."

"Oh, God, you're right." The blond boy fought not to bite his nails from the anxiety pooling in his system. "Mom and Dad would be so worried if we *did* tell them, though."

"So would my parents."

"What do you think, Paige?"

There he went again, asking for Paige's input. He had noticed her slowly rolling her chair away from the two of them when the topic of "families" came up. Periwinkle sparkles fizzled around her fingers under the table. Paige needed something other than their conversation to focus on. Dread filled her when her opinion was requested.

"I don't have a family, so why would what I think matter?" Paige grumbled to avoid answering the question.

Leo and Peyton looked at each other in disarray. Neither of them expected such a response from Paige. Well, maybe Peyton did because she had snapped in this way towards him before. Leo appeared to be visibly unsettled by Paige's sudden silence. Peyton, on the other hand, trusted his instinct and let his heart speak.

"*We're* your family. You saw how my parents reacted to Penny - well, you - when you came over for dinner that one time. They would love you regardless of who you really are."

"I don't know..."

"Can you please try? I think I have a plan to tell Mom and Dad about you," Peyton reasoned with her. "They have the right to know if anything happens to any of us."

Paige wished her right leg would stop bouncing up and down. "I can try."

"I'm in," Leo offered his two cents.

"Me too," Peyton added on.

It was up to Paige now. She saw how Leo outstretched his hand and Peyton put his own on top. Paige now had two pairs of eyes looking at her, watching her. Those calculating - no, *caring* - eyes were what finally led Paige to agreeing to this spontaneous idea. Tentatively, the sparks around Paige's hands faded to the floor and she placed her hand on top of Peyton's.

CHAPTER TWENTY-SEVEN

"Me three," she concluded with a smile.

The rest of the school day passed by like clockwork. Paige attended her final two classes of the day while Peyton and Leo finished up whatever they were doing. She was still unsure of Peyton's exact schedule, but expected them to meet up like they always did for her to collectively transport the three home with the flick of a wrist.

Time ticked by like a bomb waiting to go off. There was no way that Paige could deny the inevitable moment of truth ready to explode over the Finlays' household. How would Peyton's parents react? How would Leo's? Living in the unknown was a necessity, but also a terror to Paige. Even though she had a multitude of powers, she wished either a pause button or a fast-forward button was one of them. Paige knew better than to try, though; she figured that would be a bit too "OP," which was a phrase she had learned from one of Peyton and Leo's Crush Bros gaming sessions. "OP" stood for "over-powered" and Paige did not want to be that. From what she had been subconsciously taught from the two boys, that meant "annoying."

She did not want to be annoying.

When five o'clock finally rolled around, Paige, Peyton, and Leo were lounging in Peyton's room. The television was on and a random show from a streaming service was playing. Paige could not pay attention, though, as her focus was on something else. Peyton and Leo were the same way–the show was on merely for background noise as the three of them plotted.

"Okay, so Leo, your parents are coming over soon. Right?" Peyton asked to confirm.

"Yup," the redhead replied, putting down his phone. "They should be here any minute."

"My parents are thrilled. They haven't seen your mom and

dad for a while because of work, so this should be a big event for them."

"Yeah...a big event for all of us...," Paige silently worried.

She did not realize she was rocking back and forth on the bed until a firm, but gentle hand was placed on her shoulders. "You don't need to be nervous. I understand why, but my parents don't bite," Peyton assured her and bent down to her eye level. A quirk of a smile emerged on the left side of his lip. "You know that."

Paige suddenly forgot how to breathe. "I don't think they'll be expecting such news coming from a college friend who they think is a nerd."

"You never know."

"Oh, God. Keep your hand there. Please keep your hand there...dammit."

"So, repeat the plan back to me so I'm completely on board," Leo requested.

Peyton stood from the bed and started walking around his bedroom while explaining, "So, everyone is invited over for a spontaneous dinner. Paige, you turn into Penny for now when you answer the door *after* Leo's parents so they don't see you coming. When everyone's seated and having dinner, I can bring up the topic and then Leo can help me explain. Paige, you can say whatever you want when you feel comfortable. Is that okay?"

Leo nodded, taking mental notes. "Fine by me."

"Paige?"

"Yeah, that sounds good," Paige squeaked out with her eyes averted towards the floor.

Peyton frowned at her fear. "We don't have to do this right now if you're not ready."

"We already have everything planned out. I don't want to

be a wuss and back out now. This isn't just for my good. It's for *everyone*. I need to suck it up."

"But we're worried about *you* right now."

"I can do it."

"I can tell you're scared."

That observation stabbed Paige right in the heart. She *couldn't* be scared. She just couldn't. "No, I'm not. I'm anxious. There's a difference."

"If you say so." Peyton furrowed his brows in uncertainty, but did not push her. He knew a strong boundary when he saw one, but secretly pleaded, *"Come on, Paige. Talk to me... I'm right here..."*

It seemed that Peyton's silent request was somehow heard, because Paige's next words were: "Fine. I'm scared. Okay?"

"Woah. Can't believe that worked." Peyton tipped her chin upwards with his finger and looked her straight in the eyes. "So am I, but we'll get through this. We both will."

"Uh, hello?" Leo waved his arms around like a penguin from across the room.

Peyton's tongue was caught in his throat. Paige grasped onto his wrist and removed his hand from nearly cupping her chin. It was not something she wanted to do–if Leo were not in the room, then she would have simply let whatever motive Peyton had to continue. She had the same desire flaming in her chest, but she washed out the fumes before they became intoxicating.

Not yet.

Not now.

She was grateful for the dinging of an alarm coming from downstairs. Her train of thought finally reached a detour.

"Hey look–the doorbell!" Leo interrupted both of their active imaginations.

"Are you ready, Paige?" Peyton inquired while Leo dashed towards his bedroom door.

Paige offered him a curt, but sincere nod before passing through the floor. Peyton had to shake his head to let reality hit him. He was still getting accustomed to the fact that superpowers were real, and someone he knew very well happened to have them. Either way, he followed Leo downstairs with the lingering thought in his head. Then, the reality of what the three of them were going to do hit him.

How in the world was he going to break the news to his parents?

The plan was already put in place, though. There was no turning back now, especially since Leo opened the door to his parents, Dan and Rebekah, who both had smiling faces. Peyton stopped at the bottom of the stairwell before approaching to hug his "second parents."

"Hi, Rebekah and Dan!" he exclaimed while embracing them.

"Peyton, my boy! How's life?" Dan greeted him with just as much enthusiasm.

"It's...going." Peyton backed away and shifted his weight from foot to foot. "You know, with school and stuff."

"I totally understand. Is it going well, at least? Semester's over halfway done."

"It's been a very interesting semester." Peyton then thought anxiously, *"You'll soon know the darker half of it."*

Dan patted him on the back. "I'm sure it has."

Caroline then entered the foyer, dashing to prepare herself. "Rebekah! Dan! Come in; come in!" She hugged the two of them just like her son did seconds before. "How are you both?"

"As good as it gets," Rebekah replied. Peyton could hear the smile in her tone; the fact he, Leo, and Paige would be taking that gesture away felt awful.

CHAPTER TWENTY-SEVEN

"Make yourselves at home," she insisted to her two guests. "Dinner should be ready in a couple minutes. Lucas is making sure I somehow didn't screw up the spaghetti."

"Mom. You *never* screw up the spaghetti," Peyton complimented, albeit a little snappy.

Leo nudged him in the arm quite hard.

"Hey!"

Caroline's lips curved downwards. "Are you alright, Pey?"

"Yeah," he quickly assured her. "I'm fine."

It was then, and only then that Paige decided to knock on the open front door while dressed - literally and metaphorically - as Penny Hamilton. "Uh, hi!" she chirped to get everyone's attention.

"Hey, Pai-er...Penny!" Hurriedly, Peyton corrected himself and engulfed her in a hug. There surely were a lot of hugs going around. "Long time no see. How are you?"

"You just saw me yesterday," Paige giggled into his shoulder. "And I'm good. You?"

"I'm alright."

Paige leaned forward to hug Leo at Peyton's side. "Hi, Leo. Good to see you."

"Good to see you too...Penny." The redhead returned the gesture while also struggling to say her name right.

When Paige let go of Leo, she smiled at Caroline, who also embraced her. "Hi, Darling. It's a pleasure to have you around again."

"*Holy—how many hugs am I supposed to get tonight?*" Paige grimaced but gave back the same energy. "You too, Mrs. Finlay."

"Oh, please. It's Caroline." The blonde woman rested her hands on her shoulders and gave her a smile identical to Peyton's. She then directed her attention to her husband. "Lucas! Can you put the spaghetti on plates, please?"

"Yes, Dear! Already on it!" he called from the kitchen.

Rebekah's eyes were friendly as she introduced herself. "I'm Rebekah and this is Dan. We're Leo's parents."

"Hi, there." Dan waved kindly.

"It's nice to meet you two."

Paige smiled and shook both of their hands. She remembered the both of them, alright. The fact she paid back her debt in the form of McDanny's cheeseburger meals would forever remain a relieving secret. Rebekah and Dan were two of the sweetest people she had ever met, going out of their way to help her unknowingly when she needed it the most. Their generosity was something Paige would never ever forget.

"Oh, you're a darling!" Rebekah reached out to pinch her cheeks. Leo's face became redder than his hair. "I heard you go to college with my son. What are you studying?"

"Uh, my major's undeclared for now," Paige squeaked from the sudden confrontation.

Thankfully, she let go a second later. "You'll decide soon enough."

"I'm sure I will."

"Dinner's ready!" Lucas announced from the kitchen.

Like a stampede, Peyton, his parents, Leo, his parents, and Paige paraded into the kitchen where Lucas was trying to carry all seven plates to the table on both of his arms. Caroline dashed over to take half of the load and set each plate of spaghetti on the wooden surface between a fork on top of a napkin and a knife on the right side. Peyton pulled out a seat for Paige, which she did not expect, but took anyway. She nodded in gratitude and sat down, letting Peyton push her chair in. Then, he sat down next to her.

The seating arrangement was simple. Lucas was on the far-left end of the table while his wife was on the far right. Leo was sandwiched between his parents, Rebekah next to Caroline and Dan next to Lucas. That left Peyton and Paige a side to themselves. Paige's mouth could not help but water at the enamoring aroma of her dinner placed in front of her. Unfortunately, that was when everyone decided to hold hands and say grace.

"Who would like to say grace?" Caroline inquired to the table.

"I'll do it," Peyton piped up before anyone else could.

Everyone around the table bowed their heads. Paige was not used to some sort of thing, even though she had been pressured into saying the prayer herself last time she was at a family dinner. Even though Peyton must have done this thousands of times, he still neglected to appear comfortable. He made up a prayer on the spot.

"Hey, God. Thanks for the food and let us enjoy it. Thanks for Mom not burning the spaghetti. Amen."

All four of the parents chuckled at that before digging into their meals. The spaghetti was too good to be put to waste. Cold spaghetti specifically was not the way to go, apparently. The only sound that could be heard for the first couple of minutes were utensils scraping against plates and quiet chewing around the room.

Paige *hated* the sound of chewing. She gripped her fork tighter and shoveled noodles twirled around the prongs into her mouth.

Once conversation started, no matter how bland, Paige was relieved that the awkward silence had been taken away. Peyton's parents asked Leo about school and Leo's parents asked Peyton about school. It was routine, as both of them said it was going "okay." When the question came around to Paige, she had no idea what to do other than to agree and say her studies were going "okay" as well. She knew of no other way to describe her academic life.

Then, the parents began to speak about their work. Paige discovered that Lucas was a doctor working at Arkford General Hospital. That fact probably should have been obvious due to the doctor's kit kept in the bedroom. Of course, Caroline and Lucas did not know about that, so all Paige needed to say was "That's cool, Mr. Finlay." The parents left it at that.

The dreaded moment of everyone's plates being halfway consumed finally came. That was the time that the three of them had agreed on to break the news. Peyton looked at Leo and gave him a curt nod. He returned the gesture and then did the same for Paige. Despite her nodding back, he noticed her leg bouncing up and down under the table; she was nervous. Peyton chose listening to his instincts over the annoying voice inside his head and placed a gentle hand on her thigh to keep it from jittering about. Paige's eyes snapped towards him, but she remained still.

Peyton cleared his throat. This was it.

"Mom, Dad, and Leo's parents," he started out. "There's something you all should know."

All eyes were on him. Caroline smiled innocently. "What is it, Pey?"

"How am I supposed to say this?" Peyton fumbled but trusted his gut and spilled everything at once. "Penny isn't really Penny–her name's Paige and she's a shapeshifter and is really a super cool superhero with superpowers but she had to escape an organization that wanted absolute power and that gave her the superpowers, so she came here and has been staying in the guest bedroom since September and now everyone's in trouble because the organization wants to control the whole city so we made this huge plan to stop them a week from Saturday at the National Championship game."

By the time Peyton was finished, he was panting from how long that sentence was. When he finally looked up from catching his breath, Leo had his face in his hands and Paige... well, she was as still as a statue. She stared down at her food like it was some sort of green-eyed monster. He knew he was trying to avoid the gaze of the six other people at the table. Peyton did what he thought was right. He slid his hand that was on her thigh into hers to keep it from shaking. It was not much, but it was something

What he didn't expect was for her to squeeze his hand tightly.

What neither of them expected was Lucas to eye Peyton with raised eyebrows and ask, "Peyton, are you drunk?"

"No, I'm not drunk!" he yelled louder than he meant to. "This is all true. Leo, tell them."

Leo just nodded and hid his face. "It's true," he muttered sheepishly.

"Um, Honey..." Caroline put a gentle hand on her shoulder. "Are you feeling alright?"

"I'm fine!" Peyton took her hand off of him. "This is all true, and none of us are drunk."

"I thought superheroes were only in movies," Rebekah commented somehow casually. "There's no way that one could exist in real life."

Dan added with the same tone, "Me too."

"Oh, for the love of God!" Paige decided to make her presence known and shift into her true form, a blonde with hazel eyes and no glasses. "See?"

The entire table was silent. Lucas' fork clattered onto the table, knocking spaghetti sauce and noodles from the prongs everywhere. Every single one of them–Dan, Rebekah, Carolina, Lucas, and even Peyton and Leo were trying to take in what had just happened. None of them expected Paige to break down so quickly–including her. Paige's stomach turned in circles. For a moment she thought her dinner would end back up on the plate, but she swallowed down the anxiety crippling her. She clung onto Peyton's hand with a death grip. He held her hand gently, but firmly, as if it was a soft presence, but a necessary one.

Dan was the first one out of the four parents to speak. "Well, damn."

"You're telling me." Lucas awkwardly picked his fork up and cleaned it off with his napkin.

"Peyton, you...," Caroline softly stuttered out, pointing at her son and then Paige. "You had her stay in the guest room and we didn't know? No wonder you always got two helpings of dinner. Paige, is it?"

Paige nodded fearfully.

"You're more than welcome to have a helping of breakfast, lunch, ro dinner whenever you'd like. Why didn't you say so?"

Wait. This was not right. Why was everyone being so nice? This was not what Paige was expecting at all. In fact, Leo finally lifted his field of vision, but not to a table of angry people. At that very moment, the three of them were very blessed to have such kind, loving families who had open minds even when it was never anticipated.

"I think that having superpowers is pretty darn cool," Rebekah announced cheerfully and smiled at Paige. "Be proud of yourself, Sweetheart."

Paige could not help but blush. "Thank you, Mrs... um...Rebekah?"

"You're welcome," the middle-aged woman chuckled.

"Wait a minute," Caroline interrupted the happy moment with a concerned question. "Pey, you mentioned you three have a plan to stop an...organization thing? Is it safe?"

This time, it was Peyton's turn to squeeze Paige's hand. "Probably not."

"Oh, I don't know about this..."

CHAPTER TWENTY-SEVEN

Lucas nudged his wife from across the table and looked at Peyton crossly. "Son, you lied to us, hid an extra person in the house for over a month, and kept all of this a secret just for her safety?"

"Mhm, yup," he gulped and averted his eyes.

"I'd say that's very admirable of you, and I'm proud of you." His expression changed to one of pride. "Thank you for trusting us with this. We'll work things out and make sure everything and everyone is safe and taken care of."

Caroline hesitated, contemplating the situation, but then broke. "How can we help?"

Peyton, Leo, and Paige all three let out a sigh of relief in unison.

That went much better than any of them thought.

Chapter Twenty-Eight

INDIGO

A blue mechanical pencil scribbled on a large poster board. "How does this look?" the wielder questioned almost self-consciously.

"It looks like the top of a building."

"Great!" Peyton cheered while waving his arms around. "Because that's what I was trying to draw."

"I can see that," Paige offered him a sarcastic retort.

Peyton rolled his eyes and clicked his mechanical pencil to dispense more lead. "I'm drawing a blueprint of the baseball field that Leo found on the database so we're completely sure that we know what we're doing tomorrow."

"Why didn't you just print out the blueprint?"

Peyton looked at Paige, his poster board, and then at Paige again. "Oh, I really could've done that, couldn't I?" he asked, utterly dumbfounded.

"My *God*." Paige hid her face in her hands at Peyton's obliviousness. She knew it was due to his worries surfacing more each day, but it was something she was not compatible with.

She inhaled a deep breath and elaborated, "This works too. What were you saying?"

"You don't have to pity me," Peyton half-teased, half-excused for her kindness. He looked down at the floor, past his drawing.

"I'm not pitying you." She cocked her head to one side just a notch.

"The hell you're not."

Paige decided to avert her eyes once she heard the slight snap in his tone.

"I'm so sorry." Peyton suddenly realized what exactly he had done and instinctively held his hands out. "I didn't mean to be rude. I'm just...stressed. I know you are too, and that was no excuse for me to lash out."

"You didn't lash out, Peyton," she assured him in a whisper.

"*God...*"

Peyton wished he knew where his mind went on vacation for the past few weeks, but all he was aware of was that he wanted to go there too. Certainly, it could not have been in the clouds for nearly a month, but it surely seemed as such. Peyton had to scratch the back of his neck and shake his head to return to reality. There was nothing about his thoughts that was fictional. He needed to keep his head in its atmosphere and pay attention to the task at hand.

Was this how Paige felt about the missions she used to go on for the organization?

The boy released a long exhale while his imagination continued to run a marathon. The crummy baseball field he drew on a large poster board he purchased from the dollar store looked quite dumb. In fact, he thought *he* looked even dumber. Paige pointed out a simple mistake he had made that would have saved him so much time. Now, he felt like an idiot, especially since the girl he was trying to impress pointed out his error.

Being pressured was like a crossword that had no correct answer.

"Seriously, Peyton," Paige continued. Slumped eyebrows and a pitiful frown were an odd look on her. "It's okay. Don't pressure yourself so much."

"How does she know what I'm thinking?" Peyton snapped out of his imagination. "I'm trying. I'm sorry."

She scowled at that. "Stop apologizing."

There was the old Paige he knew and loved.

"Yes, Ma'am." He mock-saluted and directed both of them back to the drawing board...literally. "We don't know where the four corrupted people are going to be, but from Leo's observations, they will definitely be present to help corral those who become exposed to the Endiridium. Hopefully, it won't ever get to that point, but if it does, you know what to do."

"Right." Paige kept her focus on his face rather than the drawing. "If the chemical gets released before we can stop it, I can try to remove it from everyone at once. There's no telling how much energy that will take, but I'll do my best."

"That's all we're hoping for."

Paige could not help but wonder if Peyton meant to express "I'm" instead of "we're" in that simple statement. The fact someone actually took the time and patience to believe in such a *mess* of a human being was something that she was unable to comprehend. How was she in the same house as she was over a month ago–nearly two at this point, with two loving parental figures and a boy who was *not* like a brother, but...something else. Paige forced the idea back down her throat. It was not going to happen.

At least, she *thought* it was not going to happen.

Then again, another fragment came to her. What if Peyton meant "we're" as in "us?" Was there an "us" at this point between Peyton and Paige, or did he mean it in a mundane, friendly sort of way. Peyton had been more than courteous to his guest who was more of a resident in the Finlays' household at this point, especially since Mr. and Mrs. Finlay were newly on board. The two of them were hesitant at first, but after Peyton - with Paige at his side - reiterated how dire the situation at hand was, they agreed to be of service in any way.

Peyton put down his pencil when Paige failed to fabricate a response. "How about we take a break," he suggested–for his own benefit as well.

"Yes, please." Paige was quick to agree.

Peyton and Paige arose from their seats on the hard, yet carpeted floor, and made refuge out of the former's bed. Paige sunk into the comforter perpendicular to the way a person was supposed to lie down–with her head nearly touching the wall and her legs dangling at the knees above the floor. Peyton did the same, seeing how easily Paige was able to relax once buried in the feathery, fluffy shelter.

"I never got tired looking at the ceiling when I was stuck in a cell," Paige commented out of the blue, tossing a lilac energy ball between her hands and watching it float.

Peyton watched the sphere pass through the air. "Really? How come? When I look at the ceiling, I get bored really fast."

"I had nothing else I *could* do other than toss a ball against it like in the movies or count how many bricks made up each surface." She shrugged casually.

"I'm...I'm sorry."

Paige rolled over on her side to face him. When her dominant hand cupped her cheek, the energy ball vanished into small sparks that faded into the comforter. "Why's that?"

"What do you mean "why?"" Peyton's gaze locked on the

ceiling fan twirling overhead. "You've been a prisoner for most of your life while Leo and I have been living ordinary lives as ordinary people without a problem other than an intense amount of homework every so often. How can I *not* feel bad about that?"

"It's nobody's fault other than the organization's."

It was Peyton's turn to roll onto his side towards Paige to better prove his point. "You're just like Leo and I am–still practically a child. Nobody, *especially* you, should have to endure such suffering."

"It wasn't "suffering" after I got used to it."

"I don't think you fully understand what I'm trying to say." Peyton looked directly into Paige's eyes–they were so close, yet so far. "You never got to experience life like we did, like my parents did, like my *grandparents* did. I wish I could change that."

"*Those eyes...*"

Paige was instantaneously enamored by Peyton's authentic dusky irises bearing into her own. Her heart stuttered in her chest once she realized how close their proximity really was. She had never been so near to another person excluding her parents for the first few years of her life. This, however, was much different. She had nothing to do with the two people who left her behind, but with Peyton–Paige wanted *more*.

"You know..." Paige could hardly hear her own voice over her heart pounding in her ears. "I think you might be able to do just that."

Peyton blinked open his eyes the rest of the way. "What do you mean?"

"What I mean is..." Paige ignored the voice in her head screaming at her not to as she reached out and cupped Peyton's chin. "I'm tired of being on the outside looking in. I want to experience life from within the walls."

CHAPTER TWENTY-EIGHT

"W-What do you mean?" Peyton stammered, taken aback by Paige's sudden forwardness.

"I think you know what I mean."

Peyton almost did not recognize the girl in front of him. Such sudden confidence was unheard of. Sure, Paige was protective of herself as well as those she cared about, but bravery was not the same thing as being confident. This, however, was a mixture of both. His eyes were intoxicating. Paige simply could not pull away.

Paige knew little of what possessed her to do so, but she could not resist any longer. The pull was too strong for her not to. Paige guided Peyton's face towards her and engulfed his lips with her own. The simple act of affection, the first *kiss* between them both was soft and slow, jumping no hurdles but instead steadying a fallen one upright. Even though her eyes saw nothing but the backs of the lids, her heart saw Heaven.

The boy's eyes widened for a split second before his mind registered what exactly was happening. He returned the favor, not as much as he wanted to, though, because Paige pulled away before he was able to.

"I'm sorry." Paige looked to be as surprised as he was when she squeaked. "I don't know what came over me. I just..."

Peyton held a finger up to her lips. There was a different look in his eyes, one of kindness, but also desire, as if he was wanting more. "We'll have none of that."

"What?" she croaked despite what he was insinuating.

"You said you wanted to experience what life had to offer, so why stop now?"

Paige's advances, as gentle as they were before, seemed subdued until Peyton began to pull his own weight. Cautiously, he rolled Paige over onto her back and noticed a tiny twitch of a smile anticipating what was to come. He decided not to keep her waiting. Their lips collided as Paige sunk into the bed, almost laughing with the abrupt pleasure such affection had given her. The way Peyton cupped her face in his hands was with the utmost care. This was not a battle of dominance, but rather a surrender of the trance the two of them had put each other under.

Before Peyton knew it, Paige had flipped the both of them over so Peyton had his back sinking into the mattress and his head onto the pillow. At that moment, nothing mattered other than the girl on top of him. The two kissed each other as if they were two helpless individuals suffocating from a lack of oxygen, but at the same time, drowning in their own satisfaction. They say two halves make a whole, but this was not the case. Both Peyton and Paige were whole within themselves, but they built each other up past the breaking point.

Neither of them absolutely needed each other to be successful—both had the capability to get by on their own, but right then and there, times were different.

Paige had never experienced such gentleness, such *love* from another human being before. It was an emotion family had always failed to give her, but on that day, that hour, that minute, and every passing second that Paige and Peyton were in each other's arms, they felt full and yet still could never get enough.

Somehow, someway, the both of them made their way under the covers. Neither of them knew how much time had passed, but by the glimmer of the moonlight shimmering through the window next to the headboard, at least a little bit had ticked by. By that point, it was not like they had grown bored of each other's lips, but decided to take a different approach. Peyton's mouth left hers and instead experimented in different places around her jaw before descending past her chin. Paige jumped - a mere twitch - at the sensation, which made Peyton hesitate until she whispered a strained *"Don't stop"* through her enamored vocal cords.

"Peyton..." Paige craned her neck upwards as his kisses traveled down her neck and close to her collarbone. "Right there, right...*oh, my God*..."

Peyton continued creating a love-bite on her collarbone until she started prodding him, causing his head to shoot back up. "What-...what's wrong?"

"Someone's coming," she hissed and slunk further under the covers.

"They can wait." Peyton covered his head with the comforter and joined her. "All I want is you."

Once more, Paige could not stand the way her stomach fluttered at such simple words. She captured Peyton's lips once again and fought back yet another giggle from how he started trailing butterfly kisses up her jawline. She tilted her head upward to allow access to her neck for a second time. Peyton quickly took the hint and began nipping gently at several spots in every direction. Paige's breath hitched in her throat as he began creating yet another love-bite near the first one on her collarbone. Her entire body stiffened at his touch and her hands made their way into his hair, softly tugging at the tufts. A low hum rumbled in the back of his throat and that somehow contributed to her euphoria.

Peyton detached his lips from her skin for just enough time for the girl to yank her tee off the upper half of her body and throw it across the room. The boy took this as an invitation and did the same with his own before he reattached his lips a tad bit lower. Paige shivered under the touch of his fingers grazing over her rib cage. Despite the petite crevices that each of her ribs placed just above her stomach, he did not seem to mind, instead caressing her body with the adoration it deserved. Her small frame had gotten her this far, and it would continue to carry her to the final battle.

Paige grasped onto Peyton's wrist and rolled him over for a second time so she could somewhat straddle him. His head sank into the pillow just like her teeth nipped tentatively on the lower portion of his neck. Her lips gradually elevated in the form of delicate butterfly kisses just like he had done for her up the most sensitive part of his throat - closest to the windpipe - and up his jaw. Paige fought the urge to suck on a spot by his ear, figuring their illicit affair would be soon discovered, and instead plunged her lips on top of his before he could catch his breath. Nevertheless, both of them silently planned on taking the next step further. Peyton fumbled with the button on his usual jeans and nearly got it undone. Paige heard the pair of pants unzip and her heartbeat accelerated faster than it already had been, resembling a hummingbird's. *This* was what she meant by experiencing life how it should be lived.

Paige thought back to that simple game of Twenty Questions they played in the middle of a Dairy King and what their favorite colors were. Oh, how it had escalated by then. Blue and purple mixed created indigo, a limbo between the two shades. *This* was their indigo, the molding of their bodies and spirits into one. While not all the way, the paintbrush twirled these two cooler colors on the wheel into one. There was no blue. There was no purple. There was only indigo splattered onto their canvas, ripped at every edge but it was a masterpiece.

"Live a little," a quote from some television show had advised her, but she had forgotten the name of it in the heat of the moment. She was ready to do just that.

That was...until the door swung open and Leo walked in snacking on a bag of chips.

"Hey, Peyton!" he exclaimed obliviously. "I thought I'd stop by and bring some late-night snacks to help with our nerves for-...what the hell is going on?"

Peyton almost flinched off the bed from how much he was startled. Paige made herself vanish despite being under the comforter, leaving Peyton to be holding nothing but air. She crawled off from on top of him and instead curled into a ball between his body and the wall. He awkwardly turned around and popped his head out from under the covers.

"Oh, hi, Leo," he exclaimed between subtle gulps for air.

"Good God, Peyton. You're sweating bullets." Leo munched on a chip despite his shock. "Are you feeling alright? Why are you shirtless? Do you have a fever?"

"Uh, yeah." Peyton offered him a wonky smile. "As good as it gets. And...no, I'm not sick. I just got...*hot*! I got hot during my nap—that's it."

Paige clamped her hand over her mouth to keep herself from bursting out into laughter.

Leo popped another chip into his mouth. "...I see. Guess we all should be resting up for the big day tomorrow."

"You know, we really should." The blond tried to hint at Leo to leave...just for the night.

"What snacks do you want?" Leo set down a plastic bag full of treats. "I brought Doritos, Cheetos, Oreos, lots of 'O's, but you can take all of it—maybe even share some with Paige. I know how much of a pig you are."

"Hey!"

The redhead gestured to his peace offering and began backing out of the room. "Well, get some sleep. You'll need it."

"You too. Love you, Man."

"Love you too."

Leo tipped an imaginary hat and exited the room backwards, shutting the door behind him. At once, Paige reappeared and stuck her head out of the covers as well. Peyton needed to take a second to take in exactly who he was looking at. Paige's loose hair pooled around her shoulders and her forehead glistened with tiny droplets of sweat. Still, though, she was the most beautiful thing he had ever seen. She rested the side of her head on the abnormally large pillow that Peyton slept with, eyeing the boy with a grin that had more than good intentions.

"So, where were we?" Peyton smirked with harbored delight now that the two of them were alone again.

Paige nestled into the pillow with fond eyes. "Remind me."

The boy leaned in unfortunately at the same time his phone from the nightstand next to him buzzed. Peyton stopped abruptly, leaving Paige to stifle yet another laugh as he held up his finger and excused himself.

"One second."

Paige waited patiently as Peyton sat up in order to reach his phone. A familiar messaging ID popped up with his best friend's three-letter name on it. His heart sank when he read the contents:

"I'll let you two lovebirds get back to work. Don't think I didn't see the second lump in the covers. ;)"

"Damn him." Peyton rolled his eyes, yet somehow still amused; Leo surely knew how to instigate.

Paige took the phone from him before he could throw it across the room. "What is it?" she inquired, knowing full well what had just happened.

"That asshole sure knows how to ruin the mood."

"Well..." Paige's eyes drifted towards the bag Leo left on the nightstand. "We have snacks."

Peyton's gaze followed her own. He smiled at the idea even though nothing could match the pure euphoria he felt just minutes ago.

"Snacks it is."

Chapter Twenty-Nine

MAROON

Paige had never felt such bliss before.

There was no unnatural light necessary to illuminate the bedroom as a whole. Rays of the morning sun beamed down over the entire room. The space in between the four walls was at a perfect temperature that the ceiling fan regulated; it was just a bit cold, but the blanket covering her balanced it out flawlessly.

Being protected was something Paige had never truly experienced, but right then and there, she felt just that. The two gentle, but strong - maybe not the strongest, but that was the only instance she underwent such treatment - arms fit snugly around her torso sealed the deal. Paige's hands clung onto both the pair of appendages and a substantial portion of the dark blue comforter. The rhythmic rising and falling of the chest belonging to the person behind her was more soothing than she ever expected.

She procrastinated opening her eyes for as long as she could. Paige heard Peyton's soft snores from behind her and felt them as well when her hair moved ever so slightly with each respiration. That only made her want to soak in as much warmth, as much *affection* as she could. Maybe it was her imagination, but she thought she felt Peyton's arms tighten just a little bit around her and his cheek resting daintily on the back of her head where it hadn't been before.

All she wanted to focus on was the fact she actually felt loved for the first time in her life.

Paige wished with all her heart that this moment would last forever, but the inevitable was upon her once the alarm on Peyton's phone started to sound. It was not loud and obnoxious, but rather quiet and calming, almost soothing to the ear. Peyton let out a whiny exhale and was about to roll over when he realized exactly what kind of predicament he was in. Cautiously, he reached over with one arm to turn the alarm off. It returned just in time for Paige to clasp onto and to pretend to be asleep.

Well...for the most part.

"I know you're awake," Peyton murmured into her hair.

Paige kept her breathing as steady as possible and her eyes slammed shut to avoid confrontation. She had enough of that the previous night.

Little did she know, Peyton began gently prodding her shoulder with the hand that was closest to it. "Stop faking it," he smirked teasingly. "I know you can hear me."

"I don't care," mumbled Paige as she took a tighter hold of the blanket.

"Come *on*."

"No."

Peyton could not help what he did next. Carefully, he turned her around and placed a delicate peck on her forehead. "Is that what you wanted?"

"Not exactly, but I'll get up." Paige rolled her eyes and shoved the comforter and sheets out from on top of her.

"I didn't mean for you to get up this quick, but I-...I-..." Peyton stuttered to a halt when Paige got to her feet, still without a tee covering the upper half of her body. Only a sports bra left half of it to the imagination. *"Good grief, I'm such a blubbering idiot."*

Paige just smiled snarkily in his direction. "You...what?" She decided to tease him just a little bit. "Now, if you don't mind, I'm going to take a shower."

Peyton scurried to a standing position before he could stop himself. "Can-"

"Before you say a word, my answer is no."

"What? You can't do that! I didn't even say anything!"

"You already almost saw me without a towel once," Paige reminded him playfully. "I'm not risking that again. This is as much as you get."

Peyton tried to follow after her, but she stopped him by generating an energy field in the middle of the room. "But I-"

"No!"

"I hope you know I'm teasing."

A grin curled onto her lips. "I know."

Once Paige walked through the door, it seemed as if everything returned to normal for at least a little while. She took her shower, changed into a set of clothes that was more her size—a white band tee that went down to mid-thigh along with jeans with a hole in the knee and her shoes that she wore every day topped off with her favorite black sweater. Paige brushed out her hair in the guest room and decided on placing a hair tie around her wrist. She had no idea what the day had in store for her.

Breakfast, or more like lunch since it was half past noon, went in the same fashion. Both Paige and Peyton made sure they were each filled to the brim with pizza that the Finlays ordered since the two of them were probably not going to have anything until much later. Paige discovered she thoroughly enjoyed cheese pizza much more than pepperoni. For a moment, Peyton thought she was crazy, but then, he remembered she could throw him across the room with a flick of her wrist.

It probably would not be a good idea to argue with her.

The afternoon blurred together into several hours of watching cartoons and playing video games. Peyton and Paige had their plan set in stone, as well as Leo, but all of them figured he had slept for the maximum time allowable for the first ten hours of daylight. Nevertheless, he was more than awake when the time came for the two families to drive - in separate vehicles - to the Arkford Blue Warriors' baseball field just outside of town.

Paige simply could not sit still during the drive to the field. She sat on the right hand side of the back seats while Peyton was on her left fiddling with his phone. Paige decided to lean over and check out what exactly was going on in the little device he held in his hand. It turned out that he was switching between a text conversation with Leo, whose vehicle was directly behind them stopped at the same traffic light, and a spaceship shooting game that looked retro. When Peyton realized he had an audience, he tilted his phone towards her so she could spectate.

That kind gesture, no matter how small, made Paige's heart flutter into oblivion. She absolutely despised not having control over her own emotions around Peyton anymore. It was merely something she would have to get used to. Of course, she had plenty of time to do that if everything went well with their mission that crept up to them sooner than either of them thought.

Paige continued watching Peyton play his space game that he gave up trying to show her how to play - even though all the player needed to do was tap to shoot - and text Leo funny pictures, or "memes," as he had called them before. She dreaded what was about to become of what would be a fun day for the entirety of Arkford if it weren't for the organization. Paige's whole frame tensed at the thought of it. Her eyes watched the flying colors out the window until a warm hand slid into one of her cold ones.

She snapped her gaze upwards to meet a concerned pair of eyes. "Are you okay?" Peyton whispered just out of earshot of his parents in the driver's and passenger's seats.

"I'm fine. Worry about yourself." Paige nodded with a sudden numbness.

"But I'm worried about *you*."

That led to an abrupt half in Paige's train of thought. "You don't need to worry."

"Yes, I do," Peyton insisted softly.

She tried to hide a smile on her face, but miserably failed when a rosy hue grew on her cheeks. It stayed there until the Finlays' vehicle entered the parking lot and picked a spot as close as they could get. The Rhys' car snagged the parking spot right next to them, and the group of six exited their cars all at the same time. Leo tugged the straps of his black backpack over his shoulders. The three of them tried to avoid the odd look Leo's father was giving him.

"Are they going to let you bring that in?"

Leo shrugged at that. "We'll see. Otherwise, I'll just stay in the car."

"Oh, no you won't." Rebekah tugged him forward. "We bought you a ticket for this game even if you aren't going to watch it. Maybe we should've gotten Ollie to come with us instead."

"Mom," Leo whined at the woman staring up at him. "I can

try to convince the bag checker dude to let me bring it in when we get up there."

Rebekah looked like she wanted to argue, but decided not to, instead offering him a hesitant, motherly smile. "Alright, then."

For the first time since before she could remember, Paige finally imagined herself as if she was a part of a family. She was surrounded by people she had grown to love and trust–Peyton on one side and Leo on the other. The two sets of parents walked behind their kids and spoke to each other out of earshot. The tension in the air was so thick it could be cut with a steak knife. Paige warmed her hands by stuffing them in the pockets of her sweater, one that was occupied by a ticket for the game. The cool breeze outside did nothing to aid that factor.

"Tickets, please," a kind, elderly man in a reflective vest whom Paige assumed was the ticket master or whatever they were called requested.

One by one, the group of six removed their tickets from their pockets or bags. The man smiled as he scanned each ticket and welcomed each one of them into the next portion of the entrance procedure. This was where the entire process became more difficult. Paige walked through the large metal detector first since she did not have any bags or metal on her. Then, Peyton entered second after placing his phone in the plastic bin. Leo was third, taking off his backpack and placing it in the bin along with his phone. With a goofy smile, he started to strut through the metal detector when a security guard standing by the baggage check stopped him.

"Woah there, young man," he halted him politely. "We don't allow backpacks into the field for security reasons. You're going to either have to put that back in the car or we can't let you in.

Paige stood stock still. She leaned over and hissed to Peyton, "They aren't going to let him in?"

"Watch," whispered Peyton with a grin. "Leo can squirm his way around it."

A frown that both Paige and Peyton knew was fake grew on the redhead's face. "Oh, *please*, Sir. The Blue Warriors are my favorite team and Mom and Dad only said I could go if I did some homework during the game. I'm very behind but can multitask efficiently. Right, Mom?"

"Huh?" Rebekah was clueless until her husband nudged her. "Oh! Yeah, I told him that."

"See?"

"Can we check your bag?" the security guard asked.

"Of course you can." Leo unzipped it for him and revealed the contents to him in every compartment. "I only have my laptop for homework and a charger just in case it dies."

The man who looked like an off-brand police officer hesitated, checking each of the contents of the bag. He looked at Leo, who had already snuck by the metal detector and was deemed all clear. The guard then looked at Leo's parents who played the part as well as they were capable of doing. Then, he exhaled and passed the bin across the table towards Leo.

"Enjoy the game, Son."

Leo conjured up the biggest smile he could at that moment, zipped his backpack up, and slung it over his shoulders. "Thank you, Sir."

"See?" Peyton asked Paige quietly. "Works every time."

Paige just rolled her eyes at the two of them. "If lying was a sport, you two would have a medal."

"Thank you."

When the rest of the big family went through the metal detectors, Leo started walking next to the two of them. "What are we talking about?"

"Don't worry about it," Peyton dismissed the subject and changed it entirely. "Ooh, popcorn!"

"We'll get food when everything is clear," Paige insisted, taking a hold of his wrist and dragging him away from the concessions stand.

"Nuts."

"They have those there too," Leo teased.

"Hope you guys don't mind we got seats close to the top," Caroline interrupted their pre-argument by gesturing to their seats. "They were the only ones we could find on such short notice. We're here."

"This is perfect." Leo plopped down in a seat directly under the shade of the interior portion of the field. "Thank you."

"You're welcome." Caroline smiled and took her seat between her husband and Rebekah.

Peyton made sure Paige had the aisle seat, something she requested when the families were purchasing the tickets to the game several days ago. The girl was wonderstruck by the view she suddenly possessed. She had only seen baseball fields on television, but in real life, everything looked to be so much bigger, larger than life itself. Then again, Paige was small in stature, which made everything around her bigger than they really were.

Paige watched Peyton play the retro shooter game on his phone before the game was to begin. Leo whipped out his laptop, set it on his lap, flipped up the lid, and accessed the database he had been researching for weeks. Paige never truly got a good look at it, so she leaned over a suddenly flustered Peyton to do so. Once she did, though, she was instantly overwhelmed. How on God's green Earth did Leo navigate such a complex universe within his device?

Thankfully, that was his niche–not hers.

"When should we start investigating?" Paige asked Peyton, who was entranced by his game.

Peyton paused the game, albeit reluctantly. "I guess when Leo starts getting information. Do you see anything, Leo?"

"Nothing by the organization has been booted up quite yet," Leo replied while typing and clicking. "All I can do is watch and wait until I get a signal."

"What kind of signal would that be?" inquired Paige softly.

Leo pointed to a window inside of his screen. "Do you see that?" he questioned, and she nodded. "The organization can see what the corrupted people see because of the Endiridium that's in their system. Once the organization is ready, so will we."

"Got it."

Time flew by like a gaggle of geese overhead in a V-shape but also ticked agonizingly slow. It seemed as if the pre-game announcements took a millennium rather than five to ten minutes and the National Anthem felt like three verses instead of one. Finally, the game started and the players from Arkford in blue and Cambridge in white uniforms took the field. Paige did not bother asking Peyton how the game was played, but she did remember how he promised her he would take her to an Arkford Blue Warriors game on the night of the fraternity party.

How Paige did not realize her feelings then, she had no clue.

Rather than having his eyes on the game, Leo's gaze was glued on his screen waiting for some sort of change on the screen. He turned the brightness all the way up in order to see any type of discoloration on the blank window. Everything was there on his computer. The group of three had prepared for days upon days for this very moment. Now, all of them forgot exactly what they were supposed to do when that moment truly came.

A feed coming from someone else's point of view popped up on Leo's screen. The redhead turned to the two of them and gave them a curt nod.

"It's showtime."

Both Paige and Peyton swallowed nervously when they realized their time had arrived. "Mom, Dad—Paige and I are going to get some snacks." The latter leaned over and notified his parents.

Caroline grasped onto Lucas' hand with worry. "Be careful, Pey."

"I will, Mom," he solemnly promised and fistbumped Leo, who removed three headsets from his backpack, handing one to Paige and one to Peyton. "Where in the hell did you hide these?"

Leo grinned innocently. "Secret pocket."

Peyton looked as if he was about to retort, but then patted him on the shoulder. "Keep in touch."

"What do you think these things are for? Decoration?"

"Oh, shut up."

Leo chuckled but then turned serious. "Be careful, though. Both of you."

"We will," Paige and Peyton replied in unison.

Before anything else was said and done between the group of six. Peyton and Paige broke off in their own direction, a planned route according to Leo's instruction. Paige led the way while Peyton trailed behind, the two of them placing their headsets over their ears and switching them on. Once they both reached a quieter area, Peyton tried communicating with Leo.

"Leo, can you hear me?"

CHAPTER TWENTY-NINE

Seconds later, the ginger's focused voice came through crisp and clear. *"I can hear you. Paige, can you hear me?"*

"Affirmative," Paige confirmed with more gusto than Peyton expected.

The blond boy gave her an odd look–furrowed brows, and tight lips.

"What?" she innocently questioned. "Just trying out a big word I learned in English class."

"I see," Peyton chuckled.

Paige quickly changed the subject even though she desperately did not want to. "Where are we headed, Leo?"

"It looks like Subject A is headed for the cotton candy stand on the far-right side of the stadium. The feed is live and has a three-second delay, so I'll let you know if they move."

"Got it. Let's go."

Paige dragged Peyton along as she started speed walking towards the cotton candy stand that Leo mentioned. Since the Blue Warriors game had just begun, not many people were purchasing concessions or using the restroom quite yet. Instead, all eyes were on the sportsmanship in front of them. The Knights batted first, which was always suspenseful for the home team's fans. Paige hardly saw anyone wearing Cambridge merchandise, but rather a sea of navy blue.

"What does Subject A look like?" Peyton asked Leo once he and Paige reached a distance of several yards away from the cotton candy stand.

A couple of seconds passed, but Leo answered, *"Subject A has dark blonde hair and is wearing a red sweatshirt with black leggings. I believe her name's Ivy."*

"Got it." Paige quickly scanned the area and found a girl fitting the description. She pointed in her direction. "There she is. Peyton. You drag her out of sight and I'll do the rest."

Peyton nodded and yanked the hood of his faded blue hoodie over his head. "On it."

Paige watched from afar as Peyton strode over to Ivy, who appeared to be contemplating the menu with emotionless glazed-over blue eyes until Peyton clasped onto her wrist.

"There you are, Babe," he said just as he had rehearsed. "I thought we were going to get popcorn at another place. Let's go there first."

"You wish," Ivy spat with surprise, but was not strong enough to run the other way. "Let go of me! Let *go*!"

"You'll thank me later, Ivy."

"No! Let me go!"

Peyton ran around the corner where Paige was waiting with outstretched hands. "Are you ready?" he asked, fighting against a struggling Ivy.

"As I'll ever be."

Paige stepped forward and ignited the lilac flame that always sparked whenever she concentrated hard enough. Ivy glared directly into Paige's eyes, brightened by the hue. The periwinkle energy began to encircle Ivy like some sort of tornado. Both she and Peyton tried to ignore the muffled screams from under Peyton's hand clamped over her mouth as he held her steady during the entire process. Paige was not anticipating how long it truly took for all of the Endiridium to exit her system, a pale blue mixing in with the purple swirls until it faded away completely. When it was finally finished, though, Paige's body was substantially more fatigued than it was moments earlier.

Ivy, on the other hand, was slumped down on the ground, held upright only by Peyton's grip underneath her shoulders. He dragged her carefully until she was leaning against a wall in an alleyway leading to the exit of the stadium.

CHAPTER TWENTY-NINE

"What happened?" Ivy groaned, clutching her forehead and blinking her eyes open.

Paige was relieved to see they were a chocolatey brown. "You were under the control of the organization, but you're safe now. Stay here and out of sight." She kneeled down to her level. "We're helping your friends as well."

"My friends? What happened to my friends?"

"They're suffering the same fate, but it will be over soon."

Ivy was too weak to argue, so she complied, nodding her head. Paige stood back up and spoke into her microphone. "Come in, Leo. We've restored Subject A. Where's our next feed?"

"*That's great news!*" Leo yelled louder than he thought he would, summoning odd looks from his parents, Peyton's parents, and spectators around them. He quieted down. "*Subject B is approaching the ladies' restroom near the center of the field, between two concession stands. She's named Ayla with brown hair and is wearing a black tank top and ripped light washed jeans.*"

"We're heading that way." Paige already started to dash off when Leo interrupted.

"*Wait! I'm intercepting a second feed that's on the far-left side of the stadium. Subject C is heading for the main exit. He has blond hair and is in all black.*"

Paige stuttered to a stop when she realized what kind of situation they had put themselves in. If the two of them went together, one of the subjects would escape, leaving the whole endeavor to be much more difficult than anticipated.

Then, it hit her.

"Peyton!" Paige sharply grabbed his attention. "You catch up to Subject C and I'll get Subject B in the ladies' room. I'll come find you when I'm done."

Peyton hesitated, however looked as if he agreed. "Split up?"

"That's what I'm suggesting, yes."

"Okay, just…" Peyton leaned in and gave her a spontaneous peck on the lips before she could retaliate. "Be careful. *Please.*"

Paige brushed her fingers across her lips, wondering if what he even did was real. "I will." Her words were a stunned whisper.

Once she started walking away, she realized she could not leave just like *that*. She whirled around just in time to see Peyton start to head off. Paige dashed over to him, spun him around, and smashed her lips against his. It was an unexpected turn of events for the both of them, but not an unwelcome one. Paige absorbed every drop of him that she could for the few seconds the two of them were connected. She pulled away and then sprinted towards the location of Subject B. Peyton watched her depart, a statue of emotions, but then decided to do the same.

Paige dashed to the ladies' room near the center of the field. She knew exactly what to do, but was never ready to do it, especially when she passed through the entrance of the bathroom and saw a young brunette with a black tank top and ripped jeans adjusting her mascara in the mirror. She leaned towards the glass and extended her eyelashes with the small brush in her right hand. Even though the makeup enhanced her eyes, they were still dull from the chemical that Paige was about to extract.

She figured since Ayla was distracted that she would come in from behind. That was exactly what she did. Before she knew it, Paige stepped into the bathroom with energy surrounding her fingertips. She extended her arms and then did the same as she did with Ivy, generating a whirlwind of sorts around her small, thin figure. Ayla let out a surprised shriek when she realized she was trapped in pure nothingness.

"What the hell are you doing?!" Ayla screamed in horror.

Paige was more than confident with her response: "The right thing."

The young woman continued to scream with tears cascading down her cheeks as the Endiridium exited her system and entered the lavender tornado, disappearing without a trace at least half a minute later. Once the supports holding her upright vanished, Ayla collapsed. Paige launched forward to catch the girl before her head hit the ground. She clutched her forehead and blinked her brown eyes open.

It worked for a second time.

"What's going on?" Ayla's question was nearly inaudible.

"You're safe," Paige assured her, avoiding the query. "I'm going to transport you to be with your friend, Ivy. Both of you are okay now."

"What hap-"

"Everything will be explained later. Just trust me. Okay?"

Ayla could do nothing but nod.

Paige opened a vortex underneath Ayla's body that teleported her to the alleyway with Ivy. She heard a small yelp as the ground separated below, but it quickly vanished along with the brunette's body. Paige attempted to get to her feet, but was noticeably slower than before, her body seeming to be weaker than before. She decided to ignore it, tapping into the microphone on her headset.

"Leo, Subject B is reversed and safe. Is Subject C still heading towards the exit?"

"Great work," Leo complimented her from his seat.

Peyton interrupted from his end, seeming to struggle. *"I've got Dylan! Hurry so we can get him reversed!"*

Paige broke out into a sprint towards the far-left side of the stadium. By now, more civilians had gotten up to use the restroom or purchase concessions from all of the possible options scattered around the walkways of the massive stadium. Paige despised how she had to weave around crowds of people just like at Azure University or even among the streets of Arkford. It was something she never became completely accustomed to, especially now.

She suddenly knew exactly where she was supposed to go when she began to hear the furious profanities coming from a deep voice that she had heard only twice before. Paige ran further to view Peyton on top of Dylan in an attempt to hold him down. Dylan was much larger and had quite a bit more muscle than Peyton did, especially considering the latter's lanky build.

"You asshole!" Dylan cursed and smacked Peyton's arms and chest while the poor boy was trying to keep him still. "Get the hell off of me!"

"You'll thank me later," Peyton gritted out, taking the hits and punches with a grain of salt.

Paige skidded to a stop. "Peyton! Don't move," she demanded.

"What do you think I'm trying to do?" he snapped, yelping from a slap to the face.

Paige did the same as for Ivy and Ayla, generating a whirlwind around Dylan's flailing, screaming body. Peyton jumped out of the way just as Dylan was restrained from the energy surrounding him at every corner. Paige found herself to be struggling more with each person she extracted the chemical compound from. Peyton watched as the blue Endiridium mixed in with the lilac energy tornado until it disappeared. Paige caught her breath as Dylan fell to the ground. Thankfully, Peyton was able to catch him before he hit his head.

"What the hell?" Dylan tried to shake himself awake, his head swishing from side to side. That only made him dizzier, causing him to limply lay in Peyton's arms.

"You're okay now," Paige told him between quiet puffs for

air. "You were hypnotized by someone named Dr. Kelley, but you aren't under the influence anymore."

Dylan held his head up woozily and fluttered his brown eyes open. "Am I drunk?"

"Unfortunately not. I'm going to transport you to a place where you're safe. Stay with the other two girls there."

"Why?" All of a sudden, he was more alert. "What's going on? Can I help?"

Peyton stood next to Paige after Dylan was sat up. "Thanks for the offer, but it's too dangerous," he politely declined. "What would be most helpful is you staying safe and protecting those two girls who were also influenced."

"Got it." Dylan offered him a thumbs up.

"Good," Paige concluded and opened a portal underneath him.

He was instantly transported to where Ivy and Ayla were in the alleyway away from the action. Once he was gone, Peyton and Paige looked at each other, smiled slightly, and gave each other a high five, something that Paige learned about from him and Leo. This was wonderful news for the both of them, having revived three of the four corrupted people from the organization's control. There was only one left, and Paige had a bad feeling.

"This is too easy," she muttered breathily.

"I'd say we're getting a good sweat from running." Peyton then noticed how fatigued Paige appeared to be. "Hey...you don't look so good."

Paige straightened up once attention was brought to her. "I'm fine," she lied through her teeth. "Let's just get this done. Leo," she directed into the microphone, "Any word on Subject D?"

"I think Subject D is....oh no."

Both of their hearts sank in harmony. "What is it?" she asked the dreaded question.

"I lost my feed."

"What?!" Both Peyton and Paige were in utter disbelief.

"I lost my feed! I don't know where Subject D is."

"Okay, okay, don't panic," Paige instructed an anxious Peyton. "We'll find them."

Peyton began pacing around her. "How? She could be anywhere by now. You're right. This is way too easy."

"Or maybe you two are just idiots," a crisp, snarky female voice exclaimed from behind them.

The duo cautiously turned around to view a smirking Hannah, her dull, but somehow piercing blue eyes scanning over them like a copying machine. Her long brown hair was tied up in a high ponytail. She wore a designer denim jacket, black leggings, and much newer Converse than Paige's. Paige thought she had been zapped by a lightning bolt of pure stamina. Now that the end was finally in sight, she knew exactly what to do. Determination filled her veins.

"Hannah, stay put," she demanded while slowly walking forward. "This is for your own good."

To Paige's surprise, Hannah chuckled at her words. "That's just sad," she mocked, backing away as Paige crept towards her. "Isn't that what your mommy and daddy told you? *It's for your own good.* Look at you now. You're weak. You're pathetic. You're *alone*."

"Let us help you." Paige ignored the comments despite their sting.

The corners of Hannah's lips twitched upward along with her eyebrows narrowing. "You want to help me? Then, you'll have to catch me."

Paige did not quite understand what she meant until she started sprinting the other way. She looked at Peyton and the

CHAPTER TWENTY-NINE

two of them wordlessly agreed to chase after Hannah. After all, it was the only way to make things right when it came to the control of the Endiridium.

"She's headed for the roof!" Paige announced when Hannah disappeared up a flight of stairs.

"I'll take the stairs and you go another way so we can corner her at the top," Peyton suggested before pedaling himself behind her.

Paige was left at a standstill. As far as she knew, there was no other way up to the roof. "Leo," she called the boy still in his seat, "where's the nearest way to the roof besides the stairs?"

"*I'm looking.*" Leo seemed to type on his keyboard for a bit before replying, "*There's another stairwell, but it's on the other side of the stadium. You wouldn't get there quick enough.*"

"Okay, I'll think of something."

Paige continued running until she approached the stands of the baseball game that was already in the third inning. The audience loomed in front of her, focusing on more than just the scoreless game at this point. Instead, the commotion from above caused several spectators to get up and turn around from where they were facing. Paige's brain clicked with an idea, but she was hesitant to go through with it. What were the consequences?

That did not matter right now.

"*You could've thought of a better way to go about with this,*" argued Dr. Kelley.

"I did the first thing I thought of."

"*The first thing you thought of was publicizing your abilities in front of the whole city? The whole state? Maybe even the whole world?*"

"I couldn't just let those people die!" The sphere quietly shattered as Paige rocketed to her feet, knocking the wooden chair she was formerly seated in onto the floor with a crash.

Paige made the ultimate decision not to hide anymore.

"*Fuck* publicity," she ridiculed Dr. Kelley's teachings over all of those years she spent in isolation.

Paige did what she knew only she could. Without caring what those around her thought, she generated those same lilac energy fields she grew up learning how to create and positioned them as spontaneous stairs leading up to the roof. As one foot touched a surface, the field behind her vanished. Everything was in slow motion: her steps, the gasps and confused exclamations from the baseball fans, and her own mind discerning whether this was the right thing or not. This continued until her shoes were upon solid concrete, the roof of the Arkford Blue Warriors stadium.

At that same moment, Hannah appeared through a door near the middle of the room from the stairwell with Peyton hot on her heels. She stopped in her tracks when she realized Paige was in front of her. Hannah turned around desperately and realized Peyton was on the other side blocking the entrance to the stairs back down. She swung her eyes from left to right before ultimately realizing she was trapped.

"Let's get this over with," the blonde girl snarled.

Paige clapped her hands together. When they delicately pulled apart, a large ball of purple energy broke into several shards that eventually became a fourth whirlwind to extract the harmful chemical from Hannah's system. The brunette tried to escape, but was caught in the current. Paige and Peyton fought the urge to plug their ears as Hannah began to scream like a banshee trying to deliver a warning. Paige struggled to keep the tornado intact as the blue Endiridium blended with the lilac winds before disappearing completely. Just like the others, Hannah fell towards the ground, but Peyton caught her before any important part of her body made contact.

"Oh, my...," Hannah murmured as she opened her eyes, thankfully brown once again. "...What happened?"

Paige could have shrieked with the joy she suddenly felt. She and Peyton high fived each other before she engulfed him in a hug after he sat Hannah gently on the ground. The two of them hopped around and embraced like never had before. Nothing amounted to the unmeasurable joy the duo felt when they realized the Endiridium was truly gone and their plan had worked.

That was when a door opening near them followed by a slow round of applause stopped them in the midst of their celebration.

"Very impressive," Dr. Kelley complimented with a sneer. "Very, very nice."

Paige loosened her grip on Peyton with a start. She spun around in his arms until the both of them were facing a hunched-over, balding old man in one of the nicest tuxedos that either of them had ever seen. He was adorned in all black with a tie the color of blood tucked under his blazer. His yellow teeth grinned past his chapped lips. For a second, Peyton thought even his eyes had wrinkles. Paige's heart stopped in her chest. This was not happening.

Not today.

Not now.

Dr. Kelley shut the door behind him and stepped forward. "You see," he started to explain, "I needed the both of you up here so I can further go ahead with the organization's plan that your redheaded friend so cleverly discovered."

Paige was stunned by the pure rage - the *darkening* - in Peyton's eyes that had become slits by that point.

"You son of a-" He started to step forward, but Paige grabbed him by the wrist.

"Now, now," the old man tsked. "You don't want to end up

like your *friend*, do you? It's a wonder how she helped you escape before, but this time, neither of you are going anywhere."

Paige chose her words carefully. "What are you planning on doing with us?"

"Oh, I just want a proper audience." Dr. Kelley removed a remote from his pocket and fiddled around with it in his hands. "You see, I needed to have you two distracted so one of my men could start up a drone filled with the rest of the Endiridium that I didn't leave out in the open for you to take and investigate. No, that was not an accident," he denied an unasked question by Paige's expression. Hearing the drone start to fly over the field made him grin. "We used this research that your friend found to vaporize the chemical into a gaseous form. This way, it is much more transmittable to unsuspecting civilians. All they have to do is breathe it in."

"No, you can't do this," Paige pleaded with the man who was seconds away from fulfilling his so-called destiny. This time, it was Peyton holding her back.

Dr. Kelley exhaled a maniacal laugh, "Too late."

When he pressed the button on his remote to release the Endiridium over the crowd, Paige had to think fast. She wriggled her way out of Peyton's grip and ran towards the edge of the roof. Extending her arms and splaying her fingers like a routine, a massive energy ball formed and surrounded the drone just before the Endiridium began to spread. Beads of sweat fell down Paige's face as more and more of the chemical was absorbed into the violet force field. Paige summoned as much electrical energy as she could to contribute to the sphere. To her, Peyton, and even Dr. Kelley's shock, the force field hardened around the chemical, trapping it inside. Paige telekinetically pulled it towards her and placed it safely on the roof.

"No! The Endiridium!" Dr. Kelley screamed, running as fast as his brittle legs could take him towards the orb.

Peyton looked as if he was about to chase the older man, but the sound of a body crumpling against the floor made him adjust his attention. His eyes widened in terror as he realized Paige had collapsed on the concrete from the amount of energy it took for her to contain the chemical compound. Her body twitched and trembled. Her fingers shook numbingly. He ran over to her and started to try to help her up, but she stopped him with a frail hand raising.

"I-...I need a minute," she gasped weakly while her chest heaved up and down.

Peyton knelt down anyway. "Jesus Christ. Are you okay?"

"I'm fine..."

Paige shut her eyes and rested her head on the solid ground. She ignored how the small pebbles and bumps dug into her skin at every point on her left side. A flash of black metal to his left caught his eye. Peyton's heart launched itself out of his throat when he realized Dr. Kelley had pulled a gun out of his waistband. The man had to fight his devious smile as he cocked the pistol and aimed it towards Paige's motionless frame.

Nothing but pure adrenaline went through his mind as Peyton shot up to his feet and lurched towards the weapon, grabbing a hold of it. Dr. Kelley was much stronger than he anticipated since the two of them put up quite a fight, yanking the gun back and forth like two kids fighting over a toy. Peyton let himself slightly loosen his grip when he realized the barrel was not pointed in Paige's direction anymore. She was not going to be hurt. He had saved her. His heart stopped pounding as hard against his chest.

Lowering his guard was his biggest mistake.

Paige's eyes snapped open once a loud *bang* protruded

through the air. Her entire body fought to writhe in horror when Peyton's thin body fell and landed in a heap on the ground. While he was small before, seeing him so vulnerable made him even more petite, shrunken by the morality that he was promptly reminded of.

"*No!*" Paige screamed when what had happened clicked in her mind.

She saw *red*.

Without thinking, her eyes drifted over to the ball full of Endiridium. She squinted and outstretched her hand in its direction. To her relief, the ball began rolling towards her. Paige forced herself to sit up and use both hands to lift the energy sphere off the ground. With her one last remaining ounce of strength, she let out a shriek and catapulted the ball towards Dr. Kelley.

The unsuspecting demon screeched like a banshee at the top of his lungs when the sphere hit him directly in the face. Paige watched with wide eyes as the Endiridium began to circle Dr. Kelley in all directions, practically consuming him with the energy. He continued to scream and yelp as the whirlwind grew faster and larger. Paige had to hold herself down, clamping onto a bar connected to the roof as the gust became like a hurricane. The tornado lifted up into the air, dragging Dr. Kelley with it. Suddenly, though...

...it stopped.

Paige clamped her hands over her ears as a loud explosion erupted from where Dr. Kelley was once standing. Now, there was nothing left other than lilac sparkles cascading from the sky and disappearing into the concrete. Screams chorused from below. The baseball game had been called off when the first bout of danger was sensed. Now, there were news helicopters hovering overhead along with reporters and cameramen racing in every direction. They had done it.

CHAPTER TWENTY-NINE

When Peyton began coughing and spluttering from a couple of yards away, the reality of what the doctor had done to him hit her like a ton of bricks. Paige crawled over to him with whatever stamina she had and sat over him, placing his head in his lap. She fought back a shudder when she realized blood was pooling on the concrete below and from a large spot on his chest. The maroon liquid made her want to gag, but she still leaned down and smacked his cheek to grasp his attention.

"Peyton, can you hear me?" she stammered, desperately trying to keep him conscious.

All she received was a gurgling cough.

"No, no, *no*!" Paige ripped her sweater off and pressed it against the wound on his torso, causing him to grunt loudly in pain. "Listen. You're going to be okay. Talk to me."

"It's...alright," a whisper croaked from under her.

Paige pressed down against his chest, ignoring the crimson beginning to stain her hands through her sweater. "You're right. It's okay. You're going to be okay."

"I-It's over..." He cracked a small smile. "You're safe..."

"And you will be too."

Peyton tried to say something else, but instead began coughing harder. He was too feeble to speak, much less sit upright as his condition started getting worse. This was when Paige officially started to panic. She could not remember the last time she cried - possibly when her parents left her at the organization "for her own good" - but this time...was by far the worst.

"Help! Somebody! *Please!*" Paige yelled for someone - anyone - to come to their aid.

"*Paige?*" She had forgotten she was still wearing the headset. Somehow, she must have called in to Leo's feed. *"Are you crying? I heard the explosion. What's going on?!"*

She fought back many sobs threatening to clog her throat.

"Leo! Peyton's been shot! We're on the roof. Come here. We need you!"

"What?! Oh my God! I'm coming! We're coming!"

"Peyton, *listen*—you're going to be alright," she repeated, mostly for her sake.

"You know...," he choked out between labored gasps for air. "I...I didn't want to...t-tell you this way..."

Paige cupped his chin with one of her bloody hands. "Then don't. Wait until you're all better. Then, you can tell me."

"But Paige... I-... I-..."

"*I called an ambulance,*" Leo announced. "*They'll be here soon.*"

"Thanks, Leo." Paige kept her teary eyes, the salty liquid cascading down her cheeks, on Peyton's heaving frame. "Keep going, Peyton."

"...I love you," Peyton rushed out with a fatigued grin. "There. I finally s-said it."

Paige tried to mimic his expression through her weeping gaze. "I love you too, Peyton. Just stay awake. Help is on the way."

The girl kept the declining, but smiling, boy in her arms while everything around her occurred in slow motion. Before she knew it, Leo, followed by Peyton's parents and his own parents, burst through the stairwell's door. She could not even look at their devastated, horror-filled faces. Peyton's mother let out a gut-wrenching scream when she saw her son struggling to breathe on his friend's lap. Soon enough, sirens began blaring from below that Paige fought an urge to flinch away from. She held her sweater against Peyton's wound where blood was still pouring out. When his eyes rolled back in his head, she thought her heart stopped beating.

Everything else was a blur.

A purple blur.

Chapter Thirty

TRANSPARENT

Was this what heartbreak truly felt like? Was heartbreak the sensation of laying the table for a lavish dinner–plates, forks, spoons, and knives placed to perfection around the plates only for no one to use? Was it when every napkin was expertly folded into a three-dimensional pyramid on top of each plate only for no one to eat? Was it the fact that every glass was filled with a perfect amount of water and ice to reach the top only for no one to drink?

Was it when the table was set for a guest that never showed up?

Heartbreak was when someone tried their very best for someone who never appreciated it, only merely sanctioning the act as if it were a chore or even a crime committed. It was the stroke of black paint amongst a bright, heavenly sunrise. It was the absence of stars on a clear night. It was as if a dagger was prematurely removed from a chest wound only for the victim to helplessly bleed out.

The joys of life should have been celebrated, but instead, they were only tolerated.

Heartbreak was the dark brown hair dye bleeding into the running water in the bathroom sink. It was the sense of hopelessness that Paige felt as she dried off her straight hair and looked at a face in the mirror she hardly recognized. Her bloodshot eyes stung as they met the cool oxygen in the room. Dark bags circled her under-eyes and her chapped lips that were glued shut with remorse. She grabbed a towel off the rack and engulfed her hair with it, attempting to dry it and let the color sink in any way that it could.

"I'm so sorry, Paige."

Heartbreak was the way the few clothes she had easily fit in an ebony suitcase given to her by one of her closest friends. Every single article of clothing except for her black knit sweater, which was now in the trash can in the kitchen, laid loosely at the bottom. Her now-brown hair hung over her face as she collected everything that she owned, which was not much at all for that matter, and zipped the bag shut. Paige hated how a teddy bear given to her by the same friend gazed up at her with its beady, lifeless eyes that mirrored her own.

"There's nothing else we can do."

Heartbreak was the way Paige kept her eyes glued to the television screen belonging to the hotel room she had lived in for the past month. Her stomach rumbled with hunger since she had barely eaten for days, even weeks at that point. It was set to a local news station that was still covering the events from thirty days prior.

"We're still searching for the young woman who risked her life on top of Arkford Stadium in order to protect the city from immediate danger," Rita, the enthusiastic reporter, announced. "Who knows what type of supernatural phenomenon this is? Who is this mysterious woman, and what will this hero do next?"

CHAPTER THIRTY

"*Give up already,*" Paige grumbled to herself. She picked up the remote and turned off the TV before Rita could say another word.

Heartbreak was the way her suitcase rolled out the door and down the hallway, breaking the only silence Paige was allowed. The heavy door slammed behind her, possibly disrupting other guests, but she could not care less. Her hotel key along with a folded-up sheet of paper rested in the pocket of her jeans with a hole in one knee. The rest of her body was buried in a dark, navy-blue sweatshirt she knew all too well. Getting rid of it was out of the question. She housed memories that were swaddled in it.

"*He's not going to wake up, Paige.*"

It was the way that Paige rode down the elevator's hotel watching as the numbers above the doors declined until the walkway opened up to her. She felt nothing as she walked through the lobby and to the front desk to check out. Paige had already paid with someone else's money for her stay. No matter how much guilt threatened to spill from her veins, she was convinced to do it to help herself heal from the scars her life left.

No matter how many times she tried to cover them up with whatever artistry she could think of, she felt as if she was going to bleed out...just like *he* did.

"*I'm so sorry.*"

All Paige wanted to do was cry, but she needed a change in routine. That was why as soon as she checked out of the hotel, she passed through the automatic glass doors and waited outside for a familiar vehicle. She fiddled around with the sleeves of her - no, *Peyton's* - sweatshirt while she waited, seated on a bench on the edge of a busy city sidewalk. She watched as cars drove by without a care honking, weaving around others, and skidding on brakes to get their points across. Everyone was in a hurry to get where they needed to go. Birds chirped overhead, zipping and swooshing their way through clouds and leaving their mark on the streets in the form of shadows.

Nothing had changed. Life went on with or without her.

She had lost her blue. Now, there was only purple.

The soft beeping of a car horn jostled Paige out of her grim contemplations of society. Sure enough, the worn-down tan Nissan she had seen only a couple of times was parked against the curb with a head of fiery hair operating the machinery. Paige's hazel, but red-tinted eyes glued onto the passenger side window as it rolled down and a friendly voice called out:

"Hey! Need a lift?"

That simple gesture was *almost* enough for Paige to crack a smile. "As a matter of fact, I do," she replied as she opened the door and sat down, placing the suitcase at her feet. "You didn't have to do this."

"I wanted to," Leo countered smoothly and looked straight ahead.

"Well, then..." Paige brushed imaginary dust off of her jeans just after shutting the car door behind her. "Thank you."

"No problem."

Silence ensued for just enough time for Leo to shift the gear into "drive" and to start inching along. That was when Paige solemnly broke it.

"I don't understand why you're doing all of this for me."

"How come?"

"Because of what I did to Peyton."

The vehicle slammed to a stop, causing Paige's torso to fly forward before it was caught by the seat belt and pulled back. Leo shifted the gear back into "park" and laid back, eyeing Paige with a knowing brown stare.

"Paige... I've already told you several times you've done

nothing to Peyton," Leo assured her in the strongest voice he could muster up. "It's not your fault."

"But it *is* my fault." Tears began to well up in Paige's eyes for the fourth time that morning alone. "I wasn't strong enough. I wasn't fast enough. I couldn't save him."

The redhead fought back a potential crying spell of his own; he needed his sight to navigate the streets of Arkford safely. "Nobody could. It was an unexpected tragedy. Not even someone with super cool superpowers would have predicted it."

That made Paige crack a sliver of a smile.

"You think so?"

"I know so." Leo rested his hand on her shoulder. "Don't blame yourself or I'll have to dump a glass of water on your head."

Paige giggled in just the slightest. She wiped away a lone tear from her cheek, remembering when he did the same for his best friend. "I'll do my best."

Leo removed his hand from her shoulder and used it to shift the gear into "drive" for a second time. He guided his beloved tan Nissan forward and into the maze of roads making up the city Paige had become fed up from. It just...kept going, having no relevance or initiative to wait for the stragglers swiftly swept into a state of no return. Paige thought of herself as one of the lost sheep trying to keep track of the shepherd and his ninety-nine and eventually becoming separated.

This time, though, the shepherd never came back.

Paige watched in the side view mirror as the skyscrapers, busy streets, and careless civilians grew smaller and smaller until they disappeared altogether. A sense of the unknown threatened to swallow her up with each passing second. She made the ultimate decision to look forward even though her mind screamed and begged at her not to.

"I never got to say goodbye..."

The tan Nissan passed under a sign stating "Arkford International Airport" directly before Paige realized what exactly she was doing was, in fact, real. She felt the piece of paper in her pocket, the *plane ticket* she had bought using Leo's credit card after he refused to let her say no. She thought back to when she first began staying at the hotel, once again using Leo's credit card when he insisted it was the "least he could do."

The least he could do was absolutely nothing, but Paige refused to complain about the fact many finances had been taken care of for her.

The roar of multiple engines operating a winged vehicle that Paige had never seen before filled her ears despite the car radio being turned on a moderate to low volume. Paige peered out of her window in awe as a large blue and white Boeing 747 aircraft shot its way down the runway only for its nose to tip upward at the last second and take off into the sky without looking back. She craned her neck in order to see the long body and wings rocket into the blue until it ultimately vanished. Paige wished she had that sort of confidence. It took a month for her to consider her next step.

Leo turned around in his seat to parallel park into a spot next to the airport that looked larger than humanly possible. He squeezed his tan Nissan in between two cars with plenty of space to spare because the size of the vehicle was diminutive. Paige watched the tedious procedure, but when the car stopped entirely, she could not find it in herself to move. Leo turned off the car, unlocked the doors, and exited his side, walking over to Paige's side and opening up the door for her. Despite her silent protests, Leo picked up the suitcase by the handle and set it down on the sidewalk to make plenty of room for her to exit.

"Are you sure you want to do this?" Leo lowered his voice with uncertainty.

Paige nodded, swallowing back the doubt in her throat. "I'm sure."

Leo looked as if he was uncomfortable, watching as his weight shifted from one foot to the other. "...Should I come inside with you, or...?" he asked timidly.

"Honestly, I think this is something that would be easier if I do it alone," Paige politely rejected Leo's offer.

"Okay." He dragged his foot against the concrete and then mustered up the strength to look her in the eyes. "So... I guess I'll be seeing you, then?"

Paige nodded, waging war on her mind that wanted her to cry so desperately. "I guess so."

"Oh, I almost forgot." The redhead reached into his pocket and revealed a phone that looked like it was brand new. "I may or may not have talked with mine and Peyton's parents and since they're so loaded, they offered to buy you a phone for your travels. I put my number along with my parents' and his parents' just in case you need anything."

Right then and there, the waterworks arrived on cue. Paige could not argue with it anymore. She let the dam break once she saw the brand new phone in Leo's hands. Instead of taking it from him, she barreled herself into his arms. She bawled into her shoulder like she was a toddler who had just dropped an ice cream cone on the floor. His hugs were nothing like Peyton's, but they had the same warming comforting factor. The affection was not the same, though. This was purely platonic. What she and Peyton had...was something more.

"You did *not*," she sobbed into his shoulder.

Leo rubbed soothing circles on her back despite the urge to burst into tears himself. "Yes, we did. I didn't tell anyone where you were going like you requested, but we all love you. You're family, and you always have family here with us."

Paige half-heartedly smacked him in the back of the head. "Ow!"

"I had to," she laughed behind her tears. When she pulled apart, she wiped away the salty moisture on her face. "Are you sure I can take this?"

"Would I have brought it if I wasn't?" Leo passed her the phone and enclosed her hand around it.

"Thank you. Really...thank you."

Leo just smiled and placed his hands on her shoulders. "You're welcome. Now, do me a huge favor."

"What's that?" She cocked her head to the side.

"Be safe."

"I will."

"Text me when you land."

"I will."

"Maybe even send me a funny meme or someth-"

"I think I get the idea," Paige teased, which was seldom as of the times given.

Leo chuckled and embraced her in one last, long hug. "Take care of yourself," he mumbled against her damp brown hair. "I mean it."

"I'll do my best."

Saying goodbye was something Paige had never been good at. The first reason was that she had been isolated for much of her life–she needed not say parting words to anyone. Now, though, her voice got caught in her throat; therefore, her farewell was silent. When she eventually let go of Leo, which - admittedly - was not as hard as letting go of Peyton, she lifted the handle of her suitcase, turned around, and started walking the other way. Her mind screamed at her to look back, but she refused, only keeping her eyes ahead of her.

If she had turned back around, then this adventure would barely begin.

Paige passed through the large double doors of the Arkford International Airport and joined the crowd of hundreds of people waiting to embark on or complete their next journey. Paige was one of the former, patting the folded-up plane ticket in her pocket. For once, Paige did not feel the need to invisibly weave around the civilians making their way to the check-in desk. Instead, she was one of the travelers, unknown and at peace.

Before she knew it, Paige had checked in, registered her bag to carry onto the plane, passed through security like any other person would, and then waited at her gate. Another Boeing 747 was patiently hibernating outside the window. Paige could hardly believe this was happening, but it needed to be done–for her and her mind's sake.

Starting anew was something Paige never knew she needed, or desired. Ever since she set down roots in Arkford, she thought that there was nothing else to the world. Peyton, Leo, and their families taught Paige that there was so much more to life than merely existing. That was why Paige dropped out of college and left everything behind. She could only keep her eyes on the prize...on the outside. Her one-way ticket exemplified that.

This time, though, she would not be looking into places she could not reach, but rather the journey ahead of her.

And for her...it was more than enough.

It *had* to be.

Epilogue

TWO YEARS LATER

If a wish was to come true, it was better left unsaid. That was an age-old rule from a tale as old as time. Every child on their birthday before blowing out the warm, flickering candles was told to make a wish. If they were to say it out loud, it would not be granted. At least, that was what the ancient legend had passed down from generation to generation.

The crisp autumn air whisked its way through the streets of York seated in the northeastern region of England. The sun was covered by large cumulus clouds invading the azure hue of the sky, transforming it into a dreary wonderland. Despite the gloom of it all, pedestrians walked the sidewalks and even the streets vacant of cars except for the occasional four-wheeled vehicle or bicycle pedaling down the left side of the asphalt.

Tucked away in The Shambles, a historic street just southeast of the city's centre was a wide assortment of wall-to-wall medieval architecture. Each building was a different variety of colors, from off-white to auburn to a gray that matched the cloudy landscape. Uneven rooftops were scattered about, shingled in every shade of brown and black. Windows of every shape and size alligned with their own special building–each one was unique. The street had a warm, busy, but somehow nostalgic feel, as if every person had walked it a million times. The street was full of hustle and bustle. At every turn, at least twenty pedestrians were crossing the street, entering and exiting stores, or merely discussing trivial topics to the very last block. York was much different than Arkford. Seeing as everyone was busy, every civilian would never think to stop, take a breath of fresh air, and absorb the world around them. This was a complete turnaround from the States. Not all cities in America were like that, but Arkford certainly was. York was a lovely change.

In between this vivid collection of intricate, ancient buildings laid a little cacao shop with a faded ebony-shingled roof. The premises had just enough wear and tear to appear used and loved, but not enough to be considered a messy establishment. The words *Cozy Covers & Coffee* were etched in cursive calligraphy on a wooden sign hanging perpendicular to the front, rounded door that almost looked like a tall hobbit hole described by J.R.R. Tolkien himself in *The Hobbit*, also known as *An Unexpected Journey*.

Through this burgundy "hobbit hole" with large black hinges was another world even more magnificent than The Shambles. While keeping the rustic feel of the outdoors, any visitor was welcomed with a brown table of popular books of every shape, size, and genre handpicked by the employees above an auburn densely carpeted flooring much less vibrant than the door. Even if a customer would walk through the front door, no employee would dash up to them and promote their bestsellers or suggest their favorite drink. Instead, everyone was free to roam as they pleased and could ask for assistance when they were ready.

Shelves upon shelves of books lined every wall except for the ordering counter of the café portion of the shop, which was on the right-hand side. This section displayed an entire menu above a floor of white tile that was calming to the eyes–not too bright, but just soft enough to bring light to the room. Chocolate couches and cushioned chairs surrounded every table to give the small restaurant a homey feel. At least five to ten people were in this café at a time, either ordering some sort of caffeinated drink, devouring a delicious dessert offered behind the glass counter, reading a book they were contemplating purchasing from the store, or all of the above.

The sheer number of books in *Cozy Covers & Coffee* was almost overwhelming. There was a wing for every genre imaginable, from Teen Fiction to Drama to Nonfiction to Romance. Each row of books was lined to perfection, making a browsing experience much more enjoyable. Every single employee knew the shelves by heart. It was how they were trained, after all.

Speaking of the employees, each one wore a burgundy dress shirt paired with some sort of sleek black bottoms and any pair of shoes they liked. The dress code was not very strict; the only rule was to maintain the "aesthetic" of the store. Anything red, black, or brown would do.

In this particular employee's case, though, she wore a collared short-sleeved dress shirt with two off-white buttons, a pair of black leggings, and a pair of new black Converse that she adorned on the daily. Her mahogany hair was tied with black scrunchies in two Dutch braids that rested daintily over her shoulders. A mismatched stack of books that rose above her head were cradled in her arms as she carefully navigated her way towards the Coming-Of-Age section near the front left portion of the store.

She hardly kept her balance as she set the pile of books on the muted red carpet. The young woman picked up the first book and then directed it to its proper place. She then began shelving books at a quicker momentum when she caught herself getting into a rhythm. That silent rhythm was interrupted a couple of minutes later, however, by a gentle tap on her shoulder.

The woman turned around to view a small girl who was about ten years old in a dress the color of pure sunshine with black shoes with white lances just like her own. Her brown curls hung just past her shoulders and her green eyes sparkled like emeralds. Her paper white teeth were easily revealed in a kind smile that the brunette could not help but reciprocate.

"Hi, there," she greeted the child with a grin she mastered over the past couple of years.

"Hi!" the girl chirped. "I was wondering if you could help me with something."

The young adult bent down to her eye level. "Of course. What's that?"

"This might sound silly, but...I was wondering if you had any books about strong girls doing amazing things. I know I can do anything I set my mind to, but more encouragement would be awesome! So, do you have any suggestions, please?"

"Oh, um...," the woman faltered. She was not expecting such a thought-out request. Then, her eyes lit up with a sudden thought. "I think I have just the right thing for you."

"Really?!" The small girl visibly glowed with excitement. "Cool!"

The girl's smile mirrored her own. "Right this way."

The brunette led the child to the other side of the Coming-Of-Age wing of *Cozy Covers & Coffee* a couple of aisles down. She skimmed the second shelf from the top until she found exactly what she was looking for: a perfectly plump book with a vibrant cover. She eyed the periwinkle jacket tie-dyed with multiple shades of purple and gray that looked as if it created a whirlwind of some sort. She handed it to the girl with an engaged, but nervous smile.

"*Indigo?*" she asked as she read the cover. Her enthusiasm never faded. "What's it about?"

The brunette shrugged, trying to hide her anxiety. "It's about a girl who's different from everybody else. She's special in her own way and figures out how strong she is with two friends by her side. I think it's exactly what you're looking for. I might be biased, though, because I'm good friends with the author."

The curly-haired girl was instantaneously intrigued. "Really?! Who is she?"

"*Well, this girl's going to find out soon enough anyway.*" The employee swallowed back any nerves she had and replaced it with a smile. "I'd happen to know because...she's me." She opened the very back of the book and revealed her photo on the inside flap of the book jacket.

"Oh, my gosh!" The child looked in between the photo and the girl holding the book, utterly wonderstruck. "*You're* Paige O'Connell?"

Paige nodded and closed the book, her cheeks reddening as she handed it to the girl. "Pleasure to meet you."

"I'm Hayleigh." Hayleigh grabbed her right hand and vigorously shook it. "I'm so excited to read your story, Paige! I have one question, though."

"Sure. What's that?"

"Can you sign it? I want everybody to know I met a famous author!"

Paige blinked back the confusion bubbling in her expression. "I'm nowhere near famous, but yeah. Of course I can. Just let me get a pen from the register."

Hayleigh's smile was contagious as she trotted behind Paige with gusto. She followed her all the way to the register, which, admittedly, was not far, but Paige felt a little bit awkward going out of her way to sign her name in a book that happened to be on the shelf. She grabbed the nearest pen and clicked it open. Hayleigh handed her the book and she opened it to the title page where she wrote a note.

Never be afraid to be on the outside looking in. You were put there for a reason, so use it to your own advantage. As an outsider myself, I can tell you this: you are special in your own way. Don't blend into the rest of the portrait. Never forget that.

Your friend,

Paige O'Connell

Paige unclicked the pen, turned the book around, and passed it over the counter to Hayleigh, who practically snatched it from her. Her fern green eyes darted from side to side as she read the note Paige had left on the title page. Paige would never forget the wide eyes scanning over her with pure joy. Hayleigh ran around the counter despite the "employees only" sign and engulfed her in a hug.

"Thank you!" Hayleigh squeezed the life out of her, but not the happiness. "I'm so excited to read this and I'll *definitely* leave a great review online."

Paige hugged the girl back timidly, but tight enough to know she was there and that she meant it. "Just knowing it inspires one person is enough for me."

Hayleigh gave her one more solid squeeze before letting go and hastily dashing off to find her mother. "Mom! Mom!" she squealed as she ran away quicker than Paige thought her little legs could take her. "I know what book I want and I met the author! You can meet her when we check out!"

Paige did not hear the rest because Hayleigh was long gone. She fought back joyous tears in her eyes knowing her book had already aided just one person. She decided to return to her work, shelving the rest of the pile of books she left behind in her haste. Paige quickly walked towards the Coming-Of-Age section of the store, right back to the aisle she came from, and continued where she left off.

There were at least ten books left in the pile that Paige had to sort in alphabetical order. She did so with not as much speed as before, but was catching up fast. Paige was about to shelve another book when she lost her grip and it fell to the floor with a thud. Without breaking pace, she bent down to grab it and place it back on the shelf. Before she did, though, a tapping on her shoulder commenced for a second time.

Paige turned around not to see the little girl from before, but someone completely different. Somehow, she recognized this young man in an instant. His lanky build, chocolatey brown eyes, apparel, - consisting of a baby blue hoodie, dark jeans, and worn-out tennis shoes - but most of all, his open-lipped grin gave away his identity immediately. He never changed. Paige, on the other hand, had drastically. Her brunette hair and form-fitting clothes were only the exterior elements. The inside was much different.

She had not used her "supernatural abilities" as society called them since the incident.

She almost dropped the book for a second time when the realization hit her like a ton of bricks. Her jaw ran dry from words other than one. How could this be remotely possible?

"*Peyton?*"

Acknowledgments

This book is dedicated to my only sister who is three years my junior. Despite this, she is wise, humorous, and always knows what to say to make me feel better. She is my built-in best friend, and I cannot thank God enough for blessing me with a better sister. Sure, we may not get along all the time, but blood is thicker than water, and we storm through every complication that comes our way. Happy birthday to one of my favorite people. I love you more than words can express.

About the Author

Cassidy Stephens is a nineteen-year-old author focusing on the Teen Fiction/YA genres, but this is her first fantasy novel. Indigo is her first standalone work. When she is not writing, she can be found playing her guitar, the piano, the ukulele, or singing some of her favorite songs. She is currently in her third year at Regent University to get her Bachelor's degree in English and a Minor in Music.

Follow her writing journey on Instagram: @_casswrites.

Also by Cassidy Stephens

The Huntington Avenue Series

Huntington Avenue: Part One

Nearly perfect grades, a loving family, and being a guitar prodigy seem to be attributes of the ideal teenage life, right? In his case, there was a debilitating catch.

Zachary West - a blind teenage boy - had no clue what he was getting himself into when he stepped foot into Oceanview High School. After recently moving to the suburbs of Kitty Hawk, North Carolina, the seventeen-year-old desired a chance at the normality of being a teenager. Being homeschooled for the past eleven years after a traumatic accident caused his condition was a nightmare for an optimistic extrovert.

Soon enough, and consequent to a couple of encounters with resident hothead, Jaylen Hunt, Zach crosses paths with the bully's long-term girlfriend—Kelsey Davis. In contrast to what her peers might assume her personality to be due to her boyfriend's nature, Kelsey was a sweet soul who made the best out of every situation. Her life seemed to be perfect, but everything changed when the teenage girl noticed Zach's intriguing sight impediment. She wanted to learn more about it.

As questions, an unlikely friendship, and possibly more begin to arise, life continues to wreak havoc for the both of them. With Jaylen and his close friend, Lyla Walker, becoming a problem, Zach and Kelsey find themselves growing closer together and further apart from the people they had been familiarized with.

Would Kelsey flip her life around for the unique boy on Huntington Avenue who needed a friend, or would she remain with the people who might not have been the best for her?

Huntington Avenue: Part Two

Supportive friends, an eligible love interest, and an opportunity to obliterate the concept of blindness seem to be the dream of Zach's, right? Unfortunately, it was more of a nightmare.

Following an unexpected confession of lies, concealed emotions, and an unconsented first kiss from Kelsey at the airport, Zach had no idea what to think of his life crashing down upon him. He finally had the chance to regain his eyesight after eleven years of confining darkness. Kelsey had proved to be his light and guide throughout his adjustment to his new home and school. There was nothing distrustful about her...until the airport incident.

For the duration of the two teenagers spending some much-needed time apart—Zach being in Florida for his procedure and Kelsey remaining in Kitty Hawk, tensions begin to rise between the latter and her significant other: Jaylen. The relationship between Kelsey and her "so-called" best friend, Zach, caused too much insecurity in the seemingly confident teenage boy. He wanted their friendship to end as quickly as it came about, but it was easier said than done—oh, how much easier.

While several attempts, lies, and pure toxicity tear Kelsey and Jaylen's "golden" relationship to pieces, Zach attempts to readjust to society. With the help of his friends, family, and trust issues, it was nearly a walk in the park. Alas, a recurring string of nightmares, confidential information becoming jeopardized, and dishonesty sprouting from Zach and Kelsey's new chapter of romance kept the situation from remaining peaceful.

Would a simple mistake drive Kelsey and Zach apart for good, or would the two of them work through their struggles side by side?

Cambridge Bound

What could go wrong if you follow your dream? It might become a nightmare before your very eyes.

Being accepted to Harvard University had been August's dream ever since he discovered the school existed. Because Harvard was one of the most prestigious universities of the United States, August made it the "Holy Grail" of his high school experience. With a 5.0 grade point average, a perfect standardized test score, countless Advanced Placement classes, and even a published novel under his belt, August thought it would be the teeniest bit of a challenge.

Despite beginning a new life away from his annoying sister and otherwise friendly environment back in Kitty Hawk, August found his college experience to be more difficult than it seemed. With a nuisance of a roommate, a puzzling schedule, and homesickness as the icing on the disappointingly bitter cake, the eighteen-year-old began to give up hope on his goal. With his mental health on a downward spiral, there seemed to be no hope for return.

Would August continue to hold up and commit to his lifelong dream, or would he leave everything behind for a second time?

Being The Bystander

Being in middle school was tough to begin with. When his only three friends abandoned him and he was left on the verge of academically plummeting, Mason had no idea what to do.

Mason Cooper was the epitome of a middle-class middle schooler on the brink of his teenage years. Friends come and go, but in Mason's world, the latter seemed to be the only applicable aspect of his social life. Despite not being the sharpest knife in the drawer, Mason's attempts to end up on top were nothing short of honest work. His trio of "friends," though, did not appreciate his company, leaving Mason alone on a dying oasis of low self-esteem.

After a good deed sends him into a battle between two of his classmates, the bullets of self-hatred continue to ricochet, but not in the direction he hoped. Mason's desperation for friends left him in one of the most difficult spots imaginable. Despite wanting to do the right thing, the first person Mason could consider a true friend led him down the wrong path, resulting in a sticky situation that Mason had no capacity to know how to get out of.

Would Mason do the right thing and discover who authentically cares about him, or would he succumb to the peer pressure egging him on?

The Behind Series

Behind The Lens

Nobody knows what happened to Abigail Bartley. Ever since one fateful day near the end of her junior year, paranoia clawed its way up her throat, latched onto the crevices of her mind, and didn't let go. Joined by her best friends, Keagan, Jade, and Brielle, along with her supportive parents, she is tasked with yet another challenge: navigating through her final year of high school with a brave face.

When an innocent dare leads Abigail to reluctantly attempt to steal an unusual pair of glasses right off the face of Hillwell High School's "new boy," she and Noah Howell cross paths that she thought would forever run parallel. That notion was quickly proven wrong when the very person Abigail fears returns to where she thought she was safe. Her only choice to get away from him is to enlist Noah's help. As one situation snowballs into another, Abigail starts to crumble and slide into the decrepit avalanche she was before.

Will a silly pair of glasses, her friends, and a spontaneous request save Abigail from flying through the free fall of her flashbacks, or will her already-cracked resolve shatter to pieces?

Behind The Motive

Ever since a restraining order was placed against her abuser, Abigail Bartley has been thriving. She graduated high school with flying colors, just turned eighteen, and was planning to attend Hillwell University with two of her friends: Keagan Lopez and Noah Howell—the latter gradually becoming just a little bit more. Her other friends, Brielle, Jade, and Ryder all had successful futures ahead of them. What could be better than that?

Life, however, was not perfect. When Abigail begins receiving mysterious letters from the person she fought to avoid, she willingly seeks help from those closest to her for the first time. Meanwhile, her friends are all struggling with their own difficulties. Noah's family is still grieving the loss of his father. Keagan begins craving attention from her adulterous mother, causing her to rebel. Brielle and Ryder's family is struggling with money and hiding behind their walls. The latter's best friend tries to help in a controversial way. With everyone else falling apart around her, how will Abigail possibly manage to stay afloat herself?

Will Abigail and Noah piece back each of their friends like a jigsaw puzzle, seeing the beauty within the fractures, or will everybody eventually go their separate, broken ways?

Printed in Great Britain
by Amazon